THE SOFT FALL

LUNAR SIEGE, BOOK 1

MARISSA BYFIELD

THE SOFT FALL
Marissa Byfield

Ellysian Press
www.ellysianpress.com

DEDICATION

For my love, Patrick,
and for wild women everywhere

THE EMPIRE OF MYRE

THE ASHEN SEA

RUINS
THE VILLAS

SHOLE
PORT OF ELALU

THE VINAEM RIVER

PATH SOUTH

THE ENCAMPMENT

WHEELOCK POINT

VALTA
THE CAPITAL
THE CITADEL
THE ACADEMY

SHIMAERAN

AWL-FETH
THE CATHEDRAL
THE VILLAGE

THE GITIK MOUNTAINS

TEMPLE OF THE LORIS

L'HESTE

THE OTAENE RIVER

KRETAIM
SARDIN CITY

THE SIEVITH BOG

THE FORTRESS OF TELOENA

THE FOUR-FORKED RIVER

CENTRAL CERRO-MYRE

PROLOGUE

Ram

Mighty men fall when they dare to rise above the heights of gods.

This is what my father told me, not long before his voice failed him in sickness. I'm not sure I believed him then. Though he sought great heights, and his reign was mighty indeed, it was the sickness that proved to be his downfall.

But my father's throne remains empty. It is not my place anymore.

I am elsewhere, cloaked in a power that I do not control. I watch my people from afar, but they do not see me. I watch and wait for a lurking shadow to reveal itself so that I may finally meet it.

I watch my empire under the siege of my enemy, but I cannot save it.

Mighty men fall when they dare to rise above the heights of gods, but also when they descend below the depths of the damned – I believe this now.

I am Prince Ramus Baines, and this is the story of how I Fell.

PART I: THE DEMON

"Woman to man is either a God or a wolf."
– English proverb

CHAPTER 1

Red moon, new
Four years after siege

There was no god but Mactus.

Since she'd been small enough to sit on her mother's knee, Dianna knew this truth. Every summer, from the farmstead overlooking the field, she had watched her father tying sheaves of golden wheat.

"He's cutting the hair of the goddess," her mother would say, but Dianna never quite understood what she'd meant, and the chance to ask was gone.

The pestilence came with the first cold snap. Underneath the snow, it seeped into the soil, sapped roots dry, choked the life from every green thing in the village. The fallow earth bared itself in the thaw.

That summer, in a lingering patch of yellow sweetgrass, Dianna harvested the last crops her family's farm would ever yield. She dropped the shriveled radishes, ugly and scabbed as diseased hearts, into a wicker basket. She dared not turn from her work.

Ravens hovered over the scaly, sunbaked land, scouting for vermin, prattling in throaty, elegiac couplets. The High Elder had warned that looking a raven in the eye ensured terrible suffering, that the birds were harbingers of demons. Since scores of them cloaked the village in black, their gazes seemed inescapable.

Just beyond Awl-Feth, a craggy mountain range cut the horizon, and Silbarran edged it like a lush green scar. There in the wooded depths, among the pines and sawtooth oaks and creeping scrub, life moved. Dianna heard it in the distant song of migrating finches, smelled it in the rich wet earth every spring.

But nameless and unseen to her, death moved faster yet.

Liam knew its name – perhaps he'd even seen it, once. Her elder brother knew just about everything and had meticulously composed theories for all the rest.

So, she had asked him with her fingers mashed into fists, her throat burning with anguish, and her face too hardened for a child of fourteen: "What took her, Liam? What took our mother?"

"You cannot know," he had said, his voice iron.

Their father forbade her to leave the farm without Liam at her side, mistakenly believing vigilance would put an end to her longing to know. Instead the ache of not knowing swathed her heart like thorned vines, growing sharper by the day.

Since Liam wouldn't ease her grief with an answer, he placated it with poetry. Dianna recited a particular verse every morning when she stoked the hearth fire and every night when she lay awake with gnawing thoughts. As she turned the sun-warmed earth in her fingers she murmured, the breeze snatching at her words.

> *And I shall not fear the solitary fate of death,*
> *For as surely as we are born,*
> *the weight of death grows inside us all.*
> *But while there grows one true death—*

A flicker of black caught her eye, and her heartbeat

vaulted. A raven skimmed low on the wind, descending like a shadow opposite her.

Dianna's breath quickened. She focused on her blackened fingers, working the delicate roots out of the dirt. The raven rummaged and prodded the earth for insects, its body gleaming in the sun, sleek as obsidian.

> *But while there grows one true death,*
> *lives upon lives are collapsed within us,*
> *sleeping, folded as wings.*

At last, she glanced at the raven. It stared at her, its head turning in curiosity, and gave a guttural rasp.

Dianna leapt backward, overturning her basket. The radishes spilled and spun away like red-painted tops.

"Fly away," she murmured, squeezing her eyes shut. "Fly away."

The bird's claws scrabbled faintly in the earth. She could still sense its beady gaze upon her.

"I'm not afraid of you," she said, louder now, but her voice trembled.

The world around her faded to the drone of cicadas, punctuated by the steady drum of Liam's forging hammer from the barn. Taking a breath, Dianna tasted ash on the air. Sweat rolled from her hairline into her eyes as she blinked, scanning the crest of the hill.

At the heart of the village, the stone spires of the cathedral pierced the skyline like fanged jaws. Awl-Feth had been a thriving locality of the empire many years ago, its people prospering with the ebb and flow of goods along interwoven trade routes – but those times had long since passed. The opulent cathedral remained as though a memorial, a last bastion, a sanctuary. There, under its magnificent vaulted ceilings, Awl-Fethans believed their livelihood could truly be saved.

There, a black tongue of smoke had begun to rise.

"Liam," Dianna said aside, almost a question. Her eyes did not break from the distant haze, dark fear twisting uneasily within her. "There's a fire, Liam."

The breeze stirred again. A radish toppled down the hillside and vanished among the rocks.

"Liam!" Dianna cried out again, but the sound of her brother's hammer smothered his name.

Below the hillside, she picked out the shapes of villagers weaving among the thatched roofs of mud huts, urging one another on, fervor in their shouts. A bewildering exchange:

"Is it the Caenani?"

"No – he's burning them!"

Crumbling the earth from her hands, Dianna stole a glance at the barn. Its weather-beaten walls reverberated with the force of the hammer's strike.

The decision gripped her as she turned to face the hill's bare slope, rocked forward on her feet, and began to run.

The lone raven took flight in a billow of black as Dianna descended, deerskin boots beating clouds of dust in her wake. Her hair came unloosed from its coil and flagged bright in the sun, long and wild.

Awl-Feth reeled by in a smudge of dry sagebrush, brown moorgrass, gnarled trees. As the ground leveled, she slowed to catch her breath. Already her nerves were simmering beneath her skin.

She turned to face the hill, hair whipping in her eyes, half-expecting to see Liam racing down after her. But his hammer struck on with the same harsh cadence. As a flurry of villagers hastened toward the cathedral, panicked voices mingling, Dianna followed close as a shadow.

Smoke curled over the windows of the cathedral facades. Inlaid with mottled stained glass, they glittered like jewels in the sun. A throng of villagers one hundredfold had gathered at the foot of the steps like bees to the honeycomb.

A tall, thin man in deep scarlet robes stood before them.

The High Elder's features – coal-dark eyes and a strong aquiline nose – commanded respect. He was reading a passage aloud and, though middle-aged and gray-bearded, he dictated with a force befitting a man in his prime.

"Though I have tested ye with dearth, with pestilence, with fiendish beasts unto thy land," he cried out, "ye who have not forsaken me shall rise up from the clay as the budding flower, to replenish thy losses, spread thy seeds, and thrive in the light of glory. For only when thy land has been razed and thy faithless have perished can ye begin again in the eternal life.' Scripture Twelve, Verse 118. This is the will of Mactus—"

Dianna had reached the edges of the crowd, feeling small amid the shuffling feet and scattered, low conversations. One man had begun speaking in strange, wild tongues.

"Excuse me," she murmured, pushing through the gaps between bodies, avoiding elbows, eliciting grunts of irritation. "Excuse me—"

The High Elder's dark eyes swept over the faces of the villagers. Unsmiling, he raised his palms in front of him, arms draped in scarlet sleeves as though dripping with blood.

"My flock," he bellowed out over the mass. "Today we cast out a great wickedness from our village. Silbarran has corrupted their souls and blackened their hearts. They shall walk among us no more."

An eruption of voices – prayers for justice, mutterings of shock and dismay – welled forth. Many made the blessing of Mactus, kissing the backs of their fists, then opening their palms to the ground below them.

"Excuse me—" Dianna gasped, straining to glimpse the front, her skinny limbs twisting clumsily through the pressing heat of the crowd.

And then she saw them.

Beneath the cloth that bound their mouths, the women shared similar features, as if they could be sisters. They were tied to twin stakes close together, and their fingers were tightly entwined. Their feet were bare upon a ground piled with dry wood. A row of men in buckskin hunting clothes stood before them, carrying smoldering torches.

Dianna's heart clenched like a fist. Her stomach lurched.

He's burning them.

"No," she said, but her own voice was feeble in the turmoil, a pebble in a rushing river.

Her gaze wheeled over the faces of the crowd, clapping upon a small knot of young men Liam's age. Their black-banded sleeves designated them as scouts training for the hunt. She watched their arms swing back and forth as they pitched stones.

The women bound to the stakes recoiled with each strike. Dianna flinched with them.

"Let this not be a cause for alarm," the High Elder cut across the clamor, raising his hands high as if in praise. A respectful silence fell, hard as an axe to timber. "Let this be a call to action."

The row of hunters began to approach the women, torches raised above their heads.

"Honor His will, and He shall spare you," the High Elder called out, even as his gaunt features spared no empathy. "Women and children must not set foot in Silbarran. Men must ready their weapons and defend our village to the last breath. Let us pray."

Dianna turned to the adult nearest her, a grim-faced man who she reasoned must have a family of his own.

"Do something," she pleaded.

The man looked at her, but not with pity or distress. He looked at her as if she knew nothing.

6

Dianna watched helplessly as the hunters lowered their torches. The fire crackled as it crept over the woodpile.

"Most holy Mactus, may your will bless and keep the people of Awl-Feth. Keep our families fed as you feed our souls," the High Elder began.

Struggling against her bonds, one of the women began to scream.

"Most holy Mactus, may the poisonous blight borne of the Baines dynasty be severed from the vine," the High Elder continued.

The smoke swelled monstrously as the flames rose. The screams of the women pitched higher, grew wilder, sharp as animal teeth. Dianna felt their bite sinking to the bone, numbing as death itself. The bitter stench of burning hair and flesh mingled with wood smoke.

Her eyes swept over the crowd, the rows of heads bent in prayer. Mothers cradled swathed babies to their breasts, hushing their cries. One man recited the orison with purpose in each word, his upturned palms flat and balanced, as though holding an invisible weight in each.

She recognized his daughter, Cathrin, frozen in horror beside him. Behind a cascade of dark curls, the girl cupped her hands over her mouth, stifling her sobs.

"Most holy Mactus, may you purge this evil from our village." The High Elder spoke louder, as the growing flames spit bursting embers and thrashed in the summer wind. "May we remain servants and foot-soldiers of your holy order. May it carry us into the dawning of a new empire. Praise be."

"Praise be," the susurrus of a hundred voices echoed all around Dianna, making the small hairs prickle on her skin.

A wall of fire veiled its victims entirely. The intense blaze shimmered in the thick air, and Dianna thought she could still see faint movement within it: a twitch of a limb, or a jerk of the head. But it was only the relentless, consuming flames that moved over the women's still bodies, and only the memory of their screams stung her ears.

They had struggled so little in the grip of their doom.

After a few moments, the crowd began to disperse. Dianna willed her feet to bear her away from the sweltering place, but the ground seemed to hold her there. Her eyes followed the tumble of ashes in the air, falling and catching, sticking to her sweat-laced skin.

From the edge of the crowd, a young man's piercing gaze found her. It was as if Dianna could sense her tormenter watching before she saw him too.

"You're a lucky rabbit, aren't you?" he said. His voice was cool and smooth as the draw of a hunting blade.

Dianna ignored him, staring ahead at the columns of smoke.

"Your mother," he continued. "The shepherdess. She should have known better than to venture into Silbarran alone."

Dianna kept her voice low and even. "Leave me be, Actaen."

Actaen instead crept close enough to touch her. He moved with a lazy, liquid arrogance, looming at least a head taller.

"But you should feel lucky that they never found her. That she didn't come back," he said, gesturing at the burning pillars, keeping his eyes on her. "This is what happens to women who abandon the village. Never seen a Judgment before, have you? The Lead Hunter wouldn't want his innocent daughter bearing witness to such unsavory spectacles, would he?"

"I said leave me be."

Actaen smiled wolfishly. Curled a hand around the nape of her neck, as if she were ripe fruit to pluck from a tree. His calloused fingers slid, then settled in the grooves of her spine, making her shiver with revulsion.

"Innocent Dianna." Her name dragged slow and soft on his tongue as he savored its sound. "I can't leave you any more than you can leave me."

Dianna wasn't sure what compelled her to say anything in defense. It would have been easier to remain stone-faced. If she could be cold, refuse to deign to his goading, he might give up at last.

But his taunt about her mother cut deep as steel to flesh, and she wanted to hurt him the same way. To scare him.

From the corner of her eye, she glared at him.

"I'll bite you," she said.

Actaen's eyes widened. The smirk at his lips broke into riotous laughter, tapering only when Dianna began pulling away.

Snaring her by the arm, he leaned in close and breathed in her scent. His own was rotten leather, the sharp tang of salt and rust.

"Not if I bite you first, little rabbit," he murmured, his words lingering hot on her neck. "You look good enough to eat, and I've half a mind to trap you someday."

Dianna wrenched herself away from him, even as another hand caught fast to her wrist, turning her on the spot. Her brother's flushed face appeared haloed in sun, behind spectacles glinting rose-gold.

"You shouldn't have come here, Dianna," he said through gritted teeth.

Actaen studied Liam, sizing him up.

"Made your first kill yet, Aergyris?" he asked, catching the glances of a few fellow scouts.

Liam pulled Dianna to his side. "I've more important duties than hunting."

"The black sheep thinks he's smarter than us," Actaen said, his voice rising. The other scouts turned to listen in, their interest in the execution waning. "With his shiny scholar-eyes."

9

One sidled up to Actaen, ribbing him. "You haven't heard, then? Lead Hunter's son ain't ever fired a crossbow!"

"The man's got virgin hands," added another.

A howling torrent of laughter broke among them. Fury welled in Dianna's throat.

"He makes your crossbows, you dim—" she began, but Liam's hand tightened upon her wrist as he looked down at her, his green eyes steady and apollonian.

"Don't," he said.

But her insolence had already provoked a clamor of indignation amongst them. Actaen only stared at a tendril of Dianna's hair flashing white-gold across her cheek. He licked his lips.

"Teach your little sister to hold her treacherous tongue," he warned Liam. "The demons will come running for her yet."

Liam turned away at once, taking Dianna's arm, the scouts' insults at his back. Dianna clung to him as they jostled through the crowd. He wouldn't tell their father about this, she knew. He wouldn't dare, because she'd been under his watch.

But he hadn't reprimanded her, either.

Dianna squinted at his profile in the sunlight. His back was ramrod straight, and a muscle quivered in his jaw.

"What did they mean by 'demons,' Liam?" she pressed.

Liam pretended not to hear her among the chatter and mumbled prayers, wagging his head. His grip was rough and protective.

"What did they mean?" she repeated, desperate.

"It's all crock and horseshit," Liam muttered.

"What demons?"

"Forget it."

The two broke free from the raucous mass, and Dianna sucked in a heavy breath of fresh air. But she still tasted an echo of flesh and smoke in her mouth. The smell of death always lingered, just like the bones of the last goats sacrificed for Mactus, fertility god, cultivator of land and people. The barren, yawning village meant they had died for nothing.

A truth, hard and weighty, settled in her stomach, and she trembled. Liam's hand fell away.

"Dianna," he began, faltering. His stare was filled with knowing.

"There is no Mactus, Liam," she said under her breath, hot tears pricking her eyes, and the words released her, as though her body was lifting and spiraling away into the ether with the smoke. "There is no Mactus."

CHAPTER 2

Cold moon, waning
Two weeks after siege

A gainst a desolate, white winter, a ravening mouth of jagged teeth had opened.

The leafless trees had been cut down, then staked into the earth by the sweat and struggle of human labor, forming a barricade. Palisades, the commander had called them. Their gnarled, naked trunks stood apart from the living: the lush forest looming just beyond the sloping grade and snow-filled ditches of the encampment.

Within the palisades, rows of crude leather tents shuddered and flapped in a stiff breeze. Thirty had been pitched in total, aside from the larger commander's tent, the lictors' quarters, and a partitioned row of wooden barracks called the reformatory.

A group of boys had filed neatly alongside it, still and silent. Snowflakes settled in their hair and eyelashes. The commander paced opposite them, stopping beside a great, craggy stone half as tall as he. He brushed snow from it with a gloved hand.

"This is the killing stone," he said darkly, watching the boys as if daring them to break formation. "Read it."

Obediently, each of the children recited the engraving upon the stone. All but one – a waifish boy, dressed in a tunic made out of a tattered grain sack, his pale limbs gangling against its shapeless form.

All night, in the cold void of the encampment, the boy had listened to the quiet scraping of steel blade against stone and the labored breathing of the Valtan man who had toiled at his futile composition. The bleak light of dawn cast the bloodstained letters in sharp relief:

If a man shields his bloodkind from wickedness in the name of Mactus,
he shall be marked bloodkind of Mactus.

The boy's luminous blue eyes stared from beneath a thatch of mussed, jet black hair, but the words meant nothing to him.

Pausing mid-stride, the commander slowly doubled back. The boy looked downward as the others' recitation faded to silence.

"Read it," the commander repeated.

"I can't," the boy said.

The commander's brow knit. He stooped, bringing his face level to the one who dared to disobey his order. His voice came hot and spitting.

"Read. It."

The boy's murmur was hollow, as if the breath had been kicked from his lungs.

"I can't read."

The commander seized him by the hair.

"Think yourself above my orders, little bastard?" he demanded, jerking a finger in the direction of the killing stone. "Think this amusing, this blasphemy?"

"No, sir," the boy gasped. "No, I— "

The commander's rough-hewn gloves rasped at his nape, shaking him.

"You Valtans think yourselves equal to Mactus? To the god himself?"

A voice carried across the encampment, low and strong:

"Commander Havril."

The commander gave a start, and his grip fell away. Slowly, he turned around.

The speaker approached with an arresting grace, smooth and powerful as a sidewinder, flanked by lictors outfitted with halberds. He wore a heavy fox-fur cloak and lavish silks in the bronze and oxblood colors of Caenan, a striking figure in the dingy encampment.

The commander swept into a firm salute.

"Legate Tryntus," he returned, as the Legate of Caenan's piercing gaze regarded him.

Something in the slant of the legate's brow and the set of his mouth terrified the commander. Not because of what was there, but precisely what wasn't: his face could have sooner been carved from stone than shaped from living flesh, betraying no emotion.

"Were you inducting my apprentices, Commander?" the legate asked. "You know that is my responsibility."

"Yes, sir. Teaching a lesson. It will not happen again."

"At ease," the legate ordered him, turning askance to survey his legion's handiwork: the palisades driven deep into Valtan soil, the killing stone that had tasted Valtan blood. He appeared satisfied enough. "Clearly you aren't aware of what occurred here in the dawning hour."

"No, sir," the commander confirmed. "I was on watch with the fifth sentry."

"Perhaps the boys should care to explain to you." The legate's stare swept over the procession and settled on one of the older adolescents. "You, boy. What is your surname?"

The boy tensed, doffing his cap and dipping his head.

"Skintson, sir," he said, breath frosting the air.

"And the Valtan man brought here last night, bound to that post over there. What was his surname?"

"De . . . Demetriou."

The legate nodded. "Demetriou had something with him, didn't he? Something he shouldn't have had."

"A knife, sir. He smuggled it."

"Demetriou had a knife," repeated the legate, taking a step forth to examine the killing stone, stroking its coarse surface. "Which he used to carve his own epitaph here, in the dark of the night. And what did he proceed to do with the knife?" He looked at another boy pointedly. "Your surname?"

"Bracken, sir. He . . ." the boy began, but trailed off, as though forcing himself to remember the nightmarish scene. "He tried to kill himself, sir."

"How?"

"With . . . with the knife, sir."

The legate's monochrome gaze glittered as he turned to the smallest boy, who was pale as a silkworm, shock of hair gummed to his brow with sweat.

"Your surname."

The boy gaped, terror-stricken, at the legate's tall, draped figure. An older boy nudged him.

"Itsip," the smaller boy whispered.

"Itsip, why don't you tell me how Demetriou tried to kill himself."

"He . . . he cut . . ."

But the boy couldn't finish, and instead held his palms out, tears prickling his eyes.

"And did Demetriou die quickly?"

Trembling, the boy shook his head, blotchy face streaming.

"He bled to death, didn't he?"

That was the phrase he used, but they had all seen it happen, had been awakened by the screams, had heard the Caenani soldiers come running. The soldiers stood mocking Demetriou as he begged for the mercy of Mactus in his final breaths. They called him a worthless Valtan. They beat him against the killing stone and dragged his body to the pyre.

His bones lay cold in the snow-choked coals, but his

ashes still lingered on the air.

The legate straightened, addressing the boys collectively as Itsip mopped his nose on his ragged shirtsleeve.

"'If a man shields his bloodkind from wickedness,'" read the legate. "Demetriou wrote this particular scripture because he had a family, you see, and there are no other Demetrious in this encampment. He smuggled them out of Valta like he smuggled in his knife. That is why he was being reformed. He thought himself a hero, a martyr. He thought himself clever." He paused, and his voice tempered until it was as soft as wings on air. "But do you know what I think? I think, in your deepest nature, you are all animals. You are meant to function beneath a master. And you will learn, very quickly, that there is nothing heroic or clever about a dead Valtan."

A delicate snowfall laced the space between white sky and white earth, clean as untouched canvas but for the open jaws of palisades striping the horizon.

"I see Caenani features in some of you," said the legate. "Tainted with the blood of Valtans. Wasted. But we can make you serve a purpose, more than you ever had in this empire.

"You have been here, how long? A day?" He paused. "We have positioned fourteen Caenani encampments across Valta in only a fortnight. Each of them filled with your kind, working themselves to the bone. Hard, character-building work. I hand-select my workers for their skills. What is your skill, Skintson?"

The boy swallowed. "I suppose I'm strong, sir."

"You shall move stones." A brush of wind caught the legate's cloak in a billowing crimson flare. His hawkish eyes tightened, ensnaring his next quarry. "And you, Bracken?"

Bracken squared his shoulders and declared, "I'm strong too, sir. I can lift my own weight."

"You shall dig trenches."

Murmurings among the boys bubbled forth, each growing more determined to prove himself.

"I can cut wood—" one cried out in a reedy voice.

"I can catch rabbits," one insisted with an agitated glance all around him. "I can make traps—"

Some of the younger boys looked uneasily aside, knowing that they could offer little.

The legate paced opposite the row of boys, stopping to face the skinny, black-haired boy in the peculiar, grain sack tunic.

"You."

The boy shrank in cold shock at the sudden acknowledgment.

"Tell me," said the legate. "What is your surname?"

Beneath a snarl of black hair, the boy's intense blue eyes met the legate's face.

"I'm an orphan, sir," he said. "Aimes is the only name I've known."

The legate studied him. A shade of disappointment twitched at the corner of his lips.

"How old are you, Aimes?"

Aimes paused a moment.

"Thirteen, I think, sir," he murmured.

"And you can't read."

"No, sir. I can't."

Legate Tryntus sighed, folded his hands behind him again, and took a few measured strides against the length of the procession. His thick fur-trimmed cloak dragged in his wake, hissing in the snow.

"Let me tell you something, Aimes," he said. "And I will speak plainly for you. Around here we've little use for people who can't do things. So, if you want to stay alive . . ." He stopped pacing. His face twisted and his roar ruptured the air, echoing throughout the encampment: "*Do not tell me what you can't do.*"

A flurry of ravens rose shrieking in the distance, blotting the white sky. The legate's eyes lingered on Aimes, burning.

Petrified, heart hammering wildly, Aimes blurted, "I can heal."

Commander Havril's hand swept upon Aimes. The sharp crack of knuckles struck his ear like a rock, pushing him forward into the icy ground. He thought he felt his brain jostle in his skull.

"Liar!" the commander snapped.

Aimes gasped and doubled over as tremors reeled through him like waves. He clasped a hand to the side of his head as though to quench the searing pain. Squeezing his eyes shut, he tried to close his senses to the world.

It was a trick he'd learned, whenever things were very bad. From the slums, he would stare out at the swaying pines of the woods, and he could almost smell their crisp green, the damp of fungi and wood rot, the strong perfume of sweet woodruff. He could hear the warble of the whitethroat among the shrubs, the high clicking of beetles and other crawling things. He could feel the decomposing forest floor underfoot – slick rock, supple clay, spongy moss.

He could see the black wolf.

I am there, he would tell himself. *I am there.*

It took him a moment to realize, his lips numb, that he was mouthing the words under his breath.

But the bite of cold against his stinging ear wrenched him into the present, where he lay squirming sideways beneath the commander's leather boot. It pushed once, grounding him into the snow.

"I can heal," he uttered throatily, desperately.

The commander eased his boot away slightly, if only so Aimes could hear him.

"And I suppose you learned that at the goddamn Valtan Academe?" he said scathingly. Then, to the legate, "Bastard can't even read."

"Please, I can heal—"

Thoughtfully, the legate smoothed his hands over the

supple tawny fur lining his cowl. From within his cloak's interior, he withdrew his shortsword, then knelt directly in front of the boy who called himself Itsip.

He took the child's hand and cut it clean off at the wrist.

The screaming was instant and earth-shattering. The ground seemed to lurch underfoot like a breath had rushed from it.

The legate rose, stepping away.

"Heal him, then," came his dark undertone from beneath the upheaval.

Aimes stood frozen in horror. Bile crawled up his throat as he watched the snow turn red.

But the legate's words sank into him like teeth, reviving his senses, quickening his pulse. He stumbled toward the child whose inhuman shrieking ruthlessly gutted his reality.

"I need," Aimes gasped. "I need . . ."

The image sharpened in his mind. He blinked at the wash of blood before him, at the child's twisted, tear-streaked face.

"Yarrow," he whispered, voice cracking. He took a breath and bellowed, "I need yarrow!"

The group of boys' wails were thick on the air, and Aimes searched frantically for someone to hear him. His eyes clapped on Commander Havril.

"Small white flower," he said in a rush. "It grows in the woods, under the redwood trees. Bring it by the roots. Quick!"

"Stupid boy," snapped the commander, turning askance to face the legate. "The ground is frozen solid! Nothing can grow there in winter!"

The legate's hands remained neatly folded behind him as he paced, savoring the madness he'd unleashed. He paused to address his lictors, who stood at attention.

"You heard the boy," the legate snapped, and they broke across the encampment.

Aimes looked at Itsip's hand where it had fallen in the snow, bright red against pristine white. The tiny fingers curled like claws.

Snowflakes began to seep under his tunic, melting into his skin. He seized the edge of his grain sack tunic, ripping a piece of it away, binding Itsip's arm with the makeshift tourniquet.

"It will be all right," he said, voice stifled amid the child's cries. A pulse of doubt thrummed through him as each precious minute elapsed. "You'll be just like new."

Itsip was unconscious when the lictors reappeared, clutching sprays of the flowering plant. The legate continued his slow pace, showing no indication of surprise as he awaited the moment of truth. The row of boys, who remained cowering in their places, watched with pallid faces as Aimes grasped the brittle stems.

Itsip's little hand was cold. Trembling, Aimes wrapped the severed appendage in the budding stems. He lifted the bloody stump of the child's arm. Fitted the hand to it, like a gauntlet.

"He's insane," murmured the commander with a chuckle of astonishment, but the legate watched with a pensive frown.

Aimes counted the seconds under his breath, feeling the sweat bead and slide down his spine.

Slowly, he let go.

The child's arm fell limp at his side, entirely intact. His tiny body breathed like a broken doll made whole again, come to life.

A leaden silence descended. Only the wind howled over the frozen, obliterated landscape.

Then the commander's voice lanced across it: "Mactus walk among us."

Aimes' shaking hands disentangled the flowers from Itsip's fingers, scattering tiny white petals to the wind.

Beneath the makeshift dressing, the skin was clean and pink and fresh.

The legate considered the boy from the slums, blinking as though to clear his eyes.

Suspicion, cold and serpentine, uncoiled in his tone at last.

"How?"

Aimes cast an uncertain look at Itsip, whose color was warming as he lay whimpering upon the snow. The older boys shifted their feet while the little ones wept.

"I don't know," Aimes whispered.

"And only you have this power," the legate surmised knowingly.

"I . . ." Aimes looked uncertain. "I think so."

The legate gave only the slightest inclination of his head, as though that answered something important.

The commander had knelt to take a closer look at Itsip's hand, marveling. "Even if he lies . . ." He looked up. "This augurs our victory, sir."

His stomach turning with the gravity of this revelation, Aimes glanced at the other boys. Their eyes were silent abysses.

"No," said the legate, voice low. He was looking at Aimes differently now. Like he was no longer a boy, but a fleck of rare, pure gold that he'd found drifting in a muddy streambed. "No, not 'augurs.' This clinches it."

The legate whirled around with a great sweep of his sumptuous cloak.

"Have your boys work, Commander Havril," he said, voice rising to full force. "But I will not see a scratch on that one. He gets full rations. He must be guarded at all costs."

"Yes, sir."

A single step. A pause.

"And you are to call him by his Caenani name," the legate added. His back remained turned upon them, but

21

there was a smile in his voice. "*Healer* suits him handsomely, don't you think?"

"Oryaen, sir?"

"Precisely." He went forth. "Carry on."

CHAPTER 3

Wolf moon, full
Five years after siege

Abram Aergyris held his blazing torch aloft. Its fire gleamed in the silver of his breastplate and his watchful eye. Gray-grizzled and battle-scarred though it was, beneath his visage lay a demon hunter's steeled nerve.

But around his neck, suspended upon a cord, a thin iron wedding band told the story of a different man. It rested cold against his heart, a marker of the infinite grief deep underneath it.

The crude amulet had once adorned his wife's delicate finger. He'd found it two winters ago – in these woods, nestled in the bloody hollow of a massive wolf track, with her bow and arrows scattered nearby.

It reminded him of his purpose.

Patches of late winter snow clung to the trees, iridescent in the light of the full moon, as Abram led twelve men on the hunt. Each wore thick leather and chainmail, carrying crossbows and shouldering stocks of bolts, but none knew the trigger of the crossbow or the twist of the knife better than he.

"Steady your arm," Abram warned his right-hand man, Ledras, whose weapon's angle had begun to falter. The hunter stiffened at once, his gaze searching the trees into the edges of obscurity.

A stillness lay thick over the woods, punctuated only by the small sounds of the hunters' movements. The primal perfume of damp pine and rich earth were fresh in every pull of breath, swirling ghostly mists into the frigid air.

From the dark of the leafless trees, an owl hooted low. Closer, a cavernous howl smothered the woods.

Abram held up a gloved palm. The band of hunters stopped short, crossbows primed, and listened as the sound rumbled and sank away. It was that of a creature too fierce and too mighty for the mortal world, the yawn of Death's own gaping jaws.

"Mactus keep our eyes sharp and our bolts unswerving," prayed Ledras under his breath.

Something in the snow caught Abram's keen eye. He knelt, touched the ground, studied the partial print made there, still fresh.

The Lead Hunter's gaze narrowed, scanning the trees. A single snowflake fell across his line of sight. Motioning his men to come with him, he bore left. The hunters covered the ice-crusted ground, safeguarding all sides, moving as one entity.

They had not taken more than ten paces before another howl resounded, rattling the woods like an earthly tremor. A shroud of shrieking birds exploded from the treetops and spilled across the moon like ink.

"Aergyris," murmured Ledras, his eyes flitting between towering silhouettes of firs. His knuckles, gripping the lathe of his crossbow, shone white in the moonlight. "It could make for the village. Perhaps we should turn back."

"No," Abram said with a hard finality, marching onward. "We head it off now. Get a clean shot."

"I can hear it moving," whispered Cott. It was the young man's first hunt, and he tensed at the chilling wind, raising his crossbow by an inch.

"Hush your whimpering, boy," growled Fyrin, a bearded boulder of a man. "A demon stands no chance against thirteen men."

Abram spearheaded the way, calm and watchful, into the heart of the night. The hunters' boots trudged through thick underbrush, over brittle branches and rime-glossed streambeds. Breathing softly, they searched for the slightest movement within the trees.

A pine bough twitched close by, and Ledras stopped. "There," he said.

The men pointed their crossbows, and the trees rustled again.

Cott's eyes darted, wide as silvers. "Good Mactus, it's here."

Fyrin hissed in frustration. "Boy, I told you to keep—"

A shadow tore into their midst, slammed Fyrin to the ground with a splintering of bone against ice and gorged into him. The hunter gasped, the wind smacked from his chest as his great hands scrabbled for his crossbow, now knocked out of his reach.

Abram did not hesitate. He speared his torch into the ground, cocked his crossbow on his heel, and let fly his bolt.

But the demon was faster to react, wrenching out of range with impossible speed before returning to its victim. Fyrin's horrifying screams rent the air.

For the first time in two years as Lead Hunter, a shard of fear slid through Abram's heart. He sized up his target, gauging their odds in silence.

Though most demons loomed at least a head larger than natural wolves, this one was as large as an oxcart, pinning Fyrin with claws the length of daggers. Its bristling true-black pelt steamed in the bitter cold, and its wild, hellish eyes blazed yellow.

This one was enraged.

The hunters leapt to combat with a clang of iron, freeing

their bolts one after the other. One bolt bit the beast's shoulder, yet it hardly flinched. Veering straight for Abram, it sent a spray of snow airborne, gnashing its teeth in a bloody snarl.

"On my left!" roared Abram to Ledras, as the wolf feinted with a rasping of claws against ice. Ledras, crossbow extended, thumped his back against Abram's and swerved around to face the monster head-on.

He released a bolt with a metallic clap. It soared and fizzled into the snow as the wolf leapt.

"Come on," Ledras panted. "Come closer, you son of a bitch!"

Brandishing their weapons, the hunters rushed in. Crouching on flexed haunches, the wolf blew hot steam through its furrowed snout. The falling snowflakes had begun to thicken, dusting the beast's black fur with white, veiling Abram's sight.

"Stand clear!" he ordered, jamming a second bolt into place. On his belt hook he engaged his weapon, punching his foot hard through the crossbow's stirrup.

The hunters heeded him, abandoning their attack, but two were slower to move. The wolf plowed its hind paws into the snow and vaulted forward. One man dropped beneath its underbelly and was trampled underfoot, rolling like a felled tree into a snowbank. The other was seized by the throat in a tangle of sinew and bone, silenced, dismembered.

The remaining hunters withdrew, readying their weapons, catching their breath, cursing.

There was no time to regret a command. Abram steadied his aim.

"Now!"

At least half a dozen bolts soared through the cascading snow, almost simultaneous, almost beautiful. Within the flurry, the wolf's shriek shattered the air.

The men closed the gap at a wary crawl, forming a

semicircle around their wounded target. Some began to taunt the beast, hollering and raising their fists in the air. Nearby, Fyrin still lay screaming in agony on the frost-hardened earth. His blood pooled a halo around his body.

There was the scuffle of feet on ice, and the roar of the wolf rose above the chaos. It emerged from the blur of snow, one ear glossy with blood, just shy of a death blow. Red frothed through its bared fangs.

The men hitched and released a hail of bolts, even as the wolf darted and evaded them. Abram pulled his trigger as it lunged, but its body twisted in midair and the bolt streaked past it. His hand was whip-quick, drawing and cocking another bolt.

The viscous thud of bolt against flesh seemed to secure his victory. In the passion of the fight, the moment was too fleeting to tell. Abram blinked snowflakes from his eyes.

The shot had pierced the wolf's foreleg, but the beast merely staggered and righted itself. It gave a great shake, clouding the air with the seething heat of its body.

Abram scrambled to reload.

Locking the bolt in position, he kicked down on the bow. Even in the bitter cold, sweat dampened his hair. The other men were beginning to back away, bolts poised. Abram bellowed a command from the depths of his throat.

"Do not retreat! Do not—"

Another hunter fired. His bolt connected, and the wolf skidded mid-stride, scattering fragments of ice as its vast paws clambered to gain purchase. The bolt jutted from its hind leg, seeping blood.

Stunned, the panting wolf pivoted its monstrous head from side to side, searching for its assailant.

With a clattering of iron and a rallying cry, the hunters raced forward to finish it off – but this time, the wolf did not meet the challenge.

Balking, it heaved a great echoing roar. For a second, its

livid stare flickered to the Lead Hunter. The flame-eyes, sharp against the coal-black face, would come to haunt Abram.

Even thrice wounded, its speed was unearthly as it fled. Its great paws scattered a spray of blood and snow before any pursuing bolts could strike. A handful of hunters made to follow it, but the beast's shadow melted into the endless black, and it was gone, a fleeting nightmare, just as it had come.

Abram knew when a hunt was over. He saw no reason to lose more of his best hunters over a single head.

"Fall back," he ordered them, wiping his brow.

The hunters turned to linger in the clearing, faces wan and glistening in the moonlight, catching their breath. Three lay dead. The snow was falling soft upon the ground.

Ledras remained at Abram's side, still watching the wolf's path of escape in disbelief. Cott's eyebrows mashed together in consternation, his lips set in a grim line. The expression aged him in the sputtering torch light. He was staring at the man writhing in the bloodstained snow.

"Kill me," Fyrin pleaded. His mouth contorted, gushing rivulets of blood. "Do it – now."

Abram's face did not betray a shred of sentiment.

"It's too late for him," he urged the straggling hunters, who looked on as he drew the final bolt. "Fall back."

Hesitating, the hunters allowed Abram passage.

Fyrin's strangled cries fell to the bitter whip of the winter wind. Abram approached him with a crunching tread, lowering his crossbow. Beneath his snow-choked beard, his lips mouthed a soundless orison.

He pulled the trigger. The bolt drove into Fyrin's chest with a force that made his body jerk, then lay still.

Homeward to Awl-Feth, the hunters slogged the acres of forest in silence all night, carrying the bodies of the fallen.

CHAPTER 4

Snow moon, waning
Two months after siege

The day he'd revealed his ability to heal, Aimes knew time had given him an advantage. The effectiveness of his healing, and the potency of sylvan plants, depended on the freshness of a wound. Little though he understood it, he knew that much: with time on his side, he could perform miracles.

The commander tasked him with the messy work of ailing Caenani soldiers each day. There were bones to be mended, infections to be sterilized, bloody gashes to be sewn up and dressed. He was supplied with surgical tools, all the materials for making balms and tonics, and cuttings of any woodland plant he requested.

Once, the commander brought in one of his best men, whose ribs had been run clean through with a pike. When the mutilated soldier wasn't making desperate, gurgling gasps for breath, he was screaming with a near-unearthly force. His insides, glistening and blood-marbled, oozed from him.

Aimes' breath had rushed from his lungs as sweat darted over his skin. Seeing the human body opened up like that stopped his blood like a dry spigot, snuffed all thought from his mind.

Only the screams pulled him back to reality. The face of the commander swam before him, all clenched jaw and sweat-laced brow, his breath hot and hissing:

"Oryaen. *Fix him.*"

The other soldiers watched on, grim. Aimes had looked at the soldier on the brink of death, and back again to the commander's ruddy face.

Fix him, or you die, too, it said.

So, he did. And the commander would bring him another patient. And another.

Tending the worst injuries gave Aimes pangs of nausea. The stench of gore clung to him long afterward, and his hands never scrubbed clean enough. He applied poultices of red trillium to gangrene-eaten flesh, tinged like dried, wrinkled moss, reeking and rotten. Worms and parasites called for a tincture of horehound.

They kept him in the reformatory during the interims, isolated from the other prisoners. It was dark and dirty as a chimney flue within the tall, decaying palisades and stones piled high for reinforcement. But there was a small firepit for warmth, and a bed of straw. The ground had been leveled flat and packed with loam to keep out the damp. The lictors supplied him clean water to drink, hearty rations of dried meat and hot gruel. He realized with a strange ache of shame that even that was better than life in the slums, where his meals were usually stolen or found in moldy scraps, and shelter was never freely given.

Time smudged into obscurity. Aimes became only subconsciously aware of it, when light slanted in thin gold bars through the palisades. If he put his back to the wooden posts and turned his head at just the precise angle, he could feel the warm sunlight against his face. It would be all right, he thought, so long as he could feel the sun.

One sunlit day, he listened to the commander call out the family names of Valtan refugees. He presumed it a head count, or a rotating respite from daily labor in the encampment.

The Caenani called them Reformation Days. Aimes heard the iron fetters rattle, the muffled protests as the Valtans were led, one by one, to the killing stone. He imagined them standing in a neat row, just as the boys had stood alongside him.

Some executions lasted minutes. Others were soundless as a summer wind.

***

Every evening, as the lictors stood guard outside and the light faded above the palisades, Aimes tried to sleep. But oftentimes, he lay awake watching the sky fade into dusk like a smothered fire, from rose-gold sunset to smoke-black oblivion. Only a sliver of the moon split the night, like the curved blade of a scythe.

It was on one of those nights that he wept for the first time. He couldn't fathom why, of all that he'd witnessed in his confinement, it was the color of the sky that brought him to tears.

Anchoring himself against the palisades, he listened to the pattern of his breath, felt for rhythm of his pulse, and remembered the miracle of life within him, still fresh and crisp around the edges like a leaf in spring.

He remembered the day he was supposed to die.

***

It had been the worst winter he'd endured, the damp kind that chilled to the marrow and dragged in the lungs. A day had passed since the Caenani had laid siege to Valta, the

31

capital of the empire, without warning. Families fled as murmurs spread through the slums: *They will strike here next, and they will kill, rape, and enslave us.* But there was no family to claim Aimes, a bastard child, another mouth to feed.

He'd known friends once, orphans like him. The eldest of them had gathered the knot of children together, huddled to keep warm in their tattered clothes.

"If they catch you, you must surrender," she had told them. "Or they'll kill you."

But Aimes had no intention of being caught. His feet were the quickest among them, and he knew his way around the slums and the wooded land beyond them.

It was the last and most ancient forest in the empire, spanning more than sixty thousand acres. Crossing it to reach any village would be a day's journey at least. If he could make it through the cold, he thought, he could hide there. He could learn to chop firewood, to catch game, to build a wattle and daub hut where he would sleep and wait out the war.

Go now, he told himself. Every night, in the darkest hour, as he lay awake in a goat pen, he told himself: *Don't be a coward. Go now.*

The night the Caenani came, there was no time left for cowardice.

They came by the hundred, masked and helmed, clad in dark shrouds and steel armor. Valtans scattered like insects, their nests raided one by one.

Aimes saw men begging beneath the bite of whetted blades. He saw a woman dragged by her hair, her face a crumpled and sodden mask. He saw the snow turn red, and he ran.

In hindsight, he'd been foolish to believe he could survive the winter, taking shelter in the cobwebbed depths of a redwood tree hollow. But it was better still, he had thought, as freezing rain battered its branches and a fatal chill crept into his bones. Better to succumb to the unfeeling cold of the woods than that of Caenani steel.

Despite his stolen woolen clothes, frostbite stiffened his fingers after a few days. The food he'd foraged ran out, the only remnants a smattering of empty nutshells and the desiccated carcasses of small game birds, long buried under the hoarfrost. In one distinct moment he had felt his own heartbeat lurch, slowing to a dull murmur, and realized he was freezing to death.

He didn't want to die. He knew that more than anything. But as he had looked out upon the wooded grove smothered in glistening snow, thick as a grave upon all living things, he could not curse it even as it killed him. It simply was, and he thought it beautiful.

When the soft sound of footsteps fell, he'd been almost certain the Caenani had come to take him – quietly, just as they had broken Myre's borders in the half-sleep of daybreak, creeping like a nightmare over the land.

He'd waited as the crunching tread in the deep snow drew ever nearer. Then he saw its legs like blackened pyre logs against so much white, its hirsute body as large and lean as a cavalryman's mount, its regal upward-turned face.

The wolf appeared in a flurry of snowfall, pitch dark but for its eyes.

They were perfect yellow circles, fiery as two suns fixed upon Aimes. He was drawn to their orbit, stunned in their consuming glow.

When he blinked, he was alone again.

Not real, he'd thought numbly. An illusion of death. A shadow cast and swallowed by the light – that was all.

But there were fresh tracks in the snow.

With the last of his strength he had crawled from the hollow and lay in the snow, whimpering softly under his breath at the bitter pain in his chest. The wolf's print was much bigger than a handspan. Around its edges, evergreen buds were just beginning to push upward through the thaw.

As an orphan, innocence blunted by the scavenging life of the slums, Aimes was not easily given to childish bursts of feeling. But it was almost magical, the changing of the season, the burgeoning of life in the midst of the brutal winter.

A sob had welled in his chest, catching in his throat. He had held his face close to the tiny growing things, cupped the leaves tenderly in his shaking hands. His fingers, blue and deadened with cold, could not feel their velvet softness.

Then a warmth began to spread. It kindled the sensation in his nose and teeth as he sucked in feeble breaths, feeling his muddied lungs unsticking and his heartbeat deepen all at once, like the cogs of a jammed mechanism greased and turning again.

And the woods gave him life.

Chapter 5

Wolf moon, full
Five years after siege

Dawn had barely broken the horizon when Abram crossed into his village. Just over a smooth expanse of snow, his small plot of farmland rose into view.

The rising sun cut a stratum of light across his battered old barn, and beside it, the modest yet hardy farmhouse of clay slab. Upon the hillside, the naked branches of fig trees spread like hands to catch snowfall while their roots became buried beneath it. Not since Armina's disappearance had the trees borne fruit. Abram first thought a disease had ravaged them, until other crops came up thin in harvest time. Seedlings refused to take to the soil. Wheat fields withered to brittle stalks. It was as though the earth also felt her loss.

Only a single horse remained in the ice-choked pasture, Liam's lanky roan stallion, picking his way among sparse grasses. Before Abram sold his livestock for slaughter, the family used to sell wool skeins and goat cheese on market days.

The sheep were the most difficult to part with. Armina had liked to name them, as though they were people. But Abram couldn't bear to hear the plaintive bleating of her beloved, aimless flock in the pasture, just as he imagined he could still hear the prickle of her laughter upon the air.

"You'll become too attached to tomorrow's supper," he'd said once, long ago, watching her nuzzle her cheek against the downy fluff of a spring lamb.

The shepherdess had smiled in a way he could only describe as full: in her full-hearted way, belly full with a growing Liam.

"All the more reason to adore them today," she'd said, as the lamb bounded away from her. "All lives must end and serve their purpose in death."

But there was no purpose in your death, my Armina, thought Abram as he passed the snow-caked pasture, pausing only to rest his crossbow against the solitary dogwood tree. *Not in yours.*

The heat of the hearth fire, reduced to a heap of smoking coals, warmed his frost-numbed face as he crossed the doorway.

***

Dianna had decided to surprise her father. Too many nights he'd returned from a hunt to find her awake as early as blackbird song, terrified he wouldn't come home. After all, her mother never had.

At the sound of the door unlatching, she threw a moth-eaten quilt over herself, curled up by the window and lay still. Her breath fluttered tendrils of mist on the glass, illuminated by subtle blue daybreak.

She heard the rasp of cloth as Abram brushed snow from his beard, cast off his gloves, and paused. He breathed a sigh, and his boots plodded over the floorboards.

"My dear *fenlet,*" he murmured, relief in his voice. Dianna felt the lightest of kisses on her temple. "You sleep at last."

Her plan had worked.

But she knew his gaze would turn toward her brother Liam. The young man was slumped in the wicker chair sound asleep himself, a dog-eared, half-read book open on his lap. On the table beside him, the stub of a tallow candle sputtered light over a large map of the empire.

Dianna rolled over, and under the cover of the quilt, opened her eye a sliver.

She watched as Abram approached the map, unfurled its corner, and peered closer at it. Routes were dotted in careful penmanship to a marked destination in the foothills of northern Myre: The Valtan Academe of Science and Medicine.

Once he glimpsed the lumpy shape of a rucksack at Liam's feet, stretched at the seams with a stack of heavy books, Abram scowled.

With a rattle of old parchment, he thrust the map away like it carried a disease. Liam woke with a start, blanching at his father's cool stare. In the dim candlelight, Dianna could barely distinguish her brother's dark figure as he scrambled to his feet.

Abram jabbed a finger in the direction of the offending rucksack.

"What," he said, "is that?"

Liam's eyes followed the indicated path.

"Books," he said.

"That's plain enough," Abram said, and it seemed it was only for the sake of his sleeping daughter that he kept his voice low. "Why do you have them?"

"The man at the market sold them for a pittance," Liam said. "An inheritance from his father, a Valtan scholar, but he had to put bread on the table—"

"So, you're to give up smithing weaponry, now? That's the plan, is it? Become a scholar instead?"

Liam shrugged, but looked aside. "No one wants a dull smith," he muttered dryly.

There was another pause as Abram took a step back, studying his son.

"You could be a greater hunter than I," came his hard undertone. "It's a pity. A waste of arms."

"I'd rather put my mind to use."

Dianna thought she saw Abram wag his head in denial or shame. The movement was too small, and her father too impassive, to tell which.

"You are a man now," he said. "Your mother would have wanted to see you become one."

"Mother would have said that being a man means more than being a soldier. She always told me that."

"You know times have changed. You know Awl-Feth needs men at its defense—"

"Yes," Liam interjected, "and Myre needs educated women. I could travel to Valta when this war is over. I could teach them. Think of all the empire could accomplish, Father, with women in the Senate. Women with autonomy! No more of these blood feuds with neighboring provinces; men stealing women for wives—"

"Enough," Abram said, the timbre of his voice intensifying. "The empire has renounced its people. The princes fled in cowardice from their duty, just as you are doing. It's because of them that the Senate has yet to elect a successor. It's because of them that the war in Valta rages on, and we must take up our own arms when the Caenani come for us. It's not the rights of women that will lead us to victory, but the courage of men."

Liam shook his head. "That's exactly what the High Elder would say. He's given up on the potential of the empire at large. As if he wants us to lose."

"The High Elder has kept us in the good faith of Mactus, fed and clothed," Abram retorted. "He is owed our respect."

"The poorest villagers are not fed nor clothed. They cannot survive on faith alone."

"And the trade routes cannot reopen until Silbarran is deemed safe again. We must make do with our rations now. Our best chance of survival is to clear the woods for passage."

Liam rubbed a hand over his head in exasperation, rumpling his fair hair. It was only then Dianna realized they'd had this conversation many times before.

"I can't hunt like your men," he said. "I'd be as good as dead."

"I lost Trajan and Valeris tonight." Abram's voice rose, cutting as sharp and cold as steel. "I lost Fyrin to the beast's accursed teeth. It's not about avoiding death. It's about a man's honor."

But Liam's tone subsided to a murmur, cool and aloof. "Then for what purpose did Mother die?"

Abram drew his great shoulders back, his eyes heavy as storm clouds. Dianna nearly expected him to strike Liam for his nerve.

"And what of Dianna, if I die with a man's honor?" Liam pressed. "We're to leave her without family?"

"She shall have a husband soon. Or else I will find one for her. And then, soon enough, a family of her own."

Liam stiffened at the words as though stung. His face softened, paled in the shadows, and he took a single step backward. He looked as though he might weep.

"Mother surely can't have wanted that for her," he said. "Not when she married for love."

"Your mother was a skilled archer from Kretaim when she came to Awl-Feth," Abram reminded him. "Her customs were different. But when Dianna comes of age, she will have a duty to our village."

There was a long silence, heavy and solemn. The two men stood so still in the flickering light, Dianna held her breath. Abram turned away with a sigh of resignation.

"Keep your books," he said. "But to the best of your

otherwise squandered ability, you must protect her in my stead. The horrors of Silbarran still breed."

Dianna remembered the women bound to the stakes. Their faces like gaping masks in the inferno. Their dripping, burning flesh.

No horror in the woods could be worse than that.

"She's old enough to know," Liam said.

"There's no need for it." Abram's voice simmered low. "Better it remains a nightmare."

His heavy tread gnawed through thick snow as he left to report the hunt's casualties to the High Elder, the door swinging shut behind him.

Dianna sat upright, flinging away the quilt.

"I could be a hunter instead of you," she said at once.

Liam wrenched around. He squinted through his spectacles at his sister, as if the childish angles of her face betrayed the drawn, lackluster eyes of her sleepless night.

"Damned snake oil, that insomnia tonic," he said, shaking his head.

"It made me a little faint," she said helpfully.

"I'll be having a word with the apothecary."

But he was changing the subject. Dianna glanced out the window, where her father's crossbow, propped up against the dogwood, gleamed in the dawning light. Mouth pressed in determination, she rose to her feet with a whirl of hair.

"I could be a hunter," she insisted. "Like father is. Like Mother was—"

"And just where will you find your courage? Where, when Silbarran frightens you out of your wits and your imagination runs wild every night?"

"But she could still be out there," Dianna's voice fell to a whisper. "She could be—"

"She's gone, Dianna." Liam's tone was final, and Dianna felt its weight. "Do not speak of it again."

Dianna swallowed the words that threatened to creep up her throat. Like a lump they lodged there, uncomfortable and unspoken, and she was left with only a hollow reverie.

Liam looked aside, hiding his face. As if to soften the reprimand, he murmured, "Shall I show you the books?"

Dianna eyed the rucksack he had hauled home. She suspected this new find made his collection the largest in Awl-Feth, since the only other books she'd held were the crumbling hymnals they used at the cathedral.

"Come on, then," he coaxed, extracting them one by one.

Liam introduced each of their subjects – history, botany, art and architecture and arithmetic – with his warm voice and careful hands, treasuring them all like children. Dianna admired their pages, fragrant with dust, old parchment and the tannic acid of oil ink. Her mother had taught her to read, unconventional as it was for women and girls, and Dianna could nearly hear her voice in every word.

She pulled a slim volume from within the stack, the most ragged of them all, which groaned at the spine with the effort of being opened. It was written in the old Awl-Fethan tongue, and delicate illustrations laced the margins.

She studied the picture of a strikingly graceful figure, almost human in appearance but largely featureless. It stood like a dancer, arms aloft, bearing a chalice in offering. She couldn't tell if the figure was a woman or a man, both or neither.

"Liam, look," she said, enthralled.

Liam only glanced up from *Ecology of Vinaem: Riparian Flora and Fauna*, making a kind of grimace before returning to the preface. "Imaginary stories don't interest me," he said.

"I don't think it's imaginary," Dianna said, brow furrowed. She showed him the book, titled *A Compendium of the Minor and Arcane Deities of Ancient Myre.*

41

Liam squinted again, contemplating the cover's gilded lettering, before a fleeting dread passed over his features. He reached over and snatched the book, tucking it back into his rucksack, and Dianna made a plaintive noise of protest.

"Sorry," he said, searching the stack. "But you ought not to read that one. The High Elder wouldn't take kindly to it. In fact, it shouldn't exist at all."

"Why not?"

"Because that," Liam said darkly, glancing at the book that contained the drawing, "was a god."

"But it didn't look at all like Mactus. The scriptures say he's a powerful man, horned like an ox and many-eyed."

"That's because it wasn't Mactus. And that's not our scriptures. It's a book of the old gods."

Dianna frowned. "Must you be an owlish know-all?"

"Must you be a common loon?"

Chagrin sharpened Dianna's tone as she regarded her brother. "If you bothered to explain, I wouldn't be."

To her surprise, Liam chuckled at this, eyes sparkling with amusement before his features smoothed again. "Fair enough. Long before you were born, An-An – quite long before – our people worshipped not just one god, but many. An entire pantheon of gods called *lares*. Each was a guardian of a particular domain – the hearth, the crops, the forest, and so on. It was believed they took the forms of ancient animals or plants. Massive things.

"It was still quite long ago when Awl-Feth was formally settled. When the original High Elder wrote the scriptures of Mactus and destroyed the temple of the lares with fire. He enforced conversion, condemning all pagans to death. His religion spread to other provinces in the empire and even beyond. And in doing so . . . he rewrote our history." Liam handed her another book. "Here. You can have this one instead."

Dianna took the book without taking her eyes away

42

from her brother.

"Now that sounds imaginary," she whispered.

"It's not," Liam said, adjusting his spectacles on the bridge of his nose. "Read your book."

Dianna thumbed through it in silence, tracing her finger over the fine parchment grain. It was a book of old folktales – stories of worlds peopled with exceptional heroes who battled fearsome monsters, always ending when the light of a star called Faeralis guided the hero homeward.

"Can I read this all night?" she murmured.

"Since you barely sleep, I don't see why not."

"Good," she said, settled. "Then I won't dream."

Liam looked up, a flash of candlelight in his glass lenses. A worry line creased his brow. He dog-eared his page and closed his book.

"You need not truly fear Silbarran, An-An," he said softly. "You'll never set foot there, except in nightmares."

Dianna turned the page to another story, another illustration: a strange, prowling creature of myth, small enough to appear innocuous but larger than a child. She couldn't decide whether it was meant to be the hero's divine companion or his doom.

CHAPTER 6

Snow moon, waning
Two months after siege

Aimes waded into the fresh ankle-deep snow, skimming the trees for a cluster of branches that would obscure him.

"On with it, boy," snapped the lictor from the edge of the woods. "You'd have just as well pissed yourself by now."

Ignoring the humiliation of eyes on him, Aimes turned away and unbuckled his trousers. He finished urinating and had begun stumbling through the snow back to the lictor when the commander's voice clapped through the woods like thunder.

"Southbound intruder!" The warning wavered over the trees in a gust of wind, sending birds billowing to the skies. "Alert the legate!"

Gutted with cold panic, Aimes stopped in his tracks. Instinctively he flung himself upon the nearest tree and began to clamber up its branches.

The lictor bellowed after him and gave chase, but Aimes was already high in the prickly pine boughs, clinging with freshly scraped hands, heart racing with terror.

The muffled beat of horses' hooves echoed from the encampment as soldiers took to their mounts. Aimes looked down at the lictor, whose mouth was pressed into a hard line as he unsheathed his sword.

"Stay there," he ordered Aimes between his teeth as a knot of soldiers on horseback broke from the edge of the encampment, racing into the northernmost region of the woods. Others hung back, their mounts switching their tails and blowing steamy breath in the cold air.

Aimes heard one of them say: "He wears the robes of a holy man, sir."

When Commander Havril's voice rang out again, Aimes saw his balding head through the thick branches below.

"Bring him in alive!" the commander hollered.

It had taken all of a minute for the Caenani to capture the trespasser, and there were no signs of a struggle. Soldiers flanked him on all sides, pinning his wrists behind his back. His head was bowed low in respect. Behind him trailed a swath of gilt-trimmed crimson robes, like blood laced with liquid gold spilt upon the pure white ground. One of the foot soldiers led the man's unsaddled horse by its reins.

They stopped at the edge of the encampment. The commander dismissed the soldiers, helm doffed. Aimes tucked his chin low, muffling his own breath in his tunic. A light snow laced the air.

The legate appeared from the edge of the woods. With all the steady, smooth-muscled grace of a big cat on the prowl, he approached the commander.

"Alive?" he noted almost dispassionately.

Commander Havril nodded. "He's a holy man, sir. So he claims."

"A holy man," repeated the legate with a touch of amusement, his eyes flickering to the trespasser.

There was a moment's pause as the two regarded one another.

"Name yourself," the legate ordered.

"High Elder Orcarrus of Awl-Feth," the man answered,

unafraid. "A humble servant of Mactus."

"Do you know of these woods?" asked the legate at once. "Of the dangers you've ventured by crossing them?"

"More than you do, legate."

The legate let out a wild half-laugh, as blithe as a man trading jokes with his comrade. He wrenched his sword free from its scabbard and held it flat against the trespasser's throat.

"Then you know you have no business here," he snarled.

The weapon's weight forced the High Elder to his knees, and his dark red robes pooled around him. He averted his gaunt, bearded face.

He looked gray, Aimes thought. Everything about him seemed gray and beginning to crumble, like a burned log splitting into ash. His robes were the exception, its fine gold brocade like rivulets of glowing embers that threatened to catch flame again.

"I come to you as an envoy," he said, calm as ever.

"On behalf of what province?" the legate demanded.

"On behalf of Caenan."

At the High Elder's neck, the blade's bite began to draw blood. A small leather satchel escaped from within his robes, swinging from a piece of twine around his neck.

"You are not Caenani," murmured the legate.

"Myre is a dying empire," the High Elder choked, but his upward gaze kept its hard focus. "My village, Awl-Feth, is dying. And I, too, wish to put it out of its misery. To be your ally."

"You feign treachery against your empire so that your true treachery shall be against me. I don't make deals with traitors or fools. Get off your knees."

"Then you will lose."

The legate's brow knotted. "What did you say?"

"You will lose," the High Elder said, his voice rising.

46

"Just as your men have been lost to Silbarran!"

The faintest twitch of recognition passed over the legate's face. Or was it fear? Peering through the branches, Aimes watched snowflakes spiral over the scene below. He couldn't imagine the legate fearing anything, least of all this old holy man at his feet.

Hesitating, the legate pulled back his sword. He returned it to the sheath at his side, his gaze turning to stone.

The High Elder's upturned face was resolute.

"Something lives in these woods," he said. "It is slaughtering your men like calves in a field. And worse still . . . disappearing them."

Slowly, the legate straightened. His lush, fur-lined cowl flickered like an animal's mane. He hissed a whisper between his teeth.

"How do you know I have missing men?"

"I know that, in our tongue, Silbarran means the Blood Woods." The High Elder's voice darkened. "And soon others will know them by this name. I know there are scores of your men either killed or made wicked here. I know this because its wickedness has touched my village. I know how to destroy it."

The legate's face had gone ashen.

"The wolves," he murmured.

The barely spoken word moved through Aimes like a memory: icy frostbite creeping over his skin. The ever-watching eyes of the great, smoke-black wolf. A warm pulse returning to his fingertips, spreading through his veins.

In that moment, he had been brought to life. In that moment, he had come to know how the woods gave life, in a way that even the legate could not refute.

He did not understand how a moment so precious could be wicked.

"The men of my village are highly skilled hunters," the

High Elder said. "To say nothing of your soldiers. But the two are distinct animals. And our common enemy is another animal entirely."

He reached for the leather pouch at his chest. Carefully, he removed the twine that secured it around his neck, pulled it open, and let its contents fall. Wolves' fangs, polished to an ivory gleam, clattered in a pile at the legate's boots.

The High Elder plucked one from the collection, rolling it absently in his palm. It measured the length of his thumb. His voice fell to a whisper.

"Have you seen how it corrupts men? How it moves under the skin?"

The legate's face was unreadable. "Corrupts?" he echoed.

The High Elder smiled. "So you haven't."

A gust of howling wind rattled the tree boughs, and Aimes scrabbled to keep hold from above, his face furrowed against the cold.

The legate was silent as the High Elder returned the fang to its brothers.

"These creatures are like no enemy you've faced before," he said. "But our god Mactus has willed me to come to you and aid you. Awl-Fethan men will fight mercilessly for their people. They will clear a path for you."

The legate stared at the array of deadly teeth upon the earth.

"I will take this empire by force, the same as your Imperator has taken ours," the legate warned. "I do not believe that you, a godly man, should allow your people to burn."

"And so they won't, should they heed my word and follow you into the dawn of the new empire," the High Elder promised. "For yours is the path of Mactus."

The legate's eyes narrowed, as though to seek out the false note in his praise.

"What would you demand of me in return?"

"My village is destitute, legate. Crops south of the woods have been barren since the winter solstice. My people will suffer terribly this year."

The legate considered him for a long moment. In one swift motion, he stooped and swept up the loose fangs into his own hand. He upended them into the leather pouch, and they clicked into place.

"Bring me another of these," he said, tying the pouch taut and thrusting it back to him, "and I'll pay you triple its weight in silver. I'll send lictors to mind your way. You will not return until it is done."

The High Elder rose in a ripple of crimson, settling his bounty around his neck. He made the blessing of Mactus, releasing his fist in a gesture of deference.

"Consider your bidding done, then," he said.

Turning away, he mounted his horse, his red robes swaying. His gray head inclined as his eyes charted his course homeward.

"About the wolves, legate . . . " he added, voice low. "Tell your soldiers to attack only at long range."

The legate did not move from his position until the High Elder's robes, flagging in the wind, vanished among the trees.

Aimes watched him go, mesmerized by the entire incident. Only when the commander's murmur carried on a flurry of snow did he glance back to the clearing below.

"Legate. It's Oryaen. He's in that tree overhead."

Aimes' fingers gripped the rough tree branch as the legate looked slowly upward. A cold smile crept across his lips.

"Oryaen," he called, almost gently. "Come down from there."

Aimes exhaled, willing his tense limbs to move. He took footholds between branches and slowly made his descent,

49

dropping to the ground with a scattering of pine needles. The snow's unforgiving cold enveloped his skinny legs.

The legate, not taking his eyes from the boy, excused Commander Havril with a leisurely wave of his hand. They were alone in the frozen woods.

Aimes shivered against the biting cold, his pulse a rapid drumbeat in his chest, terrified to return the legate's hard stare.

"You shouldn't have been here," the legate said. "Eavesdropping, were you?"

"No, sir," Aimes said quickly, watching his own breath twist into a wintry vapor. "I didn't mean to, sir."

"Do you dare look me in the eye now?"

Aimes didn't move a muscle, though his heartbeat ran wild.

He heard the rustle of snow and leather as the legate closed the distance between them. Then, silence. The legate's fur-heavy body loomed over him, waiting.

"Come then, Oryaen," he said at last. "Look at me."

Aimes glanced up, just barely, through a thatch of his dark hair.

A flash of silver lanced across his sight. The sharp tang of the legate's blade sliced him from cheek to jaw. Hot blood spilled down his neck. Aimes cried out, choking on the taste of bitter iron, clutching at his face.

"Do not presume that your safety rests with me, Oryaen," the legate spat. "You think yourself a weapon in our favor, but I have many irons in my fire. You are still a husk of Valtan flesh. If you cross me again, it is your tongue I will cut out next."

Aimes curled in the packed snow, silent sobs racking his body.

"Never look me in the eye," seethed the legate's voice above him. "Look down, where your kind belongs, and forget what you heard here."

He turned away. Aimes, blinking stinging snowflakes from his eyes, cupped a hand over the bleeding gash. He followed the legate back to the encampment, stepping in the deep footprints left behind.

He healed the wound like any other. But just as the legate intended, it left a scar.

CHAPTER 7

Flower moon, waxing
Five years after siege

From every branch, the ravens descended.

They fell like drops of ink, peppering the ground, covering Armina's corpse in black. As they settled in for the feast, with crackling bones and rippling feathers, they transmuted into a single massive raven. The bird's gleaming eyes fixed upon Dianna, its grotesque beak gaping.

It spoke with Actaen's voice, cold and rasping.

This is what happens to women who abandon the village, it said.

Dianna woke at the words, heart leaping like an arrow fired. The nightmare shattered and fell away, and the last image left in her mind was that of her dearest friend: Cathrin, amid the throng of villagers, hand crushed over her tear-streaked and wide-eyed face in horror.

Dianna closed her own eyes again, catching her breath. She wanted only to remember a time when Cathrin had been happy, and Cathrin had always been the happiest bride. When the village girls played their childhood game of "wedding rites," they took turns adorning her with crude jewelry made of osprey feathers, marbled stones, and twine. They anointed her with sacred oil and scattered flower seeds at her feet as a blessing of fertility, singing festival songs all the while. They would tell her to be brave, that she was serving the highest order of Mactus, speaking softly as they held her hands.

Dianna had never said such things. She thought it was wrong not to give the chosen bride a choice herself, even though Cathrin seemed eager to be one.

But just for a moment, she lay in darkness and let the memory come back to her.

***

"Why don't you wish to marry, Dianna?" Cathrin asked her teasingly, as Dianna braided feathers into her friend's ebony curls. "You could choose anyone you wanted."

Dianna grabbed a feather and tickled Cathrin's ear, making her shriek with laughter.

"I will take no husbands," Dianna declared through her own laughter, making a face. "Because those boys are all too callous in their ways. And they'd not have me. I'm only half Awl-Fethan, remember."

"Then they are fools also. I'd have you," Cathrin said, settling into place again, a grin stealing over her face.

Dianna paused, her face warm and her touch tremulous as she tucked one of Cathrin's fluttering curls into the elegant braid. *I'd have you.* The tenderness and ease of the words held her, cradled her.

"And why do you wish to marry, Cathrin?" she asked. "Why do you give up your freedom so willingly?"

Cathrin's smile faded upon hearing the word. She turned around, her eyes dark and vacant as a doe's.

"Freedom?" she had answered, softly.

***

Liam was jumbled in the quilt upon his hay-filled cot, golden hair an unkempt lion's mane. The shutters were open, letting in cool spring air, sweet with budding honeysuckle and clover that carried for miles from the distant woods. Lining the wall was an array of crossbows, spears, and blades forged by his hand.

Dianna hesitated, her mother's soft sheepskin fleece gathered tight around her.

"Liam?"

Her brother stirred beneath the heaping quilt.

"Still can't sleep, can you?" he answered thickly.

"No." Her voice emerged hoarse.

Liam sat up with a shuddering yawn, putting on his spectacles. "Come here, An-An."

Dianna padded toward her brother, settling beside him on the cot.

There was a shuffling in the darkness as Liam lit a tallow candle. The glow illuminated his books, nestled in stacks at his bedside like precarious cairns.

"What do you want to hear tonight?" he asked, selecting the volume of folktales. "The one about the magic geese or the one about the magic bridge?"

"No magic. Something else. Something real."

Liam closed the book and glanced at his collection.

"*Classification of Infectious Human Ailments; Lecarus: The Philosophical Oratories; Astronomical Theory—*"

"Tell me the story about the demons," Dianna said.

Liam's brow crumpled as he turned askance from her.

"I can't."

"Please, Liam."

"No."

"I just want to know how she really died."

Liam closed his eyes and was quiet, his profile still against the star-speckled sky beyond the window.

"You must know something, Liam," she said. "You know so much."

Her brother rubbed a hand through his tufted hair with a sigh and moved to sit cross-legged opposite her. A dark frown furrowed his face in the glowing light.

"I'll tell you your bedtime story, Dianna," he said at last. "But it won't help you sleep."

Dianna waited.

"What do you think Father does to keep us fed?" he asked.

"He hunts wolves in Silbarran," said Dianna. "He pays tax in wolf heads."

Liam's voice dropped to a barely audible murmur, as though afraid to be overheard.

"Did you know that wolves rarely attack humans unless provoked?"

"No."

"Do you think our mother would have provoked a wolf when she hunted?"

"No. I don't."

"And she was good with her bow."

"Yes."

"So you see," Liam said in his sensible way, "when she went missing in Silbarran, Father knew it wasn't just wolves."

"Then—" Dianna started, but Liam cut across her.

"Do you remember when the woodcutter went missing? The very next moon? The High Elder called all the men to scour the woods for him, and Father took our horse and his crossbow, and he made you stay inside. Do you remember that?"

Dianna nodded. The High Elder had closed the trade

routes not long after, declared Silbarran unsafe to all but the hunters.

There is only blood there, he had said. *There is only death.*

"Father found the woodcutter at the edge of the woods. The man's chest had been ripped open, but he was alive. I heard the trigger of the crossbow in the fog, and Father came out of there, leading him on horseback. And in his other hand, he was dragging a wolf's head. That was the day the High Elder appointed him Lead Hunter, and Awl-Feth called him a hero."

"A hero," Dianna echoed, nodding. That sounded right.

"But the woodcutter fell unconscious," said Liam. He held up a finger. "They called it the first stage. Stupor. And once he recovered, he'd forgotten the attack. He couldn't even remember crossing the woods to gather firewood. Shock, perhaps. It blotted out his memory of that night." Two fingers flickered in the candlelight. "Fugue. The second stage. And another moon passed, and we were called upon again."

Liam's voice dropped low, heavy with the weariness or pain of remembering – Dianna could not fathom which. His features were half-obscured in shadows.

"It was the middle of the night, under that full moon. The villagers had barricaded the woodcutter's home, and his wife was screaming. Deliriously screaming, over and over, *'his bones broke themselves.'*

"The High Elder came and anointed the doors with lamb's blood. They blessed the earth with the sacred salt. The villagers gathered and chanted prayers all through the night."

Dianna felt a chill creep over her skin. Liam held up three fingers.

"The third stage," he said, "is corruption."

His hand fell away, and his stare was hollow in the

56

sputtering light, searching into some deep void beyond her where she could not follow.

"I looked into the window, Dianna. I saw its eyes. It was like a fire had touched them. They burned like smelted gold. And it was . . ." He stopped, breath deepening. "Thrashing. Wild. But when dawn broke, he was just a woodcutter. Just a naked, bewildered man. And the High Elder set his home on fire. With him inside it."

Dianna was wordless for a moment. The truth seeped like cold ice-melt into her bones. She closed her eyes and saw the flourish of the High Elder's vivid crimson robes. Heard the apotropaic cries of the villagers. Tasted smoke in her throat.

"So demons live in Silbarran," she whispered. "And they . . ."

"Metamorphose," Liam offered.

"Metamorphose . . ."

"Every full moon."

"But you don't believe in folktales."

"Some of the great scholars claim we are made of stardust. And that is a kind of folktale," said Liam, but he sounded doubtful.

The sheepskin fell away as Dianna went to the window, and the vast night sky pulled her into its embrace. The stars became almost tangible, like pieces of silver she could reach out to touch.

One glowed brighter among the others. Faeralis, she thought. But it was still only a mote, a little white fish in the bottom of an ocean.

"Listen, An-An," said Liam, his voice soft. "I promised Father I'd protect you. He must never know that I told you this."

"Why did you, then?"

Her eyes met his, and their steadiness seemed to surprise him. His brow knitted in contemplation.

"Because we fear what we don't understand," he said. "The more you know about something, the less power it has over you."

Dianna looked at the moon. That night it was barely a crescent cradling earthshine, a white wisp of silk or a sliver of creamy birch bark. Incomplete, but there. It would grow, as night-blooming jasmine would grow, or a blot of spilled milk, or a hillside gathering snow.

"Are all places so full of fear?" she whispered.

Behind her, Liam's voice was low and measured.

"No," he said. "There is much to fear in Valta now, but also in Kretaim, in L'Heste, and even in places far, far across the sea. There are wars, there is sickness, and sometimes there are both."

Liam paused. Dianna sensed that her brother was choosing his words with care.

"But our people are beset from all sides," he said. "And worse still, when people can't harm what threatens them, they harm each other."

Dianna turned, a question on her lips, but Liam spoke first.

"Maybe we can go together someday, An-An. Beyond Awl-Feth. See for ourselves what the world can offer us." The smile on his face looked real, but Dianna could see the pain in his eyes, the worry he tried so hard to keep from her.

From the edge of the woods, another pair of eyes watched her.

CHAPTER 8

Raven moon, waning
Three months after siege

In the middle of the night, dull footfalls and the groan of the steel door roused Aimes from sleep. The commander's face appeared at the threshold, his expression unreadable.

"Up, Oryaen," he said. "I've a job for you."

Aimes clutched a woolen cloak around him against the cold and followed the commander into the encampment, watching the dawn light shift through rows and rows of crooked wooden palisades. Valtan captives were digging trenches all along their periphery.

The sun had just barely risen over the horizon, casting a golden blush on the Caenani soldiers. They milled around their tents, some sharpening their blades and chatting, some eating a cold breakfast of dried meat. At the center of the encampment, he glanced briefly at the deep red and russet Caenani flag hanging on its post.

Aimes squinted against the swelling sunlight, watching the flutter of tattered fabric in the wind. Gently it swayed, flesh-toned and scarlet. Terror seized his heart.

It was not the flag, but a Valtan man. Rope bound his hands to the post, and his back was flayed to shreds and hanging slack.

Aimes looked around at the soldiers who showed no concern for the man, chewing their meat and scraping their whetstones and carrying on conversations. A muffled laugh rose up among them.

Blood pounded in his ears. He felt unbalanced on his own feet as he approached the man, as though the earth's grasp upon him had begun to slip. The commander gave an indistinct order.

Aimes stood feet from the unconscious Valtan now, close enough to see the face smashed to a bluish pulp, to hear the feeblest flicker of breath stir the air. He was a hefty-looking man, one who would fare well in battle, but slumped as lifelessly as a steer left to bleed out on the butcher's hook, half-frozen in the late winter chill.

"Oryaen," Commander Havril said sharply, and Aimes recoiled. "I said, '*is he alive?*'"

"He's alive," Aimes said. The words soured his mouth.

The commander drew himself up, folding his hands behind him. His glimmering eyes looked down the bridge of his nose at Aimes as a smirk played at his lips.

"Yes, Oryaen," he said. "Good."

Aimes' eyes drifted toward the man on the post.

"You keep him that way, Oryaen." The commander spoke low. "You fix him. Tell me."

"I fix him," Aimes said, looking down. His eyes traced the pattern of blood crisscrossing the stones, fighting the urge to vomit.

Aimes began to work, feeling for the Valtan's weak pulse, examining the deep lacerations striping his tortured back with featherlight fingers, until the intuition came to him, until he knew what to do.

Rocks clattered against his feet as he retreated, giving a single wag of the head.

"Well?" the commander probed. The dark, smirking eyes met the piercing blue ones.

Aimes swallowed the livid heat creeping up his throat. A rage like nothing he'd felt before was unfurling within him.

"The wounds are very deep," was all that he said, methodically.

"Yes?"

Aimes took a breath. "So, it will take longer this time."

The commander clapped his hands together, satisfied. "Quite right, Oryaen. That's quite right. You see, we've got all day."

He called his lictors over to fetch Aimes the herbs or plants he needed from the woods. Oak leaves, he said, and snapdragon, and a purple flower called orpine.

***

Late that afternoon, the Valtan man opened his swollen eyes. Aimes saw that his pupils were dilated like a snake's, a sign of trauma.

"Mactus," the man rasped in a voice as dry and brittle as hot sand. "Mactus."

It took Aimes several attempts to make him drink water. The man kept shuddering, choking and spitting. A fine sheen of sweat shone on his gray-tinged skin.

His flat eyes pleaded with Aimes. "Mactus . . . Hah . . ."

The soldiers had long ago trickled from the encampment to carry out the day's raids and patrols. Only the lictors remained at its defense, pacing the palisades. Quickly Aimes glanced at them before reaching out to the man's face, hushing him.

"You're going into shock, sir," he said, as softly as he could. "You're going to be all right now. You're healing."

The Valtan man lolled forward, sucking hollow breaths between hacking coughs, then fell silent, twitching. The bruises covering his face were already fading to yellow.

Aimes crouched upon the stony ground, a lump in his throat.

"What is your name, sir?" he asked.

But the man's gaze didn't move from the ground.

"Don't matter a damned thing," he said. "Hah. Just a servant to the citadel, boy. Don't matter a damned thing."

Aimes paused, then tried a different tack.

"Why did they choose you?" he whispered. "Did you make them angry?"

The man's tight stare flicked toward him and sweat dripped from a thatch of his hair. He looked like a caged animal startled by a noise.

"What did I do?" The man gave a single, chortling cough. "Boy, you're not asking the right question. What did our Imperator do? What did the Valtan nobility do? That's what it comes down to. Noble damned blood."

Aimes thought the man might be delirious, but he seemed lucid enough as his pupils slowly contracted and his quivering subsided.

"What do you mean?"

The man's eyes narrowed to pinpricks, glittering in the heat.

"You're a slum boy, aren't you?" he murmured. "Folk like us are just collateral in the wars of bigger men. Plenty of rich, educated Valtan men, see. Not enough women of caliber. So, our Imperator sent for Caenani women for wives, right? Took what he wanted. A power play, see. Starting fires from kindling. S' the only way to build an empire.

"He . . . sent for them?"

"Like cattle."

Distantly, metal clanged and grated against stone as one of the trench-diggers struck a rock. The man started, trembling uncontrollably, fighting to speak through his coughing fit.

"Then the Imperator passed on," he said, swallowing. "So here we are paying for his crimes, right? And now his cowardly sons have fled the empire like rats fleeing a shipwreck. Gone. Mactus knows where."

"Gone? Why?"

"You really are in the dark, aren't you?" The man shook his blood-matted head. The cuts and welts peppering his face dissolved as he spoke. "Listen, boy. The princes were our only hope. They left. They abandoned us. The Caenani won't rest now until the whole damned empire's scoured of Valtans. And then they'll build theirs with our bones."

Aimes had gone quiet.

"Why're you—" The man shuddered with another bout of violent coughs. "Why're you trying to heal me?"

Aimes looked down at his hands.

"Because I have to," he said. "Because I can."

"Don't."

The cold singularity of the word confused Aimes. He looked up. Tears were sliding down the man's face, making tracks in the dirt.

"I should've died. You should've let me die."

"You can't say that, sir," Aimes said helplessly.

The man bowed forward and huffed through his nose. It was nearly a laugh, except he wasn't smiling. His glassy eyes were pinched with pity. "Look at me. Look at what happens when you try to survive."

Aimes looked back at the lictors stalking the horizon.

"You're more alive than they are," Aimes said, low. "They're dead behind the eyes."

The Valtan man's mouth pressed into a hard line, nodding his head as if in awe. "You're a good boy," he murmured. "They took my boy from me. And my wife."

Aimes' heart plummeted like a dead weight. Distant footsteps sounded, scattering rocks at the center of camp. The man clapped his gaze upon Aimes urgently.

"You want to try to live through this war?" he said. "Learn to feel nothing. Be a good boy, and learn to be a man: feel nothing."

The footsteps edged closer, grinding over the rocks. The commander's face, haloed in sunlight, came into focus.

Without saying a word, he checked under the Valtan man's bandages, giving a grunt of approval.

"Well done, Oryaen. You can go back now."

Rough hands snatched Aimes from behind.

"No," he gasped.

He stumbled over the rocks. The lictor dragged him upright, pulled him away.

"No, don't hurt him—"

One of the hands clapped the side of his head. Bright pain washed over him.

"Quiet," the lictor hissed, and Aimes went limp as he was wrenched away, back to the reformatory, to the palisades, to waiting and nightmares. He saw the flash of fear in the Valtan man's eyes as the commander stripped him of his dressings.

"But I fixed him . . ." Aimes whispered under his breath.

The other lictors converged upon the man with bone-whips. Each lash against his flesh made a sound like a deep lake rupturing in a hard rain.

Aimes shut his eyes, feeling the crush of rocks beneath his feet as the lictor bore him away.

"I fixed him!" he cried out. "I fixed him!"

***

Aimes' eyes followed the wood grain patterns of the palisades. As night entombed him, his weeping became silence. Curled in his bed of stiff straw, he closed his eyes and tried to forget. But the nameless Valtan's voice, low and urgent, emerged from the darkness of his memory.

Feel nothing.

He repeated the words in his mind. Each time felt like plucking his own heart out, leaving a void as cold and dark as the hollow of the old redwood.

In time the silence consumed his voice.

In time he felt nothing at all.

CHAPTER 9

Flower moon, waxing
Five years after siege

Rites for Armina had been swift and crude. Without her body to bury, the Aergyris family had anointed the earth. Dianna had touched the rose oil to her lips first. It smelled of fading innocence.

In his wise, rational way, Liam had done his best to offer her solace that evening four years before, as they watched the last embers of incense flake into ash and smoke.

"Grief passes over us like a shadow, little sister," he had said. "It can leave indelible marks upon the soul, and our minds can become all the darker for it. But it is still an ephemeral fact of human existence."

Grief had flecked their father's beard gray and traced his haggard countenance with crow's feet. And though his eyes were murky with grief, Dianna saw the glint in them every night he left for the hunt. A flare ignited, twofold flames. The purity of rage.

She knew that when the moon was full, when he slaughtered the demons that had stolen his beloved and damned his village, the flames must devour him. And for the first time in her life, Dianna thought that Liam must have been wrong. Grief did not pass over their father like a shadow. It burned and burned.

But upon the morning of her fifteenth birthday, Abram's stoicism gave way to a smile and a low hum of greeting as he glimpsed her by the window, up with the sun again. He knelt by the hearth fire, prodding the coals back to life.

"I swear that a sprite came in the night and danced on your cheeks in your infancy, *fenlet*," he said. Dianna felt too old for the Awl-Fethan term of endearment, roughly meaning *little trinket*. "You've barely slept a wink in your life, and now Liam's telling me you walk and talk as you dream."

"It wakes him up sometimes and makes him cross," Dianna said. She glanced up at the fading impression of the moon through the window. "He told me to count sheep, but then I dream about how she used to tend them, and I—"

She stopped short, her chest aching with the memory of her mother. The way she made garments from wool with quick hands and fine, precise stitches. The way she showed Dianna to knead bread as she recounted stories of Abram's courtship in their youth. The way she dared to walk into the village with strong shoulders and head poised high, and passersby would mutter in disdain that she had no humility for a woman of Awl-Feth.

"*Mesbithen*," Abram murmured. *I understand.* He set the fire iron aside, staring deep into the coals. "I miss her, too."

Dianna rose and went to him. He gathered her into an embrace of bristly beard and woolen cloak, where they stayed for a silent minute.

She could not remember a time her father had mentioned Armina so directly since her death. She only remembered the steadiness of his marksmanship in practice, the hollow rattle of armor as he dressed for the hunt. Only the bittersweet mead on his breath when he used to kiss them goodnight, a vacancy in his eyes that made him unreachable. But those four words had finally emerged as a measure of acceptance: Armina was gone.

With a sigh of finality, Abram released her.

"Wait here, *fenlet*," he told her.

He returned cradling an angular object wrapped in a

67

silken tapestry, his expression doubly serious as he instructed his daughter to sit down. He did not speak for a long moment, great hands holding the mysterious bundle like a swaddled child. He placed it in front of her.

"Today you are another year," he said. "And soon you will learn the traditional work of Awl-Fethan women. One day you will burn the hearth fire, be wed, and bear children of your own. This is the will of Mactus."

Dianna thought she heard a broken note disturb his voice. When she looked again, however, her father appeared taciturn as ever.

"But these are hard times," he said. "The land has turned against us. You must learn to defend and provide for yourself. Perhaps you'll take to it better than your brother."

With great care, he unfurled each corner of the tapestry, lifted the objects from within it, and placed them in her hands.

"Were she here today, she would be the one to bequeath it to you," he said.

The shortbow was all too familiar – well-crafted yet simple, its limbs carved from yew wood, lissome and smooth. Alongside it was a deerskin quiver, full of a dozen slender, milk-white arrows fletched with raven feathers.

Dianna traced the grain of the arrows with her fingertips lovingly, hardly believing they were hers to keep. Another, less explicable emotion formed a tight, hard knot in her throat.

They were a hunter's weapons, a man's weapons – but they had been her mother's.

Abram was soft-spoken now, but the weight of his tone was unmistakable.

"You are not to go looking for trouble because I have granted you defense against it. Is that understood?"

"Yes, sir."

Abram watched her, folding his arms. "It will take more practice to master than a crossbow."

At this, Dianna looked up.

"You'll teach me?" she whispered.

The Lead Hunter's unshaven jaw was stiff, as though chewing over his next words.

"Small game only," he said.

Standing, Dianna slung the quiver across her back. The leather lay soft and heavy against her spine, comfortable, a second skin. The feathered arrows caressed her shoulder like a single wing. Adorned in her mother's weaponry, she felt a thrill of untouched strength.

"Now?" she asked.

Abram inclined his head the way one might admire a phenomenon like sunshine during a rainfall. His gray brows knit together, and his mouth twitched in the ghost of a smile.

He nodded. "It suits you already."

***

In the barren pasture, Abram scored the dogwood tree with an X: her target.

He helped her balance her square stance – *you're as stiff as a scarecrow; relax your form; let your wrists give a little* – and showed her how to nock the arrow and measure the length of her draw. Dianna listened and grounded her feet, though her heart skipped with anticipation.

"The trick is to maintain a smooth sequence of movement," Abram said, tapping her elbow as a reminder not to let it drop. "Now nock it."

She slid the arrow across the riser.

"Set up."

She raised the bow.

"Too high. Keep your shoulders down."

Dianna adjusted her posture, looking askance for approval.

"Better. Now draw."

The bowstring pulled taut between her fingers.

"Aim."

She directed the point of her arrow at the tree.

"Breathe—"

Dianna released the arrow too soon, sending it flying off her mark. She lowered the bow, grimacing.

"See, now?" Abram said, looking down at her. "You were anticipating my next command. You misfired because your eye is on the target, not yourself."

"What does that mean?"

"Marksmanship is not all about the end goal. You must map the trajectory of each arrow. Line them up correctly."

"Line them up," Dianna repeated, hand closing around another arrow shaft.

"Moving targets are more challenging," Abram warned. "Deer are flighty and skittish. A good hunter does not depend on the actions of his prey. He can only preserve the purity of his own. Can you do that?"

Dianna thought for a moment, testing the weight of the arrow in her palm, enamored of its exquisite shape.

"I think so," she said.

Abram gestured to the bow. "Again, then."

He repeated the same round of commands at rapid fire, pausing now and then to correct her form. Dianna missed more than she struck, her arrows sailing across the field and plodding into the soil. But the friction of each pull and the flight of each slender arrow sent exhilaration humming through her fingers.

At length she reached again for her quiver, heart quickening, but realized that no arrows remained. Abram began gathering the scattered ones in the yellow grass.

As he was restoring them, Dianna spotted the bobbing head of a small quail several yards across the field. It poked in the peat for insects, unwitting.

"Look there," she whispered, pointing it out.

"Keen eyes." Abram leaned down, steadying her with a gentle hand. "Remember, the bow is an extension of the self."

Dianna's fingers twined around the fletching. Slowly,

70

she slid the first arrow from its quiver.

"Go on," Abram urged.

Dianna made her stance, steadied her bow, and released the arrow almost soundlessly. The quail fell like a stone, flapping its pierced wing with a flurry of feathers, screeching.

Realizing what she'd done, a hard knot of shame clutched her stomach. She dropped the bow and ran toward the wounded creature, her heart racing.

"No," she gasped, falling to her knees. "I'm sorry, I'm sorry . . ."

"Don't be soft, now," Abram scolded her, advancing as the quail's cries shrilled to a peak.

"It wasn't clean." Dianna turned to her father as tears clouded her eyes, feeling foolish beneath his gaze. "What can I do?"

Immediately Abram crouched, scooping up the writhing bird. With a calm, quick turn of the hand, he snapped its neck.

"You see?" he said, showing her the kill. "Purity."

Dianna stared down at the dead bird, its form limp as an empty glove, tears falling on its bloodstained feathers.

She would practice every day after that, she decided, until her fingers went raw and her back ached, until the pluck of the bowstring became as familiar as her own pulse, until she could kill as calmly as her father.

She took a deep breath.

"Purity," she repeated.

CHAPTER 10

Frost moon, waxing
One year after siege

She arrived in the dead of night, on the brink of another winter.

A thin, white snowfall had powdered the charred firepits of the Caenani encampment, now mixed into a grimy slush. Only the snow upon the thatched palisades was clean and fresh, sparkling as though flecked with burnished silver.

A group of four lictors made steady snow-tracks from Silbarran, carrying between them a figure, either unconscious or dead, upon a bloodstained shroud. Aimes heard the rasp of their footfalls crossing the encampment, where he lay curled and unmoving in the corner of the reformatory.

Aimes' black, matted hair had grown long enough to obscure his forehead, beneath which his eyes fixed on the threshold as the lictors entered with their patient in tow. His blue irises had lost their luster, like precious stones abraded by the elements, peering through the pall of smoke rising from his smoldering firepit.

It was a woman's body they carried, the only indication being a willowy hand and a wavering of long white-gold hair protruding from the edge of the shroud. As they lowered her, she reminded him of a slain doe, the way her slender shape slid bonelessly to the ground. Her features were elegant, as strong and even as sculpted marble. Torn, muddied hunting clothes clung to her.

"Oryaen," hailed one of the lictors. "Brought you another present. Just like a flower, ain't she?"

Aimes stared blankly at them.

"Found her in the woods, see," the lictor said. "The legate wants her for questioning, so make sure she's conscious and she'll prove good for something."

"Something," echoed another lictor, smirking.

"She's got the look of spy about her," one of the men added, sparing a disdainful glance for their wounded captive. "Dressed like a man."

The fourth lictor waved them away. "Don't bother yammering to the boy. Brain dead. Only knows one thing anyhow."

He pointed at the motionless woman on the ground. "Fix."

Aimes nodded. He knew fix.

"And make it swift," the lictor ordered. "She's nearly bled out."

As the lictors left, the barred door rattling closed behind them, Aimes looked at the woman and quickly, quietly, went to her.

With mindless obligation he checked her pulse, her vitals, the fresh wound underneath her blood-soaked collar. Thoughts began rising to his subconscious not from a perception of his own, but as though another hand scrawled them into being.

Impressions of incisors. Two-inch punctures, inward-shaped. Circumference . . .

Wolf.

Its bite could have easily crushed her windpipe, but by some stroke of luck, she was breathing. His eyes followed the high cheekbones of the thin face, the almost peaceful slant to her lips. She was about the age he supposed his own mother might be.

He delved into his medicine box, extracting a vial of wild indigo root. Uncorking the glass, he paused.

A faint murmur shivered from the woman's body, at once strange and familiar to his knowing mind. It came from deep in her breast, cosseted and incubating, like a clutch of warm nest eggs.

Aimes set the vial aside, mystified.

Leaning forward, he tilted his head until one ear rested just above her heart.

An energy in the air quivered like a single harp string pull.

Aimes drew back with a sharp breath. His eyes widened, and he was more awake than any dawn of his life.

The wound had manifested a sickness deeper than the physical mark of teeth, incurable. It was pulsating through her blood at that very moment, slowly consuming her.

Changing her.

A shiver traced his spine like snowmelt.

Carefully, Aimes finished cleaning and dressing the wound, which would heal by morning. The woman did not stir from her slumber as he curled in his straw-bed and waited for her to wake. But his vigilance grew fraught with delirium, and all increments of time muddled into unreality.

In the quiet half-light before dawn, delirium – or a dream – brought the black wolf out from the shadows.

It stood in the middle of the encampment, in the empty space between the long-smothered coals of yesterday's fires, firm as cast iron. Its glowing eyes burned.

***

Her voice sliced finely through the darkness.

Aimes stirred and squinted at the woman's rising

outline, the hair that fell around her like gilded silk, contrasting her warm, fawn-hued skin.

"Where am I?" she asked, with unexpected calmness. She held one hand to her head, bolstering herself against the palisades with the other.

Folded in straw, Aimes watched as she doubled over and retched, quivering. Beneath the white bandage circling her neck, a purpling bruise had bloomed.

"Ah," she gasped when she surfaced at last, and her gaze flitted around the reformatory until they found his.

Her face shone pale and feverish with sweat, but the smooth brow and steady eyes showed she was not afraid.

Catching her breath, she said, "Hello."

Aimes shrank away further still, until the notches of his spine pushed uncomfortably into the hard palisades.

"Can you tell me where we are, *fenlet*?" she asked.

Aimes kept quiet. His hands began to tremble, so he balled them into fists.

"Can you hear me?"

Aimes looked away, then nodded once.

"I'm Armina," the woman said, heartened by this small recognition. "From Awl-Feth. What's your name?"

Half-obscured in shadows, Aimes moved just enough to get a clearer look at her.

"You're a long way from home," he said simply.

Her features tightened with confusion.

"This encampment borders the woods near Valta," he said, but nothing more. He could feel the pall of apathy smother him, slow his heartbeat, like death but worse. A living death.

They'll take her like all the others, he thought. *Useless to care. Useless to explain.*

But the woman called Armina studied the wooden palisades and understood.

"I see," she said, in that same timbre as calm and smooth as glass.

"Have to check your bite," Aimes mumbled awkwardly.

"My bite?"

"Your . . ." He hesitated, gesturing to his own neck. She

mimicked the motion, feeling the thick bandage there.

Easing closer, he knelt by her side. With undue trust she angled her head and let him peel back the layers of fine gauze, watching him peripherally.

"What kind of bite?" she asked.

Aimes removed the dressings. Underneath, punctures formed a crescent moon-shaped scar curling delicately around her neck.

"Oryaen," he said, as though to distract her. "My name is Oryaen."

She turned and her wise silvery eyes rooted into him, picking out the lie. "No, it isn't."

Aimes looked up at once, taken aback at her certainty. His cheeks began to burn. Discarding the gauze and cleaning his hands, he swallowed the lump in his throat.

She waited pointedly.

"Aimes," he said at last. "I'm from the slums."

"Mm," she hummed her approval, and unfurled again into supine position. "I thought perhaps you'd grown wild somewhere. And you're a healer, Aimes?"

A sharp thought barbed him: *or torturer.*

"Maybe," he mumbled.

Her smile was warm as she closed her eyes.

The silence that followed clung to the air, and unspoken words rested on his tongue. Aimes couldn't understand why he felt compelled to speak them at all. They were futile things, insignificant, stones cast into a fathomless ocean.

Feel nothing, he reminded himself.

Armina rested, her face a serene mask.

"You are very sick," he told her at last, with a note of fear.

Her eyes opened to the sky.

"Can't fix it," he said, his voice low and detached again. "Don't know how."

She turned to him, mouth pursed in a sympathetic

frown. Not for herself, Aimes realized with an odd pang – for him.

"So, I will die," she said. A statement, not a question.

"No." He retreated to his corner, pressing his back to the palisades again, as if to quell the inkling of sentiment that threatened to burgeon within him. But the softness of his tone betrayed him. "You'll be something else."

With that, Aimes turned over, leaned his cheek against the wood grain, and didn't speak another word.

CHAPTER 11

Frost moon, waxing
Five years after siege

The first sensation was cold.

Its numbness embraced her, settled clean and raw in her lungs with her awakening breath. The sharp teeth of it needled at her nose and cheeks.

Dianna lay still, blinking. One by one, like flower buds unfurling in spring, each of her senses returned to life.

The silence was broken only by the faintest of sounds – the soft skitter of nocturnal animals, the tumble of melting snow from a tangle of branches, the wind's dull susurration. She saw darkness above; white below.

She smelled the earthy spice of pine.

A nightmare.

She looked at her body and thought it had somehow disappeared, that she'd dissolved into the snow itself. But a bitter gust unsettled her hair, making the ends whirl about her face. A white nightgown flickered around her legs.

Dianna clenched her hand experimentally. A warm rush of blood prickled through her. She tried the other hand.

No, this is real.

"No," she found herself saying. She rubbed the back of her head, tearing clumps of snow from her hair. "No . . ."

She sat up, squinting into the night. The farmhouse was

a distant speck on the horizon. The slope below it was draped in a clean, blank canvas, smudged only by a trail of her own footprints. They stopped in a spray of powder at her stocking feet, where she'd tripped and woken. She moved her ankle away from a knotted tree root and looked up.

Snow-laced pines loomed tall and motionless as sentinels around her.

Something moved among them, half-smothered in the dark. Dianna glimpsed slivers of its lupine form. A chill slithered through her as she rose to her feet.

The demon went still, watching her.

Behind latticed branches, its molten yellow stare was unfaltering. Dianna's heart was a bird beating its wings against the cage of her ribs. Though her instincts screamed to run, she dared not move.

Both girl and wolf stood with the impasse of strangers, each studying the other. Time seemed to suspend. The sounds of the woods calmed to a hush.

It began to snow.

The snow fell like fragments of moonlight, silver-flecked, before blinking out in the darkness. Dianna stood like a shivering fawn on feeble legs as the cold nipped at her skin, pushing its icy fingers through her hair. It touched her nose, swelled in her fingertips and toes. Snowflakes caught in her eyelashes.

The wolf's expression seemed serene, even curious, fringed in a soft halo of fur. Its auric eyes remained fixed on hers as if waiting for something to happen.

As Dianna stayed rooted to the spot, the grip of fear began to slacken. And slowly, a profound wonder filled her.

The wolf crept forward with a tentative grace, despite its sheer mass. It loomed over her, tall as a grown man. There was a subtle deadliness in its deliberate steps, like a snake twisting through grass, like smoke curling from a slow-burning fire.

Dianna's breath deepened. She visualized it killing her in one smooth movement – seizing her neck in its jaws, throwing her to the ground with ease.

But still she could not find the strength to move as the snow crushed under its heavy footfalls, closing the distance between them.

The wolf's head was low, flame-eyes level with hers. Something human stared out from their depths.

The realization tingled on her skin, shivered deep into her bones.

"I see you in there," she whispered.

It was so close she could feel its hot breath wash over her, strangely welcoming in the winter chill. For one mad second, she wanted to reach out and stroke its fur, just to know the feel of it.

Its muzzle furrowed, revealing glazed, sharp teeth.

Dart-quick, its fangs pierced the soft flesh just above her elbow, sinking in, drawing blood. The white-hot pain shattered through her arm like glass. She buckled to the ground, convulsing.

The wolf turned in a flash, vanished into the veil of snowfall and beyond the clustered pines, a memory to be forgotten.

Stifling her tears, Dianna clutched her wounded arm instinctively – but the bite had only just broken the skin. A thin trickle of blood warmed her fingers.

She blinked upward at the flurry of snowflakes spiraling on the soft wind. Her body felt light, detached, as if she were floating up there with them.

Minutes lurched on. The wind grew to a howl as the snow thickened, filling her footprints. The bright pain of the bite throbbed into a duller ache, like a fresh bruise. A voice called her name in the distance.

The muffled outcry rose to a refrain at her ear:

"No, no, no . . ."

She knew the fair, feathery hair, the cool green of the horrorstruck eyes as they materialized. Her brother's arms, warm and strong, encircled her.

"Liam," she choked.

Liam's brow creased as he looked at the bleeding puncture wounds.

"Don't tell," Dianna whimpered. "Don't tell Father."

Liam's gaze followed the small dots of blood dappling the pristine snow. The mangled fabric of her sleeve. The tears that spilled down her cheeks.

His jaw hardened, became resolute. He hung his crossbow over his back, gathered her in his arms, and kicked fresh snow over the blood-speckled ground.

"No one will know of this," he promised her under his breath, and holding her tight, moved as quickly as he could across the woods.

Dianna felt limp, featherlight, as he carried her toward the farmhouse, sidestepping low-hanging branches, his feet thrashing through the snow.

The faint sound of hooves startled her, and Liam stopped in his tracks. He ducked under a branch and pressed his back to a giant pine tree, clutching his sister close to his chest.

The horse pounded a thick canter along the perimeter of the woods. Dianna stiffened as Liam stole a look around the trunk of the pine. In the frigid air, steam rose from the horse's gleaming muscles. She could just perceive the outline of its rider, a village scout, patrolling the edge of the woods.

But the drum of the horse's gait carried on.

Liam caught his breath. Just on the hill, the warm glow of firelight beckoned from the windows of the Aergyris home. A storm had begun to churn, blocking the black sky with white. Dianna's heartbeat quickened as she stared ahead at Liam's trajectory, hoping the mantle of darkness and snow-choked gusts would shield them from the scout's eyes.

Liam waited until the scout was out of sight and the drumming had died. Holding fast to her, he hurtled into the dark abyss.

The icy wind whipped through their hair, stinging their faces. Liam stumbled in the snowbank, panting, but clambered onward until they reached the threshold. For the first time ever, she heard him utter a ceaseless prayer to no god in particular:

"Please let her live, please let her live, please, please—"

They were the last words she heard before she fell into the oblivion of a dream, before the light of the sputtering tallow candle faded before her eyes. Liam was careful not to wake their father, hardly breathing as he wrapped her wound and put her to bed.

Stupor.

This memory would slip through her mind like water through a sieve.

Fugue.

And at the turning of the moon, she would become a demon.

Corruption.

At her bedside, Liam buried his head in his hands and wept.

***

Winter dawn broke cold and bone-white across Dianna's eyes. Everything was too sharp around the edges, bathed in a light too bright. She took a breath and a fine, prickling pain unfurled in her chest, as though she'd been stuffed with straw.

Her own voice echoed in her ears. "My head hurts."

She touched a hand to her throbbing temple, a rough

bandage pinching the bend of her arm. The blizzard had dwindled to a few flakes, falling softly beyond the windowpane. Starkly outlined against it, Liam's figure came into focus, his eyes tinged red.

"Liam, you're crying."

Her brother's face crumpled as he embraced her.

"It's all right," she protested into his shoulder.

"It's not."

His tone, fraught with shame, struck a nervous chord in her. His arms clung to her in their attempt to comfort, but to comfort whom, she could not tell.

"Liam, what—"

"It could have killed you," he said, voice hoarse. "Damn it, if I was any later, it *would* have killed you."

Dianna made to sit up, her arm searing under the stiff bandages, face scrunched against the blinding light. Liam looked tormented, even deranged, with raw eyes and ragged hair.

"You were sleepwalking again," he said. "I woke up and saw you were gone. I saw your tracks going into the woods. And it . . ."

Liam held his fist to his mouth.

"The demon," she whispered.

Liam nodded, pale.

"Yes," he said, eyes fresh with tears. They spilled over his cheeks, sudden and frightening in their intensity. "Yes, An-An."

Dianna's pulse spiked through her veins, throbbing in her fingertips. Cold sweat began to prickle along her spine.

"I'm—" she swallowed, wide-eyed. "I'm a demon now?"

Liam paused, taken aback. Quickly, his gentle hands caught hers.

"You're just a girl," he said fiercely. "Just a farm girl with blackened fingers from pulling weeds, who reads folktales and never sleeps and asks too many questions. You're my little sister, who looks more like our mother every day."

In the harsh light, Dianna blinked away the sting of tears.

"Aren't you afraid of me?" she asked.

83

Liam shook his head.

"I'm afraid," he said under his breath, "of what they'll do."

Dianna thought of the woodcutter with a pang. She imagined the old wooden farmhouse in the sizzling haze of an inferno, crackling to pieces.

"I told Father you'd taken ill," Liam said. "I promised you I wouldn't tell him. But I can't keep my promise unless we leave Awl-Feth. We'd have to cross Silbarran to make for Shole. Take my horse and all the silver and bread we need to survive."

Dianna shook her head. "He won't rest until he finds us."

"I know that," Liam snapped, looking aside as color rose to his face. "Of course I know that. Staying is death, and leaving is death. But what else can we do, An-An? What can we do when they find you . . ."

He trailed off, covering his face with his hands. Dianna waited, but he didn't finish. She had never seen her wise, collected brother at such an utter loss.

"They can't find me if I hide," she said, voice soft.

A brief silence fell. Liam looked up from his hands. "Hide."

The word contained an inkling of hope. Dianna could almost see the plan unfolding in his brilliant green eyes.

"Liam," she said, hesitating. "When is the next full moon?"

Liam had put a hand over his mouth, lost on the slipstream of a thought, and his answer was a distracted murmur.

"Three days."

Chapter 12

Frost moon, waxing
One year after siege

In the morning, Aimes woke to a blank white sky. The crumpled shroud was vacant of its body.

Armina knelt at the threshold of the reformatory, profiled against the morning light, staring out at the killing stone. Her hands were folded in her lap, but her eyes were not closed in prayer. They rested on the bloodstained stone as though if she looked hard enough, she could extract some hidden meaning, a meaning that Aimes himself had long forgotten.

At his movement, Armina turned toward the scrawny boy huddled in the corner.

"Where are your parents, Aimes?" she asked.

The sound of his real name gripped him, and he answered without thinking.

"Gone."

The word shifted in the air like a single falling leaf, soft and final.

"They are dead?"

"Don't know."

"You're all alone?"

Aimes shrugged and averted his eyes. "Don't like people."

"I can't fault you for that," Armina murmured. "I'm an outsider, too."

Aimes focused his attention on a spot of fungi sprouting in the palisades, slowly spreading dry rot.

"I am not Awl-Fethan," Armina said. "But women cannot leave the village. Bloodlines are too valuable, says the High Elder. It's too dangerous beyond our borders, he says. But we were desperate."

She did not turn away from the killing stone, as though talking to herself.

"The first cold snap killed our crops. Not enough meat to last us through winter, either. I have a good bow, so I went into the woods, under the cover of night. I'm not afraid of wolves."

At this, Aimes closed his eyes. Darkness enveloped him like the hollow of the redwood tree, terrible and absolute, all but for a glowing yellow gaze.

"The woods are beautiful in winter, aren't they?" came Armina's voice out of the darkness. "Even in that bitter cold. Everything glitters."

Aimes blinked, stealing a glimpse at her. One of her slender hands rested over the scar on her neck.

"And then, afterward . . ." Her voice took on a low, pensive tone; her eyes became unfocused. "Everything went black."

A long silence fell. The winter wind howled and rocked the palisades, sending snowflakes whirling. They melted at the warmth of Aimes' skin.

"I have a son," Armina said. "Liam. And a girl, a little girl, about your age." Tears were welling in her eyes.

Cotton-mouthed, Aimes glanced hopelessly at the rotten wood on the wall.

"I wanted to take them and leave," she said. "I begged Abram; I said, the village is not safe anymore. The High Elder is corrupt with authority, I can sense it. All that awaits us is slow starvation. And I will not let my daughter know the life of a woman in Awl-Feth."

The weight of her words pulled his gaze back to her. Armina's knuckles whitened as her hands crushed into fists. Her jaw sharpened as she said through gritted teeth, "I would move earth and stars to set her free."

Aimes thought she was terrifyingly magnificent.

"What—" he faltered, his voice breaking. "What is her name?"

Armina's spine relaxed slowly as she turned to face him. Her delicately bowed lips spread into a wistful smile.

"Dianna," she said.

Aimes echoed the name under his breath.

Boots creaked over fresh snow as the lictors crossed the encampment, approaching the reformatory. At once Armina rocked to her feet, collapsing over the shroud.

Instinctively Aimes was at her side, hunching low over her like a shield.

"Don't move," he said, wide-eyed, and she feigned unconsciousness.

The lictors' shapes blocked the light at the threshold. They smelled of leather and iron in the crisp, frigid air. The halberds crossing their backs gleamed.

"Oryaen," one of them called out. "Time to pick our flower."

Aimes shook his head. "Not yet. Give me more time."

"By the hand of Mactus, he speaks!"

"The commander won't be pleased with 'more time,'" the other added coolly, thumbing the staff of his weapon.

Aimes shuffled around in his medicine box, pretending to pore over the contents of an earthenware apothecary jar.

"There's something very wrong with her," he said, voice clipped. "A disease. Worse than I thought. Can't fix it yet."

The lictor's frown deepened all the way to his eyes, flattening his expression. As he took a stride forward, Aimes resisted the urge to smash the jar in his ugly, looming face.

The lictor paused, stooped, and peered at Aimes.

"A day," he said, low. "You have one day."

Aimes' eyes followed their path as they retreated, snow crunching underfoot. He spoke only when they had vanished from sight.

"They would have taken you away," he said. "They would have hurt you."

"Thank you," said Armina.

Neatly, Aimes stowed his medicines.

She sat up. "I thought you didn't like people."

"You're different."

He set the box aside. Suddenly his throat seized tight, and he turned his head away completely.

Armina fell silent, until his shoulders gave a slight undulation. He'd bent his head low, exposing the dark baby hairs at his nape. *Feel nothing, feel nothing, feel . . .*

"Aimes," said Armina quietly.

"Just," he said. "I just want it to stop."

A long-held snuffle ruptured through him in a single exhale.

"Aimes, may I hold you?"

Her hands reached out to him, and he went to her without pause.

Armina's lean arms were gentle and strong, her hair smoother than white sage, carrying the subtle smell of farm dust. He sobbed childishly against her breast, the anguish finally uncoiling inside him, because it was the first time he knew the arms of a mother.

Gently she rocked him as he clung to her, small and dark. She began to sing him an old song, and he felt his heartbeat flicker like a candle, warming from the inside.

CHAPTER 13

Frost moon, full
Five years after siege

The moon had emerged in the window of the hayloft, an unblinking eye of milk glass against the purpling night. Dianna coiled her arms tight around herself, even as her nerves seemed to crawl like vines. Beside her, Liam's stallion hung his head languidly over the stable door.

"How much longer do we wait?" she asked.

Liam had hunkered in the thick straw opposite her, a lantern swinging gently from his just-raised arm, ghostly in the half-light.

"Until he's gone out for the hunt," he murmured. "Then we'll go down to the cellar. For now, he thinks we're cleaning the stables."

The old cellar underneath the barn, laced with dust and cobwebs, smelled of rat droppings and rotting wood. Her father no longer set foot there, and it had not stored mead or rations for many years.

The perfect place to disappear, Liam had called it when they first surveyed its darkened corners. The echo of his lantern gleamed as he assessed the weight and integrity of the hatch door above them. *But we'll need reinforcement for you. Something iron.*

Dianna reached up, stroking the stallion's velvet-soft muzzle.

"You'll take him out, won't you?" she asked.

Liam huffed through his nose in dry amusement. "You truly are your mother's daughter. Your life is in danger, and you're fretting about the horse."

They stayed crouched for a moment, quiet, as though they were merely playing a game of cat-and-mouse.

Liam peered through a crack between the barn doors, raising his lantern.

"He's leaving," he said at once, breathless. "He's getting his crossbow."

Dianna's palms began to itch. She rooted them into the straw, flexing her fingers.

"You have to leave too," she said. "You promised."

"I know," Liam said, though he didn't move a muscle, fixated on Abram's movements. "I'll go as soon as—"

A piercing pain stabbed Dianna's abdomen once, like the stroke of a knife. She doubled over with a strangled cry, and Liam wrenched around.

The pain grew insistent, manifold, digging. Not like knives, Dianna realized, racked with rasping breaths – like claws seeking egress. Like fangs.

Her spine gave a liquid shudder, and Liam took a single, instinctive step backward.

"An-An," he said slowly. "I'm still here."

Dianna blinked, and the barn's interior washed yellow as the wolf began creeping into her eyes. Her mouth filled with new teeth, forcing open, and her heart stuttered with fear.

"Get out, Liam," she gasped.

Liam paled. He pressed his back against the wooden doors, as though to anchor himself to something familiar and real.

Dianna felt the fangs edge over her lips, drawing blood, acrid on her tongue. Small hairs pushed through her smooth skin, tingling.

There was a sharp *snap*. A single bone broke – one of

90

her fingers – like a brittle twig, before forming into a clawed toe. All at once a long, creaking *crunch* split the air like a falling tree as her body realigned entirely. Dianna yelped, choked, gasped as tears streamed down her face.

The stallion twitched, balked in its stall with a high, braying cry. Liam sidled toward him, his footfalls soft on the creaking floorboards.

Holding fast to the lantern, Liam yanked the stall open. The white-eyed animal bolted, skittering over the straw.

"Liam?" Abram bellowed.

Liam's breath pulled taut as rope. He looked around, horrorstruck. Dianna's yellow gaze bore through him.

Her body was rippling like water, molding and whittling itself. Her limbs shriveled and her jaw thrust forward, grotesque. Her ears hollowed out and unfurled into angles, like butterfly wings.

"*Get – out–*" she rasped again, but her ruined clothing fell away and her consciousness fractured, crumbled like sediment.

Abram's voice sounded closer, and Liam brandished his palms at the rearing horse. He grasped it around the neck and spoke in a low, shuddering murmur.

"Easy," he soothed, stroking its sleek coat, leading it aside. He spared one glance for Dianna, but she was no longer there.

In the shadowed corner, the sinewy gray-haired wolf stalked over the straw, looming nearly as tall as the stallion itself. Hackles prickling, its leg muscles twitched. Its pivoting ears and quivering nose assessed its environment.

Liam looked into the unblinking yellow eyes that were not his sister's anymore.

"Go into the hatch," he said under his breath. "Please, go into the hatch."

Its jaw hung slack, teeth pearlescent in the dark. Looking aside, its shaggy head dropped as it scented the barn floor.

Silently and without uproar, as if it had heard him, the beast sought out the curious square in the floor, planted its paws inside, and descended.

Liam stared for one astounded moment before whisking across the straw-strewn floorboards, slamming the hatch door shut.

Tearing his gaze away, his jaw was stone as he guided the horse out, closing the barn doors and latching them.

Abram approached Liam, heavy in leather and armor.

"Are you all right?" he said. "I heard him spook."

"A shadow," Liam said at once. "It's all right now."

Abram looked pointedly at the barn's closed doors.

"She's finishing the mucking," Liam said.

"I see," Abram said, hoisting his crossbow over his back. His stoic gaze surveyed his son. "Take care of her while I'm away."

"Yes, sir."

Under the burnished silver moon, the Head Hunter began his journey across the village.

Liam stroked the stallion's gleaming neck, releasing a breath.

"It was just a shadow," he whispered.

***

Morning rain drummed staccato and muffled on the barn roof as Dianna woke. A cold sensation slunk under her skin and twisted deep in her heart like a wound. Every breath she drew was heavy with the perfume of petrichor and dust, painful as her lungs expanded and pushed against her ribcage.

She licked her dry lips, lurching onto her back. Pieces of straw needled at her bare skin and mice skittered faintly over the floorboards with her movement. Her joints were

92

supple as loose seams as she unfolded her aching limbs. Inspecting her body, her fingers grazed over a smattering of fresh cuts. Gently she pulled away sharp fragments of wood, flinching with each bright, throbbing pang.

Sitting up, she stared at the walls lashed with blood and splintered in places where claws and teeth had scrabbled and gnawed. The hatch door above had been flung open, torn from its hinges.

A flurry of dust whorled in the air as she held a hand to the light, spreading her fingers and studying them, but they were smooth and still.

Her nightgown was crumpled and cold on the floor where it had fallen. She plucked up the once-white fabric like a feather, now shredded at the seams, dirt-stained and covered in straw. One by one she removed the brittle pieces, shook it out, and covered herself.

Outside, morning had dawned peaceful and gray. Gingerly Dianna stepped out into the rain-dampened loam, crossed the pasture where Liam's horse grazed, and opened the door of the farmhouse.

By the window, her brother leaned over a heavy leather book, dabbing a quill in the margins. His haggard eyes and feeble lantern suggested sleeplessness. His breath caught as she entered the room, his quill still poised, dribbling ink across the page.

"Where's Father?" she asked at once.

Liam looked ashen, faltering.

"Reporting his kills," he said.

"How many?"

Liam's brow knit as he replaced the quill in its inkwell. Dianna did not fail to notice his trembling hand.

"How many?" she repeated.

"Four."

She nodded, still. A silence loomed, thin as thread.

"What are you reading?" she asked at last.

He turned the cover to face her. The embossed title read *Homeopathic Analyses and Antidotes of Bodily Plagues*. She stared at it. "How could that help?"

"In this case, it's all we have to go on." There was a slow scraping of parchment as Liam turned a page of the ancient book, pondered the diagram of a strange, drooping flower, and shook his head. "Well, we're certainly not trying aconite. It might kill a wolf, but not without killing you first."

"Liam, we could leave. Like we planned. Follow Faeralis, like in the folktales—"

"No." Liam's eyes narrowed behind his spectacles. "It's time we use logic, An-An. No more stories."

"But you can go anywhere you want to. You could go to the Academe."

"No. I have different duties now," said Liam, scrubbing a hand through his feathered hair. "It would not be noble nor wise to leave. And your future is here, as is mine."

"I have no future in Awl-Feth," Dianna said, an anger rising in her, breaking her voice. "We both know—"

"Not if Father intends for you to marry."

Dianna thought she'd misheard him. Yet the reality slithered into her throat like smoke, smothering her breath. Of all the young hunters she would be fated to wed, she knew who it would be.

She shuddered at the memory of Actaen's fingers tracing her spine.

"I've heard him talking to Ledras," Liam said quietly. "His son, Actaen—"

"I'd rather die than marry Actaen," Dianna said at once.

"He offered to protect you—"

"I can protect myself."

"By the time you're nineteen, or the High Elder will call you into Judgment. You know it is law."

"Then I swear I'll be dead by nineteen," Dianna resolved, her tone biting.

94

Liam rose swiftly to his feet, eyes flashing, face a mask of anger. He did not raise his voice, but it was both sharp as steel and raw with terror.

"You dare not say such things," he said at once. "You hear me, An-An? Not ever. Not *ever*."

Dianna shrank into herself. Liam's shoulders softened, but his mouth remained grim.

"Father's already arranged it," he said.

"Arranged," Dianna echoed, numb. The word sounded so practical and tasted so hard and cold in her mouth.

"I will find you a cure, An-An," Liam said, resolve in his voice. "It's the only way."

But Dianna's eyes narrowed to pinpricks, quivering with tears, and Liam's own face fell.

She went to her brother, circling her arms around him. He drew her in but was silent for a long time.

"Do you remember what it feels like? To be something else?" he murmured at last. "There was a moment when I thought . . ." But his voice trailed away, and he shook his head again. "I must have imagined it."

Dianna thought of lying empty in the scattered straw, remembering nothing but the rise of the full moon, like a dead weight in her heart, like ice in her veins.

"It's like remembering when Mother was alive," she said, voice soft at his shoulder. "Her hazel eyes. Her laugh, like a bell. Father says I take after her, but now . . . I wonder if my eyes look anything like hers. And my laugh doesn't sound the same. And I don't know what's real, and what I only imagined."

Liam was frowning when he let her go.

"Liam," she said, blinking away tears. "I don't think I'm good."

"Of course . . ." Liam said, but his voice broke. "Of course you are."

"I rent the cellar to pieces. I'm violent."

95

"No," Liam said, turning away, gathering up the folded sheepskin upon the mantle. "No. It was afraid, and it wanted out. That's all." Dianna looked doubtful as Liam draped the soft sheepskin over her, tugging it around her shoulders. "In fact, I think you must be very good at resisting it."

"What do you mean?"

"The men who've gone missing in Silbarran . . . they never came back. If only the moon changes them, why don't they walk among us?"

He posed the question like one of his elaborate riddles, and Dianna shrugged, unknowing.

"They all succumb to the curse," Liam answered, voice intense with the conviction of another grand theory. "They relinquish their human consciousness entirely. There is something almost poetic in it − casting off the hubris of man's desire to conquer nature − becoming eclipsed by baser instincts−"

"Liam," Dianna interjected, before he ventured off on a tangent.

Liam paused to think, idly rubbing his neck and leaving a smear of ink.

"I'm planning to forge something," he said. "Something to keep you safe."

"And the hunters' weapons? Will you still forge those?"

Liam shook his head. "Armor, not arms. Not for all the gold in the empire."

"Not even to keep the village safe?"

"Your safety is what matters to me," Liam said, firm. "I will protect you, An-An. And then I will find you a cure."

Dianna looked down at the tattered hem of her gown, at the patchwork of grazed skin covering her legs, feeling the betrayal of her own body. She nodded convincingly, she hoped.

But for once, she didn't believe him.

***

The barn was filled with sacks of iron ore from the armory and the heady reek of sulfuric fumes. Liam's back was turned when Dianna stopped at the threshold to watch him. He'd rolled his sleeves up to the elbows, dressed in a smithing apron and gloves, hair damp with sweat. With more force than necessary, he battered his hammer against the hot metal. Dianna felt the harsh clanging shudder in her bones and knew: it was not armaments he forged, but her cage.

In the crook of her arm, she carried the book of folktales. Her fingers traced its leather spine for the last time as she placed it on a high shelf.

From a hook on the barn wall, she removed her mother's shortbow and the quiver of arrows, taking them to the pasture. She marked the dogwood tree, took her stance, and let her arrows fly.

Every day, she promised herself. Every day she would practice.

Another practice she reserved for the most hushed and sleepless hour of the night, meditating upon a cool glass vial in her palm. It fetched a high price at the apothecary, but Dianna had slipped it in her cloak when Liam's back was turned. According to his book, the flower itself only thrived on mountain ranges – and though nothing grew there now, the seeds of the aconite were perfectly preserved.

Holding the vial, she thought about dying. She would be ready when Actaen came to claim her. How easy it would be in one swallow, to free Liam of her burden, to free herself from Awl-Feth forever. And for one quiet moment, a small, secret part of her thought not of the pain, but the pleasure of escaping.

The sharp beat of Liam's hammer echoed from the barn tirelessly, obstinately, into the final fading breath of winter.

CHAPTER 14

*Frost moon, full
One year after siege*

The winter cloudbank had cleared, and a pearlescent moon was on the rise, but darkness was closing in.

Aimes had dreaded this night.

Stock-still, he pressed his ear to the palisades and listened for movement outside, snowmelt dripping from his hair. Beside him, Armina had closed her eyes, adrift in some distant thought.

"They're coming soon," Aimes whispered. "They're going to interrogate you, and then they're going to – to . . ."

Armina only reached for him, smoothing back the mop of hair from his face. The gesture was natural, maternal.

"You'll be all right." Her voice was soft with sorrow. "You'll go on healing, but not for them. For me. Won't you?"

Aimes looked up at the eyes that saw into him. They were so unafraid. The thought of her fate made his breath stick in his throat.

"Go on healing," she said. "Offering comfort to the suffering is the greatest gift. It's your gift. And you must be brave. You must try to escape them if you can, but be prepared for the very worst. After they kill me—"

"No," he said, his blood going cold. "No, you can't die

"After they kill me, you'll do that for me, won't you?"

A light shifted behind her eyes, quicksilver. Tears were stinging his own eyes, and behind him, a voice exploded.

"*Oryaen.*"

Armina gathered him to her.

The commander blocked the threshold monstrously, anchored by the lictors in their tough leather hides and wielding sharpened halberds.

Armina's voice emerged, low-pitched and fierce: "His name is Aimes."

The whites of the commander's eyes and teeth gleamed through the dark.

"Take her," he ordered.

The lictors descended.

Armina's warmth was wrenched away. Aimes crumpled aside at the blunt force of a boot, the breath struck from his lungs.

Lying on the frozen earth, he blinked the stars from his eyes, clutching the blow to his ribs. Pulled upright, Armina's murky outline swam before him, illuminated only by the round moon.

"Don't," Aimes sputtered. "I told you, she's sick!"

But a cry like nothing he'd ever heard fractured over his pleas.

The lictors released Armina, stumbling backward in swift succession, drawing their weapons.

"*Mactus—* "

"What the hell?"

Aimes squinted, seeking the source of the strange sound in the shadows of the reformatory. The bloody woolen shroud, sprawled empty upon the ground like a dead thing, momentarily distracted him.

Armina screamed. The scream ascended in the night like a raven on the wing and dropped to a distorted ululation.

The hair on Aimes' arms bristled. Petrified, the lictors

watched, small and dark, as Armina collapsed to the ground. And yet, her body was rising.

Her silvery eyes lit with gold, soft as autumn leaves, calm in her unwavering way. There came a great crackling of bone, like the splintering of branches under the weight of snow.

For a moment, her face was still hers as she looked at Aimes in the moonlight. She blinked, her expression aching.

"Go back to the wild," was all she said.

A thud reverberated against the earth, and the snarling beast enveloped her, massive and pure white and – just as Aimes knew she was, knew she would be – magnificent. For a moment he was stunned still.

"Kill it!" the commander screamed, desperation in his wild eyes. But the wolf lunged, her jaws snatching upon his head. The lictors brandished their halberds and unleashed a battle cry.

Aimes found his feet.

He stumbled over the commander's defaced corpse as the wolf tossed it to the ground, turning on the lictors next. The encampment was coming to life at the familiar bellows of violence, torches flaring in the dark one by one. He ran, pushing through biting sleet.

A howl echoed, deafening and fathomless. Trees loomed before him, as though awaiting his return.

Go back to the wild, he thought.

The torch flames began to swarm the reformatory as he ran, erased in the silken cover of night. The forest ahead opened to him like a mouth, swallowing him whole.

He faltered at the first strike of the halberd, the silenced howl. The silence cleaved him to the core, just as her life was ripped from the world.

Feel nothing.

Go back.

Tearing relentlessly through thick branches, panting, he followed the moon.

CHAPTER 15

Red moon, full
Six years after siege

Poking her hand through the bars, Dianna felt for the key Liam had left for her, unlocked her cage, and ascended the wooden staircase. The monthly habit had become as ordinary as bringing in the harvest used to be, as familiar as the hearth fire on a cold night.

As she lifted the heavy hatch above her, a muted near-dawn light flooded the gloom. Sawdust fell, settling in her hair.

She left the barn, crossing the fenced paddock where the stallion softly grazed old grass. Her trembling fingers opened the farmhouse door.

The fire had burned its last, leaving the air cool and drafty. She padded on bare feet past Liam, who snored in the wicker chair, and prodded at the glowing coals on the hearth to spark them back to life.

She waited until the sun rose fully over the mountainside to start the day's tasks. Taking an empty pot to collect water for gruel, she nudged open the front door.

Sunlight gilded the desolated fields, and a creeping chill in the air hinted at the coming of fall. Abram stood outside, smoking his pipe – a rare ritual, he called it, justifiable only after a hunt. With his armored back turned squarely to her and the cool breeze twitching his wispy hair, he took on the appearance of a stone unyielding against a calm river's flow. Dianna took several tentative paces forward. Beside him, she was a fallen leaf drifting and catching in a swell.

He ruffled her hair with a large roughened hand but did not look down. His faraway gaze swept out across the field and into Silbarran as he raised the pipe to whisker-edged lips. Dianna dared not speak, recognizing that she had interrupted a moment of private reflection.

Abram exhaled a puff of musky smoke. The smell, though mostly unpleasant, carried a note of familiar comfort.

"Ever restless, you are," he said at last. "Practicing your archery, now?"

"Yes, sir."

"Good." He took another drag and went quiet for a moment, lost in thought. "When I'm withered and gray . . ." He stopped short, heaving sigh as he rubbed a hand through his own shorn hair, peppered with silver. "Well, when I'm gone, I want this farm in good hands. I want my little girl safe."

Dianna looked up at her father, but he did not elaborate. On the horizon, Silbarran's tall pines rocked in the wind.

"Claimed one last night," he murmured, as though to fill the silence. "We'll get an extra ration this moon."

She didn't need to ask what *one* meant. When he spoke the word, his voice became placid, like still water, but with a roiling undertone beneath the surface. It frightened her more than if he'd raised his voice to her.

"You know you're never to go there," he said, low and quiet. "But suppose you see one. Suppose you're unarmed. Then you get your hands around its throat and you pull. That's the weak spot." He paused to take a last, long pull from his pipe. "You get it before it gets you. And be swift about it. Do you hear me?"

Dianna nodded, frozen.

Abram tipped the pipe's dead contents aside and some ash flakes escaped, swirling in the air. He looked down at her unsmiling, but warmth softened his voice.

"You'll always be safe, my *fenlet*." He kissed her brow. "You'll always be safe."

He turned aside, disappearing into the farmhouse to hang his armor. Dianna released a long breath, watching the ravens hover over Silbarran's green edge.

Clutching the hearth pot, she turned the corner toward the well. But what she saw there made it tumble from her grasp, battering the ground with a harsh metallic clanging. A small cry escaped her lips.

Fifty paces from the farmhouse, Abram had staked a long, wooden pike into the ground. Its end gouged through a severed wolf's head, emerging at the top of its skull – the trophy her father would soon deliver to the High Elder.

The wolf's broken jaw dangled open in the ghost of a slavering snarl. Blood flowed from its fangs, crusting the muzzle. Though its yellow eyes were open, they were vacant in death. A fat black fly crawled on the left one.

The image burned itself into her mind.

As she approached it, the stench of death twisted her stomach. The slow drip of blood set a cadence like a broken clock.

A bottomless pang of empathy sliced through her as she stared into its unblinking eyes. Deep beyond their yellow sheen was a person who had died an animal, nameless and unrecognizable. A reflection of herself stared back upon their glassy surface.

"Who were you?" she whispered.

But she would never know their name. Only that her father had killed them. Only that it was possible to love and fear someone at the same time.

PART II: THE HUNT

Ulula cum lupis, cum quibus esse cupis.
"Who keeps company with wolves will learn to howl."

CHAPTER 16

Frost moon, waning
Two weeks before siege

Prince Remetus Baines paced alone in his father's massive library. The silken black robe draping his figure flowed with his every stride, as though spun of shadow itself. Servants had set the trestle with tea, but it sat cold and untouched.

The room was ornate with gilded furnishings, scarlet-painted, rich with the smell of yellowing pages and recently disturbed dust. The prince could still hear the sinuous notes of a lyre, his father's favorite instrument, weaving through the corridor. And in every looking glass, despite his every wish not to, he saw his twin Ramus.

In their youth, the identical brothers pestered the citadel maidservants with schoolboy games, rearranging the Encyclopedia Centrum Erro-Wyld out of alphabetical order, placing garden spiders in the drawers, and – most entertaining of all – pretending to be each other.

This was a game of a different kind.

Two days had passed since the Imperator's death. The burial had drawn a massive crowd. Mothers, whose ashen faces wore new lines since their sons had gone to war, stood silently. Noblemen and their wives wore black mourning cloaks and shawls over their finery, weeping with affectation. Clergymen chanted elegiac hymns, rich and rumbling as thunder, calling upon Mactus to ascend the soul of the dead. The cortege had moved like storm clouds across the mausoleum floor.

But now the clouds had parted, a hushed calm descended on the citadel in the heart of Valta. The earth itself seemed to offer a moment of silence, blotting out the windowpanes with the swirling gray fog of a winter morning. And no one, Remetus thought with a bitter taste filling his mouth, no one ever speaks of the calm after the storm. The hateful, lingering calm.

He had spent the following days in solitude, refusing the comfort of his own bedchambers as he awaited news from the consul. Waited and grieved, while his brother Ramus had been so brazen as to show his face in public, offering condolences as though he had already assumed sovereignty over the empire, shortening his imperial name – calling himself Ram – to establish a rapport with common folk. It was improper behavior, an insult to tradition and to a birthright that belonged to Remetus, and Remetus alone.

Was he not, thought Remetus as he dried his eyes, the more dutiful son?

A man's voice came from the threshold, muffled by great oak doors.

"Permission to enter, my liege?"

Remetus stopped pacing and stood silhouetted against the windowpane.

"Granted," he said.

His consul entered, a gray-templed man clad in mourning black, and bowed deeply.

"Please forgive my intrusion, my liege," said the consul, "but at last I have judicial information concerning the will of the late Imperator, Mactus rest his soul."

"Forgiven."

"If I may, my liege, he was a singular ruler and a great

hero to many."

"The empire has seen enough of heroes," said Remetus, moving to the trestle. "Heroes die by Caenani hands every day. What it needs now is a visionary." He picked up a paperweight in the shape of an imperfect glass orb, stroking its smooth mirrored surface. His distorted reflection greeted him as his brother's would, echoing the same raven hair, thick brows, and aquiline nose. "Ramus is not ready to reign. Father has primed me for years to succeed him upon his death."

"That is the general order of things," the consul agreed. "Yet some regard the Imperator's final act of offering the crown jewel to Prince Ramus as an intention to elect him successor."

Remetus set down the paperweight but kept his eyes on his mirrored likeness.

"Then what remains disputed?" he asked, voice soft.

"The Senate disputes the Imperator's judgment upon his deathbed. That is, they dispute whether the Imperator was in . . . well, the condition to permit such an election in his weakened state."

Remetus' gaze slipped away from the glass. He turned toward the consul with a tightness in his throat and a darkness in his eyes.

"Do they," he said.

"Indeed, my liege. It has caused a rift among them."

"Of course he was in no condition," Remetus murmured, curling his fingers around the paperweight again. "He intended to bequeath it to me but could not tell the two of us apart. He was senile, not in his right mind. My case will convince the Senate of this."

"They have called for a meeting after a week's deliberation. You may present your case to the Senate before then, but I must advise strongly against it. In the interim, keeping matters private will avoid public speculation that—"

"Irrelevant," snapped Remetus, rubbing his jaw in contemplation. "Supremacy is not only granted by the Senate. I require consultation from another." His eyes flickered over the spines of thick leather books lining the library shelves, lavish with history and information all useless to him now. He breathed in their smell and at once thought it musty, suffocating.

"The Imperial Legate," he said, referring to the leader of the Valtan legion. "His word could bring the Senate to the right decision."

The consul looked askance. "I would think it unwise, my liege. He is hardly in a position to do so, as he is waging a war we are presently losing."

Remetus' hand engulfed the glass orb. In one strike, he smashed it to pieces against the table. The consul recoiled, his wide eyes moving from the prince's bloody hand to his bared teeth. The shattered glass fragments, delicate yet deadly, clinked across the tiled floor.

"Is there nothing to be done, then?" Remetus demanded, a muscle twitching in his jaw. "Have all means of justice been exhausted?"

The consul paused, as though distracted by the glass shards. He spoke in careful measure.

"There may be one possibility, my liege."

"Tell me."

"There is . . . an oracle. A woman of repute, who has advised great leaders in other provinces."

"A woman!" The prince cried out in scorn. "You imply that one who begets greatness is a woman?"

His consul bowed his head in fealty. "Forgive me, my liege, but I do not imply. Upon the brow of Mactus, I know this to be true. For are we ourselves not begat of women?"

Prince Remetus stared at the man as though he'd struck him. A long silence passed between them.

"How great?"

"My liege?"

"How great," he said, "is her skill?"

The consul's lips pursed, pulling down his expression. "She makes mountains of men."

"How do you know this?"

"It is my duty to know these things, my liege."

"And she will remain silent?"

"I can assure you, her dealings are entirely confidential."

"Then summon her."

"I'm afraid that is not possible, my liege. She does not call upon her patrons. Patrons call upon her, and if deemed unworthy, she remains elusive. Only if she is to avail you will she make herself known."

Remetus ran his tongue over his teeth. Blood dripped from his closed fist. "Very well. Where does she reside?"

"She has come to pay her respects to the late Imperator," the consul said. "A fortunate juncture, in such unfortunate circumstances. The slums after dusk are an old haunt of hers."

"The slums! Like a peasant . . . like a vagrant?"

"Humility is her condition of service. It is as the proverb goes, my liege – 'all the greatest men begin unknown; shaped from the clay, they shall strengthen into stone.'"

"I remain indifferent until I am witness," Remetus said, stepping forward, crushing the glass beneath his boot. "I will leave this evening. I will play along with this game. And if I do not win . . ." His sharp eyes, youthful yet promising in their threat, settled on the consul. "Consider your position held liable."

"Observed, my liege," the consul acknowledged, bowing deeply once more. "But I would advise you to conceal yourself. It is not befitting the prince to walk among those . . . unsavory folk. And to accompany you, lictors—"

But the prince held up his hand, silencing him.

"I will travel alone."

CHAPTER 17

Snow moon, waning
Nine years after siege

Dianna crouched low to the ground as she examined the black earth underfoot. Her sleek golden hair had grown long in womanhood, but she kept it pinned at the nape of her neck beneath the cowl of her father's old traveling cloak. At her hip, she clutched the broad, arched riser of her shortbow.

She crept low along a craggy expanse, reaching out to touch patches of dry scrub or a fallen leaf. Drawing in a lungful of clean mountain air, she caught the scent of a nearby animal.

Shooting birds was simpler. In springtime she could sit in the skeletal dogwood tree, half-concealed under its lattice of bloomless branches, and pick off passing grouse. But this terrain belonged to active predators – the cougar, the red fox, the wolverine. She'd observed them closely, mimicking the stealth and sequence of their movements as they stalked prey. The hunt was instinctive to her now, a dance between likeminded partners, a courtship well-rehearsed yet delicately tread. One clumsy move meant the difference between a hearty meal and an empty stomach.

The path she'd been tracking all morning led straight to

her quarry, a lone elk browsing in a grove of aspen at the base of a slope. He was young, crowned with a single unshed antler covered in velvet, and Dianna inwardly cursed herself for killing such a noble animal in its prime. Plucking a slender arrow from its quiver, she slid it into place.

That fleeting moment was the most precious of all, in which none of the physical world existed but for the space between her and another life. Nothing else mattered but for the courage it would take to end it. She knew such focus as a viper cradled upon warm sandstone, armored in her keeled scales, primed to strike. She had known such focus at the end of each day, contemplating the vial of aconite, her quickest escape from her own life should she need it.

Her aim converged on the elk as she drew the arrow taut.

She gave an intake of breath as though it was also her last, a silent acknowledgment of kinship: *I breathe your air, too. I know the cling of death, too. It comes fast and almost painless like the snap of a neck, or it devours languidly from the inside out, like a poison.*

Her fingers twitched on the bowstring, releasing. The elk fell, its large dark eyes almost peaceful. Dianna's chest stirred with a strange ravenous rumble, and she pressed a hand to her heart as though to hush it.

The death was quick and clean – her intention for every kill.

She approached the elk with her gutting knife in one hand, extracting the arrow with the other. It slipped out, awash with red. With a gesture quick as an eye-blink, she knelt beside the animal's flank and brushed its velvet fur once with her lips.

"Thank you, dear friend," she murmured, with a real and tender regret.

Her deft hands set to work paring the flesh of her kill. Hungry ravens had already descended but had learned well to keep their distance at a radius of several paces. As soon as Dianna left, they would pick the carcass clean, leaving no evidence of its untimely demise.

In thick burlap she wrapped the elk's generous meat, enough to feed a family for a week or more, stowing it in Liam's rucksack. Concealing herself in her father's traveling cloak and shouldering her heavy load, she made her way down the mountainside toward the village. Hare carcasses dangled against her hip as she navigated the flinty, uneven ground.

At the foot of the mountain, she found a streambed to clean her hands and arrowheads, scanning the sparse landscape. A group of scouts had just finished their rounds in the area, retreating from the edge of Silbarran, soon to be replaced with others.

A quarter mile from the stream, she crossed into Awl-Feth like a phantom unseen, her weaponry concealed in the folds of her father's cloak. She picked her way across the dry, sterile, windswept land dotted with the thatched huts of the poorest villagers.

Dianna wound a path between each residence on soft feet, glancing at bolted thresholds, abandoned garden plots. The usual springtime auguries were absent: no villagers out planting seeds, no pollen thick upon the air, no children's laughter.

Outside one hut, she paused and tapped at the weathered wooden door.

From inside came the padding of footsteps and a woman's low, hesitating voice. "Who is it?"

Dozens of Awl-Fethan women knew the watchword well. "A sister," Dianna answered.

The door opened just enough to allow a glimpse of the woman's face, haggard and ashen for one so young. She was clothed in black, the marking of one of the village's many widows.

Dianna removed the hares from her belt and extended the offerings to her. The wide-eyed woman took a breath and opened the door further, revealing a belly heavy with child.

"Mactus, Dianna," she said darkly. "You mustn't keep ghosting about like this. If the High Elder doesn't catch you, the scouts surely will—"

"They can't catch a ghost," Dianna said with a smile. "A mother needs meat for her strength, Melit. And suppose I heeded you? You'd both be fodder for the ravens. I wouldn't have it."

Melit pursed her lips and wagged her head as she accepted the provisions. "You are so kind. I wish it were enough to soothe my fears."

Dianna glanced at Melit's round belly. "Do the midwives see an uneasy birth?"

"No." Melit's whisper was hollow. "I'm afraid it may be a girl."

Dianna met the young woman's eyes knowingly. A quiet moment passed, and she reached out and touched Melit's hand, where it rested over her growing unborn.

"Then let her be a strong girl," she said. "Let the earth shape her into a wild thing, and let her dance like the wind and stand like a stone. Let your fears not become hers."

Melit looked down, blinking away tears, a smile spreading slowly over her face.

"You echo your own mother's bravery," she said wryly. The smile faded, and she met Dianna's eyes. "I must be as brave . . . when the time comes. *Kel-brys.*"

In the Awl-Fethan tongue, the word meant *sisterhood.* She spoke it in a whisper, like a soft wind. But her dark eyes were fierce as a storm. In them Dianna saw the desperation of a mother.

She also saw an uprising.

"When the time comes, you will," Dianna said, low. "It won't be long now."

By spring, she had promised each woman. *Take your husband's crossbows, and I will bring the rest. I will take straight from the forge if I must. We will go to the High Elder together and we will demand freedom.*

But there must be enough of us. We must be all or nothing.

By spring, I will call for you.

"We all will," Melit agreed, giving Dianna a furtive look. "But I fear yet for the Cathrin girl. Her father's more foul-tempered than usual these days."

Hearing the name of her childhood friend made Dianna's heart stutter. She had not seen Cathrin in several moons. Her father, a veteran of the Valtan legion, was a deterrent enough to any visitor. Villagers said he still carried a soldier's dagger under his cloak whenever he ventured out, a tool made for killing and killing only, its blade broad and flat like a leaf.

"I'll see to her," Dianna promised, swallowing her misgivings.

Melit grasped her hand tenderly. "Stars protect you."

Dianna returned the nontraditional farewell. She much preferred stars to Mactus. Stars gave comforting light in the dark; they could guide her footpath; they offered corporeal hope for another day. Mactus protected no one.

As she closed the door, Dianna pulled the cloak around her face, turned around, and became motionless as a target in the line of fire.

Yards away, a new group of scouts crossed the village toward the woods. The crossbows slung over their backs nodded as they walked. They moved with a swift assurance on their way to begin watch, the beat of their boots scattering ravens.

Although well out of earshot, Dianna held her breath as if it could give her away. From some deep place in her bones, a chill bolted through her as the wolf raised its hackles.

Stay back, she warned it, stock-still.

But one of the scouts' gazes passed over the mud huts. His eyes locked upon her.

Half-concealed in her wool cowl, Dianna watched him.

117

The wolf bared its teeth. Her lips twitched, curled back.

The scout looked frightened now. He nudged another as they marched along, and both turned their intense eyes to her, intrigued.

Dianna waited until they passed. A snarl lurched in her throat.

***

Cathrin was alone, hanging linens to dry on the withered branch of an ash tree. Her dark eyes flickered to Dianna in fear as she approached. But as soon as Dianna lowered her cowl and removed her rucksack, the fear slid away, and Cathrin's face was blank again, haloed in jet black curls, her delicate chin raised.

It had been so long. Dianna felt the same rush of love for her as when they were girls – a sudden yearning to run to her and embrace her as if an aegis, to laugh like they used to, when they knew so little of the world.

Her gaze skimmed the bruises smattering Cathrin's skin, like that of a fallen apple left to rot, and she took a long breath.

"Hello, friend," she murmured.

"Dianna." Cathrin's tone was odd, both grateful and anxious.

"Is your father on patrol?"

"Yes."

Dianna exhaled with relief. She wanted to lean in close while she had the chance, to beg her *run now, far and fast; take my cloak; I will cover you.*

But the memory of burning women stared out of the deep, almost-black of her friend's eyes, and within them the dream twisted away like smoke. Instead, kneeling, Dianna extracted her heavy cargo of elk meat and handed over the bulk of it.

"For you and your brothers," she said.

Cathrin's hands fell to the bundles, but she did not take her eyes away from her benefactor.

"I thought you'd be dead by now," she said softly.

"I'm careful," Dianna answered.

Two small, scrawny boys peered out the door of the hut like mice from their den. Cathrin motioned them over.

"Bring this inside," she told them, doling out the cuts of meat. "A young man brought it by, do you hear me? A hunter who took pity on us."

The boys carried the rations inside, marveling at the bundles as if they were made of gold.

"Thank you," Cathrin said, her eyes flitting downward. "Father hasn't been bringing in enough wolf kills, and . . . I struggle to feed them on my own."

She stood for a moment, lost in thought, wringing her dark hands over and over. She picked another threadbare linen from the basket, throwing it over the branch.

Dianna spoke in a low, hard whisper.

"He's been violent again, hasn't he?"

Cathrin's tremulous hands smoothed out the fabric.

"He is right to be," Cathrin said in a hollow undertone. "He is a hunter, and my brothers will be hunters. But I am good for nothing. It upsets him."

"How can you say that?"

"'Good for nothing,'" Cathrin only repeated, a tremble in her words. "It's what he said. 'Unfit for marriage now.' But I was returning from the market around midday, and it was so hot, and he – the man – he had a waterskin. He offered me a drink, and when I was close . . ."

Dianna's stomach gave a sickening lurch as Cathrin's words fell away, her eyes black abysses.

"He offered me a drink," she repeated.

"Who was it?" Dianna asked, voice dark.

"I don't – I can't—"

"Cathrin," Dianna said, as calmly and gently as her voice could muster. "Who raped you?"

Cathrin, her hand crushed over her mouth, said, "The one you will be given to, Dianna. The one who calls you his."

Actaen.

Dianna swallowed back the wolf, feeling a ferocious anger dart in her veins. She cupped her hands gently around her friend's face. Cathrin's hands fluttered to clutch hers briefly, and she looked like a child again.

"You mustn't believe your father," Dianna said, voice quivering. "Listen. You mustn't believe him. And when your brothers are grown, you can leave the village—"

Like a skittish animal, Cathrin twitched away, the whites of her eyes emerging.

"Stop saying wicked things," she said at once. "The will of Mactus forbids it."

"Cathrin—"

But Cathrin had bowed her head and began reciting a scripture from memory, eyes pressed shut.

"*And if a woman serves her bloodkind in the name of Mactus, she shall be a servant of Mactus,*" she said under her breath. "*And He shall smite the wicked, and He shall deliver the true woman, the long-serving woman.*"

Dianna watched Cathrin with an ache wrenching at her heart, deep as a mourning for the dead, as though the time they spent as young girls must be buried and revisited only in memory. Like angels strung up in the crooked tree, the damp linens shuddered, pulled by the wind.

"You need not marry to make yourself worthy," Dianna said softly.

Cathrin looked up in a ripple of dark curls.

"They'll make you, you know," she whispered. "Like my cousin. That's why she ran away. And she will burn in hellfire for it."

She plucked the last ragged cloth from the basket at her feet, casting it over the branches.

CHAPTER 18

Snow moon, waning

Even on the cusp of spring, the sickly perfume of decaying foliage hung heavy on the air. Low voices thrummed through it, like wings.

Dianna followed the sounds into the center of the village, where the cathedral opened like a great stone cave, bolstered with pillars. She let her cowl fall to her shoulders and walked several paces alongside the outer reaches of the pews, concealed in shadow.

A group of villagers had gathered beneath the apse, chanting a somber hymn. The altar was laid with incense, diffusing an earthy smoke into the nave. Daylight seeped through the mottled glass windows, but the belly of the cathedral was dark and cool.

The pews were dotted with more villagers, eerily quiet but for the high, keening wail of an infant, likely stricken with fever. Dianna surveyed the downward-turned faces, some rapt in wordless prayer; some gray with age, sunken with desperation, lined with loss. There were ragged peasants, stalwart young hunters, widows in black and girls in white. She counted them, noting the absences, and her heart sank.

Someone dies every day now.

"Miss Dianna?"

The small voice came from behind, startling her. Turning, Dianna saw it belonged to a fittingly small girl, her tiny form shrouded in a handwoven cloak. Her eyes were wide and glistening in the gloom of the cathedral.

"Are you Miss Dianna?" the girl asked.

"I am," she answered.

The girl spoke quickly then, almost breathless. "Can you help us? Me and my aunt? She told me . . . She said the rations are running out. Please, can you—"

Dianna crouched, hushing her. "Slow down, now. Speak softly."

The girl nodded reverently.

"Tell me," Dianna said in an undertone. "Where are your parents?"

The girl swallowed, her eyes darting to the rows of empty pews, the silent congregation, the sunlight in the cavernous archway.

"Your mother?" Dianna tried again.

"She got sick."

Dianna felt a wrenching ache in her heart. "Your father?"

"Silbarran."

Dianna couldn't find the words she wanted. Instead she reached out, stroked the child's hair.

"But my aunt heard — she heard the women say you can find food," the girl said, sotto. "They said you're a — you're a—"

She stopped speaking, biting her lip. Dianna studied the girl's pinched face as she trembled with unwept tears.

"What am I?" Dianna asked, her voice gentle, neutral.

"A saint," the girl whispered. "A saint sent by Mactus."

Dianna's brows tightened, and she offered a brief smile. She hoped it looked consoling, not fearful.

"I am for you," she murmured. "I will come tonight with provisions for you, all right? Where are you?"

122

The girl sniffled, holding out her little palm, touching the center of it.

"The cathedral," she indicated, and drew her finger across the heartline. "Us. Between the elder tree and the aqueduct."

Dianna nodded.

"Go, then," she said, tenderly clutching the girl's hand. "Tell no one you saw me."

The girl vanished in an eye-blink, into the sunlit mouth of the cathedral. Dianna was still for a moment.

She rose, taking measured strides into the interior of the archway. Ravens' wings whisked in the high rafters above. A few feathers fell, floating like soot from a chimney.

Turning to face the stone wall, she gazed upon the twin princes of Myre.

She remembered the unveiling of the massive portrait, a gift to the High Elder from a Valtan merchant many years ago. It had become a shrine after the Imperator's passing, where villagers kept fruitless, nightly vigils for hope of a new reign, leaving their candles to burn out upon the marble floor. As the war in the north raged on, the princes remained missing.

But Caenani boots had not yet touched Awl-Fethan soil. It was as though Silbarran's wooded expanse, like a living barricade, had kept the enemy at bay. As though the threat of wolves could possibly daunt the Caenani's equally vicious legion.

Dianna studied the princes, their oil-painted features echoing each other's exactly: the slight aquiline nose, the olive complexion, the dark and ever-observant eyes. They looked out from their gilded frame mockingly, their faces revealing nothing.

"You've been gone too long," she told them at last.

***

Liam's hammer struck a spark on the edge of the mottled armor. He paused at the running cadence of booted feet through the pasture, setting aside the half-formed piece of hot iron and shedding his gloves.

A cluster of ravens shrieked and fluttered aside as he wrenched open the barn door, striding out. Turning the corner, he collided with Dianna, sending her rucksack flying.

She scrambled for it, but he was first to snatch it up. His mouth pressed into a hard line, and she fell quiet beneath his stare.

Liam shook the rucksack in his fist. "You said you were going to the cathedral."

Dianna looked down at her mud-crusted boots.

"I did," she murmured.

He followed the path of her gaze. The rucksack landed with a thud as he cast it upon the ground.

"*Fiiskavt*," he swore. "You went into the mountains, didn't you? You know women are forbidden to leave the village!"

"I only go when Father's training hunters every midday. The scouts already made their rounds on the east side. There's a shortcut leading to the cliff faces."

Liam's breath deepened as he raked a hand over his tired face.

"You're risking your life," he said, "for target practice."

"No." Dianna lowered the cloak's cowl, looking her brother squarely in the eyes. "For our people."

"Let the hunters help them."

"The hunters are dying. They're dying every moon. Who will help their widows? Their children? Who will help the unmarried women like me?" Heat rising to her face, she lowered her voice and leaned in close. "I have keener senses than any hunter. And you know I can't marry, Liam."

"But you will, An-An. You are nineteen years, and as soon as Actaen becomes fully initiated as a demon hunter he will come asking for you. It's hard enough keeping you hidden."

"I can still say no."

"Not if his father, Ledras, and our father strike a deal. That is the custom."

"No one owns me. No one owns another's life—"

"Your life is more important than your freedom, Dianna!"

Liam turned aside, bracing his fists against the lintel beam of the barn. His ears were reddening with anger like heated metal.

Dianna remained still. "If you've seen what I've seen, you'd know life means little without freedom."

"Better yet than death," Liam retorted. "Stars, you're growing to be just like Mother was. Bolder than what this life can offer you. And I raised you to think beyond it, I know. But her good heart killed her in the end."

"Our people are helpless, Liam. They're afraid."

"Yes, they are. That's how these politics work. When we fear, we depend more and more on the hunters for protection. As long as the hunters are under his command, the High Elder is in power. Fear begets power. As does the belief that the famine is a merely a test of Mactus, that it will be over."

Dianna bit her tongue, hesitating to reveal too much.

"If it goes on any longer, there must be change," she reasoned. "There must be."

"Listen, An-An, you can't afford to draw attention just to feed a few families. You're a—"

But Liam cut himself short with a sigh, closing his eyes. When he finally faced her again, Dianna had drawn herself level to him.

"What am I, Liam?" she asked softly.

Liam steepled his fingers and pressed them to his lips, a familiar conceding gesture, his tone matter-of-fact.

"Awl-Fethan women are needed to sustain the bloodlines. If you are discovered, the High Elder will kill you. And whose head do you think that will be on?"

"Liam—"

"Whose?" he demanded.

Dianna's throat tightened, and her mouth closed momentarily on her next words. Wind rocked in the dogwood boughs and whisked at Liam's hair, but he stood firm. The pall of ravens had settled on the barn's awning, preening and watching the proceedings like beady-eyed judges.

"I don't want to do it," she said finally. "I don't want to kill. But look around you – nothing is growing. Now only grief is a wellspring that will never run dry. I saw the pews today, Liam—"

"An-An – "

"They were half-empty," Dianna said at once. "If we all starve, there will be no bloodlines left to keep."

Liam nodded slowly. His brow furrowed over eyes gray-washed and heavy as the overcast sky.

"I told you I'd find you a cure," he said. "But it's grown restless, hasn't it?"

Dianna pulled her father's cloak around her, retreating into its soft lining, breathing the scent of stale pipe smoke like a balm.

"I've seen it," he said, looking at her carefully. "I see it moving behind your eyes even now."

"I have control," Dianna insisted, the gold in her eyes guttering with a blink.

But beneath her skin, the wolf prowled on the edges of her nerves. It moved with an easy, fluid grace in her blood. It made subtle tracks between the notches of her spine.

It gave a low, groaning cry in her mind, like a voice: *Out.*

CHAPTER 19

Snow moon, waning

Day sank into night over Awl-Feth in a hazy, crimson blaze. The faint imprint of the half-moon emerged above the bloodred horizon, and the spine of trees in the distant foothills began melting into darkness. There, on the edge of the woods, the Lead Hunter continued his steady evening patrol.

Behind the mountain crags, Dianna watched the ravens wheeling overhead in endless loops, searching for prey that no longer roamed upon the unforgiving, fallow earth. Even in the midst of famine, there was no point shooting them down. The scavengers didn't make for good meat, and were so emaciated as to be inedible.

As they circled lazily, filling the darkening sky with their guttural caws, she felt something akin to sorrow for them.

There is nothing here for you anymore, she wanted to cry out, to make them scatter like flecks of black ash to the wind.

Instead, she remained silent as she waited.

The true hunt was a long wait, and in waiting there was contemplation. Dianna asked questions, watched the last of the withering mountain huckleberry tremble in the wind, stroked the silken fletching at the end of her arrows. She asked herself how much longer she could sustain the women and children of her village, how much longer the men could protect them from wolves. How much longer before every growing thing went to ground, before the famine took them all, before the ravens came to feast on the remnants.

She could have waited for hours there, alone and pressed to the rocks as though she herself had turned to stone, asking the same questions. In the cold quiet of night, the dying landscape gave no answers.

The barest flicker of movement in the dark made her instincts spark to life. Dianna scanned the rock-strewn range, bow poised. A cluster of hares dotted the frosted sagebrush, oblivious to the predator in their midst.

She nocked her arrow and fixed her aim.

You have one shot, she reminded herself. *You cannot afford to miss.*

A breath, a slight shudder of her hand, a refocusing of her target.

Line them up—

But she held her arrow, knowing her chance was gone as soon as she heard the sound. It made her skin prickle with a terrible awareness, her heart drop into her stomach. It was the softest stirring in the night air.

An exhale.

Dianna twisted around, holding her bowstring taut for only a second longer. There was a rustle of sagebrush as the hares scattered, their white tails whisking away like cottonseeds in a gale.

"Who's there?" she called out in a low voice.

There was no reply. Dianna relaxed her grip on the bow but remained ready to draw the string again. Beneath her cloak, her skin grew cold with sweat.

Her tracker's pulse quickened. His scent was strong – salt and earth and leather.

"I know you're out there," she snarled, glancing over the terrain.

Beneath the half moon, the young hunter rose from a rocky ledge a short range away, his crossbow pointed at her head.

"Put it down," he ordered.

From beneath her cowl, Dianna met the hunter's gaze. She placed her mother's bow on the ground with a sinking heart.

Her captor's piercing eyes surveyed her, picking out her features. His mouth went slack, and his brows drew up in shock.

"Aergyris?"

Dianna stayed still.

"Actaen," she returned.

"How—" he began, childlike. "It's been you, then. It's been you."

His features hardened into a mask of disgust. Under the moon's half-light, his cold stare pressed in on her.

Dianna didn't answer. A chill like a river washed over her, dragging at her body.

"You thought you'd outwitted the scouts," Actaen seethed. "You thought we wouldn't catch on to your scheme. Corrupting women with your poisonous tongue. Talking of fleeing Awl-Feth. It's been you. My *betrothed*."

He gave a short, mirthless laugh.

"Oh, I knew you were a half-blooded heathen like your brother, but how little I suspected your nerve! Did the great Abram seek to make a fool of me?" he demanded. "To have me wed a treacherous witch?"

The wolf was creeping on the edges of Dianna's consciousness, nudging for a point of entry.

Control it, she thought, keeping her focus on Actaen. Suppression closed on her heart like a fist, smothering the wild instinct to jump out of her skin.

"How many have you made to defy His will?" he cried out. "How many?"

Dianna's gaze was steel.

"One day they'll rise against men like you," she said.

Actaen's eyes narrowed to pinpricks. He stalked toward her with weapon raised, his body framed in moonlight, until they were inches apart. For a moment he paused, as if savoring a feeling of power over her.

"The other scouts will cover these mountains soon," he said, voice low. "Your punishment shall come by the hand of Mactus. But you're still mine. You've always been mine."

His crossbow blocked her view, the point of the bolt glinting silver between her eyes. Dianna's breath fluttered in her lungs, the certainty of death smudging her senses.

It's over.

You will die.

Awl-Feth will die.

A shard of fear lanced through her as Actaen's fingers flexed.

But he didn't fire. He inclined his head slightly, considering her. The wind picked up, howling through the sagebrush and whipping her tattered cloak.

"No, I could never have you for a wife after all, Aergyris," he said, voice velvet soft. "But I can still have you."

A sickening realization slinked under Dianna's skin. Actaen lowered his weapon and stalked forward. Dianna seized her bow and stumbled backward, catching herself on the rocks, pulling an arrow from the quiver.

Actaen snatched her wrist in an iron grip, twisting her aim just as she loosed her arrow. It sailed over his shoulder into nothingness.

Dianna thrashed like a snared rabbit, but his strong arms wrested her shortbow away. A hollow rattling of arrows, and her quiver spun and scattered with it. His fumbling hand crushed over her scream.

He had pinned her within seconds, and every sensation

was a sharp, ugly fragment: the reek of his breath in her face. The vacancy of his stare. Rocks gouging at her back.

Her stomach turned as she struggled to keep the refrain of *calm, control, calm, control,* but the words seemed meaningless and uncatchable now, sliding and falling away. With one hand at her throat, Actaen tore away her cloak, the laces of her dress underneath.

An awareness clenched at her heart.

No, she thought. *No, I would sooner die.*

A life inside her shifted, shuddered away the dust of stagnation, fierce and wanting. An echo of something elusive, muffled, but there.

She bid herself to take hold of it, to nurse it into being.

It will be over soon. She turned the promise over in her mind, let it spread through her bones. *Yes, it will be over.*

Her body coiled in resistance, testing for cracks in Actaen's hold. She felt the mass of muscles in his shoulders and arms, the pressure points in his hands.

Her mind was in another place, pushing at the raw power.

It will be—

She sank her fangs into his fingers. Their bones crackled like ice.

Actaen slumped aside shrieking as Dianna wrenched herself away, spitting aside his crushed flesh. The acrid taste of rust lingered on her tongue. An inhuman snarl tore from her mouth as tremors engulfed her body.

Actaen screamed, clutching his pulped hand, spitting a torrent of curses.

"*Fiiskavt!* You goddamn—"

The wolf plunged upon him.

In a thrash of teeth and claws and bristling fur, she darted at his throat. His head unraveled from the neck in a spattering of scarlet, ragged sinew and exposed bone.

She smelled another scout, heard him in the

underbrush, saw his face illuminated by the moonlight. She hurtled forward, snatching him by the ankle.

Voices began to rise from below, fellow scouts scrambling up the mountain. A bolt seared across the sky, missing by inches.

"*Kill it!*"

"Aim for the head!"

Another hunter, closing in and loading his crossbow, went down in a flurry of limbs. Beneath ripping, slavering jaws, a hot mush of entrails spilled.

One after another, men converged. One after another they tumbled, lifeless, over the rocks.

And a human voice surfaced to the animal mind, pressing.

No!

Crouched over a man's remains, the wolf lifted its dripping muzzle. Its hackles softened. Its yellow eyes alighted with recognition.

No.

The wolf obeyed and began to fall apart.

Dianna felt her body shrink in on itself, the inversion of muscle and bone, the convulsing in her gut. The fractal, hateful pulse of blood, like a drumbeat.

The world was reeling, nightmarish. Hunters ran up the mountainside, flocking together in the dark, their shouts cleaving the air. She glimpsed the slip of the moon and resurfaced into her own nakedness, goosefleshed and human and tacky with blood.

A deep rage churned in her breast, her breath staccato through gritted teeth. The caustic tang of bile crept up her throat. She saw the glint of a soldier's dagger, still pressed in the grip of Cathrin's dead father. The horrible gory mass that had been Actaen strewn upon the rocks, carrion for ravens, his face savaged beyond recognition. Another hunter cradled his own mangled leg, making a hard, grating sound in his throat, a contained sob.

Dianna heard the flurry of bolts whisking the air as the others executed him on sight. There was a single moment, fine and quick: the smallest sound, his last living breath, dissolving in the air.

She staggered, gasping, into a dead run.

The hunters were a swarm of shadows now, nearly indistinguishable from the dark as she bolted over thick brushwood and clattering stones, unarmed.

The rallying cry of hunters amassed, growing to a fever pitch. The sputter of torches edged closer under a sky dotted with stars, lambent with the silvery veneer of the half-moon, like a shard of glass. Dianna's eyes met the brightest star.

The collective roar of men lashed her ears; she could not make out a single word but for one voice thundering above the chaos—

"*Bring her to me.*"

The moon winked out as her sight went black, and hands pulled her into oblivion.

Chapter 20

Snow moon, waning

Dianna stirred from unconsciousness but did not open her eyes. Under the guise of darkness, a low, powerful murmur cut across a worshipful silence.

"A passage from Scripture Four, Verse 67. 'The man who commits wickedness against the will of prophets is wicked in the ever-watching eyes of Mactus.'"

The voice of the High Elder soared across the air, landing like a bolt in Dianna's chest.

She smelled a faint pipe smoke around her – her father's hunting cloak, returned to her. Cold iron chains bound the length of her body, pressing bruises into her flesh, anchoring her to a hard, wooden post. A thick rag gagged her mouth. Her head throbbed with a leaden pang.

"This is why, my flock, we must not fall prey to the folly of undue trust," the High Elder continued. "When we trust our fellow man without question, he may become our greatest betrayer."

Beneath this, soft and deep as a lion's rumble, Abram's voice emerged close to her:

"Dianna, *fenlet*," he said. "Please wake up."

Dianna opened her eyes. From her vantage point against the post, atop a mound of timber piled high, she could look out upon the whole of her village. Its huts were abandoned or else left to the women and children, hearth fires burning with a ghostly light.

She could even see the vast and untouchable empire beyond: the great aqueducts, their columns and archways of white stone, cresting the horizon like the spine of some ancient dead god. Silbarran, a green kingdom of its own, crawling with unknown magic, with beasts like her. And somewhere, imperceptible to the eye but felt deep in her bones, war had swallowed the capital.

Below her, the scene was murky around the edges, lit only by several torchbearers. But across the cathedral grounds, glittering in intermittent firelight, a hundred eyes looked on.

A scent spread among them, sweat-laced and heady as smoke: fear.

Abram appeared clear and strong in the center of it, burnished in his hunting armor. He stood at her feet, just beyond reach. A pair of hunters flanked him, holding his hands behind his back.

The flickering torchlight cast grisly shadows on the faces of the rest of the hunters, who formed a semicircle around the cathedral steps. At their apex the High Elder stood, cloaked in red, looking down upon them with dour satisfaction.

Dianna looked around. Liam was nowhere to be found.

Her eyes traced the lines of Abram's face, a dark dread engulfing her. In his weather-beaten features, she saw not a hunter's wrath – only the love of a father and the hollow despondency of a damned man.

They should have killed me, she thought, cursing her heart as it raced on. *Why didn't they just kill me?*

At the sight of her waking, Abram fell to his knees with the dull thump of iron on earth, like a broken puppet.

"Hold him," demanded the High Elder.

The hunters dragged Abram to his feet again. Dianna struggled at her chains, retching at the taste of blood, the rough gag binding her tongue.

"It is conscious, High Elder!" someone cried.

A clamor broke out and grew deafening, surrounding like walls. Hands pitched stones, battering Abram's armor. Dianna, petrified against the wooden post, only vaguely felt their bite smacking at her body, whisking at her cloak.

Raising his arms above his head, the High Elder lulled the villagers to a murmur again. His face was unreadable in the dim light as he addressed them.

"It has woken." His thunderous voice was cold and clear. "This is not a cause for alarm. The beast is weakened and bound." He turned askance, beadily eying the half-circle of hunters. "Tonight we hold Judgment of Lead Hunter Abram Aergyris on the accusation of high treason abetting murder. He is henceforth stripped of his title and authority. May he be an example unto us all: the will of Mactus holds no favor to traitors."

Dianna gritted her teeth against the gag. A realization unfurled in her chest, tangling maddening knots around her heart. This was why the High Elder had wanted her alive.

So he could punish Abram, make him suffer, when he watched her burn.

"Tonight seven hunters have been killed by this demon," the High Elder continued. "Upon closure of Judgment, it shall be slain by fire."

A roar of approval tore through the onlookers. Dianna risked a glance at her father, held fast by the hunters. His brow drew tight and his still-hollow eyes stayed fixed on her.

The flames threw flashes of light across the High Elder's empty face. "I invite Abram Aergyris to make his case," he said.

Abram managed to tear his eyes away from his beloved daughter. His gray grizzled features flattened, becoming impassive, as he turned to the High Elder.

The hunters hauled him up, shoving him toward the foot of the steps. Abram approached them with a warrior's steady stride.

The hunters' stony faces looked on. The High Elder stood still, eyes alert as a bird of prey.

"Aergyris," he began smoothly. "Is it true that you have knowingly harbored a demon against the will of Mactus?"

Abram answered without hesitation, loud and clear. "No, High Elder."

Faint murmurs wove throughout the gathering of onlookers.

"Then were you aware that your daughter was corrupt, conceivably for years?"

"No, High Elder."

"Despite the discovery of a barred enclosure upon your land, intended to confine the demon?"

Abram's stoic mask faltered, just barely. "No, High Elder."

"The evidence stands against you," the High Elder pressed, glowering.

"It is false evidence."

"How long have you kept this monster?"

"I have kept nothing—"

"You lie!"

Dianna started with a shiver of chains. The High Elder had thrust an accusing finger at Abram, red sleeve trembling with rage. The villagers jeered and shouted, but Abram appeared unshaken.

"I am no liar." His low voice was lost in the sheer volume of protests.

When they finally receded, the High Elder clasped his hands behind him in a pretense of calm. But his frustration etched hard lines in his reddening face.

"So," he said at last, pausing to allow the bite of his next question to sink in. "I am correct that you find yourself innocent of the charge of high treason?"

Abram met the High Elder's glare. With an arc of his hand, he removed his helm and came down to rest on his knee, the picture of servitude, at the mercy of the hunters.

"High Elder. Fellow men." Abram's gaze ranged over the swarm of villagers, who craned their necks at him, whispering. "Good people of Awl-Feth. I kneel before you humbled, reverent, and a wrongly accused man.

"Have I not served you in the highest order?" His voice began to ascend. "Have I not defended our village in times of despair, and saved countless lives from succumbing to the evils of the woods? Have I not paid my taxes in blood? Have I not been a loyal servant of our great Mactus?"

His words, intense and unwavering, seemed to still the air. Dianna held her breath. Then a hunter at the forefront spat at Abram.

"Traitor!" he roared.

The villagers' voices lurched into an upheaval. Some raised their torches higher, and Dianna's eyes followed the trails of embers floating down, hissing through the blackness.

"Aergyris makes a reasonable defense," remarked one of the hunters at last, when the voices settled again.

"Then explain this incriminating evidence," the High Elder cut across, his face withered with disgust. "Explain what Aergyris cannot."

Abram spoke first, his gaze unyielding. "I suppose . . . my son was attempting to cure the demon of its corruption," he said.

"And based on this claim alone, you expect us to attribute the crime not to your ignorance, but to the arrogant misdeeds of your son? A foolish boy who thought himself clever enough to defy evil incarnate?" The High Elder gave a barking laugh. "How do you answer such nonsense, men?"

"Lies," one of them said coldly. "All of it."

"His claim does seem consistent," another hunter disputed. "Lest we forget the younger Aergyris has fled, his cowardice speaks of his treachery."

He got away, Dianna thought, tears filling her eyes. *Clever Liam, he got away.*

One of the hunters cleared his throat. "Our men are already scouring the village for him, High Elder," he said, and glanced aside at Abram. "We are confident he would not dare to cross the woods. And our search of the farmstead bore evidence in favor of Abram's claims. A book."

The High Elder's eyes flickered.

"Bring it here," he said.

The hunter approached him, relinquishing the ragged leather book, its pages speckled with black ink. Dianna recognized it at once, seething with fury at the High Elder as his fingers edged the yellowed, crackling pages she knew were filled with notes written in Liam's scrawling hand.

The book fell open to a marked section. The High Elder studied the text with an ever-darkening expression, forming the words under his breath. Licking his lips, he read aloud:

On the Exorcism of Accursed Beings, the remedial stages are as follows:

The Accursed shall sup once daily at first light, the milk of the flowering yellow aconite.

The Accursed shall remain isolated for a sum of seven eves, with the sole exception of a holy guardian, who shall administer this sustenance.

The Accursed shall remain underground, at the contiguous tier to the fires of hell, so that the demon may return to the chthonic depths whence it came.

His eyes narrowed as he finished the passage. A silence descended.

"Would the girl herself not perish of this poisonous essence?" one of the hunters asked at last.

The High Elder's eyes narrowed at the book's markings.

"The beast will . . . but by the holy grace of Mactus, the girl may yet survive." His fingers caressed the leather-bound pages. "This work is a relic of the first disciples of Mactus. They have dealt with demons of old. It had been stolen long ago from our archives."

Dianna could barely see his expression in the murky light. He could easily be lying.

"I would like to propose a negotiation," Abram said at once.

The villagers' ensuing torrent of shouting, a mix of mocking laughter and incredulous objections, spread across the cathedral grounds.

"It is clear that you would find me guilty," Abram said, drawing himself up with an air of finality. "So I shall plead this on one term."

In the torch light, the High Elder's eyes flashed white at Abram.

"And what," he said slowly, "might that be?"

"If my just services in the virtuous name of Mactus have proven to be any value to you, you will spare my daughter and treat her with this cure."

The villagers' objections elevated, but the High Elder only clasped his hands, gazing from on high.

"How audacious of you," he said coolly, though his mad eyes gave him away.

"Spare her life instead of mine—" Abram pleaded.

"That is enough," snarled the High Elder, silencing him.

Dianna glanced between them and clenched her teeth. She remembered holding the aconite in her hand, wishing she had swallowed the whole damned vial.

"Shall we not grant his term?" one of the hunters called out. "Shall we not attempt this in good faith?"

The High Elder's twisted expression faltered, deliberating.

"And if this remedy should fail?" another hunter

contested, rounding on his fellow man with a glint in his eye. "Would you have an ungodly man walk free?"

"He should be punished in a manner befitting his crime. He should be put to death," a third hunter added. "And the demon should burn."

Voices rose and filled the air. Dianna searched the faces of her people, wraithlike in the dim light, knowing well they would not call for her salvation. The sisterhood wouldn't dare speak out against the High Elder, not now that they'd seen what she was. There would be no vote cast, not when the decider of her fate was a prophet of god.

"Then it is settled," the High Elder assented. "The exorcism begins tonight. If it fails, the punishment stands: the demon shall burn at the stake."

His scarlet robes threw shadows across the cathedral steps as he stared daggers at Abram, his face distorted in the torch light.

"Abram Aergyris, you have been found guilty on the count of high treason against your people and shall be put to death by beheading."

Death.

The word fell like a stone. It stopped, with a crushing enormity, in Dianna's heart.

The breath guttered out of her. The stone beat from within her heart, shattering it from the inside.

"The Judgment is hereby concluded," the High Elder said distantly. "The will of Mactus."

"It is written," the chilling echo resonated as hundreds of hands repeated the blessing of Mactus in unison, palms outstretched to the earth.

Dianna's face crumpled as hot tears stung her eyes.

Come out, she begged the wolf. *Change me. Save him. Do something!*

She writhed, rattling the iron chains, but the wolf had retreated into the shadows of her mind.

A figure broke from the knot of hunters and steadily advanced toward the center of the grounds. He was a tall, sturdy man, outfitted in leathers suited for combat. With precision, he approached Abram and unsheathed the sword at his hip, setting the point of the blade at his feet.

Abram did not flinch, addressing his friend formally. "Ledras."

"Aergyris," returned the man.

Abram lifted his gaze to the High Elder for the last time.

"Before I am to die, I wish to have my final words," he said.

"Very well," said the High Elder.

"It is *you* who has deceived us, High Elder."

Dianna lifted her head just barely, a sob catching in her throat.

Abram's voice was an even, slow burn. "You, High Elder, who promised to feed our families and protect them from harm," he said. "You have failed them."

"I know not of what you speak, Aergyris."

"You know damned well," Abram's voice flared like unquenchable fire now. "That the hunters were to carry out an inquisition upon your orders!" He turned to face the villagers, livid features burnished with sweat in the leaping torch light, and bellowed with a shuddering force. "That he would have you all questioned for treason and purged! That he would test your loyalty to the empire—"

"Hold your tongue," the High Elder snarled.

"The empire that he'd have wrought from Myre's ashes!"

An immediate uproar broke like a thunderclap. The High Elder merely assessed Abram with a cold gaze.

"It is not the will of Myre we uphold, but the will of Mactus," he said.

"Then His will be damned!" Abram roared.

The hunters shoved Abram to his knees as Ledras set

142

his sword against his nape. Others pounced forth from the shadows, shouting and cursing.

"May you rot, Aergyris!"

"Traitor of Mactus! Traitor of blood!"

The High Elder met Dianna's eyes.

"Take it away," he ordered his men.

Dianna felt the cold iron loosening and slipping away, and rough, angry hands wrenched her upright. Her scream stuck in her throat.

Her father's eyes turned to her, crestfallen. Before the night swallowed him, he mouthed three words.

"Don't be soft."

The sword fell.

CHAPTER 21

Snow moon, waning

A ragged screaming sharpened the air all around – many voices, all rising. It was a long time before Dianna realized the screams came only from her, and longer still until she stopped. Until the screaming turned inward, until she felt it in her bones, breathed it in her lungs, until every heartbeat was a small, dying scream.

She wept like a child, pushing against the smothering hands with her own, lashing out in all directions in vain.

Heavy boots scraped against stone stairs as they descended, each step shuddering through her. There was no way to go but down, into the dark underbelly of the cathedral.

A muddy spectrum of yellow wheeled over her irises. Fangs slithered against her lips, sharp on her tongue. The wolf dragged itself through her bones, veering through her extremities but still too cowed to surface, smelling the thickness of terror all around. Nothing else moved in her but a rapid-fire pulse.

As the stairs leveled into the underground, the procession entered the yellow catacombs.

Dianna's skin grazed against an unnaturally smooth surface. In the marbling light of the hunters' swinging lanterns she saw the shadowed crowns of human skulls built into the walls of the narrow corridor and smelled the damp reek of decay. Her stomach plunged.

In the depths of the gloom, a dungeon cell waited. The hands holding Dianna released her across its threshold, bolting the door shut with a clang of metal. A quivering breath escaped her as the rage kindling in her chest sparked into flame.

"That will be all," the High Elder dismissed the hunters.

Each performed the blessing of Mactus, fists unfurling. They retreated one by one, the light of their lanterns melting into the shadows. Only the High Elder lingered.

Dianna clawed at the gag over her mouth and threw it aside. Her voice ruptured from her, full and rasping—

"You bastard!" she cried. "You murderer!"

The High Elder held his lantern aloft so its light danced in his eyes. They regarded his prisoner with a silent, covetous curiosity.

"*You murdered him!*" Dianna choked, her throat a hot flume as she shook the iron door in her fists. She wanted to break it, to lunge at him, to take his neck in her teeth—

The High Elder stooped. At his feet he rested the lantern; its soft glow illuminated his knitted brow.

"Will you be cured in seven days, she-wolf?" he wondered aloud, voice steely. "Will you burn evenly?"

"You—" Dianna gasped, hot tears streaming. But suddenly the words wouldn't come.

The High Elder straightened, meeting her gaze with absolute contempt, lips pressed flat.

"No," he said in an undertone. "*You* murdered him."

Dianna crushed her body against the iron bars, the molten vestiges of her rage extinguishing in the pit of her belly as she sank to the floor. The High Elder turned in a flare of scarlet.

"May Mactus have mercy on your soul," he said coldly,

and he was gone.

Dianna watched the lantern flicker before it finally sputtered into pitch black, leaving her in a tomb of bones, alone with the dead.

***

Dianna wept until she felt empty, closed her eyes until sleep came and went fitfully. In an alcove of her mind, the wolf paced softly, lulled into submission. Time passed, but with all entombed in darkness, the night could be infinite.

Liam had been right all along, she thought. Her fight was over before it could begin. Her family was no more. The sisterhood was no more.

She swallowed, sidling up to the cold iron bars. As she smelled the air, the wolf distinguished each individual scent – cool earth, musty rot, and a strong acrid odor. Though the lantern had been relit, no one else was there.

A waterskin had been left for her, which she seized and gulped down at once, fingers shaking. When she looked down, she found the source of the foul odor: a small wooden bowl filled with a watery, piss yellow broth. The aconite they believed was a cure, but she knew to be poison.

Dianna considered it.

Alone in the catacombs, darkness and silence covered her like a grave, as though she were already dead. She stared at the innocuous-looking offering, hardly daring to move.

Almost a courtesy, she thought. *Almost a boon.*

Of course, they thought it would take more than this to kill her. But the amount of aconite would be plenty enough. It would be a quick, easy death, perhaps even painless.

Leaning back against the iron door, she rubbed her palms over her eyes. They were swollen from crying.

Taking a long breath, she reached for the poison. Her fingers edged around the wood grain. Carefully, she lifted the bowl.

146

In her belly, the wolf gave a sorrowful howl.

She hushed it, fresh tears already stinging her face.

"There is nothing here for you anymore," she told it. "Leave me."

She felt it rummaging under her skin, whimpering, making slow circles as if lost.

"Go on, leave me be," she snapped at it, clutching the bowl to her, looking down at its shimmering surface, summoning her courage.

But a memory pulled at her subconscious even as she tried to resist it. It was from a happier time, before her mother disappeared. Her father's strong, sun-warmed arms had held her close. In the air drifted the smell of damp sweetgrass and the earthy traces of his pipe smoke. His voice was pleasant and lulling as he told her a story.

"That spring we had one ewe pregnant with twins, and she was ready for lambing. One came out just fine. The other was going to be a breech birth. Do you know what that means? Well, the lamb was turned around the wrong way in the womb. Likely it wouldn't live long enough to be born.

"But your mother, no, she wouldn't have that if she could help it. She said, 'She's carried a full gestation. That ewe has worked too hard, and that lamb's been in the dark too long not to see the light of day.' So she buckled down, turned its hooves around, and pulled that lamb out herself with her own two hands. Little wobbly thing, no bigger than you.

"Every life is precious to your mother, no matter how small. You, my fenlet, you have her gentleness.

"But when ravens fly by, circling the lambs, your mother is a fierce protector. With her arrows, she knocks them clean out of the sky. We are farmers, after all. We must do what we can to safeguard our livelihood.

"So you see, your mother is as gentle as the lightest summer wind catching the pines. But when the time calls for it, she is also as steady as the stone caught in the quick, winter river. And so are you."

A ragged breath wracked Dianna's lungs. The finality of her decision anchored her like gravity as her father's last words flitted on her tongue:

"Don't be soft."

She wouldn't let them be in vain.

Tipping the bowl over, she drained the poison clean onto the stone floor. Instinctively, the wolf shook itself, urging her forward.

Dianna relinquished her command, letting it guide her.

Sliding to a crouch, she crept along the boundary of the dungeon cell. Squinting in the dim light, she felt her way along rigid flagstones. For several minutes she looked for something she wasn't certain existed.

She had almost closed the perimeter when a skittering sound startled her. She turned just quickly enough to glimpse an enormous rat scurrying into the shadowed corridor.

Slowly, she traced its path backward. Her heart leapt.

It had come from inside the cell.

Her fingers swept over small crevices in the stone as she moved to its entry point. Abruptly, her hand came down hard into nothingness.

Angling her body, she knelt and prodded the small pocket of earth in the corner. It was no bigger than her fist, intended as a kind of drainage system. Mercifully, it was unused.

She paused for breath, brow furrowed, and brushed an errant strand of sweat-slick hair from her face. A seed of an idea unfurled its delicate roots in her mind, taking hold.

She began to dig.

CHAPTER 22

Snow moon, waning

Dianna dug well into the night, or what she perceived to be night, until a small pile of sodden earth had begun to take shape beside her.

It took her precious minutes to dispose of the evidence, mashing the excavated dirt into the corners of the cell, packing it in the tight gaps between stones, filling her cloak pockets with it. The hole in the wall, now larger, would need to be covered when the High Elder brought her more of the foul poison.

With some reluctance, she slipped her father's cloak from her shoulders, gently folded it, and set it aside. She scraped away at the loose dirt until the gap grew to be the size of her head.

Time dragged on. She had lost track of it when she heard a thump echo through the corridor. Between panicked heartbeats, she brushed flat the new heap of dirt, threw the cloak over her handiwork and fell on top of it, feigning sleep.

Steady footsteps approached as a yellow glow flickered in the dungeon. Dianna listened to the decanting of liquid as the High Elder refreshed her waterskin, the hollow clack of wood against stone as he left the cold dish – and the sound of his footsteps again, fading with the light.

As soon as he was gone, she breathed again. Feeling her way to the cell door, she cupped her hands around the bowl, nose wrinkled. She tipped out the sour-smelling poison at the back of the cell, then resumed her tedious labor.

She estimated the passing time by every stroke of the earth, her hands stiffening from the continuous scooping motion. The small of her back ached with a slow burn that later spread the length of her spine. Even in the cold catacombs, her skin grew slick with perspiration, her long hair plastering to her skin like snakes.

The ache in her arms melted into fatigue. Only when her trembling fingers refused to close did she slump against the stone wall, exhausted, hunger gnawing in her gut.

She stared into the darkness, sight dull from lack of light, and mopped salty grime from her face. When her hot cheeks dampened again, she realized it was not sweat, but tears. *Childish*, she thought.

Softly, there came a shiver of nerves, a flutter in her heart. The wolf was stirring, roaming under her skin, reminding her, *I'm still here.*

It filled her with a strange warmth.

Her tears subsided.

***

When the light returned at the mouth of the catacombs, Dianna was supine, wiry limbs sprawled, staring skyward.

The High Elder placed her daily sustenance in the corner. Dianna remained motionless, waiting for him to leave, but his scent clung to the air like bitter, tarry incense.

This time he lingered, beady eyes peering at her with a disgusted fascination.

Sitting up, Dianna stared back, her matted hair falling over her breasts. Blackened by the film of earth, her hands curled into fists.

The High Elder's hand came to rest on the lock of the cell door. The lantern's light deepened the wrinkles in his features as he contemplated something.

He was a small god in the eyes of Awl-Fethans, Dianna knew well, called by his title and never his given name. But under a cave of bones, half-shadowed, she thought he appeared older, mortal. Nothing more than a man.

At long last, his hand fell away. As he turned to leave, she spoke.

"You fear me, Orcarrus."

The High Elder came to a standstill, scarlet robes swaying.

"Not the demon," she said. "The woman."

She willed her words to bite, to unnerve him. For a moment he was motionless.

He resumed walking without a word, more slowly than before, retreating into the corridor's darkness. The catacombs fell silent again.

But under her tongue, the wolf howled.

***

Time passed. Dianna dug without rest.

She saw nothing. She felt nothing but a fierce flame, feeding the hunger of the most basic instinct – survival.

In the black void, she heard nothing but the sound of her own breathing.

CHAPTER 23

Snow moon, waning

Death was near.

Dianna had no inkling if the seventh day had yet dawned. But of death, she was certain. She felt it haunting her breath like a wraith.

The High Elder would arrive to take her away. The fire would consume her.

She leaned down, reached into the earth, and swept away the debris. She wriggled in and found she could fit both arms, her head, her torso – but then the earth became a hard clay, holding her back like a corked bottle.

Shaking herself free, she sat back to view her work and felt a blow of disappointment. The tunnel wasn't nearly deep enough.

Hopelessness descended like a heavy mantle on her body, sapping the last of her strength. She flattened herself to the ground and stared into the depths of the pit, feeling each second slip away. The wolf paced restless circles in her belly.

Instinctively she hushed it.

"It's not time, friend," she murmured. "The moon isn't full."

Yet her body tingled with its memory, pulling her out of

one shape and into another.

No, she did not have the strength to tunnel upward through the earth.

But the wolf did.

Aching and weary, she blinked into the dark of the burrowed corner, her cheek pressed against the cold flagstones. Her breath came flickering, tentative. In her mind's eye, the wolf paced within a deep corner of herself, a shadow almost blending into the black.

All right, she coaxed it. *Come out, then.*

The wolf's head dipped low, ears flat, passive. Its mangy, grizzled ruff shuddered. It hunkered down on lean legs, hackles bristling like fine spines.

It's time to come out.

She heard the High Elder's faint voice.

And then her body was splitting itself, on fire. With a sharp cry she pitched forward, retching air.

Her limbs convulsed in burning twists of sinew and bone. For one terrifying heartbeat, she thought the force of her own crumpling organs might crush her from the inside, but they folded like supple fabric.

Her eyes locked on the hole in the ground, saw freedom in its depths. She gritted her teeth, willing her body to lose itself.

"Get out of the dirt," she urged it, in a half-human snarl. "Go into the light."

Footsteps, coming closer, thumped in time with her pulse.

With a last heavy breath, Dianna finally lurched into the wolf.

Its ears pricked forward as it scented the strange and stifling underground, which stank of sickly-sweet, human sweat. Like light-drunk fireflies, its yellow eyes darted, panicking. Its instincts cried out to escape.

The footsteps quickened. A man began shouting.

The wolf snuffled at the cold stone ground, but there was warmth here, too. Its nose quivered, following the perfume of earth, of river and pine and sunshine. They meant safety. Home.

It wanted out. *Out* ... Meaningless words, vaguely whispered, flickered in the depths of its animal conscience ... *Out* ...

Out of the dirt. Into the light.

The wolf ducked low, writhing, clawing into the ground. Its forelegs scrabbled in the narrowing tunnel of mud, thick and sticky, until its hind paws found purchase.

Out of the dirt, into the light.

It pushed upward with strong wiry legs. Loose earth began to collapse around it like heavy rainfall. Panting, it shook itself and burrowed deeper, head snaking from side to side.

Out of the dirt, into the light.

The wolf shoved forward, churning earth, choking. Wet clay clogged its fur, its nostrils.

Out of the dirt, into the light.

Tearing into the darkness, it began to suffocate ...

Out of the dirt.

The earth was everywhere, pinning her.

Into the light ...

PART III: THE WOODS

"If the wolf had stayed in the wood there would have been no hue and cry after him."
— German proverb

CHAPTER 24

Cold moon, new
Two weeks before siege

On the bleakest outskirts of the slums, even the most highborn man could slip into the shadows unnoticed. In the rat's nest of the empire where desperation reigned, nobility itself receded into myth.

Beneath his dark cowl, Prince Remetus sloshed through muddy snow, winding his way around a smattering of tents peopled by illicit peddlers and prostitutes. There, in the darkest of hours, they dealt under some semblance of privacy. Thieves and beggars snatched and scavenged, and vagrants and drunkards made their fleeting dwellings.

Children with grubby faces and tattered clothes meandered without guardians. Many tugged at his arm, bleating, "Spare a copper?" But the prince hardly spared glances for them, drawing his cloak closer and melting into the night.

He crossed opposite a backlit tentskin, behind which a woman wept or prayed in a strange language. A toothless vagrant plucked fragile folk songs on his lyre.

But one figure stood alone outside her tent, illuminated by a bonfire's blaze, observing the night.

A homespun robe swathed her, and her wool-gray plait hung past her waist. Perhaps she had been beautiful once, but time's handiwork had traced her face, brown as his own skin but puckered as a walnut. In one hand she dangled a half-empty bottle as a cat might dangle a mouse from its mouth.

Her gaze had already found him before he approached. Her wine-stained lips spread in a thin smile, giving the impression of geniality, though the eyes disclosed nothing.

He passed her silently, but her murmur followed him.

"You are looking for me, child."

Remetus paused, glaring through the dark folds of his cowl.

"I don't believe that I am," he said.

The old woman tottered forward, disturbing the contents of the wine bottle, dark as blood within the glass.

"Some call you the prince." Her rasping whisper crawled under his skin. "I see an imperator."

Remetus glanced about, but there was no one else in earshot. He turned, peering at the stranger.

"You have an exceptional potential, you know," she said. "A power that runs deep in your blood."

"I know not these lies you speak," he retorted.

"I do not speak lies. I speak only legends."

Drawing nearer, Remetus saw that her skin was shriveled as dry oak bark, her teeth mottled or missing. An assortment of heavy earrings swung from her earlobes. He had expected a more imposing woman, certainly one wealthier and more beautiful than this ragged, wizened crone.

"There is a mistake," he said at once, shaking his head. "My consul led me on a fool's errand. You cannot be the prestigious oracle he spoke of."

"The very same," she answered.

"No. I need proof."

The old woman extended her free hand.

"Your palm," she prompted.

Remetus paused, listening to the wild animal sounds of commonfolk, the distant clamor of brawling men, the drunken falsetto of a woman singing. He took a deep, sharp-edged breath and thrust his hand forward. The old woman took it in her own, peering down at the lines of his skin.

He had barely exhaled before she spoke.

"Prince Ramus took your mare out to ride," she said. "She belonged to you, and it upset you. You watched in secret, and with your thoughts alone, made her spook. She threw him, and he broke his arm. You were nine."

Behind a thin veil of woodsmoke, her eyes bored into his soul. "You have power, child, yet it frightens even you. You have not nurtured it, yet it remains in you. A seed."

Remetus glanced at his palm and back to the oracle, chilled to his core, knowing she was right.

She was right about everything.

"Your fee?" he asked low.

A sharp cackle met this question, more piercing than he thought her capable. She dropped his hand from her grasp, took a sloshing draft from the bottle, and surveyed him with beetling eyes, edged with crow's feet.

"For you," she said, "no charge."

Remetus eyed her with suspicion, but she pulled back the tent's gauzy curtains.

"Your grace." She stepped aside with a crooked smile, allowing him passage.

The rich smoke of sandalwood incense stung his nose. Hazy candlelight bathed the cramped, tapestry-draped interior, which held a trestle laden with an assortment of trinkets and crystals, but little else. It was a place for visiting, for coming and going, impermanent. The prince shrouded his mouth in his cloak, already skeptical that such shabby makings could house any legitimate business.

"Have a seat, my child," the old woman invited, pulling up a rickety footstool with a moth-eaten cushion. With a wheezing cough she settled into her own stool opposite, set aside her bottle, and steepled her bony fingers.

"What is your name?" Remetus pressed.

"Neither here nor there. Now, come to my table. I insist."

Upon the tufted footstool, the prince sat as well as one could without sitting. The effect was ludicrous, like a great menacing raven perched upon a birdhouse.

"Tell me, my liege," the oracle began, "what do you fear the most?"

Remetus stared, the candlelight throwing shadows upon his stony features. "Do you take me for a fool? A man does not disclose that which would ruin him. You seek to blackmail me."

The corners of the oracle's eyes prickled in amusement.

"You hold your cards close. This is wise. But a true ruler can only rise to power by killing his greatest fear: that which is more powerful than he. So tell me . . . What do you fear?"

"I will tell you when you tell me your name," Remetus said coldly, "for that is also enough to besmirch one's repute."

She dismissed this with a wave of her hand. "I have many names. Most are in the ancient language, too strange and wild for your soft tongue. Call me the Knowing One, Singer Over Bones, *sannat-rynnir* or simply Lupa Bijou, my birth name – it matters not. I am what I am."

Remetus surveyed the woman with scorn, but a crease of doubt broke his brow, and the aura of a man bested escaped from him like a sigh. The oracle seemed to sense this, and her thin-lipped smile was as mysterious as the crescent moon.

"You dare not speak a word of it, crone," he warned.

"I shall not."

"Swear to it."

"I swear upon my life."

"If you speak, you will have none." The prince's eyes narrowed to pinpricks. "I will have my best men find you and slit your throat."

"As you wish," the oracle agreed, at peace.

Beneath the bite of the prince's threatening voice was a flicker of terror. He leaned forward, bracing his weight on his strong arms in a gesture of dominance, but his face had gone pale – a fleeting glimpse of the true prince, a small man haunted by a shadow.

"It lives in the woods," he said under his breath.

The oracle regarded him through heavy-lidded eyes, the same feline smile still in place.

"One night in my youth, by the light of a full moon," he continued in a low voice, "My cavalry and I hunted elk. A female and her young calf. We had been tracking them for many hours until they led us to their grazing place.

"There was the most magnificent bull I had ever beheld. His antlers were longer than a man's arm span. His eye, this big." He made a fist with one hand. "Enough meat on him to feed the court for days. The cavalry master directed the men, leveled his crossbow for the kill. 'Steady on,' he said. And then, out of nowhere . . ."

His face hardened, but the ghost of a nightmare lingered in his eyes. "A lone wolf darted forth from the trees. Barely half the bull's size, even rangy. It was . . . starving.

"It leapt onto the bull's back, thrashing and snarling. Its fangs tore into its tough hide. First, I was angered to lose the game. Then awed. Then . . . then afraid." His voice was only a whisper now. "How quickly the great bull bled out. How the wolf devoured its still-breathing body. Never had I seen a creature so vicious, so hellbent in its quest for flesh."

The oracle's eyes glinted with understanding. She nodded.

"It struck the bull down," Remetus finished. "One wolf."

The oracle now reached over the trestle with a sagging

arm, relighting the end of a large pipe in the candle flame.

"Wolves. Strong, resourceful animals." She sucked a long pull on the pipe and exhaled, swirling a thick heady smoke into the air. "Notoriously elusive. Natural navigators: instinctively they know locations from the richness of soils, the movement of sound and wind, the shape of the landscape, the patterns of scent. And they mate for life. Essential to the cycle of things . . ."

"Enough," snapped Remetus.

"Wolves . . ." the oracle repeated, deliberating. "That is all, then? Very well. My answer to you is this: you must hunt them down."

Remetus' dark eyes sharpened.

"Hunt them?"

"Hunt them."

"What good will that do me?"

The oracle smiled. She tapped a bit of old ash from the pipe, the brass rings on her knobby fingers gleaming in the lowlight.

"Return to the root of your fear," she said, smearing her fingers in the scattered ashes upon the trestle. "Live and fast in the forest for a fortnight. Kill as many wolves as you can hunt and drink their blood. Upon the next full moon, the power you seek shall be yours."

"Drink their blood?" Remetus' features twisted in disgust. "Are you mad, woman? That shall kill me in a fortnight!"

But the oracle merely shook her head.

"It shall show you all the life in the world," she murmured.

The prince opened his mouth to speak, but she dabbed the ashes on his forehead in one swift gesture, marking him as in baptism.

"Go forth with the blessing of your god Mactus," she said, with a distant calmness.

But Remetus touched the mark upon his brow with revulsion.

"This is trickery." At once he rose to his feet, shrouding his eyes in his cowl, retreating. "Damned black magic."

"Your enemy is coming," the oracle said.

Remetus paused at the threshold of the tent, facing the night.

"The Caenani," he murmured.

"They are on the move even as we speak. They will strike here first."

Remetus chanced a look over his shoulder into the hazy light.

"How do I stop them?"

"You cannot." The oracle traced a thin finger through the black ashes, making a series of lines. "There will be a great war. This is fated. Bloodshed. And death."

She lifted her hand, revealing runes the prince could not decipher.

"But you can save your empire from ruin," she said.

"How?" Remetus demanded, rounding on her.

"I tell you again, my child," said the oracle, waggling one blackened finger and clucking as though chastising an unruly boy. "I tell you, if what you desire is power, you must tread over that which obstructs your path toward it. You must kill fear. Then you shall be feared."

Remetus lingered at the threshold with an incredulous frown as she curled a hand around the neck of the wine bottle.

"If you do not," she continued with a casual air, "it is your brother Ram who will become imperator."

Remetus' eyes flashed. "You will respect imperial rule, witch! *Ramus* is my brother's given name."

"And his chosen name is Ram," the oracle said without a change in her tone. "Ram . . . like the male sheep. Quite poetic, a wolf in sheep's clothing. Sacrificial."

164

Her rambling needled at Remetus, who shook his head as though to rid himself of it. A smile spread across the oracle's lips before she lifted the bottle and tossed down a deep draft.

"Only in death shall your empire live, after all," she said. Her red smile slurred into mad laughter. "Only in death."

Remetus recoiled as if the sound had burned him. He swept from the tent without a word, dissolving the plume of smoke in his wake. But the oracle's laugh rose to a piercing, crowing pitch, following him long into the night, and long after that.

Like a leech, it burrowed into his mind and fed there.

CHAPTER 25

Snow moon, waning

A pair of ravens circled around the midday sun. A mile away, in the course of her path through waving ferns, a rangy, brindle-coated wolf paused and sniffed the air.

Following closely, a second wolf came to linger beside her. His yellow eyes were fiery sparks, striking against fur of pure coal black. He would have disappeared in the darkest hours of the night, but silhouetted sharply against lush greenery, he was a phantom revealed in the sun.

The pair of wolves moved quietly for their great sizes, as though a god had shaped earthly creatures into visions of creeping death. The brindle wolf whined and shifted her weight to lean against the black, her ears cupped forward.

They touched snouts. Within the fleeting gesture was an exchange of language, a transmission of thought.

Fresh kill.

Tail flagged behind her, the brindle wolf lowered her head, loping over the mossy earth. The black wolf shadowed her. Together they bounded through the woods, synchronized, until the iron stink of blood grew stronger on the air, and the ravens loomed overhead.

Beneath a thick cover of blood and mud, only a few patches of the dead thing's skin were visible. One of the ravens descended upon the unfortunate creature and began picking at it with its curved beak.

The brindle wolf rushed in to claim the kill, snapping at the scavengers, who unfurled their bony wings and scattered to the wind. Snuffling, she prodded her snout into the flank of the dead thing, testing for signs of life.

But her companion balked, hackles flickering. A low growl rose from his belly.

The brindle wolf whimpered, but fell back on her haunches, dropping her head in solemn watchfulness.

The black wolf advanced at a low creep. As he stalked forward, his fur fluttered and vanished with the breeze like molting feathers, unearthing the brown flesh of human limbs.

Now a man stood in place of the wolf, his strong body tense, his dark eyes transfixed on the thing in the mud.

"Eccka," he said in a calm undertone. "Call them."

The brindle wolf let fly a deep howl that rocked in the pines, carrying for miles.

But only a moment passed – the span of a few breaths – before a second pair of wolves quietly emerged from the ferns, noses trembling. One edged up alongside his companions in curiosity, switching his umber tail.

The other wolf padded forward, lowering his head to the ground and shivering out of his own skin. A young man surfaced, naked, shaking off the animal. His yellow eyes cooled into icy blue.

He came to join the older man, staring at the dead thing at his feet.

It was a young woman, curled in the mud on her side like the crescent moon, naked as a newborn. The curves of her body shone bone-pale against the dark muck. An inflamed gash split open the length of one thigh, welling with blood. Long, silvery tendrils of hair, crusted in mud, splayed a halo around her, and her lips were cracked and ashen.

Tangled and ethereal in her shape, she gave the impression of a fallen angel.

Kneeling beside her, the young man pressed two gentle fingers to her neck. The pulse was faint, fluttering, but it was there.

His mouth parted, sucked in a breath.

"She's barely alive," the older man said, kneeling beside him. "Her body's lost much blood. Those wounds will get infected."

The young man's hands examined the bolt embedded inches deep in the woman's mangled calf, skimming over the ugly bruises cascading from the crest of her shoulder to the arc of her hip.

His blue eyes blinked and blinked. He crushed a hand over his mouth, swallowing hard.

"Aimes?" prompted the older man.

Swiftly Aimes brushed away the gleam of a tear.

The man beside him paused, closed his eyes briefly in resignation. "Take her, then."

But Aimes shook his head: no, they should not move her.

"Can you treat her here?" the man asked.

Aimes nodded. His eyes did not leave his patient.

The man beside him turned away, addressing the umber wolf that looked on in interest. "Fredric, fetch his supplies."

The wolf immediately turned tail and vanished into the tangle of bracken leaves. The brindle wolf remained, sulking, her ears flattening.

"We'll go west to hunt," the man said, his voice final. "For now, we'll settle here. Help Fredric get the supplies, would you?"

With a low growl in her throat, she was gone in a flash.

In the following silence, the patch of woods where the

three human figures remained seemed to exist only for them.

Frozen with anticipation, Aimes stayed crouched over the woman's broken, bloodied body, his gaze thrown over her like a shield. Between his hands he took her mud-caked hand, like a fading firefly his warmth could bring back to life.

"It's her," said the man.

Aimes looked up. Nodded once.

CHAPTER 26

Raven moon, new

Skeletal branches formed a latticed canopy in the sky above Dianna, bright with a mosaic of sunlight. The lofty treetops seemed to shudder and spin in circles as she returned to consciousness. Her stomach roiled, and she turned her head, heaving, but had nothing to vomit.

Rolling onto her back, blinking and drowsy, she inhaled a familiar floral scent laced with sun-dried forest pine. Subtle, underneath the earthy layers, was a third scent, rich and musky and wolfish.

She lay there for a short time, closing her eyes and breathing in the perfumed air. Her senses felt hazy with sleepy calm.

But rational thought clawed its way through the momentary fugue. The calm must be deceptive. How could she have fallen asleep when the last thing she remembered was crashing through snagging branches, running for her life?

The memory triggered echoes of movement in her limbs, but they were restrained, tight with what felt like bandages. Stirring beneath a thick fleece swathing her naked body, she felt pockets of air around her and an odd sensation, a slight pressure on her calf.

She looked down at her legs, at the outline of a man bent over her, and screamed. He flinched, stumbling backward.

A white-hot pang shot along the length of her leg as she sat up and wrenched away. With a pained gasp, she doubled over, clutching at a sutured wound splitting into a ragged flap of skin.

The stitches lining it had ripped loose. Her hand came away glistening with fresh blood, turning her stomach.

Her wild eyes snapped up at the stranger through a tangle of hair, her lip curled in the echo of a snarl. Flustered thoughts careened and flickered through her mind like birds.

Pin him like Actaen. Go for the throat.

But the young man did not move. Instead, he had shrunk into a low crouch, making himself as small as possible.

Heart pounding, Dianna studied him. His full head of chaotic black hair, shorn just above his ears, offset his striking blue eyes. A faded gray tunic and a pair of hole-riddled trousers hung a size too big on his rangy build. She caught another trace of the wolf-scent in the air – musky, warm, and all too familiar.

The source of it became unsettlingly clear.

"You," Dianna breathed. "You're one of them."

His blue eyes darted at her from under his shock of black hair, neither confirming nor denying the accusation.

Dianna felt her skin crawl, and anger lapped like a flame in her chest.

"You're a demon, aren't you?"

But the man remained silent, glancing skittishly at his feet.

"There are more of you here," she said, and her voice emerged hard, quivering. "Aren't there?"

No response. The man's eyes closed. He pulled a long, faltering breath.

171

"Answer me, damn you!"

"N-Not," he said at last, sotto.

"Not what?"

"Not . . . demons," he said, pushing the word past his lips with difficulty.

"Then who?" Dianna demanded. "Why?"

He shook his head, lips pressed shut as he looked down. Dianna's brow knit as she considered him, childlike in his uncertainty. He spoke as though illiterate, but his eyes were intelligent, sharp and icy.

Liam was wrong about you, she thought at once. *You have human consciousness. You're not a demon.*

You're like me.

She changed tack, speaking in a gentler, measured cadence, as if placating a frightened animal.

"Can you hear?"

His dark-haired head bobbed.

"Can you speak my tongue?"

A subtle wag of the head. Then an inclination, like an affirmative. Dianna wasn't sure which to believe.

"Are you lost, too?" she whispered.

His thick brows rose under his dark hair, and he lifted his head slightly. A patch of sunlight illuminated him, and Dianna's gaze traced the thin white scar striping his face.

He gave a tentative nod.

Dianna's focus tore away just long enough to assess the damage of her reopened wound. Only then did she notice a small wooden box filled with assorted medical supplies: a large jar of salve, woven bandages, costly looking herbs and medicines, and blades of various sizes. Among them, a silver stitching needle winked in the sun.

"You've been looking after me," she said under her breath. "Why?"

His posture was shy, all focused downward – shoulders hunched, head ducked low. It said, *I am no threat. I submit to you.*

172

It intrigued her, and the tension along her spine softened. Words could mean nothing, but she was well-versed in the language of movement. It rarely lied.

For a moment that seemed to stretch on, the two of them were still. Dianna felt warm blood trickle down her throbbing leg, the open air on her exposed skin.

"What's your name?" she tried, a universal question.

The man's eyes flitted downward again, tight with contemplation. His mouth formed a silent "O," holding it for a moment.

"Oryaen," he said to his bare feet. Dianna wondered if they were cold.

"I'm sorry I shouted at you, Oryaen."

The man stooped, picked up the slender wooden crossbow bolt nearby them, and showed it to her. Its speared tip glinted in the sunlight.

"This?" said Dianna, shaken. "This was in my leg, when you found me?"

He nodded.

Dianna judged the sun's position in the sky against the angle of the tree line.

"Are we far from Awl-Feth? Are we very deep into the woods?"

Another nod, firm.

"The hunters lost track. They gave up the chase." A doubtful frown pulled at Dianna's lips. "But not for long. At the next full moon, they'll be back again. And they'll be after us both."

The man's mouth formed a word clearly, but it was soft with despair. "Stay."

Dianna looked at him, unsure. She made to sit up, but her muscles felt viscous, aching down to the marrow. Her stomach was a hollow drum, and her mouth was dry.

Let him heal you now if he wants, she thought. *Decide if you can trust him later.*

173

Beside her makeshift moss-bed were several heavy clay basins. Stooping, her healer cupped his hands in one basin of cold, clean water, making a tiny pool in his palms. Wordlessly, he extended the offering to her.

She eyed him with uncertainty, so he lifted the water to his own lips. He sipped it, showing her it was safe. He cupped a fresh pool for her. Leaning forward, Dianna winced as her wounds seized with the movement.

The man's eyes caught hers, their blue depths wide and full, with some indefinite feeling. He held his hollowed palms out, filled with water.

Dianna pressed her lips to the edge of his fingers, her burning tongue tasting the cold water. She took sips that turned into great gulps.

Oryaen brought water to her again and again with steady hands, and she drank until it ran out, until the sudden lump in her throat cut her breath short. He brought her a pouch of tree nuts, which she ate at once.

Something about his gesture of providing nourishment stirred her, made death seem less welcome – or perhaps, she thought, compelled her to live.

Hot tears pricked her eyes before she could try to suppress them.

"Thank you," she said, turning her head away.

Among the contents of the medicine box, Oryaen selected a clean rag, which he immersed in another basin.

He proceeded, methodically, to lift part of the fleece covering Dianna's legs. She flinched, recoiling involuntarily.

He looked at her, and his eyebrows had drawn together in a complicated mix of sympathy and sadness. Dianna watched him a moment before relenting, melting into the forest floor.

Oryaen tried again, taking great care in moving the fleece aside. With the lightest touch, he applied the warm compress to her leg, stanching the flow of blood.

Dianna tried to read his expression, but his eyes were downcast as he washed the blood away.

Through ashen lips, she asked, "Am I going to die?"

The question was not concerned, but empty.

Oryaen shook his head, but a frown pulled at his mouth. The cloth was sopped red now, and he wrung it out.

Dianna watched him work in silence. He repeated the process until the wound was clean. Gently he pressed a crushed leaf against it, making her skin numb.

He extracted the silver needle, threaded with catgut, from its place in the medicine box. With a piece of flint and a bit of tinder from his pocket, he ignited a small fire. He held the needle under the flame to sterilize it.

Dianna glanced at his face, the dark stubble of his jawline offsetting softer features. His hands and forearms looked strong enough for legionary combat, but she couldn't help but find them distractingly beautiful in the work of healing.

"You seem young for a healer," she said, without quite thinking.

Oryaen dipped the needle into her flesh. The anesthetic he applied had dulled all surface pain, and his eyes darted back and forth while his fingers laced fine, precise stitches.

Dianna lay still, taking a deep breath. A blend of chamomile, clary sage, and lavender sweetened the air, and her limbs felt heavy.

"That scent," she said. "I know it. It smells like sleep."

Oryaen nodded toward a bundle of dried wildflowers beside the moss-bed.

It was a common aromatic remedy for insomnia, she remembered, among many from the apothecary that she had tried as a child. But it hadn't worked for her then. She must be so exhausted that anything would lull her into slumber.

"I have a restlessness," she explained, more subdued.

"Sometimes I don't know whether I'm asleep or awake."

Overhead, a bird sang. Oryaen did not look up from his stitching.

"My father—" Dianna started, and the stone of pain in her heart turned with remembering. "My father said I'd just grow out of it."

She stared upward again, vacant of all energy or will to move.

A moment passed before Oryaen drew up the long dark thread. With one of the short blades, he tied the end of the catgut and cut it.

Dianna couldn't help but admire the young healer's neat work before he covered her again, retreating from her side. She eased into the fleece's forgiving warmth, sinking into numbness.

"I should have died," she murmured aloud.

His whispered answer came from somewhere around her elbow, each syllable measured.

"Dianna," he said. "Sleep now."

As her eyelids grew heavy and her pulse began to slow, the woods slipped away. The sedative perfume of the wildflowers drifted on a breath of wind, and all was quiet but for the small sounds of medical instruments as Oryaen cleaned and replaced them.

But a half-formed thought tugged at the edges of her consciousness before it dissipated into the ether of a dream.

She had never given him her name.

CHAPTER 27

Raven moon, waxing

Dianna's breath rasped through the gag muzzling her mouth. Rough rope binding her wrists and ankles gnawed at her skin.

She was standing on a bed of hot coals, tethered to a stake, surrounded by faces. They leered at her with black eyes, chanting the words over and over.

"The will of Mactus. The will of Mactus."

Searing flames licked at her legs and she writhed against the creeping heat, frantic. Billowing smoke began to fill her lungs. It was only when she turned that she saw her father and brother tied down on either side of her, slumped forward, shapeless lumps of blackened flesh.

***

Dianna jolted upright out of the nightmare, seizing upon her aching leg as if it had really been burning. Gasping, she brushed clumps of moss and leaves from her salt-slicked skin. She wheeled around, filmy eyes blinking into a patchwork of harsh sunlight.

Her quiet healer was not there. She did not know why she expected him to be. He had no obligation to ease her pain, to wait at her bedside, yet he had done both. Already, she felt a twinge of loneliness at his absence.

She wondered how long she had slept – hours? Days? The feeling of lying folded within a dream, not meandering sleeplessly in the dark of night, was as old and strange as the softness of lush grass and warm moss beneath her. Her body cried out everywhere, and she wanted nothing more than to turn over and succumb to sleep again.

But the unwelcome nightmare clung to her like the weeks of filth. She scraped her grimy hair, matted with knots and smothered in dried mud, from her face. From the bowls Oryaen had gathered, she knew there must be fresh water close by and halfheartedly decided to trace the chattering birds to its source.

Staggering upright, she placed her weight on her good leg, rocking back on her heels and gritting her teeth. Even the slightest pressure fired a splitting pain through the torn sinews.

Hobbling forward through the undergrowth, she followed the damp earth smell and burbling sound of water. Her hands brushed aside prodding branches and sticky spiderwebs until the dancing light of a river nearly blinded her.

On such an early spring day, its surface was sparkling and clear as glass. Sun-drenched greenery sprawled endlessly beyond it, vivid as a painting. Dianna's eyes feasted upon roots, branches, and leaves, prickling with tears as she sucked fresh air in fervent lungfuls. She had never seen land so bright and untouched, and even now, in her consuming grief, she marveled that the woods could be teeming with life when her own village had fallen slowly into ruin.

She stood for a moment, simply listening. So faint it could have been imagined, more felt than heard, a steady rhythm plucked the air like a heartbeat. It drew her, riveted and wondering, over the littered forest floor.

"Who's there?" she asked aloud, unthinking.

But the sound passed, and only the wind answered as it prickled in her hair. Dianna shook her head as if to clear her mind.

You're still waking up, she decided. *Silbarran feels more alive than anywhere you know. But these woods aren't sentient.*

She took a tentative step forward. The river stones, smooth beneath her feet, rattled as she disturbed them on her ungainly way to the water's edge. She broke its shallows slowly at first, savoring the cool, slippery pulp of algae between her toes. With some reservation she glanced around but found no company except the birds. Holding her breath, she plunged into the river's depths and let the cold shock envelop her.

Minnows dispersed at her contact in a whorl of silver darts. As the water stung her wound afresh, she cried out and waited for the waves of pain to subside.

Scouring silt and crumbling mud from her skin, Dianna raked tangled hair from her face, braiding it into a neat plait and coiling it at her nape. She was up to her neck in the water when Oryaen approached quietly on the riverbank, medicine box under one arm, a bundle of cloth in the other. He looked askance again as though to preserve her privacy, despite having seen her entirely unclothed.

"Hel-lo," he murmured carefully, testing the word on his tongue.

"Hello," Dianna echoed, watchful.

Without elaboration, Oryaen stooped to place the bundle on the rocks. He turned his back to her. The wind feathered his black hair.

Dianna waited, but he remained still. Swimming to the riverbank, she pulled herself out. The cool water trickled away from her skin. For a moment she stretched out on the smooth pebbles, glistening in the sun like a stranded fish. She picked up the bundle and unrolled it. It felt supple and warm in her hands.

The color of the dress was black as a starless night, black as the mourning gowns of widows. It was unadorned except for a trim of plain silk ribbon, the knee-length hemline practical for movement. A Valtan noblewoman might have worn it like a nightgown.

What a strange choice of attire, she thought at first. But as she held it, smoothing out the thick, sleek fabric, it dawned on her that the dress was unabashedly, comfortably fitted for a woman's body – nothing like her father's coarse hunting clothes, despite their comforting smokiness and warmth.

No longer would she need to disguise her body under woolen layers.

Standing, Dianna found her balance and slipped the garment over her head, pulling her arms through the long sleeves, letting the skirt fall and caress her legs. She had never felt a material so fine in her life, like wings enfolding her.

Like freedom.

When she spoke, her voice was tight and unlike herself. "Thank you."

Oryaen turned around, his cautious gaze moving to her. His voice was soft and low.

"Fits," he said.

A light wind billowed through the trees, shaking leaves from their boughs. A wolf's distant howl cleaved the silence.

Out of sheer instinct, Dianna's hand dropped to her side. Her fingers clenched into a fist, closing on the space where her shortbow should have hung.

Oryaen angled his head as though understanding. He looked at his medicine box, slid a thin lancet from its compartment and extended it to her, handle first.

Dianna considered the delicate instrument, the glint of the sun on the blade. At first glance it seemed pathetic, but with just enough pressure flicked against a vital artery, it could be deadly.

Oryaen's outstretched hand faltered as he tried to gauge her expression, but finally Dianna shook her head.

"I'm not afraid of what's out there," she said. "We're safe, aren't we?"

Oryaen nodded, tucking the knife back into its compartment.

The howl sounded again, low and steady, and a new awareness prickled the back of Dianna's neck, hitching at her pulse.

"Oryaen," she said, faltering. "Are you alone?"

He shook his head.

Without warning, he lifted his head to the sky and released a long, throaty howl. The call shuddered through Dianna's bones, and she turned to look at him, alarmed.

Oryaen stood fixed in place, breathless and watchful as a sentinel. His eyes had lit up.

From a sparse copse of white alder, three human figures emerged, almost as though they had been waiting there all along.

Their faces turned to Dianna with a collective, feral interest. An eerie chill shivered through her as they approached one by one over the rock-strewn riverbed.

Standing at the fore was the heir to the empire himself.

Prince Ramus Baines.

CHAPTER 28

Raven moon, waxing

At a distance, Dianna would have mistaken him for a peasant. Only threadbare wovens clothed him – a pair of loose trousers faded and tattered by the elements, and a once-white tunic open at the collar. A man and a woman shadowed him. None of them wore shoes.

But his brown-skinned, square-jawed face, though thick with a beard and years older, was undoubtedly the same as in the portrait on the cathedral wall. The very one she had witnessed almost every day of her life.

In the portrait, a softness of expression and more heavily muscled stature had revealed the difference between the twins. Dianna recognized both as he proffered his hand in greeting.

She slid to her knees at once, biting back a cry at the strain on her wounded leg, palms in the dirt, face downturned.

Above her, the prince's deep voice thrummed.

"Why do you withdraw?"

Dianna did not move, speaking with a practiced cadence.

"Because taking your grace's hand is tantamount to claiming oneself his equal, an offense to the empire punishable by death," she said to the ground.

There was a rustling of leaves as the prince stooped to her level and put forth his hand a second time.

Dianna raised her gaze slowly, hardly daring to breathe.

"The laws of the empire do not apply here, child," he said, dark eyes studying her from under his brows.

Steeling herself, Dianna maintained eye contact. She took his hand with a firm grip, too many questions in her mind clamoring to be answered.

She decided on one.

"Your grace—" she began.

"Call me Ram."

"Are you a coward?"

The prince's hand fell at once. "I beg your pardon?"

In the corner of Dianna's eye, Oryaen seemed to fold into himself, drawing up his shoulders and frowning.

"Your empire is at war," Dianna said, keeping her voice steady, but it sharpened at the edges in spite of herself. "Your people are starving. Your soldiers are martyred in the streets. Your order has collapsed. Are you hiding in the woods like a coward?"

The woman behind the prince made an aggressive noise of protest, stepping forward. Complemented by high cheekbones and full lips, her rich complexion was striking in the sunlight. But her beauty was not a soft kind, as an open lily. The harsh angles of her features suggested a predatory scorn, a self-preservation – a barbed rose.

"Don't ever call him that," she growled.

But the man standing at her side caught her with one outstretched arm. Curly-haired and freckled, he had the lean and lanky physique of one who must never be idle. He wore frayed burlap trousers like a scarecrow's, while only a lightweight tailored jerkin, threaded with buttons of bone and riddled with patches of various patterns, covered his chest.

"Come, now," he murmured, in an unexpectedly lighthearted tone. "We all know I've claimed that title."

As Dianna glanced at the man in consternation, he winked.

The prince's storm-gray eyes were sober as he considered Dianna.

"I admire your courage." He spoke under his breath, his words catching her off guard – not denial, but praise. The wolf welled up inside her, squirming and seething; it wedged itself in her throat, primed to burst forth.

"I'm not afraid of you," she said.

"Of course you're not. You are the daughter of a Lead Hunter. An Aergyris."

The wolf in her flinched at this, a flutter of panic in her breast. Dianna's brow knit. "How could you know that?"

But the prince – *Ram*, she reminded herself – did not smile with malice as she expected. Instead, his mouth deepened to a frown.

"I am truly sorry for your loss. Abram was . . . a great defender of your people."

Like a foreign language, his words of empathy twisted in her ears, making little sense. Color rose to her cheeks, betraying her.

"How. . ." Dianna faltered.

"If I frightened you," Ram continued, "I am sorry for that, also. You must understand. We've had to keep a close watch on your village, and hiding, as you call it, is a tiring business."

"A close watch . . ." Dianna echoed, and her heart quickened. "Has a man passed through these woods – a tall man, fair-haired? His name is Liam."

But Ram shook his head solemnly, and her heart sank.

"No," he said. "I'm afraid we've not seen your brother."

Dianna began struggling to her feet, grimacing as her wounds panged with her weight. Oryaen extended his arm

184

for her to take, hoisting her upright. Begrudgingly, she leaned against him for support, keeping her eyes on the prince.

"But you've been hiding here," she said at last, slowly. "You're cursed, like me."

Ram followed suit, rising to meet her gaze. The lines of his body were relaxed, his face an unfailing mask of calm.

"Your people have been made to believe we are demons. But they are misguided. We are cursed, yes. We are a family." He glanced over his shoulder at the two strangers in his wake. "We are many things, Aergyris. Evil is not one of them . . . though I'm afraid something like it roams these woods."

"Then why stay here, cheating death?"

Ram drew his broad shoulders back, taking a breath, holding himself tall. Through shabby clothing, the Prince of Myre became clear in his regal bearing.

"If there was another way, we'd have found it. But to live, we must live like this. And so we have."

"For seven years," came a hardened voice.

It was the woman who had spoken this time, her intense stare fixed on them.

Ram half-smiled at Dianna, though his sunken eyes gave no impression of true gladness. The juxtaposition was disarming.

"I believe we began on the wrong foot," he said. "This is Eccka and Fredric."

The roguish smile quirking Fredric's lips seemed to hold a secret. Although he could be no more than thirty years old, the confidence in his posture was warm and true, and of a man who had experienced many things. He was not standing flat-footed, but gently rocking on perched toes of earth-stained, roughened feet that hadn't seen shoes in a long time.

Eccka turned askance, refusing to acknowledge Dianna

185

in kind. Just under her jawline, beneath her close-cropped hair, an inky black tattoo crisscrossed her dark, matte skin. It was an inscription, a series of simple but strange markings.

"And you've already met Aimes," Ram added, nodding to the man at Dianna's side.

Dianna glanced at the healer, brows drawn together, but he was already turned away, staring indiscriminately out among the trees.

"He called himself Oryaen," she said.

The friendly smile slid from Ram's face. He stepped toward the young man, hand outstretched, palm open like an offering.

"Aimes," he said softly, steadily. "You're all right now, yes?"

Aimes remained facing away, dark head bowed. He was as still as a deep-rooted tree.

"Where are you, Aimes?" asked Ram.

Aimes blinked. Stirred, as if waking from a reverie. Followed the lines of Ram's palm with his gaze.

"Home," he answered, distantly.

"Yes," Ram said, and his hand fell away. His voice remained low and slow. "Yes, you're home, Aimes."

"A-I-M-E-S," Aimes spelled, like a child. "I'm Aimes."

Ram nodded. "Good." He looked at Dianna. "He's Aimes. He forgets that sometimes, you see."

Dianna didn't understand the dark tone in which the prince spoke.

"He saved my life," she said.

Ram gave no indication of surprise. "It's what we must do for each other," he said simply. "We can offer you food and shelter, too. Nearly anything you need."

Dianna glanced at the roughened hands at Ram's sides, the twitch of his linen tunic in the breeze, his chest moving with breath: an oil painting come to life.

"All I need are answers," she said.

"I can offer these, too." Ram scanned the trees. "But daylight is burning. We must arrive at the nearest boundary of the woods before dusk."

Dianna turned to Aimes. "The boundary?"

In his wolf-like silence and too-big clothing, Aimes nodded.

The woman called Eccka settled her piercing gaze on Ram. "Is that the wisest course of action, sir?"

"There is much to explain and nothing to argue now," Ram said. "We will do so when time is kinder."

Closing his eyes, he tilted his head to the sky, exposing a stippling of coarse dark hair from jaw to neck. Curious, Dianna studied his outline against the trees.

It was still whole and human before it quivered, then unfolded.

The prince's thin, off-white clothes fluttered across the dirt like snakeskin, inexplicably intact. All that Dianna remembered from her own transformations – the awful sputter of bone and rending of sinew – seemed painless to Ram, reduced to a swift ripple of reallocated flesh, as if blinking out of existence.

The wolf, black as coal and eclipsing Dianna in height, breathed like bellows and moved like water in a flume. His thick fur ruffled in the wind as he lowered his head, fixing his gold almond-shaped eyes on her.

A seamless change. In broad daylight.

Dianna was breathless, immobile. She knew too well that beasts this size could devour her bones and all – yet he watched her with an awareness that could only be human.

Silent Eccka followed suit, not bothering with modesty. Craning her neck away, she peeled off her clothes in a snap of leather and fabric. One leap and her lithe limbs were shifting too, crawling with black-flecked fur. Fredric, his eyes yellowing, flashed Dianna an impish smile before bounding away to join them.

One by one, in their distinctive ways, they shook away their former selves like winter cloaks and emerged, monsters, in the sunlight.

Aimes watched the newly formed wolfpack, swallowing hard with something like longing.

He rolled forward into a sinuous crouch, fingers splayed in the dirt. Already Dianna could see his ears moving up the sides of his skull, his clicking spine rearranging itself like a wooden puzzle. His human skin unraveled like silk, spinning away to vanish at his feet.

The change was smooth and steady as the glide of raven wings, as quick as an eye blink, as easy as a breath. His body unmade itself, not in fits and fractures, but with tenderness.

Dianna's own voice had escaped her. But before his fleeting vestiges of humanity ebbed beneath animal skin, Aimes managed to spare four words for her.

"I will carry you."

CHAPTER 29

Raven moon, waxing

Aimes loped on light feet, lacing across switchbacks and between the scrub of coniferous trees. Pressed to the coarse pelt of the great rangy wolf, hackles gripped between her fingers, Dianna watched the woods rush by in surreal shades of green, in oakmoss and pine and spring buds.

The air, too, tasted of green – fresh and damp and glorious in her lungs. And there were glimpses of life everywhere: A flicker of winged insects and birds in a whisper of flight, a thicket fringed with trees and spun with delicate foliage.

Cradled in the gentle pitching motion of the wolf's gait, she felt time slide away. There was only the cool wind lashing through her hair, wolf-scent warming her skin, and the mix of trepidation and wonder at what she would see next.

Like a trick of the light, the woods became momentarily bright, almost blinding. Dianna's eyes tamped shut against it. Clinging to the wolf's back, she felt something in the ground *shift*.

And all at once, they had arrived.

Against the thicketed edge of the woods, the wolves slowed to a halt with the dry turning of earth and leaves underfoot.

It seemed much darker. The sun had plunged beneath the spindly branches, throwing its last slivers upon them, pinking the sky. A tawny owl chortled close by, a phantom in the coming dusk.

Dianna alighted on the forest floor, staggering against Aimes' flank as she steadied herself. He turned his great head toward her, panting hard.

Eccka and Fredric, in their massive lupine forms, blinked their golden eyes at her, tongues dangling from their fanged mouths. The black wolf at the forefront shook itself, and the prince rose naked in its place. Dianna looked away, embarrassed, but the inconvenience seemed trivial to him.

Ram approached the edge of the woods, half-concealed in the underbrush, looking into the distance.

"I was bitten while walking through these woods," he said. "After I awoke, I meandered for miles among these trees, calling for help. There was no answer." Ram paused. "But that is a story for another time. First, you must know why I left my empire to burn."

Dianna heard subtle cracks in Ram's stony voice. It pained him to remember.

"I had become lost," he said, "in a pocket, of sorts. A little-known part of the woods. Eventually, I came to the boundary – it was here where I stopped." Ram put forth his hand, rested it upon a pine tree.

Beyond its boughs, across the outlying land, Dianna could see Awl-Feth. The cathedral spire loomed over the village, the little smoking mud-huts dotted the hills, and the blue ridge of the mountains spilled across the horizon. Barren tree branches sprawled like black veins against the sky.

Her heart wrenched for her father, for Liam.

"I did not stop willingly, you see," continued Ram, "but because I was physically unable to cross."

Dianna blinked, shaking away the pall of grief. "What do you mean?"

"Try."

Her pulse skittered as she looked up at him. "I can't go back there. Not now."

"Just try."

Dianna scanned the trees, uncertain. She stepped forward, testing the soft peat moss between her toes. Twisting between trees, she lifted away branches.

"What am I to expect—"

Her hand caught on something solid. She peered through the clustered pine boughs.

Her fingers migrated left and right, pushing and prodding. There was some kind of barrier, unyielding to the touch.

Brow crumpled with curiosity, Dianna pushed the rest of her body through the scrubby pine. Like so many spider legs, its needles prickled, creeping along her skin. She thrust her palm forward until it came to rest fully on an unseen surface.

From her fingertips, ripples of light and shadow undulated, expanding thick and fast.

"Can you pass?" asked Ram quietly.

Dianna glanced back at her hand, flat against the world beyond.

"No."

Ram nodded with grave acceptance. This was not the answer he had hoped to hear.

Dianna's fingers glided over the invisible, impervious wall. Though it felt solid, the flow of light and shadow across the landscape reminded her of a wind-kissed lake.

"Is there no way out?" she mused aloud. "A break, or a weak spot?"

With a rustling of earth, Fredric's soft human voice emerged from behind her.

"I have waded through the Seevith Bog of Kretaim," he said. "I have met with great horned beasts in far Caenan which I cannot classify. And I have meditated with monks in the temples of mountain peaks in L'Heste. Never in my wandering years had I seen something like this."

Dianna's hand remained suspended in the air, pulsing with light. She turned to exchange glances with Fredric as he crouched upon the forest floor.

"Then I take it you've tested this barrier thoroughly," she said.

Fredric nodded in earnest.

"And does it continue?"

"Oh, Gentle-heart," he said sadly. "It borders the entirety of Silbarran."

Dianna thought she felt herself sinking; the hope within her slithered away to emptiness. Awl-Feth shimmered like a memory against her hand.

Chapter 30

Raven moon, waxing

Darkness had unfolded over everything, vast and consuming, blunting Dianna's senses. Only the cold flecks of stars offered illumination.

The trees thinned out over the miles, and the snagging scrub and twigs of the undergrowth became sparser. An open clearing – a clean thumbprint of land crushed into the unfathomably strange wilderness – came into view as they drew nearer.

Dianna slid inelegantly from Aimes' back, feeling the soft grass underfoot. The wolves loped beyond the pines, where she could not see their changing shapes. Ram's deep, steady timbre materialized out of the shadows.

"Eccka, I'll leave you to sort out supper," he said. "Aimes, please stake out the perimeter."

Dianna could just make out the faint contours of the prince's figure as he emerged under the starlight, pulling on a tunic.

"This is our den," he told her. "We move sometimes, but we keep most supplies hidden in this cache." Stooping, he extracted a flint and steel from the hollow of a tree, like a magic trick. "Rations, medicine, clothing – you're welcome to it."

"And a pair of calfskin boots in there, if your feet get cold," Fredric added from somewhere in the dark, his own voice muffled by folds of fabric as he dressed himself.

"Thank you," Dianna said faintly as she looked around her.

At first glance, the small clearing where they stood seemed like any untouched patch of woods. Yet the acidic muddle of wolf-scent was as thick on the air as incense. Footprints, both human and wolf, laced the ground. Shallow indentations in the earth covered with peat moss suggested beds, and the trickle of a stream meant drinking water was close by.

All along, it was here where the wolves lived, Dianna thought. It was here where the demons slept.

Eccka's voice was sharp in her mind: *seven years*.

Ram set to work making a fire. The dry tinder crackled like old leather, snapping Dianna from her stupor. Flames sputtered into the atmosphere, shimmering but not burning black around the edges.

Fredric's expression was serious as he approached her.

"They grow here in places," he murmured. "The kind of trees with bark that doesn't smolder. No smoke trail; hardly a chance of being found."

Breathing the clean air, Dianna passed a hand over the fire.

"But the light can still be seen at dusk," she said.

"Well," Fredric said with a shrug, "it never has. But if it ever did, then we are nothing more than vagrants enjoying a meal. Excepting Ram, of course," he said, a proud smile illuminating his face. "So, I made him the Earthencloak."

Ram sat back from the fire and, seemingly out of nowhere, hoisted up a heavy cloth in a sweeping gesture. Textured with rich earth tones, woven of leaves and twigs, the traveling cloak had rested imperceptibly upon the ground.

Ram draped the cloak over his shoulders and pulled its thick cowl over his head, and covered by the aegis of greenery, became the forest itself.

"But it becomes harder, doesn't it?" Dianna whispered. "Staying human."

Within his camouflage, Ram looked at her profile in the light. His features were compressed with a frustration she imagined had eaten away at his soul over years of exile.

"It becomes easier," he said, "becoming the wolf. But as long as we have each other, we have our humanity. Our consciousness. You understand?"

"I understand."

Ram nodded. He looked across the miles of dark, steepled pines, and folded his hands. The gesture was diplomatic and so small, and Dianna felt a rush of sympathy.

"There is no leaving Silbarran," he said. "It is time I accepted this truth. We scout on the edges when we can, even after the hunters caught on and began to patrol. When we realized how you came to be here . . . we hoped there was a chance you could cross the boundary again. That you could show us how."

Dianna followed his gaze. "My brother rescued me when I was bitten here. I had to be caged."

Ram paused, as if comprehension was dawning on him.

"He saved you before the woods could claim you," he murmured. "Before its curse took hold . . . I see."

He turned back to the dancing fire. Eccka had reappeared like a ghost on the fringes of the camp with two large squirrels, throwing them haphazardly on the kindling. Without a word, she crouched and stoked the flames.

Soon the headiness of charred food wafted on the air, and Fredric helped ration the gamey meat, all stringy muscles and little bones. Dianna's insides rippled with a loud growl. It had been far too long since her last hot meal.

"Go on," Fredric insisted, handing her a portion.

She gave him her thanks as they ate in silence. The blackened meat was still scalding hot, flaking apart on her tongue. Memories of suppers with her father surfaced in her mind. His tough, scarred hands upturned in grace to a god who would forsake him. His flinty face veiled by a cloud of steam as he sipped his tea. The scarce moments when he smiled across the table from her, and she glimpsed the stirrings of happiness beneath the stoic mask.

The last bite was difficult to finish, tacky in her throat. Dianna brushed her hands of the ashes, blinking.

There was a scuffling of leaves and clothes as Aimes emerged from the shadows, half-dressed and disheveled, but human again.

"In the clear?" Ram asked him.

Aimes gave a nod and slumped beside the glowing fire. His eyes flickered once to Dianna.

"Clear from what?" she asked.

Ram's eyes skimmed the faint outlines of the sawtooth pines. The fire threw splashes of light upon them, casting oddly shaped shadows.

"I promised you answers," he said. "There are more of us living here."

Dianna's blood stopped cold. She stared at him across the fire.

"How many?"

"Dozens, probably. An unusually large pack."

"And you see them often?"

"Seldom."

"Seldom in seven years? But how deep must the woods be?"

Fredric made an enigmatic hum of knowing in his throat.

"The woods have a life of their own," he said. "Within the boundary, they're fluid. As we move, they change."

"As we move," whispered Dianna, struggling to understand.

"I've seen the tracks of this pack," Ram said. "I've heard their calls at night. They don't leave their territory often, but we remain vigilant. They are . . . volatile."

"How do you know?" she asked.

"Because we have tended their bitten and buried their dead," Eccka cut across.

Dianna chanced a look at the glowering woman in the dimming firelight. Her sharp tone was familiar, so often heard in her father's voice – that of one who knew the brush of death.

"Nothing can cure the curse of their bite," Ram added. "They are the origin of it. We're almost certain of that. We are the few who survived their attacks and found each other."

"And how do you survive the hunters every full moon?" asked Dianna. "When you have nowhere else to go?"

To her surprise, Ram's mouth broke into a sly smile.

"Have you ever run, Aergyris?" he said. She knew what he meant and shook her head.

"I don't quite remember how it feels."

"Your mind has obstructed the wolf. When you allow for its presence, you'll remember. We use evasive tactics if necessary. We can move fast."

"And until she can 'allow' for it?" Eccka said, her tone barbed. She pitched a fistful of tinder into the fire and muttered an Awl-Fethan word Dianna knew well. "When the hunters come tracking her? She's a *hauntoun*, Ram. A burden."

Dianna's stomach plummeted in a sickening realization: she would slow them down. The High Elder would send for her head. And he would kill them all.

Ram's dark eyes turned toward Dianna as his portrait had once seemed to do, but they were real now, full of a warmth that an image alone could not capture.

"You escaped for your life," he told her. "It was instinctive—"

"It was a goddamn catalyst," Eccka seethed.

"Eccka." Ram's jaw grit on her name with a flash of teeth, his noble demeanor falling away, and Dianna's breath caught. But when his eyes returned to hers, they had calmed again.

"When they come, we'll be neatly hemmed in. Our best strategy, if they find us, is to flee. We'll have to carry you until you're healed."

Dianna could not help but notice Aimes' outline shift slightly, folding as small as possible in the shadows.

"The hunters are few," Ram said. "We will elude them, as we always have."

"For how long, Ram?" Eccka pressed, though he did not reply.

But Dianna shivered with a chill that the fire could not warm. She watched the embers rise spiraling into the air before glinting out of existence.

Slowly dying. We are all slowly dying here.

Fredric's glistening eyes mirrored the pain in hers. In a careful, natural movement, he gathered her in his arms.

"It's all right," his voice soothed.

Dianna rested her head against the patchwork fabric over his heart, and his scent was of cedarwood and an unfamiliar spice. There, accepting the condolences of a stranger, folding herself in his embrace, was the loneliest feeling she'd ever known.

"We have all lost," Fredric continued in the same gentle murmur. "We have all lost."

"Aergyris." Ram's voice was soft and low.

Dianna did not stir from beneath the crook of Fredric's arm, feeling like a child, swallowing each wretched sob threatening her mouth.

Ram came to crouch before her, meeting her eyes. His brow creased, aging him.

"You are angry. You are grief-stricken," he said.

"Perhaps you are in a great deal of shock. So was I."

When he spoke, she heard a long-suffering man, a man whose life had been plunged into the unknown without reason.

"That is how we've all woken – frightened, wounded, without memory. We knew little of the woods before Fredric joined us, and we suffered far more casualties. He is our navigator. He needs no compass to point us, no map to see the lay of the land."

Fredric tapped his head gently. "All up here."

"And without Eccka," Ram said, "we'd have lived on a steady diet of mushrooms and grubs."

Eccka snorted, spearing a large piece of sooty meat from the coals with her knife.

"Understatement," she said, tearing it with her teeth.

"And Aimes . . ." Ram's voice grew tenuous as he looked into the darkness where the young man huddled, a quiet inkling of a person. "Well, Aimes can heal. Together we're a family. I am no imperator, but I can help you survive. Do you want to survive, Aergyris?"

Though not devoid of compassion, his tone was forthright, authoritative. A call to arms.

Dianna's breath deepened as she clenched her hands, and the tremors darting over her skin subsided.

"Yes," she said. "For my father."

Beneath his handsome cloak patterned with firelight, Ram's weighty stare held hers as he nodded. "I understand your desire to be brave like him. But let me tell you something." He leaned in, as if divulging a long-kept secret. "I am not my father. Trust my command, and you have my word: I will give my life to protect you."

Dianna searched his face for traces of deceit, but his gaze remained constant as the sun.

"Yes?" Ram prompted.

"Yes," Dianna whispered.

Ram's hand rested on her shoulder briefly, with a tenderness of which she felt undeserving. His gaze was faraway, ranging over the trees again.

"Please forgive me," he murmured. "I think we've had enough parley for one day, and it has made my mind heavy. The lure of sleep has bested me." He rose to his feet, drawing up his cloak.

"Goodnight," Fredric called after him.

Ram gave a nod. The Earthencloak stirred in a flutter of leaves, and he withdrew into the dusk.

When Dianna looked up, Aimes was also gone.

They were three, sitting in deep silence. Eccka was watching the shriveled remnants of coals crumble to white ash.

"I'm sorry," Dianna managed feebly.

Eccka's stony eyes regarded her. Her slender form unfolded, and she too vanished into the night.

Almost shyly, Fredric glanced down at Dianna, like a reed overlooking a shallow pond.

"Don't mind her," he said. "She wears a hard armor to cover her softness."

"She's right," Dianna said. "I was not supposed to come here."

"We don't always end up where we meant to go," Fredric said thoughtfully, inclining his head. "And if we're all supposed to be elsewhere . . . perhaps we're truly meant to be here."

But Dianna was worlds away, mired in thoughts of warm blood in her mouth, the iron rasp of Abram's helm against the killing sword.

"I hurt people," she whispered.

"Everyone does. What matters is if the hurting is consciously done."

Fredric's tone had darkened a shade, and Dianna looked at him. He was sitting cross-legged, staring deeply into the firepit, one finger at his temple beneath his curls.

"Who are your people?" she asked him quietly.

A small, proud smile tugged at his lips. "Vagrants. Nomads. The always-moving feet. Outcasts and bandits, too, but most of them are good people. There are many wonders beyond these woods, beyond this empire, we dearly longed to explore. Yet you'll find the woodland flora here a great mystery."

Dianna marveled at how one could keep such morale under the circumstances.

"Doesn't it sadden you? That you can't leave this place?"

Fredric pressed his hands together, studying how his fingertips aligned with an almost childlike intensity. He nodded once.

"As much as it saddens one to be parted from one's own flesh and blood. From the place one calls 'home.' And yet . . . I enjoy the pull of every direction." He let his hands fall, surveying her conflicted expression. "Oh, it's not born of homelessness, but a sense that I can make something like a home anywhere I desire and uproot myself as I please. Like the rambling ivy."

His eyes shifted to the sky, surveying sidereal lines and the silver gleam of the partial moon.

"Movement," he said. "Movement keeps me alive. Without it, my wanderlust is confined to these woods. So, in the bodily sense, I am too still for my own liking. But as for my heart – it belongs here, with my family. They are my true home, you see. They surround me. And I am no longer saddened."

The sounds of nocturnal animals had subsided, and the night fell quiet around them. Like a cloak of dark silk, it hung on his words. Dianna heard the depth of their idealism, saw the earnest gleam in his eyes, and ached for such a feeling.

"Even within these woods, in many ways we live like gods," Fredric said, his voice subtle as the last feeble wisp of flame. "Outside them I sought adventure, but are we not now living the greatest adventure? We feared the terrors of the woods, but are we not now the greatest terror?"

"You don't seem terrible."

Fredric's laugh punctuated the air, making his curls tremble. "Pah! Not any more violent than you are."

Biting her lip, Dianna looked down at her hands, remembering the tear of claws through flesh. Her knuckles shone white.

"Speaking for myself, of course," Fredric went on. "I'd be dreadful in a fight. Fortunately, I'm far too quick on my feet for these hunters, and Aimes can heal us. No small wonder the other villages consider us myths, hmm?"

"Not Awl-Feth. To the High Elder, we're a threat worse than famine. He wants us dead."

"Well, then, Gentle-heart," said Fredric, "he must double his endeavors if he is to succeed."

The laugh lines around his eyes deepened, and his broadening smile was eerily akin to a fanged grin.

"Would you like to hear a story?" he asked in a different tone.

The wolf began to roam beneath Dianna's skin, and she shuddered. Fredric seemed to take this noncommittal gesture in the affirmative, because he gave an odd little wriggle of delight.

"Well, in the words of my people," he said, "The fire makes even the most heart-cold travelers warm. And all the longest, twice-told tales make the best tinder." He swept up a dry pinecone and gave it to her. "Go on. Throw it in. Then the story can begin."

Chapter 31

Raven moon, waxing

Dianna tossed the cone into the firepit, and a great dazzling blaze of embers ascended into the cool night air, where they guttered and died. And Fredric began his tale, his voice low and lulling.

"It was the bitterest winter night of the year. My old family of vagrants was but a company of seven. Seasonal nomads, or folks who could afford the comforts of a more permanent home, had migrated elsewhere. We were the true ones, the ever-unsettled, but on this night we were desperate for shelter. The truth is, even in our desperation, our hunger for adventure made this worthwhile.

"We'd been on foot for a fortnight, making for our first destination at the springs of Nabkhat, when we found ourselves in the thick of a stinging blizzard. My beard – I had grown a handsome one then – was choked with ice chips. Cold numbed my ears and gnawed at my cheeks. Snow fell into my boots and melted between my toes. We were trudging along, nothing but thick sleet for miles, when we spotted an outcropping of basalt rock with a cavern in it. Its black shape seemed a dream in so much white. The navigators, leading the way, thought it promising.

"In the cave, we formed a great shivering, gasping pile

in our furs and rationed half a bottle of mead. You would have laughed at the sight of us, self-proclaimed intrepid explorers sevenfold and huddling for warmth." He paused for emphasis, and Dianna mustered a halfhearted smile. "Brant and Reya – our navigators – had scraped kindling together for a fire when we heard something rumble from the depths of the cave.

"My companions and I were not only freezing and exhausted, but food-poor and weaponless to boot. Expert travelers will arm themselves to the teeth, but we'd been raided by bandits on the wayside. So, my Gentle-heart, alone in that cavern, we were soft as an old man's maw."

Fredric spoke so low, Dianna had to bow her head to hear him against the crackle of fire, its heat nearly licking her throat.

"There was the clatter of rocks," he said. "A vague scuffling. There was a groan of something – something huge." He paused as if to savor her curiosity.

"What then?"

"Then," Fredric said at leisure, "rising up from his slumber, the great bear lurched into our midst. His eyes shone beetle-black, his snout had crumpled in a fang-filled snarl, and fur hung thick from his massive bulk.

"The bear swung his paw – wider than a puncheon oak cask – and struck down three of us at once. They toppled, smacking broadside into a rock with a crunch of bone. Brant and Reya ordered us back, submerging their torches in the fire and waving them wildly. And then we discovered our bear was not alone."

"Cubs," Dianna guessed.

"Correct."

"A she-bear! You led me astray."

Fredric flashed a guilty grin. "A storyteller must keep his audience wondering as long as possible. Often unto the very end, and ever after still."

"You could be spinning the whole yarn."

Fredric rested a palm over one ragged lapel. "On my honor as a vagrant, which means nothing to you but the earth and sky to me, every dreadful scene thus far is true as a shoe."

"Which you are lacking."

"The better to sense the earth," Fredric explained, warming his calloused feet in the fire's glow. "But point taken. Now, don't you dare interrupt again if you want the rest of it."

Dianna rested her chin on her hands, feigning an air of patience.

"The cubs huddled behind their mother as she lumbered forth. With only fire for protection, the best we could do was dodge her attacks."

"Impossible."

"True as a shoe," Fredric repeated, brisk. "Some were strewn about, bruised and bloodied. Brant cried out, so the she-bear charged him with open jaws and nearly tore his arm clean off, but Reya seared her torch into the beast's shaggy flank. And the bear turned and knocked Reya out cold, sending her torch sputtering."

Fredric cleared his throat, and his voice grew fervent, building to the climactic point of the tale.

"We do not abandon our own," he said. "I watched the whole gruesome skirmish unfold, too petrified, I think, to act immediately. I could have fled for my life. But seeing my companions struck down one by one, the blood began to flow in me. Soon enough, I was the only one left standing.

"And I knelt. And with my hand I hollowed out the crystallized snow. And I took aim at the great bear. And I pitched that ice hard at its nose."

Dianna listened with rapt attention now. Fredric had closed his eyes as if to recount the events as he had witnessed them.

"I stunned it," he said. "Yes. And I scrambled like mad for the fallen torch and cracked my hand against a stone." He stretched out his skinny arm, inclining the wrist to show that his littlest finger was crooked. "But by the stars, I brandished that torch in the face of the beast and its kin, and they began to retreat. And our entire party came away from that cave, battered and broken, but alive."

Dianna watched him uncertainly. At last his eyelids fluttered open, and he chanced a look at her in the fading firelight.

"The moral of my tale – oh, yes, there must always be a moral," said Fredric as she made a face, "is that formidable beasts do not simply emerge out of nowhere. For there is one thing a vagrant knows – never call nowhere Nowhere, and never call Anywhere yours, for Anywhere is always someone else's."

Dianna gave a short, bemused laugh. "Your stories are well told, but they are folktales."

"Who says folktales can't be true?"

Fredric's radiant eyes studied her, but she couldn't think of a satisfactory answer.

"Your turn, now," he said, feeding another pinecone to the flames. "Tell me about yourself. Tell me about your village, and of farming, and how you made the bread and tended the crops when your land was plentiful. Tell me about your father."

"My father?"

"Yes. What was he like?"

She thought Fredric's question a trick, squinting at him in the fire's dim glow. But her new friend's beaming countenance betrayed nothing.

"Why would you care to know of the man who lived to kill you?" she whispered.

Fredric's words were both somber and warm at once. "You have accidentally confused your words. You must know there are times we must kill to live. Don't you, Gentle-heart? Just as there are times we must grieve to heal."

Holding his gaze, Dianna felt the fire's heat stinging her eyes.

"Now," Fredric said softly, "tell me all about him."

Dianna hesitated, feeling the sorrow well in her chest again, but it did not spill over this time. She gathered her breath. And she told him.

Chapter 32

Raven moon, waxing

In the morning, the charred scent of burning wood laced the damp, earthy air. Crouched on bare feet beside the firepit, Aimes was cooking a breakfast of rabbit. He was naked but for a pair of grubby trousers, hair a snarled mess.

His wild eyes flickered to Dianna, following her path as she sat across from him. The lines of his body drew tense.

She spoke uncertainly, not expecting a response. "Good morning."

Aimes blinked, silently mouthing words before beginning to vocalize them.

"You . . . slept well. I am . . ." He thought for a moment. "Glad," he said at last.

Dianna smiled, impressed by his progress. "You speak well," she returned.

Aimes returned intently to his work, but a shy smile flitted across his lips. His earth-darkened fingers turned the spit over the fire with a delicate touch.

Dianna glanced around the sunlit den, but they were alone. "Where are the others?" she asked.

Aimes circled the perimeter of trees around them with one finger: "Ram." He pointed toward the river: "Eccka." He gestured directly at a tree behind her: "Fredric."

Dianna looked over her shoulder. The dozing man was draped across a low mulberry bough thick with a bedding of gathered moss, a mangy fur hat covering his eyes. The dawn refrain of a grey catbird rasped somewhere within the thick leafy awning, but he did not wake.

Aimes had plucked the dangling rabbit from the spit, stripping away a generous piece with his hands. "For. You."

Dianna said a quiet thanks as she accepted the food and ate. From somewhere deep in her belly, the wolf rolled and growled with appreciation.

Aimes' eyes darted away again. "I had to . . . remember . . . how . . ."

He trailed off, touching his throat.

"How to speak?" Dianna gathered.

"Yes," he said emphatically. "That."

Watching the fire, he rocked to his knees and splayed his palms on the ground, like paws. Dianna couldn't help but study the strange posture of his gangly limbs.

"I didn't think it was possible to forget," she murmured. "It must be difficult."

Aimes glanced up, his stare piercing. His irises shimmered blue-yellow, unsteady as water in sunlight, and Dianna blinked as a realization sank in: he was barely staying human.

"Aimes," she said, "how long have you been a wolf?"

Aimes lifted one hand, unfurling it. The other followed, flickering two fingers.

Dianna threw the rabbit bone, picked clean, into the fire. "Seven . . . months?"

He shook his head.

"*Years?*"

He nodded but didn't elaborate. The unnerving truth of this information hung between them, and Dianna couldn't look away from him as she calculated it.

"All this time," she whispered. "But you were so young."

Maybe, she thought to herself, *even younger than I was.*

Aimes' gaze had drifted back to the fire, distant now, as if his mind was in another world.

"I need . . . to tell you," he said. "But it hurts . . . to remember." He swallowed hard as if to force back a feeling.

"Tell me what?"

Aimes' eyes focused on her then.

"They . . . killed her." His words came in garbled increments, tangling and untangling on his tongue. "They killed . . . so many of them."

Dianna's brow furrowed. "Who—" she began, but Aimes' head jerked as though a sudden pain seized him. Yellow sparks of light smoldered in his irises.

In a fluid movement, he rose to his feet.

Dianna instinctively followed the motion, but her voice faltered. Looking down at her feet, at the soft impressions they made in the cool clay, she felt only the fading ghost of pain.

She reached down, unwinding the gossamer dressings binding her calf. Underneath, the stitches had been removed. Nothing but a long white scar remained.

"How . . ." she marveled at it.

"No," Aimes said, shuddering. "Not now."

Dianna looked up, but Aimes wasn't talking to her. He was talking to himself.

"Shh," he hushed, squeezing his eyes shut. "Stop . . . changing."

Bristles of dark gray hair prickled over the muscles of his shoulders. His fists were taut as stone. But his outline flickered like a breeze, distorting at the edges.

"Aimes?" Dianna said, hesitating.

"Need to . . . tell you . . ." His breathing deepened and guttered, and his hands began to tremble. "About *Armina.*"

His mouth closed on her mother's name a tone darker,

a hair's breadth slower. It was the low, fractured mumble of an animal, culling the warmth from her blood.

The sound of the crack and shuffle of bone, the lurch of compressing organs rent the air as Aimes changed with a gasp. Layers of muscle and fur swelled over him, burying his body.

As if instinct devoured him, the wolf darted away, sleek as smoke, into the shadowed copse of pine. Aimes' whisper seemed to echo in his wake. Dianna stepped forward as if to snatch it from the air.

"Aimes," she said, soft at first, followed by a cry drawn from deep in her lungs and sharp in her throat, "*Aimes!*"

Adrenaline tearing through her, she scrambled after him as quickly as her ungainly human legs would allow. His wolf-shape had navigated the uneven ground seamlessly, but the bite of coarse rocks and scratching pine boughs hindered her pursuit.

Heat flushed over her skin, a rising anger. The wolf in her chest pressed against it, seething and growling as she gave chase.

What does he know? What hasn't he told me?

"Aimes!" she cried again. "Wait—"

Just as the wolf flickered beyond the trees and out of sight, a white light glinted across the wooded expanse ahead, like a sunbeam through crystalline stone. Momentarily blinded, Dianna gasped and stumbled to her knees, churning sharp stones underfoot.

But when she collapsed, it was a patch of damp peat moss that broke her fall. Catching her breath, Dianna felt a nauseating reeling in her gut, as if the wolf had changed its mind, settling behind her ribcage, afraid. She shook her head, blinking shattering stars of light from her eyes. The air smelled faintly of clover and lingering rainfall, although the sky had been cloudless a moment ago.

All was eerily quiet. Even the birds had stopped singing.

The Soft Fall

Dianna turned around. The den was gone.
And she was elsewhere.

Chapter 33

Raven moon, waxing

The earth was strewn with fallen leaves, weeds, and a moldering body.

Pausing on the trade route through Silbarran, a Valtan envoy on horseback drew up his reins, peering down at the corpse. His mare tossed her tail at the lingering haze of fat flies. The ravens had all but scoured the bones clean, and any identifying clothing or weapons had been stripped away.

It was said only the bravest or the most foolish travelers dared to cross Silbarran, but the envoy was a skeptical man. If he believed anything, it was that serving the empire was a duty, not an accolade, and pride became irrelevant in wartime. The greatest warriors would be venerated in death, if their legacies were preserved, but the flesh decayed. Nature reclaimed. To her, all men went to ground nameless.

This dead man was not a warrior, having fallen so far from the Caenani's range. Most likely, some vagrant had starved or succumbed to cold, and the envoy thought no more of it.

"Foul place," he murmured in disgust, clucking his tongue and spurring his mount onward.

The envoy wore a simple traveling cloak, and his mare carried supplies for at least a week's journey: water-heavy skins, a knife in its scabbard, a threadbare haversack of cured meat, a smoking pipe, and some coin of mixed denomination. Fastened upon the saddle clattered several sealed tin canisters. Their contents were unknown to all but the Imperial Senate and the envoy alone, the only man with the necessary tool to extract them.

The envoy had traveled many muddy miles and sleepless nights to reach his destination. In the final stretch, his mare plodded along with a hefty snorting of her nostrils. The envoy dismounted at last, patted her neck, and led her for the rest of the way.

"I could do well with a pint, couldn't you, lady?" he said. "An apt one, mind you, none of that well-watered piss from the slums. Fucking cesspool."

The copse ahead thinned as the envoy passed into Awl-Feth. The ground softened under his feet and the sun shone free on his face. From his vantage point, the whole village spread end-to-end before him. It was not at all like the sprawling network of Valta, but contained, efficient.

"In the clear now," he huffed. His mare nudged him on the back, velvet muzzle twitching.

"Who goes there?" someone called from the edge of the treeline.

A figure on horseback approached him, equipped with a battered sword, and the envoy drew up short. It was not uncommon for raiders to bereave merchants of their cargo. But as the stranger drew closer, clad in the faded forest green and silver colors of Myre, the envoy realized it was an Awl-Fethan patrolman – likely one of those hunters he'd heard talk of – and heaved a sigh of irritation. *These poor, rustic folk were not any better than beggars of the slums up north*, he thought.

The patrolman, stinking of stale ale, had a nasty scar

between his brows, making him look permanently cross.

"Business?" he demanded, surveying the man on foot.

"None o' yours," returned the envoy, but surrendered his hands when the patrolman unsheathed and brandished his sword. "All right! Good Mactus, do I look like a Caenani to you, man? Strike the messenger, indeed." He shuffled around in his pockets for the appropriate key, which he used to open one of the gleaming tin bottles. From within, he fished out a scroll of parchment. A wax seal marked its outer edge, bearing the crest of the empire's capital. "See that? Official declaration from the Valtan legion. Some respect, if you will."

"I ain't blind," sneered the patrolman, his ugly scar bulging more prominently.

"Then you'll kindly direct me to the location of High Elder Orcarrus, where I may deliver this information," the envoy insisted, returning the precious parcel to its compartment. "You do your job; I do mine."

The patrolman's lips twisted into an odd, unpleasant smile.

"Thing is," he said, "my job doesn't pay a pretty salary." His smile grew wider, peeling over rotten teeth. "And I've a family to feed."

The envoy's eyes narrowed. He reached into his haversack and thrust a couple of silvers at him.

"Any further hindrance and I'll have your High Elder cast your family out like mongrels," he threatened.

Looking down his nose, the patrolman took the coins in his filth-blackened fingers.

"Mongrels," he scoffed. "You mean demons. You one of 'em?" Swiftly he directed the rusty sword at the envoy's throat.

"Mactus alive! No, I'm not a – a—"

"A demon," the patrolman finished, eyes beetling. "Must be one, crossing Silbarran with your life intact. Coins you gave me, they're a trifle next to the share I'd get for your head."

"I've come from Valta by order of the Senate! You saw the crest, now let me pass!"

The patrolman waited a moment longer before deciding something. Giving a grunt of discontent, he returned his sword to its sheath with a metallic slither. Leisurely, he maneuvered his horse aside.

"If you were one of 'em, you'd keep clear of the High Elder anyhow," he muttered. "Eastway over that hillside. The cathedral tower."

Still fuming, the envoy rustled the reins, steering his heavy-footed mare past him. Simple village folk and their superstitious bunk, he thought.

As the envoy trekked up the hill, the patrolman called out to him.

"You'll lose."

"I beg your pardon?"

"The Caenani will come, glorious in number," said the patrolman. "And the empire will lose. Or submit to them and rise anew."

Simple, and a traitor at that! The envoy refused to entertain such treasonous thoughts. He shook his head and gripped the mare's lead, making to resume his climb.

But the patrolman remained at the bottom of the hillside, dark gaze on him. All else was still but the wind shifting in the trees.

The envoy stared back, curiosity getting the better of him.

"Then what is this 'demon' you speak of?" he shouted downward.

The patrolman smiled again. It was a smile that saw amusement in death.

"If you knew," he shouted back, "you wouldn't have come."

He spurred his mount on and continued his patrol.

***

Nestled in shadows on the edge of the woods, Ram watched the envoy recede into the distance and waited until the patrolman left.

He turned with a rustle of his green cloak, moving like the thicket come to life, releasing a long-held breath.

Time. He needed time and precise timing.

A flutter of movement in his periphery brought him to a halt. Ram's eyes settled on a spot in the undergrowth.

"You shouldn't be this close to the village, Aimes," he said.

A wolf peered through the tangle of leaves.

"No, I won't let you scout next time, either," Ram demurred, pulling his cowl tighter over his head as he swept into recesses of foliage.

The wolf's warmth was at his flank almost immediately, giving a light nudge.

"You wouldn't have understood the political nuances of this," Ram said, descending deeper into the wooded grove. "I am monitoring the situation."

The nudge became more persistent, coupled with the coarse lash of a tail and a soft whine behind gritted incisors. Ram stumbled a little against the beast's bulk but pressed on.

"A Valtan envoy crossed into Awl-Feth," he said with a sigh. "I suspect the High Elder intends to persuade the Senate that the threat of demons is real, enough to warrant military forces to purge the woods of us. He may as well burn it all to the ground – it would be faster – but he thinks we'd escape. So, armaments it is."

Ambling down the shallow embankment, Ram pushed aside the untamed branches of woody giants with more force than necessary.

"I believe he is petitioning to recruit my legion," he said, chewing his lip, the anger in his tone sharp as a whetted blade. "The High Elder has attempted this plan before, but the Senate refused to send combatants when the Caenani declared war. But now . . . now, they could."

The warmth slid from his side, leaving an empty space. Ram paused mid-stride and turned to look up.

But the great wolf seemed smaller and lankier as he retreated, rangy legs buckled, head bowed low. His grizzled snout quivered, nose blowing steam into the crisp air. No more threatening than a dog.

"Son." Ram's dark eyes met the large yellow ones. "Don't blame yourself for all of this."

But the wolf remained half-crouched, ears flat against his skull. Ram turned away, resuming his walk to the den.

"What happened has happened," he said softly. "She's here now. There's no going back."

***

The massive spire of the ancient cathedral was the first unusual feature the envoy noticed about Awl-Feth – as dominant in its scope as the Valtan Academe itself. The second was the scores of ramshackle, seemingly abandoned huts littering the village like tombstones, and the third was that all was devoid of green.

Approaching the cathedral, the envoy lingered. A shallow grade sloped into the flat and barren land below, and he looked across it. There were no children at play outside, no people going about the day's work – only a stirring of black.

Ravens fluttered and plunged in droves upon stakes in the ground, splitting the silence with harsh shrieking cries. Only when their wings flickered aside did the envoy see the charred skulls they picked at, mounted upon the stakes like grotesque birdhouses at which they came to roost.

The envoy had seen enough aftermath of the war up north to have developed a strong stomach for bloodshed, but something cold and visceral squirmed in him at the sight. Instinct told him this was not the work of a warrior upon his enemy, but that of man upon his fellow neighbor.

With unsteady hands he hitched his mare under the shade of a wilted olive tree, patted the dust from his leathers, and crossed the cathedral's threshold.

Rows of archangels sculpted from granite loomed within the interior nave. They drew the envoy's eyes like a ghoulish congregation awaiting his presence. An oil portrait of the empire's princes glazed the sepia-toned archway. The pews were empty of living souls that day, and the only sound reverberating in the rib-vaulted dome was the envoy's own tread on marble floors.

Pulling the smell of stale incense into his lungs, he felt a chill prickle his neck. Unlit, the cathedral would seem tomblike indeed, but the braziers were burning bright, reflecting gilded fixtures and colored glass filling the high windows. An unholy thought crossed his mind: the sanctuary, larger and more sumptuous than any of the empty huts that clung to the land like mites, was the true belly of the beast.

"Do you admire the realm of our great Mactus?" a voice echoed, startling the envoy.

At the heart of the nave, a red-robed man with sharp features advanced toward him.

The envoy had already decided not to ask what terrible violence befell the High Elder's village. He was there to fulfill his duty to the empire.

In answer, he removed the pronged key from his pocket and revealed it. "I come in His Holy Name, High Elder."

"He welcomes you, my son." The High Elder touched his fingertips to his caller's head in blessing. Underneath his beard, a thin-lipped smile spread. "And where are your auxiliaries? I trust your passage was without disturbance?"

"In general, High Elder. I was not afforded accompaniment from Valta, yet several L'Hestian sentinels shadowed the trade route."

The High Elder's smile slid from his mouth. "I see," was his terse reply. "What news do you bear for my people?"

The envoy unlocked the tin container he held and flicked the catch with deft fingers. "Senate election begins at summer solstice. Emissaries of the Senate, as you well know, have taken command in the princes' absence. They have approved this dispatch from the Imperial Legate of the Valtan legion." The envoy presented the scroll, sealed with the insignia of the empire in bloodred wax.

The High Elder broke the seal and read its contents thrice, fixated upon the smudgy lines of ink as though suspecting forgery. The envoy lingered in the wake of his silence.

The High Elder then thrust the sheaf of parchment at its deliverer.

"Can you elaborate?" he murmured.

The envoy cleared his throat.

"The Imperial Senate has rejected your appeal to enlist their combatants to serve your cause. It is not in the empire's interest to authorize such a venture. The Senate requires each able man at his post in defense against Caenan. Emissaries of the Senate agree that your appeal would not be in accord with the wishes of the late imperator, nor the will of Mactus."

"The will of—" began the High Elder, reddening, but he paused, drawing himself to full height, and his features cooled. "Very well. The judgment of the Senate is insurmountable." He grew quiet, casting his steel gray eyes around the cathedral walls. "Very well," he repeated with a detachment that seemed to fill the air with a sweeping chill.

"There is another memorandum, High Elder," added the envoy, hesitating. "From L'Heste."

The High Elder straightened, his interest piqued. With a ripple of his long crimson sleeve, like dripping blood, he held one hand aloft. His voice was low and resolute, sleek as silk.

"Let me see it, please."

The envoy keyed open the second of the two documents, and unfurling it with a grand gesture, slipped it into the High Elder's outstretched fingers.

The High Elder's thin lips formed the words scrawled across the crisp sheaf as his eyes shifted in recognition.

By the order of Centurion Merrinal Gansin X of L'Heste, a century of the cohort Tharknas and auxiliaries acquiesce to the High Elder's request to furnish mercenary services to his cause.

"Shall I elaborate again, High Elder?" asked the envoy.

The High Elder's eyes had settled on the L'Hestian word *Tharknas*. No word was more befitting of the mission, more exquisite on the tongue.

Tharknas, meaning chaos.

Beneath his smooth voice was an undercurrent of appeasement, even victory.

"No," he said. "Thank you."

Without further comment, he reached into his thick red robes and withdrew a handful of coins. The compensation was much greater, the envoy noted, than the amount he'd lost to the heckling hunter. He met the High Elder's gaze in stunned silence, speculating how the governor of a famine-stricken village could have so much to spare.

He said nothing of it, however, and pocketed the money with humble thanks.

"Your journey home is a treacherous one," the High Elder said. "Mactus keep you."

221

Chapter 34

Raven moon, waxing

Rising to her feet, Dianna felt a chill crawl up her spine as she looked around. No breeze stirred the trees, no small animals skittered about, and the forest was so densely packed she couldn't see ten yards in any direction.

Dianna's skin prickled, awe and fear creeping into her voice.

"I'm still here," she whispered to herself, remembering the boundary. "Still in Silbarran . . . just somewhere else here."

She moved to take a step forward and thought better of it, pausing before her heel touched the ground.

If I move, she thought, *it could move beneath me again.*

She stayed still instead, scanning the surrounding trees. From where she stood, there was no way to measure the distance to the den. If she tried to find her way back, it could be nightfall by the time she made any progress on foot.

Dianna laughed at herself. She had never been content to stay still.

She took a breath and put forth one foot, letting her sole sink into the earth. Nothing. She exhaled, took another step. And another.

"Aimes?" she called out, tentatively this time.

Silence.

Ram's warning about the wolves that stalked them in the shadows quickened her heartbeat. Raising her voice might have been a grave mistake. For the second time, she felt the hollow absence of her bow at her side.

She decided she'd have to make one.

Among the crowded patches of trees, she wandered in search of the reflection of water, or the babble of a stream. She was on the banks soon enough, rummaging in a tangle of roots for a sharp piece of chert.

She brushed her fingers against the cool damp of lady ferns and the delicate softness of draping moss, remembering the feeling of life in the earth, becoming acquainted with her surroundings. She climbed hardy oaks, tested their strong crooked limbs dripping in green, and studied the lay of twisted undergrowth, ideal cover for stalking land game.

Toeing at rocks and overturning sod, she found a fallen hardwood branch, dry and sturdy, which gave just enough at the pressure of her hands. She sat down under a tree and set to work sculpting the branch to her liking.

As a child she'd watched Liam craft hunting arrows in practice. One by one he would cut half-moon notches for the bowstring, shape arrowheads with whetstone, and attach fletching made from raven feathers. He'd fashioned a bow from a sapling once, shaping the belly of a stave from it, tilling its curve for evenness.

Remembering his work, she lost track of time in the peaceful rhythm and satisfying scrape of the chert, peeling away fibrous curls of bark to expose the smooth, milk-white flesh. With each new modification, she tested the bow's curve. The simple task was a comfort in the strangeness of the woods, but the memory of Aimes' voice disturbed her thoughts.

Armina, he'd said. *I need to tell you about Armina.*

He'd spoken like he'd actually known her mother.

Dianna shaved away at the wood with more intensity, ruminating. Why couldn't he control the wolf? Why did it run from her?

What if they were all lying?

She was just testing the smoothness of the stave when the plodding of feet punctuated the quiet. Materializing among the trees, haloed in a blaze of sunlight, was Fredric.

Seeing her, he grinned.

"I thought I'd find you here, Gentle-heart," he said, eyes briefly glinting gold. "If you're trying to run away, I'm afraid you won't get very far."

His tone was not threatening but filled with amusement at his own joke. Heat rose on Dianna's skin. Gathering her makeshift bow in her fist, she stood and faced him squarely, wasting no time.

"What do you know about Armina?" she demanded.

The grin on Fredric's lips slipped into a frown. "I've never met an Armina, Gentle-heart."

"I think you have."

Fredric's eyes seemed to lose their gleam. He ducked his head as though she'd struck him. "I always remember names."

"Aimes barely remembers his own," Dianna said. "But he knew my mother's. Why?"

"I don't know," Fredric said, puzzlement in his features. "Won't he tell you?"

"He became the wolf. He left before I could ask, and I went after him and . . . somehow, I ended up here."

Fredric's tone dropped slightly. "I see."

The peculiar note in his response piqued Dianna's interest. Fredric gestured to the half-finished object in her hand.

"You're making a shortbow," he said.

Dianna looked down at the carved wood, feeling oddly timid about her hasty craftsmanship. "I'm a hunter's daughter, after all."

"A huntress," corrected Fredric with a smile. "You'll need to string it up, of course. The den's cache holds an assortment of useful supplies."

Dianna's brow furrowed. "How exactly do you know the way back?"

Fredric paused, his gaze ranging over the trees.

"There's a rift over there," he said quietly.

"A what?"

"A rift," he repeated, holding up his hand as if testing something. "See those pines ahead? The wind there flows in another direction. Southerly, while ours is easterly. In a moment it will open, and we can cross over."

Dianna stood, staring at the slivers of sunlight patterning the pines. In the center of the grove, a faint light shifted like a clutch of fireflies.

"Where will it lead us?" she asked.

"Within the ambit of these woods? Wherever we choose to go."

"You mean to say the woods can do your will?"

Fredric flashed another lopsided grin. "Well, you certainly didn't will yourself here on purpose, did you?" he said, and Dianna gave him a withering look not unlike the many she'd aimed at Liam throughout their adolescence. "No, one must know her more deeply than one's ego. And cardinal directions only get one so far here. One can't trust in the stasis of a land that does as she pleases."

"But Ram – he called you a navigator."

"In the most basic senses, yes: sound, touch, taste. But there are times when paths simply open – paths which one can take to cross miles in a single step. It seems to bear on the proximity of others, though I've yet to discover why. I can't truly be a navigator of Silbarran. She is the navigator of my soul. She tells me where to go; I listen, and I follow." Fredric knelt, brushing his fingers over the soil, and a smile curled his lips. "Yes! This is promising. Wait."

Dianna stood with her bow in one hand, uncertain. Like a heart buried in the earth, a dull pulse swelled beneath her feet.

At once, the gentle pressure of Fredric's hand closed on hers.

"Come on!"

They ran toward the thick grove, to the light-filled schism in its depths. Fredric moved quick as thread unraveling, ducking and twisting under branch and over root, and Dianna thought she would lose her grip on him unless she spooled him in. But she stumbled after him, the wind snatching around her, howling in her ears and dying just as soon.

She turned around, still clutching Fredric's hand loosely. Their former location was gone, as though a curtain had closed over it.

The rift had swallowed them.

They stood in a spongy quagmire, half-concealed in a patch of tall sedge grass choked with weeds and cattails. Fredric turned around, sniffing.

"Different environment," he said, bouncing on his heels in the damp soil. "Riparian."

Dianna marveled at the tiny saplings sprouting there at her feet and upward at trees grown as tall as if they grazed the sky, their leaves whispering in the spring breeze.

Laughing, Fredric spread his fingers against the wind and wiggled them. "Do you believe in folktales now, Gentle-heart?"

"I must, or I'm going mad," Dianna said in a small voice, watching a dragonfly hover over the reeds, iridescent as a jewel. "Do the hunters know about this?"

"Not to our knowledge."

"But how do we get back to the den?"

"We find another rift. It may take some time and tangents, but it will happen when it does. If you follow the right rifts, you'll never lose your way. If you trust them, they will take you where you need to go. Not unlike the wisdom of your hunting: listening to the sounds of the woods, learning which to follow and which to pass by, when to strike and when to withdraw. Such wisdom is good to keep practicing. A reminder of our humanity . . ."

His rambling fell into silence, and Dianna couldn't help but think of Aimes. Of the yellow light that engulfed his eyes, involuntarily.

"To be quite honest with you, darling," Fredric said softly, "I used to be herbivorous."

The quip seemed unusual at first, even meaningless, until Dianna turned toward him and glimpsed the weight of an unspoken truth upon his profile.

"Fredric?" she said at last.

"Yes?"

"Do you think the woods will take our minds, in time?"

Fredric contemplated the question.

"Yes," he said simply. "Yes, I think they will."

***

At the den, the musk-scent of wolf carried on the wind like a warning. In the tree hollow where they kept their cache, Dianna rummaged around for a suitable carving tool. She appraised several assorted arrows they had collected, long lost in the woods.

Among the items, she unearthed a sharp paring knife, a scrap of tough buckskin, and a length of catgut. She set to finishing her shortbow, which lay stretched across her lap, while Fredric looked on.

"What is the leather for?" he asked.

Dianna dredged the strip of buckskin in a damp patch of soil. "It will help keep my bow from breaking and allow me to fire swiftly."

Fredric nodded, making a small sound of intrigue. He began picking leaves from his hair and jerkin. Dianna imagined a wolf fussing over his fur.

"That name," she said. "'Gentle-heart.' Do you call everyone this?"

Fredric's eyes widened. "Of course not! It's your vagrant name. Singular, only for you."

"But I'm no vagrant."

"We vagrants take new names upon beginning our journey. I'm known as Ragpicker, Story-weaver, The Furthermost-feet. Sometimes you recognize a kinship in people."

Dianna wrapped the leather tight around one end of the carved stave and began measuring the bowstring.

"You haven't seen what is in my heart," she said softly.

Fredric smiled.

"I saw you kill a bird," he said. "A mourning dove, it was. Caught in a hunter's crude trap, its wing snapped, making the most sorrowful cry. You knelt beside the poor thing and spoke to it. 'Do not be afraid, little beauty,' you said. You killed it on the first strike of your knife. And you lifted her in your palms, stroked her feathers, tucked her in your burlap, and made on your way."

Dianna stopped short, glancing at him. His eyes were crinkled against the sun, searching over the treetops.

"You were in Awl-Feth once?" she asked.

Fredric nodded with an air of indifference. "Passing though, as vagrants do.

I said, 'Ah, yes! Gentle-heart!' Because few would handle their kill with the care and respect you had shown."

But Dianna looked away as the sun brimmed blindingly over the mountains. She finished stringing the bow and set it aside to dry in the warm light.

"Respect is the half of it," she said in an undertone. "The other is killing only when it is necessary. I take no pleasure in it."

"Your moral compass is strong."

"My moral compass is what points me to trouble."

Fredric snorted, drawing his jerkin around his lean body with bone-pale arms. "Well, it remains that I saw you. Any huntress can try to cover her tracks, but she still leaves traces of herself everywhere. I will fashion you an Earthencloak, if you like."

Dianna frowned, recalling the taste of ash in the air and the hunters' thunderous uproar. "I would be wise to accept."

But Fredric, closing his eyes, shook his head.

"Don't worry," he said. "You'll learn."

"Learn?"

"How to become what you are."

Dianna studied his serene face. The lines of his body were alert even as he rested, his skin shivering at the shift of the breeze. It reminded her of Aimes – the feral pitch of his voice coiled tight as the wolf devoured him from inside – and her palms grew clammy.

"And when does one learn to call this home?" she asked.

"Hmm." Fredric's eyes fluttered open then, and he inclined his head. "I'll let you know when I find out, seeing as I've never had one. But I suppose it's about as close to one as I could imagine. Home implies stagnancy, does it not?" He intoned the word like it left a terrible taste in his mouth, wrinkling his nose.

Dianna paused. "Still . . . when you showed me the boundary, you seemed hopeful I could somehow break it."

"Oh, yes," said Fredric. "Yet doubtful, I'm afraid."

"But Aimes didn't look hopeful," she murmured.

"No, he wouldn't be," Fredric said, with a note of sadness. "He thinks he belongs here."

"Why—" began Dianna, but the vagrant shook his head in a quiver of curls.

"That story is not mine to tell, Gentle-heart," he said,

though his voice was kind. "I am sorry."

"Whose story is it?"

Fredric chewed his lip, his toes fidgeting in the soil. "Ram's," he said at last.

"Then I'll wait here until he returns from his sentry."

"You may wait all day."

"I'll wait as long as I have to," Dianna said, folding her arms.

There was a distant rustling of leaves as something pushed through them, too heavy for a bird or a rodent in the underbrush. Dianna stiffened as a shadow quivered in her periphery, slithering steadily between trees like a needle through cloth. The wolf's coat shone onyx black with a fine dusting of silver throughout, like mixed brushstrokes.

"Hello, Eccka," called Fredric.

But the wolf's intense goldenrod eyes settled on Dianna. They bore through her, humanlike in their directness, before shrinking back into the greenery.

"I don't think she likes me," Dianna whispered.

Fredric frowned.

"Her trust is the earned kind," he said.

Chapter 35

Raven moon, full

By the time the cloak of night fell over Silbarran, the others had still not returned. Dianna had a sinking feeling they were avoiding her, each for their own reasons. Fredric was the apparent exception, dozing upon his mulberry branch above her, brown curls tousled against greenery.

"For a pack, you don't seem to stay together often," she mused, her back against the tree's trunk.

"Though kin scatter the earth like seed and grow apart, their paths are rooted in the same ground," came Fredric's voice from the alcove, thick with sleep.

As morning dawned, Dianna lay awake staring at the ghostly imprint of the full moon. *Well*, she thought, *if the prince is to remain absent, it's only in his character — and I'm too hungry and tired of waiting.*

Unfolding, she crept a good distance away from the den, resting her shortbow and its clutch of arrows on the banks of a stream. She set to work foraging for ripe salmonberries in the bushes.

Holding the findings in the hem of her dress, she turned as the sound of muffled footsteps approached, and a figure obscured the sunlight.

Whip-quick, Dianna dropped the gown, sending the bright vermilion berries tumbling, and seized her bow. Raising it, she nocked an arrow at eye level. But at first she glimpsed only forest until the prince's Earthencloak fluttered, revealing him within it.

"Good morning," he said, raising his hands in calm surrender. "I've startled you again. Forgive me."

"Your grace," Dianna said, but did not lower her bow. "Ram. Unfortunately, my arrow is less forgiving."

Ram raised his eyebrows momentarily, then gave a deep laugh. "Aergyris, my wolf would snap your little bow in two."

Dianna drew the bowstring back. Ram went stock-still, laughter fading in his throat.

"Tell me about my mother," Dianna said.

Ram, palms still aloft, looked as stunned as if her arrow had pierced his heart. "Your mother," he murmured.

"Aimes said her name," Dianna probed, eyes locked on him. "And Fredric said you know more. I want—" Her voice broke. "I need to know what happened to her."

Ram took a deep breath. Gave a small, weary nod, as though he knew he'd been discovered.

"Will you walk with me?" he asked.

Dianna lowered her bow, allowing her grip to relax, and that was answer enough. Ram turned away. A mouse scurried from the underbrush at the rustle of his cloak.

Dianna followed the careful placement of Ram's steps through a bramble-choked thicket. Whatever he had to explain, it weighed on him like stones. The gravity of unspoken words dragged in the depth of his strides and the angles of his shoulders.

But they walked onward in silence, scaling an upward path which meandered around the trees. Dianna had to quicken her pace to match Ram's surefooted tread. Tall, flowering grasses prickled at her bare calves, sweeping at the hem of her dress. There was a subtle pleasure in the squash of black, fertile soil between her toes, a faded memory of a time when the plot outside the farmhouse yielded crops as abundant as the thick undergrowth in Silbarran.

Only when they reached the top of the shallow ravine did Ram face her. A warm wind sighed through the treetops, and the fresh green fragrance of spring was sharp on the air and in her lungs. There at the apex, above dense foliage and beneath open sky, it seemed almost easy to believe the woods had collapsed away. For a moment, the scenery's beauty distracted Dianna, soothing her stiff breath and quick pulse.

Ram let his cowl fall back so they might speak freely, rubbing his shadow of a beard. The gesture lent him a rakish charm. In his features, Dianna could still see the portrait of his younger self – a man who would have had a promising reign, led his legion into battle. Even in his ragged clothes, she could envision him in the finest silks.

"I cannot tell you about your mother," he said, "without first telling you about Aimes."

Dianna nodded, but waited like a thirsty traveler who had crossed a hard mountain range knowing a river was just within her reach.

"Aimes was abandoned in the filth of the slums when he was very little," Ram continued. "He'd managed to survive there scavenging on pig slop, and if he was lucky, scraps from pitying strangers. Others weren't so kind. It's a brutal life in the slums, a life of vagrants and addicts and the mad."

"When he was enslaved by the Caenani, he saw . . . he was subject to . . . their wrath. He had become a gifted healer." He paused, eyes flickering to Dianna from under his cowl. "They made him heal wounded, captive Valtans and made him watch as they wounded them brutally again. Over and over, just for sport. They terrorized his mind."

Dianna was still. Only a cold, dark horror moved through her.

"So you see," Ram said, "he rejected humanity like it had rejected him. Until he met Armina."

Every childhood nightmare folded upon itself until Dianna was left with the worst truth unfolding before her.

"They—" The words stuck like sand in her throat. "The Caenani killed her."

Ram's voice was barely a whisper. "Yes."

Dianna nodded, and her breath deepened, but she couldn't cry. She was the thirsty traveler again, collapsing at the riverbank. Only now she could see the rippling water that had kept her forging ahead was nothing but a trick of the shimmering heat. It was a truth she had known, and the child in her had wished away.

"Then she died a martyr," she said. "Like my father."

"And a wolf. Like you."

Dianna blinked, feeling the revelation slide over her. The strangeness of it plunged her into half-memories of painful transformations. It was a final cruel sting of fate, that her mother should endure an experience they could never share in words.

"A wolf," she whispered. "Then she must have been among the first ones bitten."

"Even before us," Ram agreed. "Aimes escaped to Silbarran. But when I found him . . . He was all skin and bones, sleeping in tree hollows. Fixated with guilt about Armina's murder, and all the captive Valtans he couldn't save from their torture. He wouldn't speak. He—"

For a moment, Ram was suddenly, frighteningly quiet. Even the cool morning air seemed to go stagnant. He spoke with a flat calmness, breaking the silence.

"He'd been torturing himself instead."

Tears glistened in his eyes. Dianna imagined what he must have seen: Aimes as a boy, crouched and shivering and smudged with blood, staring wild-eyed and mute into the abyss.

"I took care of him," Ram said. "I became the only family he knows, and I called him my son. But he wouldn't stop trying to hurt himself. The only thing that calmed him down was when I became a wolf. As though the only life he saw worth living for himself was as an animal. And then he asked me for that." His voice darkened. "So . . . I helped him become one of us."

A chill washed over Dianna.

"You bit him?" she whispered.

"For a while, it was an escape from the pain. It came more naturally to him than to any of us. Like breathing. I thought . . . for the first time, I thought he would be all right.

"But he began to resist his human body like a stone against the river, until he stopped being human at all. And then, he began to lose his human consciousness." Ram shook his head. "Sometimes his eyes grew vacant. He'd get confused, act on instinct. But there was one thing he clung to, fiercely. Armina's words. She died wanting a better life for her daughter, away from Awl-Feth, by any means necessary. And Aimes thought he could give you that life. That he could save you from pain . . . the way I saved him."

"He thought . . ." Dianna echoed slowly.

And then she understood, but only just, as if it were a terrible lie, and any second he would take it back.

Dianna felt a chasm open in her chest, bile rising in her throat. Her childhood came flooding back in flashes, in waves. Girls in white dresses, the High Elder's voice quaking under cathedral arches, the bloody wolf's head upon the spear—

She searched them, but could not fathom the image of Aimes, of the wolf, of his teeth. She only remembered Liam's tense answer as he knelt at her bedside.

It got under my skin.

Yes. Yes, An-An.

Dianna turned aside slowly, wordlessly. She walked a few paces, the tenderness of the sodden earth comforting beneath her feet.

"It's my fault as much as it is his," Ram said, watching her. "I thought I was giving him another chance at life, but I never thought — I never dreamed he'd turn you into one of us." The tears in his eyes slipped and fell. "I am so very sorry, Dianna."

A breeze hissed through the trees, snapping up leaves and sending them flying. Dianna stopped in her tracks.

"I had every intention of telling you. I was foolish and selfish in my desire to protect you from the start. Just as I was with Aimes." Ram spoke plainly but strained with remorse. "But your wound is healed now. You are free to go."

"Go where?" Dianna's face hardened. Her voice shuddered on the wind. "Go where, your grace? The outside world is closed to us. I have nowhere else to go. My family is dead. I have nothing left to lose."

"Your life has been taken from you. I know that nothing can change that. If I have any honor, all I can do is offer you mine in return."

Dianna turned to look at the prince, momentarily speechless. She couldn't believe he would propose such a thing. He had clasped his hands in front of his face, a gesture that reminded her so much of her father, or a soldier on the front lines of a losing battle.

She gathered her breath like kindling, and from it her words emerged fiery and raw.

"The wolf didn't kill Actaen on its own, or my father," she said. "My choices killed them. Their blood is on my hands, on the High Elder's hands — not yours. And you think your blood will absolve you? That it will appease me?"

Ram lowered his hands and met her gaze.

"I may be a huntress, but the last thing I want is more

236

blood!" Dianna couldn't help but shout now, rousing the wolf in her chest. "And you may be heir to the empire – you may have left us – but if you think I wished you dead, you don't know your people at all!"

Ram raised his eyebrows, and Dianna felt a strange rush of courage. Was it her mercy that astonished him, she wondered, or her audacity?

He held up his hands. "Then I concede, Dianna Aergyris," he said. "But I stand by my word. I will protect you. This family takes care of each other."

Dianna's breath eased and she swallowed, pressing the wolf back. "I'm not so easy to take care of."

"We leave no one behind."

"Then I'll slow you down."

"You won't. Don't let Eccka convince you otherwise. She doesn't . . ." His brow creased and he looked askance as if in shame. "She doesn't know how you came to be one of us. Nor does Fredric."

"But she's right about me. I'm a *hauntoun*. I'm better off away from you, where I won't cause any more deaths. I'm better off—"

Dianna cut herself short, mouth tamping down on the thought, and restlessly thumbed the edge of the shortbow at her hip.

A frown pulled at Ram's mouth. He looked down at his feet. When he spoke his voice was kind and deep.

"I would like you to stay with us. I would like you to live."

Tentative hope clung to his words, like drops of rain. Dianna studied Ram's profile beneath the lightening sky and saw that he knew. He had known all along.

"Before we found you, you wanted to die," said Ram softly. "You wanted to die, because it seemed easier than living."

Dianna lowered herself to sit in the dew-laden grass.

The sensation, one she would rather forget, came back to her in fragments: the force of the hunter's bolt thrusting her down, hollowing her flesh. Stumbling in a flash of light, stifling a scream as her tissues disconnected and reformed, as her organs decompressed, as her bones sprouted and grew.

She could have staggered to her feet, kept running. Instead she'd lain gasping into the mud, tremors shuddering through her, cleaving to the earth with a fevered hope that it would mercifully rise up and swallow her whole.

So many times she'd wished for death.

But Dianna closed her eyes, remembering the animal consciousness melting into her own. The power of four legs over rough terrain, culling the breath from her lungs.

"The wolf didn't want to give up," she confessed. "All it wants is to survive. To be free."

Ram seated himself upon a great stone beside her, his cloak fanning out behind him.

"You fell into a rift," he said, his low voice making eddies in her stream of memory. "That's why the hunters didn't find you, but we did. The wolf wants you to live. We want you to live."

Dianna looked down, tracing the delicate bones on the back of her hand, contemplating what they had done. The reek of blood, the angry faces pressing in all around, ripping Actaen's body to pieces because she wanted him to suffer—

She swallowed as if to calm the pulse in her throat. A tear escaped her in a blink, landing on her knuckles.

"Do you think this could be hell, Ram?" she asked.

Ram reached out to gently place his hand on hers. When she didn't stir, he left it there.

"It is life," he said. "I suppose I don't deny such a place exists. But if so, it's not here. I also believe in redemption."

"And in Mactus, like your father?"

The question slipped from her before she could stop it.

She could almost see it tumble from her lips, wishing she could gather it up in her hands and snuff it out. It was a personal question, impolite.

But Ram didn't hesitate to answer. "I used to believe in something. I used to have my faith, yes. But I am nothing like my father. He was a ruthless strategist before his mind began slipping. Then his speech. And then, very quickly, he was a shell. I liked to imagine it was a peaceful way to go."

Dianna thought of her father with an ache in the pit of her stomach.

"Sovereignty is passed when the crown jewel is bequeathed to its successor," said Ram. "My father wore the jewel at all times, on a ring. When my brother and I were summoned to his deathbed, he removed the ring and extended it to both of us.

"But before he died, he looked at me. And I pitied him. Because it was as if he thought, if he chose me, I could undo it all. The inferno of war that he ignited. A price that our people are paying in blood."

Ram's own voice lashed like a flame, his eyes glinting before settling into coal-dark. He inclined his head, and the chatter of morning birdsong played over his silence.

"Remetus, on the other hand . . . his vision for the empire aligns with our father's, and that is why I believe the Caenani assassinated him. At first, I thought he'd run off. I ignored the warnings, crossed Silbarran in search of him . . . and here I am." Ram absently touched the notched half-moon scar on his leg. "Without knowing whether Remetus was dead, I had refused ascension. I felt I could not fairly accept it otherwise. But I remain doubtful that the Senate would have crowned either of us."

"Why not?" Dianna asked.

"My father never married. They suspected us to be bastards born of 'peasant blood.'" A troubled look stole across Ram's face. "The truth is, Dianna, our fathers were flawed men. The truth is that all is flawed, even faith. I had faith because I wanted a simple answer, an easy answer, to the world's mysteries. Now, I am faced with the strangest one yet. And I am not so certain. There is so much life here, it nearly drowns out the thought of my empire's death. And then I think of it as a sanctuary. But if it is an act of god, then Mactus plucked us from civilization and placed us in this wilderness to live as anathemas for eternity. Then perhaps others would call it hell. But not us."

Over the horizon, the sun's golden crown slowly bloomed.

"Fredric thinks it's our destiny, what we are," he said. "Aimes would call it freedom. Eccka goes where the wind takes her. And I . . . I have wrestled with this puzzle, every hour upon every one of my days here, never to come to a single finite conclusion. Except that I don't know." A mist haunted his eyes as he gazed into the distance. "I may no longer be a man of god, but I am a man of logic. Being without it very nearly drove me to madness."

Dianna was quiet as she stared at the snarled undergrowth surrounding them. A beetle struggled in the silvery, dew-scattered lacework of a spider web. A fat orbweaver clung to the threaded edge, waiting to strike.

"I've tried to fight it," Ram murmured. "So I can feel human. So I can speak like this to you. I hide away, because, as you so astutely observed upon our acquaintance, I am a coward. But I've grown weary with the years. I've given up trying to act under the pretense that I'm whole. And I learned there's no point in fighting." A tight-lipped smile flashed across his face. "We cannot disconnect our two selves and hope to survive, as much as we cannot remove the bones from our bodies. We are a wondrous and terrible amalgamation. And we shed our skin so easily now, it frightens me."

"Is that why Aimes couldn't tell me about himself?

Because he's barely himself anymore?"

Ram nodded, jaw tense, lost in thought.

"Aimes didn't just know your mother. He loved her like his own," he said slowly. "He only became human again because we found you. As though he wanted to think again. To heal again."

Dianna parsed this for a moment.

"I'd like to talk to him, Ram."

Ram rubbed a hand over his beard. "It could take time."

They sat together for a while in peaceful solitude, as the sun continued to rise.

"I have nothing but time now," Dianna said at last, quietly.

Ram smiled at her.

Chapter 36

Raven moon, full

Dianna walked among the greenery of Silbarran until the sky faded to soft blue twilight. The rifts felt like silk as she passed from one to the next. With each passage emerged a new world – a grove of massive birch trees, fit to be the walking sticks of giants. A meadow filled with the flitting sound of winged insects, lush with mushroom caps as big as her palm. A strange, impassable hedge of creepers and branches, heavy with moss, obstructing her path.

With a practiced eye she sought the clawed tracks upon the litter of forest floor. But she ended up in the mire by the riverside, bending to study the scuffed impression of a heel, and realized her mistake. She'd been tracking the wolf, but she'd found the human.

She waited a moment to approach him, her stomach tense. The river was a silver snake glazed with a gold-scaled patina of sunlight. The scent of wet earth hung thick upon the air. Aimes sat on the banks among blooming saxifrage, facing away. The muscles of his back were relaxed, and he'd rolled his trousers past the ankles, allowing his feet to skim the cool shallows. His careless hair was ruffled by the light breeze.

"Hello," Dianna called out at last.

Aimes startled at the sound, wide-eyed as he made to

get up, feet splashing in the water.

"Wait, please," she said, advancing, raising her palms. "May I speak to you?"

Aimes shivered once and became still, watching her with the gaze of a wild creature, drawing brisk, shallow breaths.

Dianna stopped short at the riverbank. Carefully, she sat beside him, sliding her feet into the fine silt. The cold, silken water lapped at her ankles. Sharing the same secluded space in such a way felt more intimate than she expected.

Instinctively, her hand fell to the curve of her calf, throbbing with the memory of the searing smack of the bladed bolt.

"Thank you for healing me," she said. "I'm not sure how you managed it."

Aimes glanced furtively at a sharp rock jutting from the river's surface. Without a word, he reached toward the rock and dragged his palm across it, as though he thought nothing of tearing himself open. Dianna flinched as he opened his gritty, bloodied hand.

He seized a cluster of the frothy saxifrage in his injured fist. Seconds passed, and he let go with a long exhale.

Red petals fluttered from his grasp, revealing smooth unbroken flesh.

"It depends," he murmured, staring at his palm, "on time. But it always works."

Dianna met his eyes, imagining the possibilities: a sickly infant's cry, hushed to a gentle prattle. Cathrin's beautiful skin, unscathed by violence. And men – Valtan soldiers – whose wounds could be mended, no matter how deep.

Myre, victorious.

"How?" She shook her head, voice rising in wonder. "How did you learn such a thing?"

Aimes withdrew his hand like a reflex, and Dianna nearly recoiled.

"I didn't learn," he said, with a firmness she had never before heard in his voice. "Silbarran gave it to me. It *chose* me. And I don't know why."

Dianna's gaze broke, turning toward the river as she floundered for something to say. A breeze stirred the air, ruffling the saxifrage and chilling her skin.

The day was already giving way to darkness, yet the full moon was on the rise, opalescent against a sky of dusky orange and blue. She thought of the last laborious transformation as she pulled herself free of the catacombs, the first burning breath of air drawn into her lungs, the thunder of her animal feet against earth.

It was a strange solace, after so many agonizing moons alone, knowing that she would be among others now. Knowing that it was because of him.

"It's odd, isn't it?" she blurted.

Aimes' breath hitched a little, but he didn't move.

"You're a healer," she went on, tentative. "And I'm a huntress. I've taken lives. You've put them back together. Perhaps that makes me the wilder of us."

When his breathing calmed again, she looked at him. His jaw had clenched as if biting back some unseen pain, and his skin had taken on a paler sheen, as though some sickness was clawing its way through him.

"No," he said, low. "I changed you. I took your life."

"Yes. You did." Dianna's fingers idly traced the scar streaking her calf. "Ram told me."

Aimes' eyes narrowed in bewilderment, searching her face. The cadence of his phrasing was still slow – a wild voice catching on a human tongue – but steadfast.

"Then where," he said, "is your hatred?"

From his parted lips, the whispered word waited between them. His intense gaze, broken by the white line of his scar, shone earnestly.

He means it, Dianna thought, marveling. *He thinks I should hate him.*

"It's not that simple." She shook her head. Remembered the glass vial of aconite, smooth and cool against her fingertips. "You changed my life, but you gave me a second chance. I think it's only right that you have one, too. To be at peace with a mistake. It's what my mother would have wanted."

For an instant – in a glint of yellow – Aimes' gaze faltered. His brow furrowed as he seemed to dredge up a long-buried memory.

"She was the first person . . . who cared for me," he said.

He shivered again until it overtook him, as if he might shiver into pieces. But the stammering rhythm of his voice grew steadier, gained weight as he spoke, like a branch beneath snowfall.

"I saw you there – in the snow, alone. I smelled death on you." His head bowed, black hair falling forward. "I knew it was you. And I remembered what she said. She said, 'I would move earth and stars to set her free.' And I thought I could. I thought I could . . ."

For a moment they said nothing, and only the forest spoke its old language: the gentle murmur of the rocky shallows, the swish of long green reeds, the intermittent harmonies of bird calls.

"Aimes," Dianna said. "I forgive you."

He shook his head. "I don't deserve your forgiveness."

"Don't you think that's for me to decide?" Dianna said, in a voice edged more sharply than she intended. "You've brought me here. But from now on, my life is my own. For once – for once, I'm allowed a decision that is *no one's* but mine."

Aimes did look at her then. He looked at her as when his eyes first met hers. As if he'd been lost, and in them he recognized a path homeward. But there was a glimmer of something else – something pure and longing, like hope. Up close, Dianna couldn't help but notice that the fine scar on his face, trailing from cheekbone to jaw, looked like the ghost of a tear.

"I forgive you," she repeated, softly.

Aimes blinked – and a tear did fall, disappearing in the river.

"I'm here now," Dianna said. "I'm here, and I'm like you. And nothing can change that now."

But the crease of worry between Aimes' eyes didn't fade. Dianna glanced at his healed hand, and without thinking, took it in hers with a firmness that was not quite a handshake, a softness that was not quite the holding between lovers.

"We're the same," she said. "So, let's be friends."

Heat rose to his face as he studied their clasped hands. Dianna wondered why he seemed so nervous, why his breath cut short, until his gaze broke away to contemplate something deep among the trees. He rose to his feet with an inhuman grace.

Slowly, she slipped her feet from the water. They glistened like pale fish in the fading light as she turned to face him.

"What is it?" she asked.

Aimes stayed as he was.

"Listen," he said.

A minute passed. Dianna felt the human need to speak, to fill the silence.

Like a shifting wind, the feeling subsided. She heard the scrabble of a squirrel upon his branch far away, smelled a rare orchid – lady slippers – growing in a distant patch of shade, and felt the subtlest draft from a falling leaf on her skin.

And, in the thicketed depths of the woods, a rustling of grass. The stalking, rhythmic plod of footsteps.

A feeling stirred in Dianna's chest — a flicker of fear. The beginnings of a life about to be born.

"Someone's coming," he whispered. "We should go back. To the den."

Dianna nodded, her stammering pulse resisting her motionless body.

As he turned toward her, she almost expected his shape to ebb away into the wolf, for him to run ahead of her again. But his eyes remained blue in their transcendent calm, like still waters.

"You'll be safe," he said. "I promised."

Dianna heard the conviction in his words, saw the determination in the set of his mouth. For the moment, she believed him.

Side by side, they set out into the dusk.

***

The den was dark when they arrived. Only by the illumination of the full moon did Dianna recognize the figures beneath the trees: the flash of Fredric's impish smile. Ram's cloaked silhouette watching the sky. A taciturn Eccka pacing beside him, hands folded behind her. A hushed expectancy had fallen over the woods, like a sky heavy with rain after so much drought.

Ram turned then, and under the cowl his dark eyes gleamed, soft and warm.

"You came back," he said as the pair of them approached, but something in his voice seemed to be meant only for her.

Dianna stole a look at the round moon, a visceral dread clinging to her like sweat on skin.

"The hunters are out tonight," she murmured.

Aimes looked at Ram, his eyes luminous. "We heard one," he told him. "Coming from the northeast."

Ram gave a grave nod. "Fredric?"

"We'll take the rifts on this side of the river," Fredric

said, folding his jerkin and tucking it safely in the cache. His golden eyes found Dianna as he added mildly, "We can't risk staying in one place, no matter how safe it may seem. The important thing is to keep moving, Gentle-heart, and follow my lead."

A thunderous growl shuddered in the air: Ram was the first to go.

Like a trick of the moonlight, the Earthencloak crumpled in a flurry of leaves. From underneath a black snout emerged, nudging away the folds, and a pair of eyes as radiant as candlelight. Eccka slinked into a crouch beside him.

Beside her, Dianna felt Aimes' warmth begin to flicker and tremble, as though a hard wind would sweep him out of his body.

"Aimes?" she whispered.

His eyes marbled blue and yellow as they focused on her.

"I'm here, Dianna," he said.

The words were unassuming, but he spoke her name with a subtle reverence. His tongue curled over it like a breath pulled from his throat, deep and sensuous, and it quivered like quicksilver through her bones.

He spoke her name like he loved her.

"The fear passes," he added, looking away again. The slope of his naked back glowed pale in the moonlight. "Like turning seasons. It passes. Like leaves of trees."

Dianna's gaze returned to Aimes, to the inclination of his head, the shocking clarity of his unblinking irises. Biting chills inched over her skin as she took a deep breath.

Slowly, gently, she placed a hand on his shoulder to steady herself. With the other, she slipped her silken gown from her shoulders and let it tumble to her feet.

Sinking her toes into the tender loam, she drew deep lungfuls of woody scents, each distinct from one another.

Pockets of air murmured in her breast, and her pulse seized, and the wolf scuffled at her from the inside.

She collapsed to her knees, shuddering, gasping for breath, a fish out of water, dying – until she saw Aimes collapse and return, sleek and wolf.

It was as if light itself opened in the center of her, its bright sudden thrill numbing her to the pain of changing. The moon lured her out of her skin in one smooth pull, consuming discord, resurrecting her.

In her mind, she imagined herself and the wolf, separate beings, together in the same darkened space. Imagined herself kneeling, calling out to it, opening her arms. Smoothing over the thick, coarse fur. Nestling her cheek into its neck, drying her tears.

Four glowing pairs of eyes converged on her in the dark, like beacons to a stranded ship. Ram was an inkblot against the spindly contours of moonlit trees.

In the distance, a rift glimmered, and together they ran to it. The cool air combed its fingers through Dianna's fur, lashed her face with intermingling scents – the sharp green of firs and pines, crisp running streams, soft floral nectars, the decay of organic debris beneath acidic soil.

They glided through the rift one by one, threading through a shifting patchwork of trees. Silbarran rose and fell around them again and again: fallen sprays of cypresses, soft underfoot. The brush of conifer bark, mellow with sap underneath. The voices of a thousand nocturnal creatures rising, chattering, singing, whooping, shrieking.

For the first time in the wolf's body, Dianna's mind was aware of it all.

She gathered each rich sensation like a collection of perfect, scattered leaves, wanting to preserve them between the pages of her mind for later, so she wouldn't forget. She wanted to run her human fingers over the edges of these dried husks of memory, a fragile yet tangible reminder to herself: *You are not death, after all. You are wild, and warm, and alive.*

Eccka tailed Fredric, her smooth pace uninterrupted by the hollows and ridges of the earth underfoot. Ram was forging ahead, his sharp-toothed mouth suspended in the impression of a smile.

And Aimes, a lean, loping silhouette, ran alongside Dianna into nothingness, skirting unseen death.

Yes, she thought. *Yes. The fear passes.*

Chapter 37

Raven moon, full

In the night, the pack had circled back to the den. Aimes was on the outskirts, the late morning sun edging his profile as he leaned over his medicine box, making tonics. His hands delicately crushed berries into pulp, dribbling purple juices into crude clay vials.

Dianna's body felt small, contracted, every drawn-out bone and muscle collapsed into its former shape and blanketed under the downy sheep's fleece. Taking a deep breath, she ran her hands over her own skin, testing its malleability. She recalled the first time Aimes touched her, a pleasant sensation in the midst of pain, his fingertips light as raindrops. It made her shiver with a sudden longing to feel them again.

She turned on her side and listened to the hollow clatter of earthenware for a moment, her hair catching in the dew-glazed grass, before wrapping the fleece around her and rising to her feet.

As she approached, Aimes stopped. He held up his palms, spreading out his stained fingers, but they did not tremble.

"It's all right," he said. "I'm steady."

Dianna didn't respond, only gazed at him with a warm,

indefinable pang in her chest.

Aimes turned back to his work, placing a stopper in one vial. There was a sheen to his eyes, but he blinked, and it was gone.

"Trying to make myself stay," he said under his breath, determined.

His mop of black hair, tangled as a bird's nest, shadowed his face. Dianna thought if she smoothed it out, it might feel as soft as feathers through her fingers.

The fleeting idea made her nerves spark to life. But hunger roiled in the pit of her belly, interrupting her thoughts.

"Aimes," she said tentatively, "I don't think we ate anything last night."

Aimes slanted his head, a subtle smile breaking on his mouth, a shade of wolf in his posture. "You remember it?"

The smile, so radiant it touched his eyes, made Dianna smile back.

"I remember," she said. "I wasn't scared. I felt . . . free."

"Good," Aimes said at last, after a breath. "That's good."

They were quiet for a moment. He seemed relieved, Dianna thought, as his gaze held hers. Perhaps he'd been worried she could never feel that way again.

"Will you hunt with me?" she asked. "Or will it keep you from staying human?"

"No. It won't." Closing the medicine box, Aimes rose to his feet. "As long as I'm near you, I think."

His voice slipped, making the briefest note of ache. It, too, seemed hungry, but with a hunger of a different kind. Dianna found her breath strangely shallow at the sound of it, her skin tingling with an unbidden rush of warmth down to her core.

But as soon as Aimes had spoken, he glanced away again, as though looking at her was too much. His hands clenched, tensing the strong muscles in his forearms. His face was flushed.

Dianna felt more naked than ever despite the blanket's cover. An unexpected thought crossed her mind: would he stay human if she invited him under it with her?

She liked the idea of that.

"I should get dressed," she managed quickly, turning back toward the den's firepit.

She followed Fredric's snores to the mulberry tree, where he had creatively arranged himself among its branches. In the cache, she found a folded pair of men's trousers and a loose linen tunic. She pulled them on and plaited her long hair. Finally, among the assorted supplies and weaponry, she extracted a hunting knife and shouldered her bow and arrows.

Together, she and Aimes set out through the sunlight-pierced woods, winding around pines beneath the prattle of birds high in their boughs. Pausing occasionally to check for tracks, she scented the forest for signs of life amidst perfumes of damp decaying vegetation, budding wildflowers, and sap-encrusted bark. She led them downwind and through a rift, where they navigated the uneven ground of a shallow embankment, snagged by twigs and sticky spider webs, kissed by falling samaras.

Aimes followed, his movements even quieter in comparison, and Dianna admired his practiced stealth.

They did not dare to speak. It was the kind of place and time that called for silence, and when words alone would not do.

At length, they paused at a thicket lush with the kind of fresh grass and lichen-smothered rocks which deer would find irresistible. Dianna stooped behind an outcropping of fern-laden underbrush.

"And now we wait," she whispered.

Aimes cocked his head.

"For our quarry," she explained.

"You don't seek it out?"

"My father taught me this way," she said. "Killing must be swift so prey need not suffer. I say, 'I am about to kill you. But I will honor your right to walk upon on this earth.' The hunters in my village have no use for such rites."

A frown twitched at Aimes' lips.

"I hated them," he said, his own voice low yet scathing as the heart of a flame. "When I pulled the bolt from your leg. I hated them almost as much as I hated myself."

Dianna propped her bow in her lap, remembering her first failed hunt: the quail with the broken wing, its helpless thrashing, its sorrowful cry. The guilt hollowing a hole in her chest.

"You only think you had every reason to hate yourself," she said quietly. "It doesn't mean you should."

When she glanced at Aimes, he was staring back – only his eyes had not yet reached hers, lingering instead on the curve of her mouth.

In that moment, the wolf was gone. She saw the man who had lived without love for too long, who studied her with what seemed like pure fascination.

They fell into silence again, a silence suddenly, contradictingly eloquent. Even in its wake, Dianna suspected he sensed the quickening of her pulse. The quiet tension thrilled her just as much as the slow, wild-edged tones of his voice.

The thicket rustled, and she straightened. On lanky legs, a doe plucked her way among the weedy grasses, too tempted by the budding lichens to heed the presence of her onlookers.

Dianna nocked her arrow and pulled back her bowstring, knowing its gentle glide through her fingers as a practiced lyrist would know the tautness of well-tuned catlines.

The doe lifted her head, but her willowy body was motionless. Her ears were like large leaves upturned and forward, and her dark eyes were serene.

The smooth extinguishing of life happened just as Dianna anticipated. When it was over, she approached her kill, grabbing the aft-end of her arrow and pulling it out in a single stroke. With an easy slice of the hunting knife, the fallen deer's glistening dark entrails spilled from its underbelly. Dianna knelt and began gutting the deer, working quickly.

Aimes looked on for a long time but did not offer his help, seeing that it was her responsibility, her kill. Dianna felt the fragility of his presence, his unspoken desire to collapse into the wolf, to tear into the raw flesh, rising and falling with his breath.

"Did your father teach you this too?" he said at last.

Dianna maneuvered the bloody knife between meat and bone, separating it with precision. "My mother."

When Aimes knelt beside her, their shoulders brushed. His palm covered the lifeless doe's flank, feeling the warmth draining.

"I watched her kill and skin a wild rabbit," Dianna said, working her knife around another cut. "That was only my first lesson on the farm. We're all just this, underneath. We all end up this way."

Aimes inhaled the luscious scent of fresh meat and fat and blood. A muscle twitched in his jaw and he blinked, as though focusing on her voice.

"She taught me to catch rabbits, too," Dianna said. She smiled then, lost in a memory. "But sometimes — when Father wasn't watching — she'd let me set them free."

Aimes lifted his palm from the doe's stagnant body and placed it on his heart.

"Your mercy is rare in this world," he whispered.

Dianna paused to glance at him, brow knit, but he was looking down and away, as though hiding his eyes.

And you know, she thought. *Lonely boy from the*

slums. You know just how rare it is.

She finished her work quietly, cleaning her knife and stowing the provisions in a pair of bags. Rising, she gathered one in her arms. He took the other, and together they carried them to the den.

Chapter 38

Raven moon, waning

"Mactus welcomes you, Centurion Gansin," the High Elder said, shaking the thick leather gauntlet of the man before him. "And your men. Our gratitude is with you all."

The Centurion of L'Heste had removed his helm, revealing old battle scars and a beard spilling over his enormous breastplate. Part of his left ear was missing.

"High Elder Orcarrus," returned the warrior, bearlike both in stature and hirsute countenance. He looked out upon Awl-Feth's hunters, seated in a semicircle around the High Elder and framed by the marbled columns of the cathedral tower, where they had gathered to discuss their business in private. "We are glad to be of service."

Behind the Centurion, in phalanx formation, a hundred soldiers uniformed in gleaming armor saluted the High Elder. Their helms were removed, revealing a smattering of youthful faces behind a front line of older, hardier men. Each man's neck was striped with a dark tattoo, though the intricate markings differed amongst them. At the forefront of their configuration, rows of additional mercenaries had aligned themselves separately, their own flesh bare of the inked inscription.

"It is a grave era within the empire," the High Elder said.

Many of the Awl-Fethan hunters nodded in assent. The weight of their hardships pulled upon their mouths, but their watchful eyes seemed to hold the reflection of silver plate mail like flickers of hope.

"The war with Caenan is a lost cause. Valta is already steeped in blood," agreed Gansin. "I have kept my soldiers well at bay, ready to strike if the iron burned hot. Then I heard the reports from both sides . . ." The Centurion paused and glanced again at the gathering of hunters, as if to take note of their numbers. "Soldiers gone missing in combat, only to turn up mutilated in Silbarran. I have suspected that what lives there is born of hell itself."

His tone darkened, fell almost to a whisper. "But when I received your missive, High Elder – I knew it could only be defeated by a holy man. So, lead us where you will. We shall follow."

The High Elder stroked his dark beard with long fingers.

"Yes, the Senate considered the war a higher priority," he said, the distaste in his voice clear and sharp. "We have taken it upon ourselves to eradicate the demons."

"My men will see it done, High Elder."

"I must remind you, however, that these are clever demons. Elusive." The High Elder paced parallel alongside the L'Hestian soldiers, admiring the remarkable craftsmanship of their spears and shortswords. Pausing, he envisioned how they might sink into an animal's flesh, lancing and sticking like the barbed teeth of a snare. His piercing eyes flicked up, and his voice was cold with vitriol. "They can cheat death."

The Centurion drew himself up to full height, imposing as a rugged mountain shadowing a valley.

"We continue to set a standard unrivaled even by the

empire's legion," Gansin insisted. "My men at the forefront are High Echelon. They will serve you exceptionally in combat."

The High Elder folded his hands behind his back. "Shall we then discuss our course of action?"

Gansin bowed his great shagged head with a grunt of assent.

"Very well," said the High Elder. "My hunters are a small defense, not nearly as qualified as your forces. Still, they are available as auxiliaries to your mission."

"We could make use of archers and cavalrymen," conceded Gansin. "But I will not allow my soldiers to rush into combat blind. Our first footfalls should be measured."

There were low murmurs among the hunters, resonating within the tower walls, and the High Elder's eyes narrowed briefly. "And how do you recommend we proceed?"

"Knowledge of the enemy is power, High Elder. We know little of these hellbeasts, including their total numbers. We must first understand their manner of attack."

The High Elder steepled his fingers neatly together, gauging the inquiry within this statement. He spoke with a slow softness now, like the calm before a violent storm.

"They may look like men," he said. "But they manifest, upon each full moon, in the form of wolves. Not common beasts, mind you. Colossal fiends, as the dire wolves of old."

Gansin's composure remained undaunted. "In my experience in battle, small strikes before the final offensive will be our most effective plan."

The hunters spoke amongst themselves, some voicing uncertainty at the notion of such a venture. The majority, however, nodded their agreement, too weary to offer counterarguments.

"Then I shall trust your experience, Centurion," the High Elder agreed. "Infiltrate Silbarran, stake out the woods. As you say, knowledge of the enemy is power. But you should kill them on sight."

Gansin turned toward his soldiers.

"You heard the holy man. *Al'daneas*," he dismissed them. "We embark at dawn."

In unison, they saluted their Centurion, turned on their heels and departed, one row at a time. The High Elder called the meeting to a close, and the men of Awl-Feth began to disband before Gansin approached him.

"I shall like to confer with you at length about the enemy, so I may brief my men before combat," said the Centurion in an undertone. "I see the strategic appeal in catching them unawares. But when the enemy can appear human . . ." He regarded the High Elder, serious. "You are a man of the cloth. We do not wish to involve civilians."

The High Elder's mouth set in a grim line, and he clapped the great warrior on the shoulder.

"Unintended altercation, my good Gansin, is an unpleasant yet inevitable fact of warfare," he said. "Silbarran has long been insecure territory. Mactus shall prevail over all who abide by His will, and Awl-Feth shall rise all the stronger for it." He smiled. "Now, first things first. Shall we settle on the matter of payment?"

Chapter 39

Raven moon, waning

Dianna opened her eyes to a canopy of stars and sat up, the undergrowth snagging at her clothes. The den was silent as the others slept.

A shiver coursed through her, vibrant and wild. She held a hand to her mouth, touched the pointed edges of her teeth. Waiting, she felt them smooth over again.

But her nightmare twisted in her heart like a sharp knife.

There was the fallow village, still lush with life in her youth. There was the musk of dust in each brushstroke of Liam's horse, her mother's strong hands kneading soft bread dough. There was resting, cradled in the crooked branch of the old dogwood tree, spent, watching the sun go down after a hard day's work.

There were also flashes of scarlet. Stripping flesh. Actaen's gaping, gurgling mouth.

She breathed in the wooded scent of Silbarran so that the nightmare felt faraway, even imagined, just like one of Liam's folktales.

Leaves rustled close by and Aimes emerged, human, in the darkness. He knelt in front of her, his gaze coming level to hers, studying her wan face.

"Are you all right?" he whispered. "I heard . . ."

Dianna shrank back into the shadows, mashing her hands into the earth. "I don't want to talk about it."

Aimes' own hands felt soft around her knuckles, and her fingers unfurled like saplings in warm sun. "Your eyes are yellow."

His voice was so mild. It was without judgment, without inquiry. She looked away, but the knowledge of his gaze upon her lingered.

The silence deepened until the words poised upon her tongue tumbled out.

"Just once, I became the wolf on my own. It wasn't a full moon. It was because hunters attacked me, and I killed them." She paused, heat rising to her face. "I feel ashamed. But not because they died. Because I think they deserved it."

Aimes held her hands for a moment before she felt his fingers slip away.

"I once thought I feared Silbarran," she said. "But the real demons lived among us, in the village, in the violence of men. The wolves aren't demons. They're . . ." She searched for the right word that would explain the strange intricacy of their nature, unsure that one existed.

Aimes' broad brows knit together as the calm blue waters of his eyes became a troubled thrall.

"They're our dormant instincts," he said, voice low. "Pure and wild and free. They're what help us survive."

Dianna's breath was shallow as she thought.

"Maybe the wolf eventually consumes our consciousness. But without it, we would die here." She looked at him fully, her mouth set. "I want to try again."

Aimes blinked. "What?"

"To become it," she said, the clarity of realization cool and striking as the brush of wind on her skin. "Without the moon. To feel again. I don't want to fight it anymore."

Aimes was quiet for a moment, barely visible in the

dark. Dianna closed her eyes.

"Then don't," he said at last.

Dianna filled her lungs and focused on the pattern of her breath. And she remembered.

Actaen's fingers grasping at her skin.

Abram's eyes on her as they beheaded him.

Scourge, the villagers had hissed as they spat upon her, as the hunters dragged her into the catacombs. *Devil child.*

In her mind she was on the floor of her dungeon, swathed in darkness, spirit thin as a leaf crushed underfoot.

She crouched, feeling the texture of earth beneath her, plant roots and rock ridges.

She lay on her side facing the wall. The burrow in the earth glowed with light, beckoning her to follow. She lifted her aching arm, fingers reaching.

She only had to touch it . . .

Outstretched, her hand reached for something in the distance.

Out of the dirt.

Into the light.

She wasn't conscious that she was on her knees, open eyes glazed yellow, until she felt a prickling in her feet.

"It's crawling up my legs," she cried out in an unfamiliar voice, animal at its edges.

"It's all right," Aimes said. "You're here."

Something lunged in her body, as if the earth moved through her – bird calls, the rustle of wind through the pines – everything living and breathing as one collective body, growing to a fever pitch, overwhelming. Buried underneath, so quiet it was almost nothing, she knew the whisper of home.

A cloudy fog smudged her thoughts. The little farmhouse was just a dot on the horizon of her mind's eye, the fields a golden blur, unrecognizable.

"You're here," came Aimes' voice through the fog.

"I'm here," she answered.

The prickling sensation slithered through her limbs, building a slow-burning fire in the pit of her belly. It was painless, but gutted hotter with each breath.

"Aimes," she said, and the fire spread.

Her hands stretched into the dirt, felt the endless roots of trees, footprints of people and creatures long passed. She inhaled, tasting the clammy, earthy air.

Here. Here. I am here.

And she was everything, then nothing, then animal, then human again. Sharp pangs like pins needled all over her skin, and Aimes' face came back into focus.

"It hurts," he said, brow furrowed.

Dianna nodded and hissed through her teeth.

Aimes nodded, putting his cool hand to her feverish cheek. "It hurts to feel."

He brushed the fringe of hair from her temple, each stroke of his fingers sweeping away the pain until she could breathe easy again. She shivered as the heat rolled away like raindrops, smooth and fleeting, along the length of her spine.

"Eventually—" he began but stopped short. His eyes moved over her features.

"Tell me," Dianna managed, wincing.

Aimes swallowed. When he spoke again it was fluid and slow.

"Eventually your two halves become whole, and you can change at will. I call it Falling. But it doesn't hurt. It feels softer."

"A soft Fall." Dianna imagined her bones gliding, folding into new joints. Wolf's fur, coarse and thick, spreading over her skin like a blanket, like an embrace. Like acceptance.

Her mouth was dry when she replied, "Tell me more about what it feels like."

Aimes smiled, and his eyes clouded knowingly.

"It feels like unbeing," he said at last. "As effortless as breathing, or a river's course."

When he closed his eyes, she could see the animal moving behind them.

"You'll know when you feel it," he said. "Take a breath."

PART IV: THE FALL

"Extinguish my eyes, I still can see you,
Close my ears, I can hear your footsteps fall,
And without feet I still can follow you,
And without voice I still can to you call."
– From *The Book of Pilgrimage* by Rainer Maria Rilke

CHAPTER 40

Cold moon, full
Night before siege

A mist lay draped over the woods like the veil of a bride. A man wandered through it, cloaked in black, beneath the milky rounded moon. He was disheveled and dirty, hollow-cheeked and sallow-skinned as a corpse. Were he seen, one might think him a vagrant, a lost emissary, a madman.

But he likened himself more to a shadow as he pressed on through the howling wind. A shadow gathering in the dark of the forest, which would emerge anew to cover all, dominant and glorious, sovereign of the empire.

He was Prince Remetus, heir of Myre, and he would kill fear.

His thumb edged over the hilt of his blade as he searched the mist-coated undergrowth for signs of his skulking quarry, listened for the soft tread of padded feet over cluttered forest floor. Though he had been no master of sport hunting like the empire's cavalry, he had sent for snares and taught himself to use them. They called them the jaws of death, traps that sunk to the bone and crushed the nerves to pulp.

He set them at night, with birds or rodents for bait, and by morning his fear – the wolf – lay tangled in it, squirming and baying like a ghastly tempest. Once weakened and helpless, it only took a knife-stroke of the throat to bleed out the beast. He had learned to find the largest veins, to suckle like an infant at the life-source, to dig out the sharp canine teeth, which he kept as tokens of his courage. Upon the final evening, his pockets had grown heavy with their weight, their number beyond even his own recollection.

Sickened as he was, sustained by nothing but blood, he felt a strange power brewing within him. The end of his struggle was nigh, the empire almost within his grasp.

Live and fast in the forest for a fortnight.
Kill as many wolves as you can hunt and drink their blood.
Upon the next full moon, the power you seek shall be yours.

He laughed as the oracle's words wormed and clutched at his mind.

As he moved through the darkness, he sang a simple tune under his breath, its cadence almost soothing as a companion.

Swift of feet and heartless
That howling hound of hell
And I, the man who hunts him where he dwells.

A hollow grade underfoot startled him. He knelt and touched the earth, caressing the imprint of a wolf track. He rubbed the soil between two fingers, scented it for the animal it had touched.

I am swift and heartless as
That fanged fiend in flight
And my bite, my bite, my bite is black as night.

A tree swayed nearby. With a violent start, he ducked

beneath his traveling cloak. Naked branches above offered glimpses of the rising full moon.

"*And my bite* . . . my bite, my bite . . ." he whispered between shallow breaths.

There, through snatches of churning mist, he saw it – the elongated face, the close-together eyes bright and knowing and vexingly human. The sight sent waves of fear swelling through him.

But the writhing wolf lay weakened, making soft whimpering noises through its snout. Its hind legs kicked, battering the metal trap against the ground with a sickening splinter of bone.

The prince stooped, plunging his knife into its neck in one methodic, swift strike. Again. A third time.

He licked his own spattered skin clean, so as not to waste a drop. He ran the knife along the soft underbelly of the wolf, spilling the innards from it. He dropped the knife, scrambling to get closer, cradling the blood in his trembling hands.

The iron tang of it spread on his tongue, and the reek of death was in his lungs. He retched, steadied himself, drank more.

Crouched over the wolf's sprawled body, he felt its warm strength filling him. He was the predator now. He was greater than this great, now lifeless beast. His smile ran red.

He lowered himself again but stopped short.

The wolf's vivid yellow eye was still wide open. From this angle, it appeared to be watching him, taunting him even in death. "*Look what you have done,*" it seemed to be saying.

Behind the thick mist slipped the movement of something. A hallucination.

Remetus stiffened. "Who's there?"

A figure as dark and tall as the trees drifted out from within them. It moved without the use of its own legs, fluid and silent.

Remetus blinked, filled with a cold dread as blood dribbled from his mouth. But in the figure's presence, he felt only captive. Helpless.

It stood there, staring at him.

It was a being neither male nor female. It was a person, and yet it was not.

It was unearthly, unnatural, garbled. Yet here, in the forest under the lambent moon, it belonged more than he.

Remetus knew old tales of ghosts and phantoms, but it was neither of these things, nor a physical being. In his deepest instincts, he knew only that it was wrong.

The entity leaned over the dead wolf. Its long body arched, graceful as the branch of a weeping willow, and it rested its lips on the wolf's head.

It spoke not in a human tongue, but in another language. To his torment, Remetus understood every word.

This is the last of them, it said in a voice broken with sorrow, as though it had seen the murder of a dear friend.

Remetus began to back away, bloodstained mouth agape.

But the face of the entity turned upward at once, and Remetus found himself immobile.

"Who are you?" he demanded.

The entity inclined its head, pale as the moon.

Here.

It hadn't understood the question. Remetus brandished his knife, hot in his pulsating hand. "Who are you?" he repeated.

Its voice was featherlight.

Here.

The entity motioned from the earth to the sky, slender fingers warped and reaching like tree branches.

Life. Death. It looked at the wolf's emptied carcass. *Eternity.*

"What do you want?" Sweat clung to Remetus' brow.

His head throbbed with the effort of comprehension, grip tightening like a vise on the hilt of the knife.

But the entity ignored this. It reached one elegant, elongated limb toward the dead animal. Its outstretched hand tenderly stroked the wolf's fur.

You have killed us.

A dark undercurrent roiled beneath its words.

"I – I have killed to become ruler," murmured Remetus, eyes darting. "I've followed the old wretch's orders. If this is your beloved beast – if you are so powerful – you'd have stopped me!"

Only you may stop yourself from making death. Help is not our doing.

Remetus gasped, clutching at his heart as a prickling spasm of terror pulled at his spine.

The entity's lips curled upward in the unsettling echo of a smile, yet its eyes remained grave, even ruthless.

Balance is our doing. Punishment.

Pale-faced, Remetus raised his blade, fist trembling.

"Stay away, demon!" he cried in warning, but it burst from him like a plea.

This is impossible, said the entity.

The edges of its figure rippled like water. In one blink, its face had come within an inch of his.

You are within us.

Its gaping mouth opened, swallowing him whole.

CHAPTER 41

Seed moon, waning

Dianna's toes gripped the pebbled river bottom as she waded into a knee-deep current, her dress tied up to keep the ragged hem from getting soaked. She scanned for the telltale flicker of scales in the cold, clear water flowing around her legs.

Her fingers curled around a long, slender branch carved to a fine point at one end. She did not brandish it but held it firm at her side.

At the first sight, she plunged her crude spear down in a splash, followed by a billow of scarlet. An enormous wriggling fish surfaced on the sharp point of the makeshift spear. Its brown-speckled body was broad and many-finned, eyes bulging, mouth agape. One quick strike against a rock and it fell limp.

She said, soft under her breath in the Awl-Fethan tongue, "My gratitude to you, *kil-de-sain.*" Brother-of-the-water.

The rosy light of sunset laced through a leafy canopy over the den. Ram had assumed the rather ordinary task of washing their reserve of clothes in the river and was hanging them to dry. Fredric had scaled a tree and discovered a few hard plums growing at its crown, which he was proudly arranging in a pyramid. Eccka was gone, taking her shift to scout the perimeter.

Aimes had already set to work building a fire, and soon the smell of trout filled the air. They gathered around the flames and ate together, Ram devouring his share like it was his last supper, Fredric gnawing at the sharp, delicate bones.

"Dianna," Ram said in his deep, warm tone, "this is truly a feast fit for nobility."

Fredric dabbed at his mouth daintily. "Pass the marmalade, please."

With a grand gesture, Ram presented him with an imaginary jar.

"And the milk, as well."

Aimes, watching this exchange, gave a shy smile.

Dianna couldn't help smiling back. "But you haven't yet starved, your grace," she said pointedly.

"No," Ram said with a chuckle, stoking the cookfire. "Though we all miss certain comforts of home. One begins to dream of them."

"Mince pie," Fredric moaned between bites. "Fried tomatoes on crispy toast."

"A cold, bitter cask ale," Ram added, his eyes half-closed, while Aimes pulled a face.

"It's deadly good, huntress," Fredric agreed. "Maybe deadlier than Eccka herself."

Dianna looked sidelong at him. "Deadly?"

But Fredric had taken another large bite. "I will say nothing more, as I've divulged too much already," he said thickly.

"Sir," called a woman's voice in the distance, followed by the faint rasping of movement through foliage.

Fredric gulped. "Speak of the demon," he said, grinning.

But Ram stood immediately, his body stiffening.

"Put out the fire, Fredric," he ordered sharply. "Take

the essentials." He broke into a run toward the fringe of trees, the Earthencloak flying behind him like a banner.

Eccka emerged, crashing into him, bracing her hands on his shoulders.

"They're coming," she panted, wild-eyed.

Toward the den, men were scrambling over fallen logs, pushing through thick underbrush, splashing across shallow streambeds. Their faces appeared in slivers between the trees. From their clamor and the beat of horses' hooves, Dianna guessed frantically at their numbers, her heart racing. She snatched up her bow and arrows.

"Sir," Eccka urged again, between gritted teeth.

Ram seized Eccka by the hand and together they sprinted to the den. Mid-stride, Eccka's body plummeted, dragging her clothes in the dirt as she slipped out of them and crumpled into wolf-shape.

"Dianna," Ram cried out, stripping away the Earthencloak and throwing it upon her. Its weight settled over her.

Dianna pulled the still-warm cloth around her, though a cold horror gripped her heart.

Aimes seemed to materialize in front of her, grabbing her shoulders.

"Don't move," he told her, voice hard and snarled and unlike him. "Be earth."

He was beginning to lose himself. Dianna was paralyzed in the glare of his yellow eyes.

"Stay. With. Me," he said, and wrenched into unbeing.

CHAPTER 42

Seed moon, waning

Swathed in the Earthencloak, Dianna vaulted herself onto Aimes' back, burying her face in his wolf's ruff.

And they were flying, plunging through the woods like a wildfire, chaotic and unyielding. Dianna pressed her weight into the wolf, legs gripping his panting belly, arms encircling his neck. Low sunlight shifted through the delicate veined pattern of the leaf-laced cloak.

Through thrashing wind, she heard the muffled shouts of hunters in pursuit. The shriek of disturbed birds. Thick and fast, the groan and slap of a fired crossbow.

Aimes' claws furrowed into the dirt, turning hard. Two bolts whistled past his flank. The glint of sunlight on metal blinded Dianna fleetingly, an image of death burned into her eyes.

Aimes lunged into a thick patch of underbrush. Dianna reached to yank the Earthencloak closer as it quivered around her, but it was like trying to catch a butterfly on the wing.

One corner snagged on brambles, ripping the edge of it. As she turned, her hair free and churning in her face, she saw several torn leaves flap into the whisking wind and melt into the greenery.

Aimes' panting breaths mingled with the dense beating of hooves behind them. Again, Dianna felt brambles tug at the cloak's edge. She risked another glance, and her heart skipped.

Not brambles, but a hunter's hand, thick fingers grasping. His galloping mount drew up alongside them, blowing and white-eyed.

The cloak's cowl fluttered against Dianna's face. She clung to the writhing wolf's body by fistfuls of fur as the hunter hovered above her, gaping with frenzied amazement.

"She's here!" cried the hunter. "She—"

Aimes leapt. Dianna recoiled as the wolf's mouth engulfed the hunter's head and *pulled*.

A snarl split the air; a warm spray fell. She blinked, spitting bitter iron. The hunter's body slid from its steed, fell behind in a heavy thud of leather and bone.

A jarring thud shook her as Aimes stumbled, and she plummeted, crashing into bushes. The wind tore from her chest in a rough gasp. The bone in her shoulder slackened from its socket on impact. Balled on her side, she choked with a howl of pain.

Her outcry was swallowed by the screams of men – at first monstrous, then incomprehensible wails of anguish. But one hunter's voice rose, his final words running like a thread through the thick of the clamor, bellowing from his lungs:

And he shall smite the wicked
and he shall deliver the true man, the long-shielding
man—

There was a barrage of wet, ripping sounds, the hollow baying of wolves, horses' squeals and galloping strides fading away.

Hidden in the dark forks of the shrub, Dianna lay

279

flattened on her belly, biting back tears. The hot, knife-sharp ache rippled from her shoulder to her neck. Her muscles clenched with the yearning to move, to fight, but the wolf had huddled itself firmly at her center.

She squeezed her eyes shut, pulling the Earthencloak around her. The lone hunter's prayer became rasping, almost staccato.

And if man shields his bloodkind from wickedness in the name of Mactus,
he shall be marked bloodkind of Mactus—

Dianna's fingers roamed, catching on crooked twigs, mashing in sodden leaves. They found a hard, roughened surface. She wormed her fingers into the earth and pried loose an oblong stone.

The squelched rending of flesh punctured the air. The hunter reciting the orison faltered; his tongue seemed to stick as he screamed.

From wickedness – from wickedness—

The visceral symphony ended, and all was silent.

Dianna pushed herself up, snagging her dress in the underbrush, brandishing the stone.

At the sight before her, she dropped it. It plodded, dull and heavy, as her heart sank into her stomach.

Four men lay face down in the dirt, almost as though asleep. But their limbs splayed at odd angles, and scarlet pooled from them, and their battered armor cluttered the mud. A mangled severed hand had landed nearby, pulped by teeth.

In the center of the massacre, his bare skin pale as milk, Aimes stood human and alone. His breath heaved from his chest once, twice. The snarl suspended on his mouth closed slowly. Blood dripped from his chin; a yellow luster ebbed from his irises. He spat aside.

Dianna swayed on her feet, clutching her displaced shoulder, and he was beside her.

"I'm sorry, Dianna," he gasped. "I'm sorry – I've got you – hold still."

Dianna barely comprehended him. Her mind was distant, floating.

He worked one hand under her arm and another just above her ribcage. In one agile pull, he shifted her arm to settle seamlessly against the joint.

Dianna screamed and saw stars as her legs buckled beneath her. Hot tears streamed into her hair, and she tasted rust as she bit her own lip.

Aimes knelt, brushing away her tears with his thumbs. "I've got you," he murmured. "You're safe now."

She nodded, rigid with shock, breath fluttering in her throat.

"You're safe now," Aimes repeated, but this did not lighten the leaden cold feeling in her gut.

Dusk had begun to fall. Fredric's trembling call came phantomlike from the trees.

"Everyone please follow my voice," he said. "Ram's been shot."

Chapter 43

Seed moon, waning

Ram gritted his teeth as Eccka pulled the bolt from his abdomen. A fierce growl heaved from his throat.

Immediately, Aimes applied a crude compress to the wound, bearing down with both arms. Ram's blood welled swiftly between his fingers.

Dianna sat motionlessly beside Fredric, watching. A pain needled her now, deeper than the ache of her throbbing shoulder. Dianna the huntress, Fredric had called her – but guilt, that scornful voice, snarled: *Dianna, harbinger of death.*

At length, Ram's breath evened. The grimace straining his mouth receded into a mask of calm again.

"I'm all right," he assured them.

But Aimes remained crouched at his side, hands folded over Ram's ribs like they held his heartbeat.

Ram reached up. Touched Aimes' shoulder.

"I'm all right, son," he murmured. "You can let go now."

Aimes blinked, his hands shaking as he released the pressure and backed away.

Ram rose, one hand absently touching the muscled ridges of his mended flank. Dark and stoic, he began rifling through the underbrush for the driest bits of tinder he could find, piling them together.

Fredric had led them to a remote pocket where they could rest for the night. On the banks of a nearby streambed, Eccka began to wash the film of earth and death from her skin.

Aimes came to kneel beside Dianna. With a healer's gentle touch, he used a cloth to daub blood from her cheek.

"You were about to Fall," he said, tentative. "But the change was uneven – it dislocated your shoulder."

Dianna looked into his human eyes, trying to see the same animal that struck those men lifeless.

"You killed them," she whispered.

"They would have killed us," Eccka said as she leaned over the stream, dousing her own face with cold water. "You see what we are to them? We're vermin. *Fiiskavt*."

Dianna glanced at Fredric. For once he had nothing to say, staring at his bloodstained palms like they were not his own.

Perhaps they had forgotten, she thought, that dead men left dead trails – widows, fatherless children. But Eccka straightened, wiping her face clean. Her harsh undertone split the silence.

"You can't help Awl-Feth anymore," she said. "You can't."

Dianna was motionless, the chill night air numbing her skin, knowing she was right. Ram's hand came to rest on her arm, and his voice was solid and warm.

"Some of the men fled," he said. "They know now that we can Fall at will."

Fredric managed to find his voice, a dismayed mutter, as his gaze remained fixed on his hands.

"We couldn't escape," he said. "We couldn't escape, because the rifts felt . . . wrong. Some were just gone. Like they're closing."

The others looked at the navigator in tense silence. His

usual merry laugh emerged little more than a nervous quaver.

"Well, the jig is up," he said. "I suppose we can all go home now."

His joke fell flat in the air. Ram began pacing, staring into the dusky sky.

"This is worse than I feared," he said.

"We need to form a strategy, sir," said Eccka.

Ram nodded, distracted as the beginnings took shape in his mind. Dianna's eyes followed his long and deliberate strides, as though only constant movement could keep his mind at ease.

"We need to find a new site to make camp," he said. "Somewhere far off the hunters' trail."

Fredric had already begun tracing his fingers in the earth as smooth and quick as brushstrokes, sketching a map of their course. Ram hovered by his shoulder, brow furrowed.

"This is the position of our den," Fredric said when he finished, tapping a spot on the ground. "The hunters infiltrated from the east. Now, this trade route winds directly through the woods from the edge of Awl-Feth, and another here." He indicated a pathway bordering the village. "This comes to intersect with the former at this point. If the rifts are indeed closing to us, and direction is all we have left, this would be the easiest passageway through Silbarran on foot."

"The easiest, but not the wisest," interjected Eccka.

"Why not?" Dianna asked.

"Well, *hauntoun*," retorted Eccka, "the easiest passage is also the most obvious. If the hunters are planning another ambush, they'll make headway off the beaten path. They'll conceal their heads and blot their breathing and cover their tracks. Like ghosts."

"Eccka speaks from experience," Ram said, stroking his jaw.

"Or," Fredric said, "they'll anticipate us, and take the opposite path we assume they would."

"It is safer to assume they anticipate everything," Ram said, voice darkening. "They attacked in broad daylight. And I'm afraid our best responsive maneuver is also the most dangerous for us."

He and Eccka exchanged knowing glances. Her cropped hair fluttered in the passing breeze, black as a raven. For a second, Ram's gaze followed the wavering tendrils.

"We have to split up," he said.

From the corner of her eye, Dianna thought Aimes bristled.

Eccka gave a firm nod. "I can work alone, sir."

"I know," Ram said. "Because of that, it's not your protection that immediately concerns me."

Eccka's lip curled and her eyes flashed. "Are you suggesting I bring the *hauntoun*?"

"She hunts as well as you. She won't slow you down."

Dianna kept her doubts to herself, avoiding Eccka's piercing eyes.

"You two will head eastward. Fredric will shadow you at your left flank, here." On the map, Ram trailed his finger parallel to their course. "Aimes and I will keep to the trade routes. We will not abandon post unless you give the signal. Fredric will act as a go-between and lay low. Eccka, if the hunters reach you first, and we are still absent—"

"I take their heads," she growled.

"You must protect Dianna at all costs," Ram ordered. "Clear?"

"You said she could fend for herself."

"I said she won't slow you down. That is different."

Eccka glowered, but Aimes was the first to object.

"I can go with them," he said.

"You will not," Ram asserted. "Dianna will be Eccka's

charge, and Eccka will take the lead."

"But if—"

"Do you distrust that I will do anything to keep you alive?" Ram said under his breath.

"No," Aimes said at last, strained. He lowered his head.

Ram stared at Aimes for a moment longer. "Would anyone else care to voice their misgivings?"

"What about the supplies?" Fredric asked. "If we can manage them?"

"Fire and water," Ram said. "And weapons. Everything else must be left behind."

"We still need to stake out our territory," Aimes pressed. "In case we need to regroup. If Dianna and Eccka get separated—"

"Fine," Eccka snapped. "I'll piss on a tree."

Aimes' eyes ignited into a blaze of gold, and a growl issued from his throat. Eccka narrowed her eyes at this display, folding her sleek-muscled arms.

"Aimes," Dianna said softly, hoping to comfort him, but a note of distress broke her voice. "It's all right."

Aimes' eyes oscillated before settling on blue. He sank back on his heels but looked sickly pale.

"Then we're agreed. For now, there's nothing else we can do," Ram said, turning away with a sweep of his cloak. "Let's move."

Eccka rounded on Dianna, sizing her up in a curt look.

"We don't know how many hunters are tracking us, so I'm your eyes from now on," she said.

Dianna nodded, her heart sinking.

"May Faeralis guide us," Fredric wished upon them as he took leave. "Be swift, my family. Be safe."

"Be safe," Aimes echoed. His parting glance lingered on Dianna as they set out into the dusk.

CHAPTER 44

Seed moon, waning

Eccka vaulted over bramble and brush, seamless as an unraveling thread, forging ahead without mercy. Dianna felt clumsy following her surefooted course, shouldering her bow, traction hampered by the mush of dampened sod.

"Can you slow down?" she panted, scrambling over the knotted log across their path.

"I stayed human so we could speak, *hauntoun*," Eccka said, without as much as a glance over her shoulder. "Believe me, we're moving slowly enough as it is."

But as they reached a rugged thicket on the outskirts of a small, treeless patch of the woods, Eccka dropped soundlessly to the ground.

She motioned Dianna over, and together they hunkered behind a thick mesh of ferns.

"Don't go further," Eccka said in an undertone. "They're over there."

Blinking through the fine-toothed leaves, Dianna tried to catch a glimpse of the approaching strangers in the dusk.

"Where?"

"Smell," Eccka reminded her impatiently. "Listen."

Dianna sniffed at the muddy air, distinguishing

between the new scents: leather, metal, sweat. Her ears picked up the vibrations of low murmurs, the dull plod of footfalls, the scrape of cloth. About five men.

Like the trees themselves had come alive, soldiers moved into the clearing. Their hands were gloved in black, their faces shadowed by short hooded mantles.

Each man was uniformed in plate and forest green clothing, rivaling the Earthencloak's power of disguise. The lightweight plate armor that adorned their backs and shoulders was a sleek, innovative construction Dianna had never seen. One that even Liam could not forge. They swept across the clearing like a wave, breaking and reforming without even a command.

They all bore swords.

"Oh," Eccka said in a strange tone.

"They're not hunters," Dianna whispered. "Who are they?"

But Eccka had gone quiet, seeming uncertain. But the strain in her spine and fixed eyes said otherwise. She knew very well.

"*Tharknas,*" she whispered.

Dianna did not recognize the word. Her knuckles were white, gripping her bow.

Eccka lifted a leather-gloved hand to bend back the ferns, peering into the clearing. Her inclined head exposed the inky symbols striping her slender neck.

Dianna's eyes widened. "Eccka . . ."

"I can handle them."

"You're unarmed!"

"I'll need my hands for this."

"*Hands?*" Dianna was stunned. "If you're going to fight them, why don't you Fall? You'd be stronger than they are!"

"I *am* stronger than they are."

Dianna blinked. She slid her bow from her shoulder. "I can cover you."

Eccka huffed a soundless laugh. "Not a chance in hell."

"I'm a good shot." Dianna's teeth grit as she struggled to keep her voice composed. "I've seen death, Eccka. At least let me help."

"Listen, girl," Eccka hissed, rounding on her. "You are beyond your ken here. Have you been in the thick of battle? Have you smelled the panic?"

Beneath Eccka's intense stare, Dianna shook her head.

"A huntress is not a warrior," Eccka said underneath her breath, and with an air of finality, turned to her vantage point. "Stay here."

Dianna bit back her reply. She shrank back into the shadows but kept a firm grip on her bow, resolving to watch for unsuspecting heads.

With a catlike grace, Eccka slipped from her hiding place, the ferns rustling after her.

Her presence disrupted the stealthy convoy at once. Some soldiers shouted, poising their swords for combat. Others, seeing only a woman lost in the woods, looked to their commander for instruction.

Eccka balanced light on her feet as a dancer but held her strong arms in a fighting stance. Dianna's instincts said to flee, to call out for Fredric, do anything to spare herself the guilt of watching the other woman die a grisly death.

"Move," she whispered, but Eccka remained rooted to the spot.

The soldiers circled Eccka, their formation smooth and coordinated.

Peering into the distance, Dianna spotted subtle movement on the edge of the clearing. She heard the locking of a bolt into a crossbow. *A hunter.*

"Move!" she cried into her fist.

A soldier at the forefront approached Eccka with a steady tread. He studied her from beneath his mantle, moving within her range.

"Woman," he called out. "You should not be here."

But Eccka did not retreat. The soldier stopped short, as if he couldn't believe his eyes. As if catching a glimpse of the inky marking on her neck.

The first kill was quick, efficient, spilling little blood.

Eccka's fist had found its mark at his throat. The force flattened him like a felled tree in a smack of flesh. Steadily, precisely, she stamped hard on his neck.

Immediately, soldiers broke from the fold, rushing at Eccka.

And the onslaught began.

Chapter 45

Seed moon, waning

Eccka dropped low to the ground, knocking the feet out from under one of the advancing men. Looking up, she seemed to hear the distant hunter's movements among the trees. In her distraction, a soldier landed a hard kick to her gut.

Dianna caught her breath as Eccka gasped, crumpling forward against the earth.

The soldier descended. Eccka whirled around, bashing him in the face with a stone she had scooped from the ground. She glanced around, and Dianna saw the bright flash of her bared teeth, her eyes burning – but not with the bloodthirsty rage she expected. It was a detached ruthlessness, more terrifying than the High Elder's zealous glare or Actaen's cruel sneer.

The hunter was in full view, taking aim at Eccka. But a third soldier closed in on her first, swiping his sword, outmatched by her dodges. She ducked, grabbed him by the shoulders and wheeled him around.

The hunter pulled the crossbow's trigger at that precise moment. The bolt buried itself in her captured opponent's back, and she seized his sword before it fell from his grasp. Throwing his body aside, Eccka eyed the surrounding combatants.

"You can do better!" she cried out through bared teeth.

The roar of fighting thickened the air as the soldiers engulfed her.

Heart racing, Dianna attempted a headcount: three had converged; one hunter remained at long range; two men already lay dead. One soldier crossed swords with Eccka once, twice, in a clash of metal. Dianna lost sight of her amid flashes of limbs and the crush of bodies.

She was drowning in battle.

Dianna's fingers found soft fletching and pulled a single arrow from its quiver. Her eyes did not break from the scene.

There was a sharp scrape of blades, and Eccka's unmistakable snarl of anguish ripped through the clearing.

Dianna aimed her bow into the tangle of struggling figures and fired true. The thud of the arrow in a soldier's neck and his gurgling choke rewarded her.

The hunter on the fringes of the battle had paused, dropping his crossbow. Beneath his dark cowl, his keen eyes traced a path toward the trees where Dianna took cover.

She realized, with a shock as cold as river water submerging her, that her arrow's flight had betrayed her position.

Her fingers fumbled to catch another arrow into the bow's notch. She set her sights on the hunter, gritting her teeth, knowing she would never achieve a clean shot at him through the leaves.

Breaking through snatching branches, she darted into the clearing and took aim.

The hunter watched her with a look of dawning comprehension, crossbow level again. "Aergyris," he bellowed from afar, features tightened like something foul had passed his lips.

It was not his poised weapon which made Dianna's breath hitch in her throat. Nor was it the anger in her name, though she heard it on a visceral depth, under her skin, in the marrow of her bones.

It was the hunter's disgusted expression. In it she recognized the features of her father's friend and delegate, a man who had once patrolled alongside him.

She lowered her bow by a hair.

Eccka's muffled cry shattered the air. "Dianna!"

"Your father was a traitor," the hunter said. His arm was steady, his words hard and prepared as they carried on the wind. "You murdered my son."

"Ledras," Dianna hailed him, holding his gaze. At the corner of her eye she glimpsed the ridge of a rock large enough for cover.

She let her stance fall in a slow, controlled movement. Slipped her bowstring across her shoulder. Raised her hands as if in surrender.

The hunter regarded her like she was mad.

"I am one of your people," she said.

The blows of swords and rallying calls seemed to fade away. Ledras' hand tensed on the lathe.

"No," he said through gritted teeth. "You're an abomination."

He released the bolt.

Dianna ducked low.

She tried to move like Eccka, like a snake in the grass, as she crawled fast toward the rock. Ledras cursed her and quickly drew another bolt.

Dianna threw herself against the rock's broad side, gasping for breath. She eased the bow from her shoulder and peered around the edge of her cover.

Ledras, remaining at long range, made the mistake of firing upon sight.

Dianna recoiled at the stark rasp of bolt against stone. A bewildered laugh burst from her, because she knew that he would be taking a beat to reload, leaving him vulnerable. The moment was hers.

She twisted around the edge of her cover, nocked arrow at the ready, but the hunter fired again in quick succession. With an outcry she jumped back, slamming into the rock.

The bolt skimmed within inches of her, landing instead in the mud at her feet. It may as well have hit her, stopped her heart, bled out all assurance.

In her anticipation, she had forgotten her father's most important teaching. This man was no target, no deer in the forest.

"You killed my son!" Ledras roared. "She-wolf! Bitch!"

Dianna's skin was alive with a cold sweat, seeping through her clothes. A deep breath rattled through her as she clenched the bow tighter in her shaking fist.

A fleeting memory of her father passed over her like a breaking tide, icy and bracing. She gathered the fine bowstring in her fingertips.

"Line them up," she whispered.

Turning around the stone, she released her arrow a stroke too soon, missing her mark, and retreated as quick as a mole to its burrow.

"Damn it," she murmured, exhaling, and tried again.

They traded shots. Ledras kept his post, watching for a sign of her, triggering always a heartbeat too late. Dianna swallowed her fear like a stone, hearing Eccka's battle cries split the air.

The tactile familiarity of the final arrow held her only remaining hope. Raising her bow, she rounded the corner for the last time, victory welling in her chest.

But he wasn't there.

She heard the rapid cadence of feet upon the ground. Ledras came sprinting from her periphery, hunting knife in hand. Dianna shrank back against the stone, her heart hammering. Throwing herself upon the mercy of her aim, she freed her bowstring.

Ledras cried out, stumbling. Her last arrow pierced his

arm, and the knife fell from his grasp, landing behind him. Hate twisted his mouth and burned in his eyes as he rushed forward at her.

Dianna scrambled for a stone or a stick, for something to throw or block with, for anything.

He lunged at her, slipping in the grass. The force of his weight sent her crashing hard to the ground, even as she pushed him away. She struck the dirt hard, breath knocked from her lungs.

Her trembling hands flew to her head, feeling the warm creep of blood over her scalp. Before she could find her feet, she found her body pinned.

The hunter's arrow-struck arm remained slack, vulnerable, but his other fist was strong as he beat her. Dianna screamed, unable to shield herself.

With each battering blow, something began to break inside her, splintering like glass. Desperately she grabbed for the arrow in his arm, wrenching it out with all her strength.

Ledras fell back howling in pain, freeing her. With the blunt end of the arrow shaft, she struck his throat, stifling his cries, and broke away. On her hands and knees, she felt the grass madly for his knife.

The world lurched as his boot struck her side.

She was thrown onto her back, seized by the neck. The wolf quivered in her gut, and a snarl throttled her chest as she thrashed in his grasp. Ledras' face swam before her, his features cold and hard-edged.

Another sensation, chilling and barren, closed the flow of blood through her body.

Death.

Fear rocked through her. She was conscious of it, like a precipice of rough stone beneath her feet. An icy black sea sloshed below.

Her senses began to slip away. The figure of Ledras

sank into darkness. His grip tamped down the scream in her throat.

The wolf pressed at her chest, nudging forward, slavering to emerge. But a cold thought pushed it back.

Why fight it anymore? Why try to Fall, when this life demands your death at every turn?

You are the wounded quail, Dianna. You know that. It's easier to end it now.

Death is easier.

Her heartbeat flickered, fading. Her legs kicked uselessly in the dirt.

A sound like sodden clothing ripping in two, a body toppling aside. The gleaming edge of Eccka's sword rising, dripping.

Dianna's airways opened again, and life seeped back into her unfeeling limbs.

Flat-eyed, Eccka tossed the bloody weapon aside. She slicked her short black hair, like the veil of Death's mistress, from her blood-peppered face. Blades had grazed her strong arms open.

Dropping to her knees, she hauled the body of Ledras aside and immediately grabbed the back of Dianna's head, exposing her throat. Dianna felt the biting pull of hair at the nape of her neck.

Eccka's bruised eye was inches from Dianna's face, her breath hot and spitting.

"You would have died!" she seethed, shaking her. "You disobeyed my order! You would have died, do you hear me?"

Dianna pressed her lips against the whimpers in her burning throat.

"Did you *want* to die?" Eccka yelled at her.

"No," Dianna gasped.

"*Did you?*"

"No!"

"Then say it!" Eccka snarled, eyes ablaze. "I don't believe it until you say it!"

"No, I want to live!" Dianna cried, tears falling freely now, waves of relief crashing over her.

She looked at Eccka through stinging eyes and could only think of Liam. Liam, if he had found her with the vial of poison in her open palm. Liam, holding her cold body to his chest as he wept.

An-An. I was supposed to keep you safe.

"I want to live now," Dianna said again, the refrain moving through her breath as if awakening her from a deep slumber. "I want to live."

Eccka struck her across the face hard enough that she would feel the hot pang of it long after.

"You are stupid and insolent, and you don't deserve my protection," she growled.

Her eyes searched Dianna's blood-matted hair and upturned face. Dianna thought her steady glare served only to further intimidate, until she realized it was to check for mortal wounds.

Once satisfied, Eccka released Dianna, stood, and turned away. Dianna wanted nothing more than to lie upon the ground, even as the body of Ledras bled out beside her.

But she looked up at Eccka, who remained square-shouldered, facing away.

"I'm—" Dianna began.

"Don't say you're sorry," Eccka hissed. "You protect yourself from now on."

Dianna wiped blood from her gashed lip. "You're leaving me here?"

"No. You said you want to live."

"What?"

"You want to live." Eccka's tone was final. "And on your head be it. Gather your arrows."

Dianna waited for Eccka to turn around. Instead the woman resumed their journey without a word, expecting Dianna to follow.

She did.

CHAPTER 46

Seed moon, waning

A wolf bounded into view amongst the trees, bottlebrush tail flagged. Dianna and Eccka turned around as Fredric lurched into human shape, giving a cursory shake of his head.

"Had to hedge past a cavalry back there," he panted, removing a water skin wound several times around his neck and offering it. "What happened? Are you hurt badly?"

"Flesh wounds," Eccka said, taking a long and hearty draft. Her lacerated arms glistened with sweat, and her tunic was soaked red. At last she took a pause to tend to herself, passing the water to Dianna.

"Gentle-heart?"

"I'm fine, thank you, Fredric," Dianna said, taking a drink with shaking fingers and spilling some.

"Will you be safe for now?" Fredric asked Eccka.

With her teeth, Eccka ripped a strip of her own clothing to bind one of her worst cuts. She scanned the treetops with eyes narrowed to slits.

"I can take it from here," she said. "Go back to Ram. Tell him I've got his back covered, but to keep his fangs sharp, anyway. Tell him not to come back for us now. And do not come back yourself. Understood?"

"Understood. Then when?"

"Sun-up." Eccka's eyes still searched the skyline.

Fredric's eyes glinted like gold in answer as he turned and Fell. The great wolf loped away, receding into the greenery.

***

Two wolves explored the perimeter of the patch of woods, their bloodied snouts snuffling close to the ground, slender legs plucking over the uneven terrain. The bodies of hunters lay scattered on the forest floor, dark and mangled among dead leaves and broken twigs. Heavy sheets of rain had begun to fall, washing away the blood.

One wolf trembled and shrank in size, shedding his coat, its shape whittling into Ram's.

"You need to heal yourself," he told Aimes at once, through the lashing rain. "Come back."

The second wolf balked, ears flat against its skull, and Ram gave him a pointed look.

"Come back, Son," he repeated carefully.

Bones shifted, sinew unraveled and contracted, and Aimes emerged smooth as marble beneath the coarse pelt. He tamped a hand over his wounded shoulder, blood seeping fast through his fingers.

"A scratch," he said, tearing up a handful of damp greenery and twisting it around his injury. "The hunters are slow. And clumsy."

"Yes. But there were many." Ram retraced his steps, prodding in the mud until the Earthencloak's leafy texture met his fingers. He settled it upon his shoulders.

"One still lives," Aimes said, pointing. "There."

Ram searched through the thick rain and darkness, following the direction. Several feet away, the fallen hunter moaned, clutching his broken leg. The shattered mechanisms of his crossbow littered the ground.

Ram let fall his cowl and stood at the hunter's side, staring down into his face with a kind of pity, a crease forming between his brows. The hunter's eyes grew white around the edges.

"Prince . . ." he choked between uneven breaths, confusion muddling his voice.

"Ram," Ram finished for him.

Rivulets of rain streamed over the hunter's gaping face, his breath forming ragged mists.

"Prince Ram," he echoed in mocking awe, mirthless laughter gurgling in his throat. "A demon."

But Ram remained straight-faced. "Why did the High Elder send you now?"

The hunter merely glowered. "Mactus will strike you down if we cannot. Your wicked disease will not save you."

"He sent you to stake out the woods, didn't he?" Ram persisted. "How many are you?"

"Rot in hell."

"How many are you?" Ram snarled, pressing his bare heel against the hunter's mangled leg. The hunter cried out through ashen lips.

"Go on," urged Ram.

"A . . . a century!"

Ram's eyes widened as he paused, lost for words. Aimes watched on like a hawk, the rain sluicing his bare shoulders, his dark hair straggling around his face and his damp trousers clinging to his legs.

"*Tharknas* is with us," the hunter panted as Ram hovered over him. "We arrived in . . . squadrons. The rest . . ." He cringed and clutched at his wound. "The rest will come later."

Ram's fist seized at the man's mantle, his demand emerging thunderous: "When?"

"Just before the next full moon," gasped the hunter.

"And what are your orders?"

300

"Kill the demons. Kill them all."

Ram released his hold on the man and rocked backward, his face wan.

The hunter turned sideways, sputtering into the mud. But a glimmer of malice, unseen in the dark, twisted his features. His hand slipped beneath his mantle, withdrawing a dagger.

Aimes Fell like a stone out of his clothes and hurtled forward at breakneck speed, snatching upon the man's figure.

"Aimes, no!" shouted Ram, but the wolf was already on him, worrying into his throat. The hunter's body thrashed against the ground, going still in seconds.

Ram marched toward the snarling beast, grabbing him by the scruff of his neck. The wolf rooted its paws into the earth, black lips peeled away to bare blood-foamed fangs. Ram looked him square in the eyes, fear and anger heightening his tone.

"Damn it, Aimes! Your life is more precious than mine!"

The wolf shrank until the young man's body took form, and Ram had him by a fistful of his disheveled black hair. Consciousness, like sunlight breaking through a storm-choked sky, returned to Aimes' features. The yellow eyes receded into blue, and the wild curl of his lips softened.

"He was—" He gasped. "He was going to kill you."

Ram's eyes were fixed on Aimes, glistening with tears. A grimace strained his mouth.

"You are more precious to me, Son," he said, with a conviction that shook his voice. "You must be more careful."

He let go and stood back. Disappearing beneath his cowl, he looked down at the dead hunter and nodded in heavy resignation at last.

"It's been done," he said, and he led the way back to their camp.

CHAPTER 47

Seed moon, waning

Dianna and Eccka began setting up camp in silence, improvising bedding from a dense carpet of toothy beech leaves. The sky had blackened to pitch, and a haze of rainclouds obscured the stars.

In the underbrush, Dianna caught a wild bird with her hands, though they were still shaking. She broke its neck with a whispered recognition for its life.

She plucked the bird clean, the feathers tacky on her fingertips. With flint and steel, Eccka lit a fire on the first strike and nurtured it with her breath.

Dianna roasted the meat with elderberries and cut up an assortment of roots with Eccka's hunting knife. The unbroken quiet became smothering. Sitting opposite the stoic woman, Dianna doled out their steaming supper onto crude planks of bark.

Eccka's almond eyes watched. Without a word she plucked at a root and devoured it, mouth taut as she tasted the complex flavor.

She asked, "What do you call this?"

"Just a peasant dish," Dianna said after a beat, hesitant to speak for fear of Eccka's wrath. "From the village. Have you not had wild grouse?"

"Not like this," Eccka said, working away the meat from

a wing bone. Under her breath she added, "I suppose Awl-Feth's traditions taught you something of value."

It was about as close as Eccka had come to expressing gratitude to her. Dianna suppressed her astonishment as she picked at her meal.

"They did not teach me how to hide or how to hunt," she said. "Those I learned from my family."

Eccka regarded the young huntress with a dubious slant to her lips. Her tongue darted over them once as she polished off the wing and flung the bones into the fire.

"How did the High Elder discover you?" she asked outright.

Dianna paused at the suddenness of this question.

"I attacked someone," she said. "I . . . I wanted to die."

Eccka gave a curt nod and looked into the fire, as if thinking, *Stupid.*

"He'd threatened me," Dianna said, a flame in her throat burning hot with the memory of his voice, his hands. "All of us, the women . . . Cathrin, and—"

Eccka's head snapped up.

"Cathrin Talin?" she asked. Her eyes bored through her.

"Yes."

"Is she all right? Did he hurt her? I'll kill that goddamned *fiiskavt,*" Eccka snarled.

Dianna looked at Eccka as though seeing her for the first time, remembering Cathrin's words: *They'll make you, you know. Like my cousin. That's why she ran away. And she will burn in hellfire for it.*

The fire crackled, its heat shimmering over the hardened features of Cathrin's long-lost cousin.

"She's safe now," Dianna said, glancing away, yet certain the truth was plain on her face. Eccka's eyes widened in realization.

"You killed him," she said, and her voice was higher, taken aback.

Dianna didn't respond immediately. Eccka regarded her with a strange expression that, for once, did not resemble loathing.

"I killed several hunters," Dianna whispered then. "Men of my village – men whose names I had known. I killed her own father. I loved her dearly, and I wanted them dead."

Eccka set aside the last of her supper. She leaned forward, dark skin sweltering in the fire's intensity. A full minute passed before she spoke another word.

"I was thirteen when my uncle sold me to an Awl-Fethan tradesman," she said.

Dianna held her gaze, but Eccka's features formed a hard mask of apathy. She did not wish for pity.

"I was a beggar from the slums," said Eccka. "My parents died of fever, and I was their only child. I went to live with my uncle in Awl-Feth, but he had little Cathrin. To him, one girl was one too many. And the tradesman offered a bounty. So he sold me.

"The man who called himself my husband was much older. He was also a drunkard." Spitting flames danced in her dark eyes. "I hid from him when I could. Until one night, I found courage. I knocked him out cold with drink, disguised myself, and stole away in the night."

"Where . . ." Dianna faltered. "Where did you go?"

"Nowhere in particular, for a time," Eccka said. "And then to L'Heste. I saw their soldiers marching through the village one day. They looked strong. Like they would die fighting. And I decided that I would be one of them."

Dianna thought of her father in his armor, kissing her goodbye before the hunt when she was young. How she'd wrapped his traveling cloak around her shoulders, sinking under the warm fabric, awake through the night until he returned.

"So, you disguised yourself," she said.

"For a long time," Eccka said, voice thick with

remembering. "It was not without great difficulty – I spoke low and infrequently, under the ruse of a non-native tongue. I bound my breasts with cloth. I would bathe only at the blackest hour of night. I kept to myself and trained constantly, like any good soldier. That I should escape a life of obedience only to commit myself to another – I once thought this the only way of womanhood.

"One does not easily become admitted to the legion. They first held trials. Many of the High Echelon hated me from the beginning. I was a newcomer to their territory, an outsider. But over time, some of my comrades became my closest companions. One was Pallix. Perhaps he understood me, being of the Short Echelon himself, and the runt of the litter. We cut our teeth sparring together. I threw him every time." Her gleaming smile spread with a fiendish fondness. "The one time he defeated me, he said something that made me falter, giving him the victory. He said, 'I know your secret.'

"I knew it was over. Knew I'd trusted him too much. The Centurion would reward him for turning me in and kill me.

"But instead, he doffed his helm and knelt before me. He recognized my strength as a warrior and my fealty as a friend. To him, the fact of my sex did not change this. He vowed to keep my secret until his dying day. And so he did.

"We ranked Half Echelon in just under five years of training. That was the time the Caenani declared war on Myre." A shadow passed over her voice. "They conscripted a select few of us. Pallix was one. I was never given the chance to prove my worth in battle, to defend the empire. But I heard that he fought valiantly. He was the best of them, Pallix.

"I vowed to live with bravery as he had died. Where he fell, I would rise." She touched the tattoo on her neck. "For six more years I trained. These insignia mark my rank among the legion's finest."

"You became High Echelon?"

"High Echelon of the cohort *Tharknas*."

Eccka's steely eyes were powerful in the fire's gleam.

"Now you know how I knew to kill those men," she said. "Because I was one of them. I didn't Fall to fight them because I wanted them to see me when they died – me, the woman – to know they had been defeated by an equal. To give them honorable deaths."

"But you said you were stronger," Dianna said. "High Echelon. Doesn't that make you unequal?"

"In skill, yes, but not in courage. And though I became strong, it was not because I joined the legion. It was because I chose strength. That is the difference between us and Awl-Fethans, Dianna. They think there is no other choice but to swallow the High Elder's poison. But I feared for Cathrin because it is all she knows. And I . . ." Eccka paused, closing her eyes. "I cannot change this. So, I have failed her."

Her face was empty of sentiment behind the crackling embers, but her voice was full of a trembling sorrow, striking in its familiarity.

Dianna could think only of Liam's hammer forging her cage, its rhythm like a heartbeat, as though containing her from the world could keep her alive. How her foolishness had betrayed him.

"I know it destroys you," she said, softly.

There was another long, unbroken silence.

"Do you think she can be happy?" Eccka asked at last. "Do you think I can save her now?"

Dianna's heart sank like a stone.

"I don't know," she said. "But I think she is brave, like you. And living is the bravest thing we can do."

Eccka nodded, and one hand flew to her face and whisked her cheek.

"After the princes disappeared," she said, "I had to see her again. See how she'd grown. I deserted my post under a

306

full moon, hoping the light would guide my way. Was I a fool? But then the whispers of demons prowling Silbarran were only that . . . whispers."

Eccka looked away, into the fire.

"I came to with one ear mangled, ribs broken, and my gut gouged by tooth and claw. Short of breath and hazy of mind. No one else around," she said dismissively, denoting the end of her story. She swallowed a hearty mouthful of the water skin, as if she wasn't used to talking for so long.

"What happened after? How did you come to know Ram?"

Eccka's stiffening posture suggested this was not a welcome line of inquiry. She lowered the water skin. Her chin lifted, defining her high cheekbones in the fire's glow, exposing the tattoo on her slender neck.

"What happened is that we endured," she said, low. "Aimes may be a sad, mad bastard mooncalf, but he's right. The wolf has only ever aided our survival. And Ram makes decisions for us, and he has made the best he can. There is more to him than you know – more to him than *he* knows – and more than I can ever explain now. I owe him my life, and I would die for him."

Dianna paused, lost in thought as Eccka's words suspended between them.

"More to him," she repeated. "Is that why you call him 'sir,' like a Centurion?"

Eccka's eyes flashed like dark jewels. Her voice was curt again, snapping as quick as sparks.

"Ram and I are bound. Do not ask me how. One of us needs to keep watch for the night."

"I don't sleep well."

"Good." Eccka stretched out on the ground, turning her head away.

Settling into her own scrubby bed of leaves and peat moss, Dianna did not bother to quench the fire.

It began to rain. Dianna drew the lush mist-and-balsam scent into her lungs and felt droplets fall into her hair. She sat awake listening to its drumming, high in the beech boughs, thick and viscous on the earth below. Like muffled thunder, Eccka's voice emerged through it.

"I was wrong," she said.

Dianna turned to face her. "About what?"

But Eccka was on her side with her back toward her, and although the curvature of her body was visible, her expression remained unknown.

"You are not a *hauntoun*," was all that she said, wearily.

CHAPTER 48

Flower moon, new

Eccka was up with the dawn. Dianna watched the soldier's dark and barefooted form as she padded across the earth, up onto a boulder and doubled into a balanced crouch, waiting.

Soon enough, Fredric, Aimes, and Ram climbed the grassy knoll toward them. Beneath the shadow of his cowl, the prince sported several cuts and a grimace.

Dianna's heart leapt at the sight of them. Aimes was limping, his loose clothes swaying on his lean frame. His anxious, wide-eyed gaze moved over her.

She ran downhill, the beat of her heels thrumming through her bones, the wind stinging her eyes. Aimes had only begun to say her name before she drew him close, and the air rushed from his lungs.

His arms coiled around her, shivering, while she became still as armor. Without a word, he buried his face in her neck. The smell of wolf was strong on his skin.

Dianna closed her eyes, listening to his rapid heartbeat. "You're shaking," she said, taken aback at its intensity.

"Did they hurt you?" Aimes murmured beneath her ear.

"Not badly."

Aimes stood back, studying the angry scrapes and the bruises smudging her skin, before asking to check the worst of them. Dianna obliged and his hands trembled as he lifted her chin, eyeing a gash across her cheek where Ledras had struck her. Seeing Aimes' set jaw up close, Dianna realized he shook not with fear, but anger at the hunter. She stole a glance at Fredric, whose mouth quirked knowingly at the two of them together.

Ram approached Eccka, gaze sweeping over her swathed arms.

"Soldier," he said.

"Sir," she returned, responding to his unspoken question. "Minced but fighting fit. News?"

"You're not going to like it."

"We had a brush with my old comrades last night. Can you explain that?"

"The High Elder is dispatching Awl-Fethan hunters and L'Hestian mercenaries to scour the woods and lay groundwork for an attack in the next few weeks," Ram said. "A dangerous task for them, which tells me these men are expendable. Short Echelon, perhaps." He paused as Eccka nodded in confirmation. "They had not counted on us lying in wait. The one who escaped us will bring their information to the Centurion . . . and then he will send the others."

Eccka had gone still. "The others?"

"Strong and agile though we are indeed – we are but five. We cannot run forever. And they are highly trained in—"

"Ram," Eccka interjected. She intoned the question low, as if she already knew the answer. "How many?"

"In total . . . " Ram took a breath. "A century of *Tharknas*."

There was a long, pregnant pause as the finality of this knowledge descended like a shroud upon them. Eccka wagged her head slowly from side to side, eyes widening.

"No," she said, her tone rising. "No, we can't hold off that many. Ram – do you realize their proficiency? We can't."

"I know." Ram swallowed. Within the dark folds of his cloak, his eyes glistened. "I know. I never claimed to be your imperator."

"No, Ram," Eccka said, firm but gentle. "You are much more than that. But what will we do about that now?"

"You know what you must do when the time comes."

"But if—"

Ram approached her, cradling her hands like flighty birds, and her hard-edged features softened. Somehow, Dianna thought, the contact seemed more intimate than a kiss.

"You know what you must do," Ram repeated. He spoke not as a superior now, but with the warmth of a lover.

His dark gaze at Eccka was a question, and her stiff nod was his answer.

He released her hands, turning toward the rest of them like a loving father, and the weight of their lives lay heavy in his words.

"I'm sorry," he said, voice hollow. "I'm so sorry to all of you. I wanted so badly for you to have hope. But the war is over. We've lost."

Dianna decided it didn't matter which war he meant. There was the war outside, the war of the empire. And there was their war, the one fought on a shifting battleground, between men and demons.

Death was coming from both fronts.

"So, this is it," she whispered.

She felt Fredric's hand as light as the wind on her shoulder. Aimes had gone still.

"I don't believe this," Eccka said. "How could the High Elder gain recruits? Awl-Feth doesn't have the means."

"The High Elder is in allegiance with the Caenani," Ram said, softly.

Dianna felt the strength leaving her body like a ghost. Eccka's staggered expression echoed hers.

"When Aimes was the Caenani's slave, he witnessed a conspiracy he wasn't supposed to," Ram said. "The High Elder paid a visit to their legate. He committed treason against the empire by offering the Caenani manpower to kill wolves in exchange for payment. Eventually, he was able to recruit *Tharknas*."

Dianna was silent as she thought. Ram's story made perfect, terrible sense: the High Elder hoarding rations. The intensity of his sermons as he invoked the will of Mactus to soothe his people, just as she soothed her prey before killing it.

Her father's last words as he met his death by the High Elder's hand: *the empire that he'd have wrought from Myre's ashes.*

Abram had known.

"Yes," Eccka exhaled through her teeth. "Of course."

"He is a pious man leading a suffering people, and that makes him more dangerous than I ever deemed imaginable. So, my frustration breeds." Ram turned to pace the forest floor in contemplation again, the Earthencloak whirling around him. "My first act as imperator would be his punishment."

Dianna remembered the cold bloodlust in the High Elder's voice as he condemned her father to die.

"He wants more than a stake in the new empire," she added. "He wants a battle."

Fredric smoothed a hand through his mess of curls, his downcast eyes flecked with yellow.

"The folly of the ages," he said. "That killing precludes killing."

"The power to curse and corrupt does not end with Silbarran," Ram said. "We all have the choice to kill or protect."

Dianna heard Aimes exhale softly beside her. The back of his hand brushed against hers, catching her fingers.

"And killing to protect?" she asked.
Ram closed his eyes as if conceding.
"If we must," he said, "then we must."

Chapter 49

Flower moon, new

The firelight at the heart of the campsite began to fade to cinders. Dianna missed its full warmth, swathing herself in a cloak against the bitter cold of nightfall.

All the disquiet of the day manifested in a half-eaten meal, over which they exchanged few words. Eccka and Ram yet again convened together a distance away, voices low and intense, heads almost touching. Dianna couldn't tell if the matters they discussed were strategic or personal.

It was Aimes' turn to keep watch. As a wolf he crept on the fringes of their campsite, padding slow and soundless through the thick copse of trees. Fredric sat beside Dianna, warming his bare toes in the fire's faint blush, picking a loose thread on his patchwork jerkin.

When at last he did speak, it was wistful, half-aware, as if thinking aloud.

"Do you think there is a place for us in this world?" he asked, staring into wind-lashed flames fighting to stay alive.

Dianna glanced at him. His expression was not compressed with despair as she feared, but faraway.

"I have been all over it," he said. "I climbed the mountains of Valta, swam the Four-Forked River. I explored deserted battlements in search of long-forgotten relics. I saw an aurora over them. I saw its bright multi-hued glow from a tor, and heard its clap on a windless night, like a godly wonder, and I named it Wheelock Point." He closed his eyes as though summoning the memory, stretched his fingers out before him as if to touch it, and gave a derisive laugh as he dropped his hand. "A crag christened with my damned name. But I have never known a thing like us."

Dianna didn't want to think about this.

"Perhaps we have no place," she said. "Perhaps we exist until we don't, and that is enough."

Only then did Fredric pull a solemn sidelong look at her. "You are much too astute for your age."

Dianna paused, frowning at his unusually disheartened tone.

"Will you tell me another of your stories, Fredric?" she asked to distract him from grief, the way he had done for her.

"I will tell them to anyone who will listen."

"How did you find them? The others?"

A smile broke on his face. It was the most mysterious smile she'd ever seen, making his eyes twinkle – yet it was also the saddest.

"It's a cold story, Gentle-heart," he said.

"The fire makes it warm."

Fredric's smile faded. As Dianna met his eyes, he looked years older, heartsick and soul-weary. For a moment he was quiet, and a light wind ruffled his curls.

"Very well." He picked up a leaf, twirled it between his fingers, and cast it into the fire. Its edges curled as it burned to ash.

"Villagers call home a place of permanence," he said. "They pity vagrants for having no permanence in this world. But you see, the road was my home. Staying in one place for too long is limiting to our knowledge, to our passions. We are creatures of movement, and I wanted to see it all. Nothing was too far or fallow for my earth-toughened feet."

He leaned forward and whispered to her, as though disclosing a secret. "There is beauty in every living thing."

Dianna smiled.

"I was passing through Awl-Feth one night," he continued. "A stopover on my way to see the chariot races in far Erro-Wyld. I was in need of a good bath, a hot meal, and a strong drink. The villagers directed me to the Bonefish Tavern, so I spent the few coppers I'd salvaged on bread and wine.

"It was by a happy accident I chanced on a former vagrant who had settled there, who once shared my rootlessness. We talked into the night of our adventures over a good many glasses." Fredric's gray eyes clouded with fond remembrance. "We became lovers very quickly. A week later, when it came time for me to pick up and move on, I felt grounded for the first time in my life. I was terribly infatuated.

"He'd offered food and shelter to me during my stay. I refused the rations, being too proud in my self-sufficient ways. But I accepted the bed." The roguish, sad smile flickered across his face again. "I'd heard talk of demons. Your people were unprepared at first, but they trained a defense quickly enough. And so he became a hunter."

Dianna felt a horrible, twisting awareness in her gut.

"Before they called them the Blood Woods, I knew this forest like the heartline of my hand," Fredric said. "Call it conceit or wanderlust, but danger doesn't sway my course. Once I'd emptied my pockets for meals, I started to set game traps here. You have to learn to feed yourself as a vagrant, and in Awl-Feth, as you well know. I'd gone to check my trap, and that was the last thing I remembered."

"You were bitten then."

Fredric nodded. "I must have snared something. Only the wolf had found the kill first, and I was the next course. And then he . . . he found me."

"Who found you?"

Darkness fell over Fredric's expression, hardening his features such that Dianna wished she hadn't asked after all. "My hunter." His voice was low and bitter. "He turned on me immediately. I was no longer human to him. I was a monster. One he was very prepared to destroy."

Dianna had gone still and quiet, shrinking into the fabric of her cloak.

"So, I fled to the woods, ran as far as I could, like a coward," he said. "I crossed paths with Ram and Eccka. And you know the rest of the story."

"You're not a coward, Fredric," Dianna said softly.

But Fredric's face crumpled.

"Oh, Gentle-heart. I am the biggest coward to walk upon this earth."

"No," Dianna said at once, shaking her head. "You're Fredric the vagrant, Ragpicker, Story-weaver, The Furthermost-feet—"

"My vagrant family is dead," Fredric said, his voice cold.

Dianna's words of solace fluttered like wings in her throat, too weak to push past her lips.

Fredric scrubbed a hand over his mouth, muffling his words. "I was the navigator. I led us into the cave. The bear killed them," he said. "They all died."

Dianna was still as tears glazed his face, iridescent in the firelight. She reached out, resting a hand on his. He gripped it fast as a lodestone to a compass needle.

He gazed upward at the scattered stars as if connecting them or deciphering some hidden meaning.

"I am a liar, Dianna," he said. "I weave my own happy endings, but I have no folktales for you. All of my stories are tragedies."

***

Dianna paced a restless loop around a stand of firs. In the cold obscurity of midnight, no sound but cricket-song and the chuckling of tawny owls disturbed the air. Ram rose to relieve Aimes of his sentry, and she heard the soft snap of twigs underfoot.

She started at the sight of a pair of vivid yellow eyes, glowing and unblinking in the dark. A seed of deep sadness, rooted in her chest, burgeoned further within her.

The massive wolf curled into a half-moon on a patch of soft grass, nosing his muzzle between his paws. If no one knew otherwise, she thought, Aimes looked like he truly belonged there – just another wild animal in the woods, though proportionately extraordinary.

Hesitating, she approached the wolf and knelt in the soft peat. He shifted his great head to fix his eyes on her, ears twitching in vague acknowledgment.

Dianna settled against his flank, melting into his thick ruff. She reached out and tentatively stroked his shoulder, smoothing over the coarse fur.

Her voice sounded strangely thin and tense to her ears.

"Will you come out of there, Aimes?" she asked.

The change was effortless, but slow. The layer of wolfskin rolled away and dissipated, and Aimes surfaced naked underneath it, like pulling off a disguise. He moved away in a kind of deference, eyes turning colors under thick lashes.

"You still can't sleep," he said, after a moment of silence.

Dianna pulled a guilty face. "Not when my mind and body are warring all the time."

His irises were blue again when they flickered up at her.

"Maybe you're just nocturnal."

Dianna smiled. "Maybe."

But her smile faded as she studied his face in the dim starlight, at the long scar splitting it, the remnant of a nightmare.

"They did that to you," she whispered. "The Caenani."

He gave a single, barely perceptible nod of his head.

Dianna looked away in contemplation, biting her lip. The sadness swelled and rattled silently within her, sudden and uncontainable. She had felt it turning the pages of Liam's book of remedies, watching Cathrin throw the linens, in Eccka's retort of *seven years*. It was a pain that clutched in the heart and never let go.

"Sometimes I wonder," she began, swallowing. "How you could let go of the wolf. How you could stand to heal me."

Aimes ran his thumbs absently over his knuckles, licking his lips.

"Because," he said under his breath, "I care so much about you."

The words lingered between them for a long time until Dianna faced him, her heartbeat drumming hard against her chest.

"Someone told me once, to be a man, I shouldn't feel," he said. "But I do. I feel so much. Being human isn't easy, Dianna. Being as strong as you, I mean."

"I don't think I know my own strength," Dianna said.

Aimes made a sound in his throat like a small laugh, searching her eyes. "Because it's more than you see. More than anyone sees. It's like the moon, pulling me in every phase."

Dianna didn't know how to reply. The softness of his voice sent fluttering pangs of longing through her.

"I was scared to be human for years," he said. "To be aware of so much pain. I thought I'd go mad again. But when I start to go senseless . . ." His expression was helpless beneath a thatch of his black hair, his gaze falling to her lips.

"You start pulling me back to my senses."

In the dark, his outline was still and faint and more human than ever before. Dianna wanted to touch him, to trace a gentle thumb over the length of his scar. She wanted his words again, warm like a river in summer, awakening something dormant in her veins.

"For one who was silent for seven years," she said slowly, "you say the most beautiful things."

A smile curled at the corner of Aimes' mouth, crinkling the corners of his blue eyes.

Dianna wondered how long it had been since he'd smiled like that – openly, genuinely, and human in every way.

"Then I'll speak until you fall asleep," he promised.

"What will you say?"

Aimes ran an idle hand over the back of his head, but his hair remained wild and unkempt.

He glanced downward, the half-smile lingering on his lips.

"Your name," he said. "Dianna. The most beautiful thing."

Dianna's smile echoed his.

"Then you may need to say it all night," she said as Aimes dipped his head lower, a deep breath escaping him. "You're in for an awfully dull one, unless there's something else you'd rather do."

She waited patiently for his response, though the silence was nearly unbearable, heightening her pulse again.

"Well." He swallowed. "I'd like to hold you, Dianna. In my arms. Until you fall asleep."

Dianna couldn't help but laugh at the innocent request, brows raised. "That's all?"

"Not in the least." Aimes' voice, deeper and more sensual now, reverberated in the air like a cool wind tingling on her hot skin. From beneath his dark hair, he looked up at her. "It's just – to sleep at your side. Just to have you near me. I'd like that very much, for now."

"I'd like that very much, too," Dianna said, exhaling. "For now."

They lay back on the grass, facing the stars. His arms felt natural around her, safe, like a long-awaited embrace she'd missed her whole life. His breath was warm on the back of her neck. Softly, his fingertips stroked her hair.

She knew then. She supposed she had always known, since the first time he had appeared to her in the woods.

I will take no husbands, she had vowed in all the stone-heaviness of girlhood, but the vow crumbled under his touch.

If she could, she would take only one.

CHAPTER 50

Flower moon, waxing

In his sleep, Aimes had wrapped around Dianna like a warm cloak. Her breath was shallow as she lay with her back pressed into his rumbling chest.

She wanted him. The feeling overwhelmed her as he nuzzled into her neck, as his arms tightened around her. She wanted to know how his healing hands would feel while making love, all the ways they could be both tender and lustful with her, clutching in her hair, learning the shape of her breasts. She would cover his skin with kisses, murmuring to him: *everything will be all right.*

She was sure that one too-quick movement would wake him, sure of his acute awareness of her body even as he slept. But his breath grew deeper, harsher, rising and trapping in his throat.

"Don't touch her," he was saying. "Don't touch her."

Dianna flinched, the tiny hairs of her skin standing on end. "Aimes?"

Aimes bolted upright, wrenching away.

"Dianna —" he gasped. "I won't – I won't let them hurt you."

"It's all right, Aimes," Dianna said, heart hammering. "It was just a nightmare."

He balled himself against a tree, as if to become nothing

and everything. His eyes were wild and wheeling, and in them she saw every terror she had ever known, but escaped – Actaen's grasp, the reek of death inside the catacombs, the bruise of her family's loss covered with *don't be soft, don't be soft.*

But Aimes relived his terrors. Aimes had never escaped.

He rocked to his knees, hands crushed over his disheveled head. His body was swathed in sweat, the sinews of his arms tensed tight.

"No," he managed to say. "No, no, no."

Dianna knelt beside him. "It's all right, Aimes." she tried again.

A rough growl swelled through his clenched teeth. His eyes were shot with yellow, filling with tears.

"It's not!" he cried. "Those soldiers are coming, and they'll take you, just like the Caenani took slaves! I know what they can do. And I hate that I was part of it. I hate being anything like them!"

He shuddered, jaw grit with anger. Dianna's gaze was steady upon him as she rose slowly to her feet.

"You're not like them," she said, glancing down at the clenched tendons of his hands. "But you're still human."

The light shifted upon Aimes' face, and the curl of his lips, the ghost of the wolf's snarl, melted away. Erratic breaths escaped him as he choked back animal murmurs.

"What if I don't want to be?" he whispered.

She knew it was not only defeat. A part of him wanted to disappear into something other, wanted it to consume him. It was a secret want, small and dark and buried deep in his mind. But his mind was breaking like packed earth, the darkness clawing its way from below.

Dianna knelt beside him, resting her hand over his. Studying his face, she yearned to trace the fine worry lines he had, smooth them over with her fingertips.

"It won't be the same as before, Aimes," she said softly.

"Oryaen is gone. It's just you, now. It's just you."

***

Hunger set in at midday, and Dianna took the chance to distract herself with finding food. After the hunt, she washed her freshly caught waterfowl of its blood, watching the cloudy red ribbons spiral downstream.

"Thank you for your sacrifice, friend," she said.

Aimes sat still by the fire, watching Fredric help roast the bird over hot coals and pull apart the brittle carcass, fingers slick with grease. Eccka paced the campsite's edges, searching for movement in the trees, and Ram approached her before touching any food.

"Come eat, soldier," he said. "Let me take over."

But she did not leave her post.

"I'd rather wait," she said. "That's all we have left to do now. Wait. Like damned pigs for the slaughter."

Ram looked out across the pines piercing the sky like arrows.

"You forget," he murmured. "Despite everything, we are people."

"But *Tharknas* doesn't understand that. The hunters never will," Eccka said. Her eyes searched the forest, never straying, never blinking. "And the other pack is still waiting out there."

"She's right, Ram," Fredric said. He looked up from the fire, a worried crease upon his brow. "I can feel them."

***

The sun had sunk behind the trees and the moon bared a sliver of its light. While the others slept, Eccka waited on the fringes of camp.

She was wolf, to allow for her sharpest senses and keep

324

warm in her fur, sitting curled within the darkness, ready to emerge as an impending hatchling within its egg. She waited out of stubborn pride, until sleep began to pull her into its murky clutches.

She waited for a sign.

Like a needle, a thin unfamiliar howl pierced the quiet. Eccka bolted upright, hackles quivering. Her head dropped low, candlelit eyes unwavering.

Who are you? She growled into the void.

As if in reply, the evening wind carried a trace of wolf-scent. He was not the alpha. It was never the alpha. His pack hid him, protected him.

But the strange wolf had been standing there for a spell, several yards away, still. Watching her.

A shadow shifted, and he swept away into the night, fur billowing like a smoke trail.

In the span of a heartbeat, Eccka held back. *To hell with it*, she thought.

Her sleek muscles cinched as she gave chase, a swift scythe cutting a neat path through overgrown foliage.

A spy. They knew, had known for years, but now the suspicion was real and physical, running from her.

She plunged forward in his wake, the metronome of her strides drumming the refrain of a promise.

I will catch you I will kill you I will catch you.

Her feet devoured the ground as a fire would spread across dry brush, alive, relentless, ravenous. Her quarry's hot breath spiraled, visible on the air current.

She was on his heels, far from camp now.

The stranger veered, changing tack, fast and jet-dark as a drop of ink on parchment.

Eccka faltered, scattering a shower of earth. She centered her focus on her fleeing target. He ducked and surfaced again in the black ether.

She swooped airborne over a dense bed of rock and

landed, claws scrabbling, blood pumping. The stranger dipped out of sight. Frantic, she searched for him.

A flicker in the distance. She had lost him to a mesh of trees, where he bloomed from underneath and slipped away into a rift.

Eccka stood panting, spent. A bitter cold disappointment snuffed out the fire of the chase. She watched the rift as it closed.

The strong scent marking his pack's territory hung over his point of disappearance, like a faultline. They had been inching closer, broadening their borders.

Sending a warning.

Her heart slowed. Everything slowed to a murmur, then nothing. The silence was hateful, deafening, smacking of defeat.

Why, she thought, *after seven years?*

Why now?

She lingered, then sank to the ground. She did not return to the campsite until sunrise.

CHAPTER 51

Flower moon, waxing

After nightfall, Dianna walked with Aimes beside the length of the river. A chill was seeping into the air, cooling her skin, silencing the woods. Gone were the mating songs of birds and the sigh of the warm spring breeze on the air.

But she could almost hear the faintest whispers of the others like them, the accursed, long lost among the trees. The whispers were like howls, monosyllabic, saying nothing but meaning everything. They rose up all around her. They filled her lungs.

"It could have been so peaceful here," she said.

Aimes paused mid-stride.

"Dianna," he said softly. "Are you afraid to die?"

She turned to him and saw that he had closed his eyes. Gently holding his head between her hands, she smoothed the edges of his jawline with her thumbs.

"No," she lied. "There's music in these woods. When I hear it, I'm not afraid."

So they paused, listening. Aimes went so still, it was as if he'd stopped breathing. But his voice thrummed beside her, and his eyes were wide open.

"That tree," he said in an undertone.

Dianna followed his line of sight. At the edge of the darkness was a monstrous old tree. The hollowed redwood gaped openmouthed at them.

"I know that tree," Aimes repeated, voice catching. "That's where I . . ."

Dianna turned to face him. His nose had wrinkled slightly, mashing his features into something ugly, petrified with fear.

A cold dread shot through her as he began to shiver. She curled her body around his, clutching him to her, as if to keep him within himself.

"Aimes," she whispered. "Listen, stay with me."

Aimes' features smoothed, his eyes softening as they focused on hers.

"Keep talking," she said, swallowing the lump in her throat. "Keep talking to me."

"I can't." Aimes trailed off. "C-can't . . ."

"Look around you," said Dianna. A tear escaped her, falling on his shoulder. "Tell me what you hear. Tell me what you see."

The silhouettes of bare trees were hellish spindly hands, threatening to pluck Aimes from the earth and keep him for their own.

"River," he said, childlike. "I hear river. I see . . . star."

"Good," Dianna urged, holding him closer. "Does the star have a name?"

"I . . . I don't know." Anxious, Aimes looked around. His chest rose and fell against hers, each breath harsher than the last.

"Where are you, Aimes?" Dianna asked. The tears fell freely now. "Do I have a name?"

A soft animal whine began, deep in his lungs, and she knew he was gone.

His body thrashed out of her embrace and pitched forward, the shape of him guttering at the edges. His muscles shifted like water, and his bones crackled like a giant pine falling. Any words poised on his tongue dissolved into a visceral hiss through canine teeth.

This time, his eyes were the last part to change. For a second they lingered in fluctuation, a muddy hue that was not his bright blue, not yet yellow. Their pupils retracted as the wildness leached into them.

Helpless, Dianna watched as Aimes folded and Fell away.

The wolf turned its back to her, his bottlebrush tail hung low. Lifting his nose to scent the air, he took tentative steps into the woods. His sinewy legs twitched, and he vanished into the night.

Dianna turned her gaze to the sky, to constellations like so many illuminated birds in permanent migration.

Deep in the trees, a howl swelled. The low, sorrowing notes vibrated throughout her spine, down to the marrow. They droned like a fine string of silver stretched thin, on and on, before breaking at last.

***

The sky smoldered gold where the sun rose over the foothills. Dianna had waited up all night for Aimes to return, facing the east where he had gone. She'd tracked his path, ending up at the same ravine where she and Ram had spoken alone, where she could see the horizon unfolded beyond the trees like a soft blanket.

Instinctively, she thought, she should fear being alone now more than ever. It was foolish to strike out from the others, knowing of the enemy's approach in due course. But watching a new dawn spread across the vast sky melted her fear, until there was only the hollow pang of Aimes' absence. She sat still, arms wrapped around her knees, feeling the flutter of her hair where the wind touched it.

"Here we find ourselves again," came a low voice from behind her.

Dianna's gaze followed Ram's long cloak to his dark-whiskered face.

"I tried to hold onto him, Ram, I did. But I saw his eyes." Her voice emerged hoarse and distant to her own ears. "He's not there."

Ram looked at her for a long time, his shoulders tense, saying nothing.

"Is there anything we can do?" she pleaded, hating that she already knew the answer.

Ram knelt before her. He took her hands in his brown, leathery ones, pressing them gently.

"You love him, don't you?" he asked.

Dianna blinked away a tear. Ram's eyes shone handsome, warm, sincere. She could not lie to him, to a question framed so knowingly.

The truth swelled in her like light shone in a dark corner: *Yes. Yes, you do.*

"I love him like the sun," she said. "I love his warmth. Each time a darkness swallows him . . ."

Ram simply nodded. "And each time he comes back."

"But what if – Ram, what if he doesn't come back this time?"

"Your heart is enough. And his will answer. I believe it."

But Dianna felt her spirits plummeting and the sting of tears in her lashes.

"I can't help him," she managed to say through the stifling thickness in her throat. "I can't help anyone now."

Ram drew her to him and wrapped her in his arms, silent as he thought.

"Lives are not clean," he said at last. "We must make peace with our suffering before we can accept the love of others."

"But why Aimes?" Dianna murmured into the warm

330

furrows of the Earthencloak. "Why *his* life?"

The tears were pooling upon the cloak's lacework of leaves, turning them a little greener where they fell.

Ram's deep, calm voice lulled in her ear. "Walk with me again, Daughter."

He had said it with such tenderness, so much like a father, that Dianna's heart ached with a strange and unexpected wash of feeling which she realized was love.

"Yes," she answered softly. She would walk anywhere with him.

Ram led the way again, and she did not ask where they were going. As they meandered through the woods, over root and rock and moss, he asked her to pick the freshest wildflowers she could find.

Along their journey, Dianna chose a pristine white lily, an unopened rosebud, and five sprays of dewy aster. On occasion, Ram spotted the ones she had missed. "That one," he said, pointing out a yellow blaze among the greenery, and Dianna went to it and pulled it by its roots with tender fingers.

Between each pause, cradling her armful of blooms, she followed the gentle sway of Ram's stride with diligent footfalls. The Earthencloak caught the light wind in a whisper of leaves.

After several miles, Ram pulled away a heavy pine bough, which gave a rasping protest and rained a smattering of fragrant needles. Without a word, he stood back to allow her passage.

Dianna ducked below the branch and stepped into a different world.

Large stones enrobed in rich, green moss contoured the ground. Dappled with splinters of sunlight, the whole clearing seemed to glow from the inside. Forming a semicircle around the perimeter were mounds of earth, a score of them.

Breathless, Dianna approached one, paused, and

looked over her shoulder at Ram in an unspoken question.

"These were our packmates," he told her. "These are my people."

There was a strange stirring within her, a dizziness turning in her head, and the fragrant bouquet felt heavy in her arms. She pressed it to her breast as she glanced around at the arc of shallow graves.

Ram stooped, touched a green stone. "Hirus lies here. He was my age. He was a proud man, followed his own rules. Without our navigator, you know, we lost our way too easily then." He spoke with a lump in his throat. "One night, during a full moon, the hunters found us. I said we could all get out alive, but Hirus refused to listen. Heroic fool. He stayed behind as if to divert them. We found his body much later, but only some of it."

With a flutter of his cloak, Ram approached the heap of soil beside this. "Osgar's grave. Same circumstances, except they shot him down as we fled. We hid him, but he bled out so quickly. With the right remedial, we could have saved him. Aimes wouldn't eat for weeks after."

He moved to another grave. "Saryn's. Only with us for a few nights. She left this life by choice. In the river."

Dianna did not want to listen any longer. The seeking clutch of death seemed inescapable here. The smell of it was thick in the air, clinging on every breath, mingling with the cloying rot of old flowers.

But Ram took her by the shoulder, guiding her under the shade of another pine. Underneath, another stone. Vines were climbing up the sides of it, curling like fingers in a loving embrace. Tiny yellow flowers, like fallen stars, dotted the moss around it.

Dianna knelt, touching the stone. It was warm where the sunlight had once been, angling through the branches.

"Who lies here?" she asked with an air of resignation.

But Ram did not answer at first. He collected each of the crumbling yellow flowers one by one. Kneeling beside her, he picked up a few stray twigs and smoothed a hand over the black upturned earth.

"Armina," said Ram. "Her name was Armina."

Dianna's eyes began taking in small details of the grave site. The porous surface of the little stone. The way the soil had settled there, the glint of a beetle creeping across it. The strangeness of knowing it somehow teemed with life even as it rested over the bones of her mother.

Ram took the clutch of wildflowers from her still hands. He arranged them wreathlike around the stone.

"You did this?" she whispered.

Ram, with a solemn bow of his head, knew what she meant, and answered only: "Aimes."

Aimes had kept her grave. He might have been the one to bury her, had there been any remains. Perhaps there weren't. She could imagine him nevertheless, a brave little boy, stealing into the encampment to recover them. Packing the soil over the body, selecting the headstone with his gentle hands. Grieving for Armina in a way she could not.

But she couldn't ask any more of Ram, not when his dark eyes had seen so much death, not when showing her the crude gravesite had been hard enough. Not now.

Instead, she was silent for a long while, remembering the scent of rose oil and her mother's smile, letting her tears fall and water the earth.

"It is beautiful," she said at last.

She felt the comforting weight of his hand on her shoulder.

His voice was calm. "If I die," he said, "you keep running."

Dianna opened her mouth to protest, but he gave her a hard, silencing look.

"On my authority, you must promise me this." It was not a request, but a command.

She raised her eyes to his. "I promise."

Chapter 52

Flower moon, waxing

Though the sky lightened, and a scattering of morning birdsong filled the woods, Ram lingered at the gravesite, taking a last quiet moment to honor the dead, and Dianna left him.

It was time to contemplate her own death, too.

Back at the camp, illuminated by a blazing sunrise, Aimes was sitting with his arms tight around himself, his face awash in pallor. Fredric had bent over him, a consoling hand on his shoulder.

"Just breathe," he soothed, but he exchanged a worried glance with Dianna. "Just keep pushing it back."

Aimes' empty eyes fell on her, and he smiled through suppressed pain.

"What can I do?" she asked, desperate.

"I think it will help if he moves," Fredric offered.

Dianna took Aimes by the hand, helping him to his feet.

"Then let's move," she urged, fierce resolve burning in her voice. "Let's run until we can't anymore."

Together they broke into a sprint, the wind rushing on their legs, wet grass gliding beneath their soles, stumbling but falling into stride again. Her hand tugged gently on his, and he followed like a kite drifting in her wake. They ran until they gasped for breath, until the trees smudged into a palette of green.

They ran as if they could escape every danger, as if the dream of safety was real.

Beneath a canopy of leaves, they spilled onto the grass, panting. For a moment they lay against the earth, basking in the warm dappled light, staring up at the fine green lacework above them.

Dianna began to speak, but Aimes pressed his hand in hers, stilling the syllable cresting on her tongue. He closed his eyes, disappearing within himself again.

"You're . . ." His voice broke. "The only thing. Keeping me human. At all. Anymore."

Dianna searched her fleeting thoughts for the right reply. Watching him lay still, she only knew she had never anticipated him, like a rainfall in summer or a bruised fruit that tasted the sweetest.

"You have the pack," she said at last. "You have Ram."

Aimes shook his head. "Not like you."

His hand trembled with the beginnings of the Fall. Dianna's fingers moved into the spaces between his and held firm to him.

"You're human now," she reminded him.

"I don't fit in my skin. I . . ."

His entwined fingers trembled in her grip. Her pulse quickened as claws unfurled from his fingertips, their sharp edges caressing her knuckles.

"I destroy myself," he finished. "Over and over. Like everyone I healed. Like you. I'm a mistake."

"No. You're a good man, Aimes. You're not what happened to you."

"How could you know?"

"Because you could never be a mistake in any shape."

Dianna drew in close enough to see Aimes' yellow-feathered irises flux into blazing blue. His lips were parted, the heat of his breath close.

"Dianna."

"Yes?"

"Will you help me do something human?"

"Kissing is human," Dianna reminded him.

"Exactly," he exhaled.

Dianna pulled him to her in answer, and his mouth was against hers, soft and open. The hitch of his growl was mellifluous on her lips, deepening as her hands explored his silken hair, the ridges of his spine, the lean-muscled strength of his body. His lush scent of oakmoss and wolf fur filled her senses, and it took all of her focus to break the kiss in order to speak.

"Please try to stay human," she whispered. "I missed you."

Aimes clung to her, his sun-warmed skin like a force that could save them both, even in the shadow of death.

"Dianna," he said, low, "I don't want to go anywhere without you."

He rested his tousled head against the softness of her breast, breath softening as though the sound of her heartbeat calmed him. At length he stopped shaking, anchored by her words.

***

The Earthencloak shuddered in the wind like the storm-caught canopy of a tree as Ram paced the ground, phantomlike in the dark. Eccka crouched on a sturdy branch above him, scanning the treetops.

By the fire, Dianna sharpened arrowheads on a stone. Aimes had come to sit across from her, watching her work. Several times they met each other's gaze, and when the corner of his mouth turned up into a smile, Dianna felt a warmth turning in her like embers in the fire itself.

Fredric emerged from the darkness, holding a

mysterious object. As he approached the campfire, Ram stopped in his tracks.

"Hid this beauty years ago," Fredric said. "I suppose I was saving it for the proper occasion." He dusted off the smooth surface of the instrument, plucking one of its strings. A crisp note quivered in the air before dying into silence.

The lyre was luthier-crafted, caringly wrought of dark wood and six strings like silver threads. It was made to make music for a happier time, another life.

Eccka dropped from her branch, brow furrowed.

"What have we to celebrate?" she asked, coldly. "There's nothing for us but bloodshed."

Fredric looked around the woods, into the blackest oblivion. It was soundless but for a cooing of owls on the faint wind.

"But tonight, for now, all is quiet," he said. "And that is enough."

Eccka couldn't argue this, watching as Fredric handed Ram the lyre.

"If you'll oblige us, Ram," he said softly.

Ram tested the lyre's light weight in his palms, caressing the curvature of the arms, the yoke, the tuning pegs.

"I haven't played in years," he said in wonderment.

Fredric gave an encouraging nod.

Ram sat, propped the beautiful lyre in his lap, and began to pick at the strings.

He drew out sounds with precise and measured strokes, bowing his head when he struck the right notes. The delicate tune strengthened layer by layer as his fingers laced notes into the framework. Eccka, as though tempered by the sound, rested her chin on one hand with a wistful look.

A deep sympathy overcame Dianna, watching Ram become reacquainted with his artistry. She realized, as waves of song broke and a smile crooked his mouth, that this must be one of the few simple pleasures he allowed himself.

The notes of his song changed course, tentatively increasing in tempo, until it could be a brisk jig played to a full tavern.

With a graceful bow, Fredric proffered his hand to Dianna. "Gentle-heart?"

Dianna mustered a smile as she grasped his palm. Taking lead, he taught her the four-step dances of vagrants, the gliding waltzes of nobility. He swept her into a twirl, grinning, and spun her around and around. Soon she too was grinning, seeing nothing but a dark and dizzying world awash with flames.

She lost her footing and they fell down glowing with sweat, clutching their sides, their laughter rising and warming from the inside out. She had forgotten how good it felt, as even Eccka joined in with a low chuckle.

Dianna sighed as the feeling subsided, knowing it couldn't last. She caught flashes of Aimes' face in the fire's light, scarred and handsome and alone. Watching her from afar, he looked like a man at the edge of a sea, admiring the sun setting over the water before wading out in the darkness.

Aimes helped her to her feet, one arm flat against her lower back, gentle but arresting. His other hand smoothed along her spine and pressed to her shoulder blade. She held herself to him, aware of the shape of his body against hers and the tingle of his breath between them, but he did not move to kiss her again.

Instead, he shifted his weight to his right foot and back to the left, unpracticed in the strangeness of the human movement. Dianna followed, and they were not dancing so much as swaying from side to side.

Aimes rested his mouth in the arch of her neck, breath fluttering on her skin. Dianna took little notice as the chords slowed like a shallow river, softening into a different tune. She heard only the powerful, precious rhythm of his pulse as she leaned her cheek against his chest.

She imagined raising her lips to his ear, telling him she loved him, that they could be there for each other when they died.

But the moment was fragile as it was. Ram's head bent low and his fingers pulled lightly at the strings. The piece was spontaneous, organic, a half-formed thought with notes of expectation, which lingered like mist after a heavy rainfall. It was altogether achingly beautiful and sad, soothing but strange, like the course of life itself. In it, Dianna tasted the warm sweetness of Aimes' lips, felt the crook of the dogwood tree, heard the cleaving of animal flesh.

It was a love song, a cry for a homeland, a death knell.

PART V: THE EMPIRE

"Oh, little did the Wolf-Child care—
When first he planned his home,
What city should arise and bear
The weight and state of Rome."
– From *Romulus and Remus* by Rudyard Kipling

CHAPTER 53

Cold moon, full
Night before siege

There was nothing else, nothing that could be seen or felt, as the power, the knowing, that moved through him.

Prince Remetus held the world in his hands, pulsing like a living heart. His world. His empire.

It slipped between his fingers like sand, and he watched the glowing motes spiral away into the ether, feeling the crushing pain of understanding but not having.

Remetus fell, disgorged, from the mouth of the entity. He stumbled backward, staring awestruck at its pale face.

"I see your power," he gasped. "It is . . . exceptional. Unearthly. I must wield it."

Why? asked the entity.

Remetus staggered to his feet, righting himself, his fear sliding away. The rust of wolf blood lingered on his tongue.

"To rule," he said, his voice darkly hungry. "To claim my birthright. To build my empire here."

Here upon this earth? Beneath this moon?

"Here," Remetus repeated. "And its people at my command. I will have this, or you will kill me."

The entity smiled.

And Remetus fell to the ground, a nightmarish agony churning in his blood, crackling in his bones, scrambling over his flesh. Brute senses opened in him, and he shuddered into otherness, into the wolf incarnate.

Then here you shall rule, said the entity. *Here you shall build an empire.*

And it vanished.

Chapter 54

Flower moon, waxing

Rain had fallen overnight, but the earth was barely dampened where Dianna had slept under the cover of trees.

She padded across the petrichor-scented camp, eyes tracing the sodden ashes of the long-gone fire, the water that had pooled in the footprints of their dancing, and the lyre propped up against a stone. The spell of evening revelry seemed like ages ago, and they would have no use for such beautiful instruments in the future. All was quiet and foreign in the light of day.

Aimes had been keeping watch for some time, it seemed, sitting by the riverbank, corded muscles of his arms tense. As Dianna sat beside him, their skin brushing, he shivered. His clean smell was warm against her, luring her back to the sweet escape of sleep.

"They want to kill us, Dianna," he said, his voice thin. "Why do they want to kill us?"

Dianna had no answer, so she slid her hand over his.

"I wanted to be empty," he said, watching the mist marbling through the sunlight. His fingers laced through hers, and his voice became velvet soft. "I wanted so badly to be nothing. But now all I want is to be alive."

Dianna looked at his profile against the woods, the

sharp angle of his set jaw.

"I know," she said, hesitating. "I know that feeling."

Aimes' brow furrowed. His fingers smoothed over her hair, and his lips met her cheek but did not withdraw. The way he held her, so close yet tense, felt like a farewell.

It scared her.

"I promised myself I would try," he said, mouth moving against her skin. "Try to protect Armina's daughter at any cost. But it's because of me that her family is dead. And now she will die, too."

Dianna shook her head. "My family did everything they could to protect me. The reverence of Mactus was stronger."

Aimes' hands were cool and gentle on either side of her face. But Dianna could hardly meet his piercing eyes. Instead she looked out at the vast green sea of pine branches rising and falling in the wind, in waves, as far as she could see.

"I would have killed myself," she said at last.

Aimes took a breath, harsh in his throat. Slowly, he pulled back from her, his hands sliding away.

"If I hadn't been able to leave Awl-Feth," Dianna said. "By the time the rations ran out, by the time I was forced to marry, I had a plan."

A silence fell. She chanced a look at Aimes, expecting disbelief in his features. Instead, his gaze remained steady.

"There are worse fates than death," she said. "You know that, Aimes. The prisoners you healed over and over knew that. You had no other choice, just as I thought I had no other choice. But you were so brave. I thought of death while you fought to live."

"But we can't fight," he murmured. "Not this time."

"Then we'll run together until they catch us. We'll die together and be forgotten," Dianna said, and she shook her head. "But our deaths are not because of you, Aimes. I lived because of you."

She studied the slant of his mouth, the scar bisecting the side of his face. Animal fear filled his eyes, but never before had they seemed so human.

"I love you," he said, softly.

And close, so close she thought he was dead on his feet, the bolt whisked past his head.

Dianna lunged for him, pulling him down. A volley of crossbow bolts rained over them, silent only until they made their marks. Hunters shouted through the trees, sending birds in flight.

"Hell-beasts!" cried one of them, and Dianna tugged at Aimes' hand, moving down the riverbank, thick wet mire sucking at her feet.

"Go!" she gasped, and together they leapt into the river, plunging beneath its frothing surface.

She felt the rapids sweep over her, wrenching at her body. Aimes' hand slid from her grasp as the current submerged him. Through white flashes of roaring water and beyond the sparsely wooded banks, she glimpsed three large loping wolves.

The pack had moved far beyond the hunters' range, free and elastic, gliding like arrows on an airstream. They flickered between the trees and vanished out of sight.

Dianna slipped through the water's course, the current carrying her around a swift bend studded with large rocks. Scrabbling blindly in the muck, she scraped her hands against one, snatching hold. Her lungs burned for breath, and she risked coming up for air.

Just ahead of her, Aimes broke the surface, choking and sputtering. She used the rocks as leverage to reach him, grasping and releasing with the river's flow. As soon as he caught his breath, she lunged for his arm. Aimes took hold of a large rock standing against the churning, bitterly cold water, straining to keep his grip on her.

The hunters' cries faded, and Dianna surveyed the far

banks around a bend downstream. In the midst of the thrashing current, she glimpsed the misty cascade of a waterfall, a rough stone ledge, and – almost obscured in the rushing white water – a cavern's dark mouth.

"There!" she cried out, and Aimes nodded. Together they let go, letting the current drag them toward the bend, fighting to keep their heads above the water.

The bend came sharp and fast, and the water slowed like a draining sieve. Pushing themselves over the ledge, they scrambled behind the curtain of water and into the shadows of the cavern, far enough away from the seething noise. Side by side they collapsed prone, gasping and drenched, overcome by sheer exhaustion.

"Did they—" he panted, frantic, his voice muffled. "The others, did they get away?"

"Yes, I s-saw them," Dianna stammered, shivering.

Aimes took a breath, measurably calmer. But the heat of his body beside her was sudden and powerful, nearly feverish. In the gloom, Dianna saw the yellow fire of the wolf in his eyes.

"It wants to keep you warm," she said, nudging closer to him. "It's all right. You can Fall."

But Aimes shook his head, a nervous catch in his voice. "If I do, I won't be able to think for myself."

Dianna reached for Aimes' hand almost instinctively, taking it in her own. His touch relieved her like sunlight against her skin in the freezing damp, in the threat of death. Deeper still, she felt the urgent, warm swell of wanting him all over again.

"Then I'll help you stay," she said.

They lay together for a long time, wordless. His fingers laced around hers, and the side of his body against her twitched. Dianna moved closer, letting the curve of her hip nestle into his waist.

Sitting up at once, Aimes released her hand. His pale

arms braced himself over her, his thick black hair falling into his eyes with the weight of water. A crease formed between his brows as he studied her face.

"Dianna . . ." he managed. The quiet word was filled with need.

Reaching up, she curled her fingers through his clinging hair and pulled him closer, meeting his mouth. The muscles of his slick-skinned back tensed but softened beneath the pressure of her hands.

"Is this—" he interjected between kisses. "All right? Now?"

"Yes," Dianna answered at once. Beneath his weight and warmth, she wanted to laugh – not at the question, but at the certainty of her answer. It was more than all right. "Yes, please, now."

She felt his body grow rigid against her, saw his canine teeth cusp in his open mouth as though he might devour her. He lowered his head to her neck and growled low in her hair, brushing the hollow of her throat with his lips. Savoring the feel of his skin on hers, she felt certainty that he'd wanted this just as badly.

Peeling off her wet clothes, Aimes traced warm kisses along the slope of her collarbone, the curves of her breasts. His tongue darted, tasting her as though using all his senses to undress her.

"You're so beautiful," he murmured as if it could break him. "Dianna."

His name escaped her in a whisper. The sound of it felt right on her lips.

Aimes touched her with delicate intention, taking time learning her softness, parting her thighs in long, deliberate strokes. He withdrew his fingertips, just once, and she ached for him.

The last touch sent shivers pulsing through her, deep and uncontrolled, and a cry racked her body. His breath interlaced with hers as she drew him closer.

So, this, she thought, *is what it feels like to love. To be loved.*

But Dianna waited to put the feeling into words until after he entered and cleaved to her, after he began keening full-throated affections into the arch of her neck, after his hands gripped her just roughly enough.

With a shudder Aimes drew a long, ragged gasp that pulled at the edges of her name. His racing heart slowed gradually to its steady rhythm.

Slowly she moved her hands to either side of his face. "Aimes," she said. "I love you, too."

Aimes looked at her like the words were new to him, a language he was finally beginning to understand.

"I love you," he echoed in a rush. He said it over and over, as if enjoying the sound, the implication of it, human and real. "I love you, I love you."

CHAPTER 55

Flower moon, waxing

Dianna lay folded against Aimes, upon a layer of dry leaves, watching dappled morning light dance across the glassy veil of water. He stirred, arms clutching her to him, chest rumbling with a low wolfish hum.

"Aimes," she whispered. "Wake up."

But he shook his shaggy head, eyes pressed closed against the light.

"Want to keep dreaming," he said, bleary with sleep.

Dianna wanted to let him. He looked so peaceful after their lovemaking, one strong arm curved over her, mouth pressed to her shoulder blade.

"Please, Aimes. Stay with me."

From her sidelong angle, Dianna saw the thick lashes flicker open to a pool of piercing blue and sighed in relief. He was human – firmly, undeniably human.

"I'm with you," he assured her, his words warming her skin.

"Your eyes are pieces of sky."

He took her fingers in his, slowly and naturally, and traced the fine lines of her palm with his thumb. Dianna smiled, but a worry line creased his brow.

"What's wrong?" she asked.

"Nothing, I . . . I couldn't tell you." Aimes' voice was shy and his face flushed, even as they lay naked together.

"You can tell me anything."

"It's too much."

"After all this?"

Aimes paused. His fingers brushed back her long, bright hair, lacing through the fine tendrils.

"I dreamt we lived here," he said. "In the woods. In a home we made, but it's safe. Away from the empire, from war, from everything. And we spent our days here. We spent our nights talking late and laughing and loving each other under the stars. We never have to go back to Awl-Feth or the slums again. And that's how we grow old. Together."

Dianna listened, the wolf in her chest circling over and over at this impossibility.

"And we are happy," she added knowingly.

Aimes leaned down to kiss the length of her neck – once, twice, three times, to the base of her throat, where his breath fluttered.

"We are so, so happy," he said.

Dianna wanted to stay curled in this imagined future with him, to let the waterfall drown out the dark voice of doubt in her mind. *You will both die here.*

In the following silence, Aimes sounded uncertain.

"You want that, too?" he murmured.

There was nothing she wanted more. She couldn't help but smile at his incredulity.

"Yes," she said. "Because in these woods I crossed paths with a wolf. And somewhere in that wolf is a man. And somewhere in coming to know him, I came to love him."

Aimes gave a small huff of breath through his nose, a small, sad laugh.

"But there's so little left of him," he said.

Dianna stretched over him, meeting his gaze.

"I've seen the little things," she said. "And I know they are the biggest things. I know the boy's shoes in the cache once belonged to you. The sun loves your skin, and the wind loves your hair, and even plants do your bidding. You are so quiet that you talk with your heart, and I can hear you."

Aimes had gone still beneath her.

"It's not what haunts you that makes you worthy of love," she said. "It's that you're a good person despite it."

Shards of morning light reflected in the water at the mouth of the cavern, a reminder that they had slept far too long than was safe. Dianna made to get up, but Aimes said something so faint under his breath that she asked him to repeat it.

"I'm worried about them, Dianna," he whispered. "I just wish we could stay in this moment."

His eyes searched hers, and Dianna felt her chest ache.

"We need to keep moving. Like Fredric said," she soothed, smoothing down the sleek hair at the back of his neck. "We'll find them."

Aimes unfolded himself with reluctance. "Then I'll go make sure it's clear."

She watched him prowl to his feet, admiring the contours of his back and curling up in the warmth he left behind. He stepped into the cave's mouth, becoming a shadow against the waterfall's downpour.

A minute passed. His figure wavered in the rippling light, taking a few tentative steps as he scanned the wooded riverbank.

At last he turned around to face her, and she heard him shout through the rushing water.

"Stay th—"

There was the trigger of a crossbow. A dull, hard sound as Aimes crumpled to the ground. In the roar of the waterfall, a hunter's victory cry ascended.

Dianna's breath cut short. Terror fell through her in slow motion, like grains of sand in an hourglass.

Running to Aimes, screaming his name, she glimpsed

354

only the bolt stuck straight up, like a sapling growing from his shoulder, its red roots sluicing his skin.

"Go on," he choked. "Go—"

"No, no, no." Dianna crouched over him, the numbness of denial spreading through her. "Please, don't say that. I can't leave you here—"

A knot of hunters advanced, reloading their weapons. Two clambered across the river toward them.

"*Run,*" Aimes cried out over the crash of water, the roars of men, the blood pounding in her own ears. His eyes pleaded. "*Fall!*"

Dianna flattened herself against the side of the stone cavern, her heart lashing at her chest, her skin humming.

She swallowed. "Aimes—"

In her hesitation, the pair of hunters at the forefront hoisted their crossbows.

Fury and adrenaline tore through her, deep and immediate, blacking out her senses. A guttural animal snarl flickered in her lungs like a tongue of flame. She opened her mouth, baring her fangs, and Fell.

The wolf plunged forward over the shallow precipice, sent them sprawling, tasted blood in a snap of the neck, a tear of the throat.

She ran, even with nowhere to go, even though Aimes lay behind her, before the others could converge.

Chapter 56

Flower moon, waxing

By the riverside, far downstream, Dianna slowly came back to herself.

She lay panting in the damp grass for a moment, hot skin steaming in the cool air. She pulled herself to the banks and lowered her cupped hands, gulping down icy water.

Sitting back, she studied the young woman staring at her. Dripping water rippled upon her reflection.

She hardly recognized herself now. Long, wild hair fell around her face, her mouth pressed into a grim line, and a pensive indent formed upon her brow. But there was a healthy flush in her cheeks, and her eyes were clear from sleep. She could discern new, lean strength in the muscles shaping her naked body. She felt the wolf settling in her chest.

Dianna, the hunter's daughter, had been left behind in Awl-Feth the moment she crossed into Silbarran. For the first time, she saw what Fredric had seen in her when they met.

"*Ket-saan,*" she whispered. The word meant many things in her native tongue, but it was an old word, almost forgotten. It meant *wild woman, she-wolf.*

Huntress.

Dianna moved like a shadow, soft-footed as time slid by. It seemed she had been walking for hours before men's voices murmured somewhere within the depths of the woods.

"Ram," she whispered, her voice cracking. "Eccka."

She spoke their names to comfort herself, even as they died on the wind. Ferns feathered her ankles; branches like claws snared and dragged at her skin. There was a faint shuffling in the underbrush.

She changed direction, following the high trill of a siskin in the treetops. Patches of vipergrass and sweet woodruff, billowing in the wind, began to appear identical to scenery she'd already traversed.

"Fredric," she whispered. "Aimes . . ."

Aimes was alive, she told herself, he was alive and had healed and hidden himself, and he would find his way back to them.

The men's indistinct voices followed her, and she stopped short, breath shallow in her throat.

Their surefooted tread meant they had spotted her movement.

Dianna became still as the woods themselves, her blood a running river, her bones straining beneath the weight of despair like branches against a stark wind. She sank, defeated and exhausted, against the moss-covered roots of a tree.

There was nothing left to do but let them come.

She looked upward to the patch of sky beyond the towering pines. The midday sun was a muted circle behind a filmy mask of cloudbank. Even as it climbed higher, she felt colder still.

The muffled tattoo of hooves throbbed in time with the ache in her head. She remained motionless, let the insides of her eyes cloak her world in darkness, and wished for a swift death.

A red haze flickered behind her eyelids. Dianna blinked, turning toward the sliver of light cutting through the greenery.

She bolted toward it.

Crossbows fired as she plunged through the rift, into the light. It closed behind her, swallowing the thicket in a silent, radiant implosion. She stumbled, falling to all fours with a gasp.

"How—" she wondered aloud, staring at the earth under her hands.

As though the woods themselves whispered it, the answer came to her: *Ram.*

Ram opens the rifts.

Ram keeps the other wolves at bay.

But he doesn't know how he can.

She remembered the way Aimes had described the wolves as having dormant instincts. Ram's empathy, his desire to protect his people, was so strong that it gave them strength. It was so strong that it opened ingresses to safety.

The memory of Eccka's words hummed in Dianna's mind.

"There is more to him than you know – more to him than he knows."

She had known. Something about Ram was more than human, more than wolf. A power that transcended even his imperial blood.

Dianna blinked away tears. Somehow, Ram's thoughts had done this. Somehow, he had led her here.

Looking up, she pressed her knuckles to her lips as if to keep from crying out.

Propped underneath the shade of an aspen tree, the bow and its quiver seemed as innocuous as fallen branches, casting slender shadows in the light. By the tree's roots, fresh prints of horse hooves marked the soft soil.

Rising to her feet, with the tread of a hunter tracking quarry, she approached it.

The arrowheads glinted silver in the sun. As she reached out, fingers short of the fletching, she saw that a delicate, pale green luna moth was perched there, tucked between the feathers.

She realized, upon brushing the silken creature with her fingertips, that it did not fly. That rather than the fine, thin wings of an insect, the object was a folded scrap of dyed parchment, ripped from the page of a book.

Her trembling hands smoothed it over. The scrawled penmanship was familiar upon sight.

I'm looking for you, An-An. I'm in hiding, and I know you are too, because I was wrong. You're not just stardust. You're forged of iron. I should have told you that.

I love you, An-An, and I will see you again, in life or in folktales.

—L

"He's alive," Dianna whispered, her voice catching, shaking. "Stars, he's alive."

She held the crumpled parchment to her lips as if she could will her brother back to her. As her gaze fell upon her mother's shortbow of yew wood and the quiver of fletched arrows, another understanding came, swift and certain.

But he can't help me from now on.

She gathered the weapon into her hands, cradling it to her in a loving embrace as Liam had held her when she was younger, when the nightmares kept her awake, when the transformations twisted her limbs and flamed in her lungs and his voice soothed, *It's all right, An-An. I've got you.*

But as she shouldered the quiver and set forth into the woods, she was no longer the farm girl frightened of the moonlight. The fear was within her still, but this time it compelled her.

This time, it was as if moonlight itself shone in her, strong and calm and clear.

CHAPTER 57

Flower moon, waxing

Three figures crossed a ravine in the woods, hemmed in by the thick green limbs of trees. The miles they had traveled were plain in their sagging shoulders and sluggish tread.

At the forefront, Ram bent low beneath the weight of his satchel, stumbling on slick stones in the streambed. The shallow, frothing current sucked at his mud-crusted feet.

"Sir, let me take that," Eccka said, mopping her brow. She leaned against Fredric, favoring her left leg.

"No need," Ram said, grunting as he pulled the satchel to him. He continued on his way over the rocks, footfalls squelching. Sweat tamped down the dark hair at the back of his neck.

"I never thought I'd say it," Fredric said over the stream's babble, "But my feet are earth-weary."

Fredric had not spoken since Dianna and Aimes had gone, and his sudden admission gave the prince pause.

"We've got to keep going," Ram said. "We've got to find them. How much longer until we reach a new site for camp?"

Fredric glanced up at the sky, noting the sun's halfway point.

"Not till dusk, I'm afraid," he said.

They pressed on across the muddy water, over rotting leaves and ragged rocks, until a bolt lanced across the wind.

"Down!" Ram cried, and simultaneously the three of them half-crouched, covering their heads and moving swiftly over the streambed.

Another voice bellowed, and there was the watery smack of a body's weight against rocks, followed by a second. Ram chanced a look behind them, faltering. He held his palm up, waiting to give the signal to Fall or flee.

In the darkening water, two hunters lay face down, run through with arrows. Ram turned his smudged face upward.

Dianna lowered her bow, slowing to a stop at the edge of the stream, exhaling with relief as she looked upon them.

"Oh!" cried Fredric as he splashed forward first, wrapping his arms around her. She crushed herself to him, resting her head against his soft patchwork vest.

"Gentle-heart," he murmured into her hair. "Where were you?"

But Dianna didn't answer at once.

They shot him, she wanted to cry out, to let the anguish in her chest emerge. *They shot him, and all I did was run.*

But over Fredric's shoulder, she saw the pall of weariness in their eyes. *Not now*, she decided. *Not yet.*

As they parted, Fredric pulled lengths of fabric from the satchel upon his back, pressing them to her. She saw that his own clothes were bloodstained.

"Sidetracked," she said, dressing herself quickly. "We can't linger long."

"Then we'd do well to cease our frivolity and make haste," Eccka said dryly, and to Dianna's surprise, pulled her into a fierce one-armed embrace. But the soldier winced as she did, clutching her side.

Ram's lip was crusted with blood, and leaves were falling away from the Earthencloak's tattered edge, trailing in his wake as he sloshed through the stream to meet Dianna.

"What happened?" she murmured.

Eccka and Fredric exchanged fleeting, anxious glances. Ram's mouth set in grim resignation.

"We were ambushed," he said. "Twice. Once with Eccka on watch while we slept. She was wounded. It was only by Fredric's quick thinking that we escaped."

"A mere shortcut," Fredric said in an undertone. "The rifts are . . . long gone."

He looked crestfallen in his spattered clothes, and to Dianna's dread, even the spark in his eyes had died.

She didn't dare to explain how she had reclaimed her bow. What if it was a stroke of luck, another false hope? How could Ram's thoughts alone lead them to safety while the woods remained closed upon them like a sepulcher?

What if she was wrong about him?

Eccka's posture was tense as she braced her weight against Fredric. More than her injury, Dianna thought it must pain her to be so humiliated, at a loss.

"They've surrounded us," said Ram. There was nothing left in his voice, no authority or faith.

"We have to find Aimes," Dianna said at once. "We have to try."

Ram's brow knit above his haggard eyes. "He Fell again, didn't he?"

Dianna felt a fist of denial close around her heart.

"We were ambushed too," she said, hesitating. "But he's still out there, Ram, he has to be—"

"Then let's go," Ram said, and a flicker of hope ignited in his gaze where none had been before. "Let's—"

"Wait," Fredric said. He was watching the foaming eddies of shallow water at their feet, the aimless twitching paths of long-legged water striders across its surface. "Do you feel that?"

Dianna looked down, feeling the subtle tremors in the silt. The murky water began to churn like a pot set to boiling over open flame.

Around them, trees swayed hard enough to shed leaves, though no breeze stirred the air. Silbarran itself was shaking, as though its magic had been pierced by a great force.

"How . . ." Eccka mused aloud, studying the rippling stream as she strode forward.

But Fredric looked like a lost child in a grown man's clothes, standing still in the water.

"Ram," was all he could muster, faint and tremulous – and Ram, wise and gentle Ram, knew.

Tharknas had come.

"No," Ram said hoarsely. "No, it's too soon. I have to find my—"

The color drained from his face. His knees buckled beneath him as he collapsed into the streambed, and the sound he cried out was inhuman.

"My *son.*"

Dianna went to the prince, and he clung to her, silent sobs racking his body.

"Ram," she said softly, swallowing her own cries. "Ram, listen."

She withdrew, looking him in the eyes. They were not the flat, painted eyes she had once scorned in the gloom of the cathedral, but the eyes of a ragged man, a shadow of his royal self. The man she now followed, trusted, loved.

He began to speak, but her hand settled upon his.

"You've said you are not the Imperator of Myre," she said. "You were wrong, your grace. You never stopped leading your people."

Ram's brow softened, his hands clasped to hers like a precious thing.

"I think I understand now," Dianna said. "I—"

But the earth shuddered beneath them, cutting her breath short, and Eccka's hand clutched Ram's shoulder.

"Aimes will meet with us soon," she said urgently,

convincingly. "We must go now."

Ram took Eccka's hand, standing. The soaked Earthencloak hung heavy around him.

"Yes," he said, faintly. "Yes, we must."

"Over that ravine," Fredric directed them, and he began to scale the steep slope. Dianna followed suit, clutching her bow at her hip. Close behind, Ram and Eccka clambered out of the river and up the rugged knoll together.

They emerged over the edge and found themselves looking down into a hollow valley. A broad hillside scattered with trees rose above it, stretching across the horizon as far as could be seen.

There in the distance, dark specks materialized, moving across the green expanse on the brink of the woods. Ram's eyes spread over the oncoming soldiers.

He paused as he saw it was real, as he came to an acceptance. He swept his cloak from his shoulders, letting the living patchwork fall to the ground. It crumpled in the dirt like an empty skin.

"I'm sorry, Fredric," he said. "I no longer need it."

Fredric looked at the cloak. He gave a solemn nod.

"We knew there may be a time," he said.

Eccka limped forward, testing her weight on both feet, watching the approaching mass as if daring them to come for her. Dianna's throat clenched, watching desolate finality descend on the faces of the people she loved.

Fredric glanced at her. "You know," he said, "I've fought a warrior or two in my time."

"I've yet to hear that story," Dianna said, her voice faint.

"Well, then," he said, sincere, "I shall have to tell it to you someday."

Dianna's mouth tightened.

"There, Gentle-heart," he said, gripping her hand. "Cheers, now."

The earth seemed to pulsate underfoot, as though it

contained a hundred steady heartbeats. Riders began to swallow the hillside.

"Cheers," Fredric murmured, "to trails yet traveled and tales yet told. May we learn the ways of long waters, of vast lands where feet have not yet fallen. Cheers to you, my steadfast family, bound by the path we share."

"The Vow of the Vagrants," said Ram. "I have not heard you recite it for some time, friend."

"May Faeralis protect and keep us," Fredric said. "May fate be on our side."

Ram positioned himself in front of them.

"Dianna," he said. "Find high ground. Run straight for it, and don't dare look back. Fredric, keep your eyes sharp. Eccka . . ." He trailed off, watching her.

She met his eyes. "Sir."

"Stay beside me."

Eccka's hands captured his face, and their lips met fiercely. When she released him her jaw was set.

"To the death, sir," were her only words, firm and tender all at once.

Ram gave a stiff nod, turning to face the breaking tide of men upon the hill. When he spoke at last, it was bereft of self-pity or fear, as plain as the final Fall that awaited.

"If this is our end," he said, joining hands with Eccka, "know that I am glad to live and die by your side, and I have loved you."

Eccka reached out to Fredric, who kept Dianna's hand clasped in his, a silent exchange of farewells.

Dianna's empty hand clenched as if she could feel Aimes with her, holding back her tears.

I will meet you, she thought, even if it would never be true.

Where you are, I will meet you.

"Forward?" Eccka asked through gritted teeth.

Ram's yellow eyes studied the full rushing scene before them.

366

"Forward," he said.

Dianna ran. The others Fell in a single leap, releasing like a flight of arrows toward their mark.

She couldn't help but look back at them once more, to marvel at the grace of the three creatures for the last time. Even as they went to meet their death, none had ever seemed so alive.

Chapter 58

Flower moon, waxing

The trample of galloping horses shook the earth in a thunderous groundswell as Dianna seized upon a tree and began a clambering ascent.

Fredric's low, baying cry as he hurtled downhill splintered her heart. From her vantage point in the highest boughs, she watched riders' swords, unsheathed and piercing the sky, form a gaping metal maw.

She balanced upon a sturdy branch, snatching an arrow from her quiver.

The bearlike, bearded man leading the front lines bellowed a battle cry. Footmen and cavalrymen, mercenaries and hunters alike echoed the roar until it burned in the air a hundredfold, swallowing the valley.

Dianna steadied her bow and nocked the arrow, straining to hear above the tangle of their deep clamor, of pounding hooves, of her own heartbeat.

A distant wind rose, its sound strange and howling, shaking her to the core. She faltered, bewildered, and turned around.

The men's voices died out, like flame expiring to ash. Their features wrenched with horror.

A hundred great beasts poured swiftly down the

hillside, a siege of dark writhing shapes.

Not wind, she realized.

Wolves.

Dianna saw Ram draw to a halt below, a dark flickering blot against green. Through the spiraling dust, the great black wolf spared a look behind him at the newcomers. "The other pack," she murmured. Only they weren't a pack.

They were an army.

Her branch pitched against a violent force, scattering leaves. With a gasp she lurched forward, fist latched upon her shortbow, and looked down.

The wolves were massive, yet moved almost formlessly, elegant as a heavy rolling fog. They swarmed around the roots of her tree, great in number yet with a seemingly singular instinct. She could barely distinguish one from another as they merged around Ram, Eccka, and Fredric, weaving past them to the front lines.

The men and their horses charged forward. The wolves arced into the air and plunged upon them, colliding like waves crushed upon shoals.

The carnage was immediate.

In a bloody frenzy of scrabbling claws and snarling jaws, they rent men apart. They leapt at riders, engulfed their horses and pitched the frightened, convulsing animals to the ground. Some attacked from below, snatching mercenaries and battering them like dolls with limbs asunder.

Tharknas countered with merciless savagery. A cavalryman swung his blade down, a silver flame streaking the air. The wolf's body slumped, its head toppling like a sack of grain. A mercenary, plunging his spear forward, lost his footing and was trampled beneath the horde. A wolf ripping a rider from his mount's back became riddled with bolts and fell away dead.

The torrent of men and wolves stretched in either direction, their endless noise coalescing with screams of anguish. Dianna watched the battle unfold below, stunned by a single fleeting thought.

They are on our side.

The charging wolves overtook the front cavalry lines. A steed's eyes rolled white with panic. Blood-drenched swords slashed, spattering the air.

Hunters flanked the rows of soldiers, releasing bolts at the command of the bearlike Centurion of L'Heste, who towered above them upon his stallion.

Dianna's gaze darted over the mass, then locked upon the darkest shape among them – Ram, surrounded by mercenaries.

She focused on the cavalryman cornering Ram, pulled the arrow across her breast, and let it soar. It struck her target in the neck, and he toppled from his mount.

Aiming her next shot into a knot of hunters, she loosed another arrow without hesitation and saw one fall back.

Below her, she heard the rasp of tree bark and recoiled.

A mercenary's gloved hands swiped at her feet. Her heel struck him squarely in the face, and he fell, landing fifteen feet below with a crunch of bone and a splitting outcry. Slinging her bow across her back, she glanced around at the shape of another soldier making headway in his climb. He grabbed hold of her, wrenching her down.

Dianna winced at the rough scrape of bark against her skin and the rain of leaves, seizing hold of a low branch. Quickly she freed herself and dropped to the ground, catching herself rolling forward as the arrows scattered from her quiver. Snatching up a fallen arrow, she lifted her bow high and felt the satisfying snap of the string between her fingers. The force of the shot knocked the second mercenary from the tree like a heavy fruit.

No time, she thought. *No time to stop.*

In the thick of the bedlam, she searched for another vantage point amongst the surrounding trees and ran for it. A spark of relief flickered within her at the sight of Eccka throwing off a mercenary with her crushing bite. The hard weight of armor pounded into Dianna's side, and a helmed face swam before her.

She struggled for purchase, slipping over the blood-soaked grass. A shortsword flashed, drawing back to strike her, and this was all, this was how she would die.

But a powerful blow knocked the soldier to the ground – a wolf, quick and sleek, had leapt into view. Snarling and screaming filled her ears as the wolf ripped into her attacker's neck. She staggered to her feet, shaking herself, choking on the stench of blood.

The wolf's eyes met hers, a yellow flash, and she would know them anywhere. His blood-soaked muzzle curled over alabaster fangs, and his hackles stood like a field of grass. He was a human mind within animal bones, animal skin; he was wildest hope made flesh, and his name moved within her like a song.

Aimes . . . *Aimes!*

She dropped to her knees and came apart like a broken thing before becoming whole again, living, breathing, unbeing—

Even as the chaos of battle churned around her, she savored the supple muscles of four legs, the grip and release of her feet over uneven terrain, the strength and swiftness of her lupine body.

She was panting, flying to Eccka's side as a swarm of mercenaries closed around her. She wrestled one to the ground, smashing his skull against rock. Aimes crouched at the edge of the fray, teeth bared, and disappeared into the midst of it.

Eccka roared, bristling, falling back from an advancing mercenary to get a better angle at him. A deep gash above her eye was bleeding.

Toppling men aside, the familiar shape of a massive black wolf covered the ground with long, flexing strides: Ram.

His head was low as he barreled through bodies, untouchable as a shadow cutting light. He glanced at Eccka with a steely calm, and only then did Dianna sense something was amiss.

Ram swept past Eccka, even as a hunter moved to plunge a dagger into her flank.

Then he lunged at Dianna.

Chapter 59

Flower moon, waxing

The jaws of the great black wolf snatched upon Dianna's thick ruff, throwing her aside as though eliminating a mere obstruction in his path. Dianna felt the razor-sharp sink of his teeth, the welling of blood in her fur. Crushed against the earth, she bared her fangs against the pain, watching in frozen dread as he turned on Aimes next.

But even if she were able, the thought of rising up to fight the prince – the man who had taken her in, who had called her "daughter" – turned her stomach. She sensed Aimes' own confusion as he cowered, and Ram charged toward him still, snarling.

Another wolf, identical – colossal, jet-black, with eyes like hellfire – tackled the first. They wrestled before he too was pitched aside, his shape sputtering into a human Ram, breathing hard and staring down the animal image of himself in astonished fascination.

The enemy's legs buckled, its wolf body folded and fell, and its fur shed away, unmasking the smooth human skin beneath.

The naked man stooped, taking a breath. His skin was dark olive, his hair black as coal.

"My cloak," said the man.

Slinking up beside him like a loyal dog, a wolf nudged a piece of cloth into his hands. The man swept the cloak over his shoulders, and it settled fully over his body.

He rose to full height, Ram's likeness in every respect, but not Ram at all. His eyes were reddened and empty as a rabid animal's, looking out upon the battle-torn valley. In the combat's short and brutal span, scores of men and wolves alike had fallen, scattered upon the grass.

A languid smile spread across his face. His voice cleft the breadth of the valley, arresting.

"Enough," he said, and his wolves abandoned their slaughter at once.

As the furor of warfare came to an eerie standstill, Remetus pressed one finger to his mouth.

"Hush," he soothed.

Dianna followed his gaze, and heard men crying out in alarm across the front lines. Soldiers began dismounting and removing their helms. The bearded man at the vanguard, the Centurion, drew his horse up, squinting. The princes were not far from his view, and he gaped with recognition.

"Hold fire!" he cried out, waving his arm back. Swords were held motionless, crossbows dropped.

Dianna staggered to her feet, body shuddering and smoothing into human limbs again. Aimes' own human arms found her, bringing her fallen bow and nearly emptied quiver to her. A short length away, Eccka was rising, panting, bleeding.

"You have come to slay them," Remetus said, and his voice echoed in the depths of the valley. Men stared at him in awe, trembled, blinked through masks of blood. "You have lived in terror, calling them demons. A blight upon you by your great Mactus. Do you believe me a demon?" He smiled in scorn. "You are mistaken. I *am* Mactus."

There were exclamations, loud cries of reverence,

confusion, disbelief. Among the broken bodies and ruined earth, Awl-Fethan men who could yet stand fell to their knees and bowed their heads. Dianna, firm on her feet, looked out upon the men making the blessing of Mactus and wondered how many of them truly believed the lost prince was their god incarnate.

"I have built my empire," said Remetus, "from the soil you stand upon. I have recruited my legion – all who crossed the woods. And I only had to taste their blood."

A cluster of wolves stalked in his wake. One lowered its great shagged head to the prince's shoulder, its eyes burning, massive fangs hanging open in a red lather.

Remetus, admiring its thick grizzled pelt, reached up to stroke its face. It could have taken his hand in one clean bite.

"They yield only to me," he said. "I made them masters of their gift. Made them mad for it. And I concealed them from my dear brother, who was taking in my strays as I confined them to the woods." He laughed, a wild barking laugh, and the sound reverberated, became distorted and inhuman. "You see, Centurion. You see now – I am worthier of the crown!"

The howling of wolves echoed throughout the valley, tangling in hollow harmony, spine-chilling as human screams.

Ram seemed smaller and thinner than Remetus in stature, despite their twin likenesses. His earth-stained face furrowed, and his fists curled at his sides as he feigned composure in his voice.

"This was a game of yours," he said.

Remetus spread his arms wide, relishing his brother's newfound recognition. "I am Mactus, after all. Mactus smites those who do not abide His will."

"You always did have a penchant for the grandiose," Ram said under his breath.

"You thought me long gone, didn't you, brother?" said

Remetus, edging closer. "Never to rise up, never to claim my birthright. But I know the worth of patience. For years I have served my time, toiling in the dirt. I have hidden in the shadows. But always, always, I have been watching, waiting for this day, for your defenses to slip. Does that frighten you? You appear frightened."

"Sooner disturbed," Ram said, jaw clenched. "Because this means I must kill you."

Remetus loomed within reach of his twin, touching his cheek almost with tenderness.

"What tears of rage you weep," he whispered. "But even they cannot quench the fire of my legion. My creation."

Ram did not move, but his dark stare burned.

"You've witnessed the destruction I can cause," Remetus' voice rang out, looking out upon the hillside littered with bodies. "This chaos I have harnessed. And this is only the beginning of my reign. You will join me or die resisting."

"You're sick," Ram whispered. "Blood and hellfire, you are so very, very sick."

"Oh!" exclaimed Remetus in a triumphant fervor, a slow smile spreading across his lips like bared fangs. "Listen to you, brother! As though we don't share the same blood. You know so little of our true power!"

Even from a distance, Dianna could see Ram's expression change, his eyes sharpen as they met his twin's.

"I know that it's not meant for your madness," Ram said at once.

Remetus seized upon his brother, tackling him to the ground, beating him in a blind rage. There was a repeated strike of fist against flesh, a scattering of blood. Men shouted, though the Centurion did not revoke his command, watching horrorstruck as the princes struggled. Remetus' wolves circled them, baying and slavering, clawing at the earth in anticipation.

"He's mine," cried Remetus, rising as Ram doubled over, howling in agony.

Another wolf circled them in a frenzy of wild eyes and frothing teeth.

"Stay back, Eccka," choked Ram.

"So attached to your pets," mocked Remetus, sending a hard kick to his gut. "This was always your greatest weakness—"

Ram took hold of his brother's ankle and dragged him down. They grappled and traded strikes, so entangled in their combat that it seemed nearly impossible to tell them apart.

Remetus gained leverage and pinned Ram to the dirt.

"And you fight like an animal," Remetus spat. "Crude – unskilled—"

"And you will die like one," growled Ram, throwing him off with a violent strength.

Remetus stumbled, mopping a hand over his bloody face. When he rose again, his crazed eyes leered.

"There is no point in fighting me," he said. "The empire is under my command now. You are a low beast under my thrall."

Ram found his footing, brushing the dirt and sweat from his bruised face.

"No, brother," he panted. "Your quest was over before it began. Your empire's walls have crumbled to dust." He pointed to the battle-torn valley, strewn with battered armor, slumped pelts of wolves, pools of red. "Already the bones of your soldiers, of your people, are scattered there. The others are war-weary and leap over your walls demanding revolution. Who will you lead when there are none left to follow you?"

A chilling, inhuman smile inched across his brother's lips.

"Well, then, brother." Remetus paused, his shoulders

bristling. "So perish all who leap over my walls."

In a distorted rupture of flesh and bones, Remetus' body rippled into the wolf. He seized upon Ram, knocking the breath from his lungs, and tore into him.

Dianna did not pause to think, nocking and loosing her arrow in one swift motion. She watched as it struck her intended mark, plunging into the earth beside man and wolf.

She cried out Ram's name. It was his kill.

Ram bit back his screams, hissing through his teeth, turning his head as though he heard the whip of Dianna's bowstring across the air. He snaked one arm from beneath the wolf. His fist closed around the slender wooden shaft of the arrow.

With all his might, he plunged it into the wolf's underbelly.

The wolf shrieked in a flash of fangs, snapping at air. Ram struggled beneath its weight, his breath dragging.

The wolf's worrying jaws slowed until they hung open in a last rasping snarl, like a final word betrayed by an animal tongue. The fire in its eyes flared, guttered, extinguished in a cold smog.

It collapsed over Ram's savaged body, sodden and lifeless.

Ram's arms pushed, rolled the great beast from him. It lay still, the arrow jutting from its bloody fur, and it could not be seen that the animal had once been man.

The victorious prince staggered, his face spattered red, sweating and paling. He glanced, panting, at the wolf incarnation of his fallen brother, tears pricking his pained eyes. One hand gripped his side to staunch the flow of blood, but his wounds were too deep. He stumbled toward a patch of grass, reaching as if to extract something from within.

Immediately, rows upon rows of hunters hoisted their crossbows, frightened. The mercenaries tensed in anticipation, but the Centurion roared in a flash of teeth, "Hold!"

In a slow, painstaking movement, Ram lifted an object above his head for all to see.

Though the ring was no bigger than a silver coin, the lustrous facets of its jewel glittered in the sunlight with a wine-red fire – a magnificent square garnet flanked by smooth, speckled bloodstones.

"I am Prince Ramus Silvius Baines," he cried out. "Last heir to Imperator Maldricus Numitor Baines, and by your witness—" He paused. Gasped. Grit his teeth and spoke the words with as much force as his last breath would allow. "By your witness I bequeath my title to my successor: *Eccka Domitia Talin.*"

His knees buckled and gave out, and his body fell alongside his brother, but human in death.

Chapter 60

Flower moon, waxing

All went silent, and all eyes converged on the fallen princes.

Someone – something – stood before them.

The entity looked upon the valley, upon the bloodshed spread over it, and it lifted its arms as if to embrace its beloved land.

Be, it said, and the earth quivered.

Living wolves became men and rose up from the earth, naked as though reborn, streaked with mud and blood. They looked in wild stupor upon the pale, ethereal being, and all they had known crumbled, and they felt the unseen threshold blockading Silbarran – like a cold wind – fall away.

But the entity was only an ephemeral vision, a blink of an unnatural reality, its presence forgotten by all who witnessed. Like silk unspinning flawlessly or ice collapsing into fog, it was solid and there, and then it wasn't.

"Aimes," Dianna said, reaching for him. "Aimes, what happened?"

Aimes gripped her human hands in his own, pressing his forehead against hers.

"I don't know," he said, shaking. "But I think . . . I think it's over."

Her eyes traced the pattern of dried mud on his cheek, fell to his undamaged shoulder where the bolt had struck him.

"A healer knows when a wound is fatal," he added.

Dianna leaned forward, stealing his words with her lips, and for a moment the valley and everything in it could have fallen away too. But they parted just as quickly, looking around at the wounded and the dead. The men who had once served Remetus under his command were coming to, rubbing the filth from their bodies, shuddering, weeping.

"Ram," Aimes whispered in disbelief.

Dianna held him to her, breathing the fading animal scent of his skin. Aside, she heard an exchange between two men. A cavalryman had drawn his horse up alongside the Centurion, his voice awestruck.

"Sir," he murmured. "What does this mean?"

Dianna watched as the Centurion turned to his men, and little though he knew of the truth, spoke like a wiser man than many.

"A divine thing has come to pass this day in Silbarran," he said. "But it was not of our doing. May the gods forgive us all."

His soldiers looked upon the earth where the entity had vanished, as though not trusting their own eyes or minds.

"The better question remains," said the Centurion. "Whose name is Talin?"

"Mine," a woman's voice answered, and Dianna knew the source of it: Eccka had knelt by Ram's body, cradling him in her strong arms. The crown jewel remained pressed in his closed hand.

The Centurion approached her, stooped, and bowed his head low, making himself lesser in her presence.

"My liege," he said. "I await your command."

At first Eccka looked up, and all that betrayed her hardened expression was the slip of tears. She clutched Ram's body to her.

Not breaking her gaze, she angled her head. It was just enough to bare the delicate skin beneath her jaw, the black markings of *Tharknas* striping the curve of her neck.

"Centurion," she said, with all the steadiness and force of the empire's ruler. "I command you and your men to move out."

Without question, without pause, the Centurion faced the last of his century, spread throughout the expanse of the valley.

"Fall back," he ordered.

Saluting their leader, mercenaries gathered the wounded and dead upon horseback. They began to form neat ranks before receding up and over the hill, followed by the last of the hunters.

"Fredric," Aimes said in the sudden absence of sound, and Dianna started. "Where's Fredric?"

Instinctively, they began calling out his name. It rose in the pines and fell to the wind. They stumbled through the valley, overturning men's corpses. Aimes cried out until his voice grew hoarse.

But there was no reply, not even a murmur.

It seemed hours had passed before Dianna found the single scrap of patchwork fabric, torn and bloody, among the roots of a tree. Her stomach plunged.

"No," she said, and her own voice was soft, hesitating, childlike to her ears. "No."

They found no body.

CHAPTER 61

Harvest moon, new
Four months after succession

Summer's last mild breath whispered in the thatched
roof of a small hut in the woods.

A short distance away, Dianna scooped the rabbit from
its hutch and cradled it in her hands, stroking its plush ears
with her thumbs. It was quivering as Aimes examined its
silky feet and beady eyes.

"She's ready," he said.

They'd found the lone kit huddled in a ransacked
burrow, the rest of the litter rooted out by a skulk of foxes
who quickly became preoccupied, squabbling over the
mother's carcass. At once Dianna had seen the knowing look
cross Aimes' face and insisted they care for the helpless
creature until it was grown.

She glanced at him now, kneeling in the tall meadow
grass beside her. His healing did not work the way it used
to, inexplicably, not since Ram's death. But he had this
warm, gray thing pressed in her palms, its heartbeat
fluttering and alive.

"You should do it," she said.

Aimes' eyes flickered to her with utter adoration as she
deposited the soft rabbit into his open hands.

"All right," he said, looking down at it.

Rising, he clasped the trembling creature tenderly to his chest. He walked, slow and steady, toward the edge of the thicket. His black hair was burnished in the sun.

Dianna's gaze followed his path, and she thought of all the ways the human body endured. The way it renewed and preserved itself, over and over. The beautiful way it became him.

Against the trees, he stooped and opened his hands, like unlocking a cage.

The rabbit burst from his grasp in a brisk leap, and it was racing through the undergrowth, wild yet entirely silent, a ghost of a thing.

"Go back," he shouted after it.

But the rabbit was already slipping into the labyrinth of leaves, white tail flickering against dark green. Aimes watched it disappear, a smile spreading over his mouth. He was laughing, raking a hand through his hair, and Dianna ran to him. He swept her into his arms, scattering kisses all over her face.

"Let's go and tell them," she said, savoring the feel of his laughter against her, and he nodded.

Taking hands, they walked deeper into the woods. The path was unmarked yet familiar, worn by footprints of months past. Dianna lifted a heavy pine bough, passing beneath it.

The mossy clearing was exactly as before, only one stone had joined the others, closing the circle. A cascading array of flowers covered the earth around them, filling the air with their sweet scent.

Someone else was already there. Facing away, she looked like she too had grown wild among the flora, crowned with intricately woven braids, a branch of blossoming purple amaranth in her arms. Her silk robes floated like a sail in the breeze.

Eccka turned toward them, a smile breaking on her lips. "How fated," she said. "She works in mysterious ways, Silbarran."

Dianna embraced her, flowers tickling in her hair. "Imperatrix," she greeted her. "You look well."

"And you, huntress," Eccka said, standing back to grasp Dianna by the shoulders, the hint of a smile on her mouth before she turned to Aimes, sizing him up much the same. She gathered him close, holding him for a moment.

"He loved you, Aimes," she said. "You know I do, too."

At her shoulder, Aimes nodded.

Eccka's robes fluttered around him as they parted. Stooping, she rested her branch of amaranth against Ram's headstone. She took a minute to look around the clearing, appreciating the many-hued, well-nurtured flowers.

"Awl-Feth is ashes," she said at last. "The High Elder carried out his purge, Dianna. It was . . . a worse sight than I feared."

The quiet hesitation of her voice quickened Dianna's pulse.

"How many?" she managed.

"Several dozen villagers."

"Cathrin?" Dianna asked, but Eccka held up her hand.

"My cousin is safe now," Eccka said. "Thanks in part to your brother."

The words seemed to fall and dissolve around Dianna, welcoming as cool rain on parched fields.

"Liam was there?" she asked.

Eccka nodded. "Loyal as you are. He'd returned to Awl-Feth to help the survivors flee. My company and I staged a coup. The High Elder has been captured."

Dianna's eyes had glazed with tears.

"As for why Elder Orcarrus did it, I cannot tell you yet," Eccka went on, clearing her throat. "Mad with zealotry, the Senate presumes. I suspect more to the story, but the interrogation remains, and I have other urgent matters to attend to."

As relief welled within her, Dianna couldn't resist the impulse. She took Eccka's hands in her own, clasped them between hers, and squeezed them gently. They were strong and soft, and she did not pull away.

At the gesture of affection, the imperatrix met her eyes with a look of mild surprise that gradually settled into a neutral gaze.

"Thank you, Eccka," Dianna whispered. "I wish . . . I wish I had been there with you. I wish my father—"

I wish he had seen Liam. He would have been proud.

But Dianna swallowed the words. There was no looking back now, she knew. Only forward.

Lips pursed, Eccka raised her head like a soldier at attention before letting go.

"I know I asked you to stay behind again," she said, watching her reaction carefully. "A huntress is not a warrior, after all. But to some, she is a goddess."

Dianna's brow knit as she waited for an explanation.

"I think it's time for you to go back," Eccka said. "I'll send your brother for your safe passage. I don't like the thought of you journeying alone, even if Silbarran is largely untraversed. I have men patrolling its borders for Caenani by the day."

Dianna turned to Aimes, whose smile mirrored hers.

"Will you come with me?" she asked. "To Awl-Feth?"

"To the ends of Myre and beyond, if you asked," he said.

Dianna gave a single nod.

"Then we're ready," she said to Eccka.

But Eccka's back was to them as she touched the edge of Ram's gravestone, watching the amaranth petals twitch in the wind. She was quiet, as if deep in thought.

Aimes spoke first, tentatively.

"Eccka," he said, "how are you?"

Unexpectedly, Eccka huffed a small, wistful chuckle.

"Can you believe they wanted to put him in a mausoleum?" she murmured, shaking her braided head. "I told them no, I wouldn't have it. This is how he wanted it. To be among his real family."

Her hand fell away, and she pressed her fingers to her lips.

"Sometimes . . ." Sorrow weighed heavy in her words, but her features were even. "Sometimes, when I hear the wind in the trees, I close my eyes, and I imagine him smiling, and he says he is proud of me in his stead. I imagine Fredric guiding me."

Fredric, Dianna thought. *He said something important about Silbarran. Something about listening and following . . .*

What was it?

Dianna looked into the wooded distance, trying to remember, when she saw it: the faintest glimmer amongst the shadows of the trees. It was so quick it could have been nothing, and so bright it could have been everything.

"She is the navigator of my soul," she whispered.

Eccka looked at her, a question in her eyes.

"Fredric said that to me once," Dianna said. "Eccka – I think he's still alive. He's *out* there. I can't explain it. But I can feel it."

The three of them stood together for a moment, wordless, listening only to the gentle wind and birdsong. But the light had faded, and it was gone.

Eccka broke the silence, speaking with an iron conviction.

"If I believe in anything about this place, I believe in that," she said. "Despite all that dissuades me. Those that Remetus corrupted are no longer wolves. They are poor, traumatized people in the care of the most experienced Valtan healers." At Dianna's side, Aimes nodded knowingly.

"And my patrolmen have not sighted a single wolf."

Eccka stooped, reaching for something at the foot of Ram's grave. With a delicate hand, she drew the cloak of gossamer leaves around her.

"But word in Valta has it," she said slowly, "that if you are to stand beneath a full moon, and if you are very quiet, you can still see one passing through the woods at night."

"Folktales, surely," was Dianna's only reply, glancing at Aimes.

His answering smile broke his mouth like a sunrise as his hand closed around hers. But it was his eyes that revealed the most, as she looked into their flickering depths, circled in blue as pure as patches of sky.

Eccka put up the cloak's cowl and bid them farewell. There was a Senate to contend with, an empire in waiting, a war to wage.

But there was hope. As she was leaving, Dianna felt it like a rift within reach.

"May Faeralis protect and keep you," she called after her. "May fate be on our side."

Beneath the Earthencloak, Eccka's eyes were tight with warmth.

"Fate," she murmured, testing the word. "Or magic."

She turned and made her way into the trees.

EPILOGUE

Eccka

I am pacing behind the curtain that stands between my small, shrouded past and the rest of my life.

I am alone in the citadel's great stone halls, awaiting the Centurion's arrival. I requested to be alone. I cannot stand the lictors who insist on shadowing my every move, dismissing the truth that I am a better killer than they.

The citadel windows are brilliant with the summer day. Outside, it will be sultry with the humming of bees scattering pollen, and later with cicadas hidden in the shrubs of the courtyard's gardens. Sunlight catches the crimson facets of the crown jewel, swinging from a long chain, where it falls against my heart. But my own heart is cool and dark as a raw stone from the ground.

As soon as I part these curtains and step into this new empire, as soon as I greet the sea of waiting faces, as soon as the sunlight touches my skin, I will no longer be able to deny this: Ram is dead. The finality of this fact, of my standing in his place, will become reality.

The Centurion of L'Heste appears at the mouth of the corridor, and I realize how little time I have to gather my thoughts.

"You wished to speak to me, Imperatrix," he says, bowing.

"Yes," I say. "Will you walk with me?"

It is a ploy to ease my restlessness. Thankfully, Gansin does not question this. He falls into stride alongside me, massive hands folded behind his back in diplomatic fashion. The many, long silks of Valtan finery trail in my wake. I am draped in their weight, dragging upon me. I am still unused to the feeling of clothing.

"I have one request which cannot wait," I say in an undertone. I do not leave my decisions up for debate, nor do I expect Gansin to challenge them.

"Please," he invites.

I take a breath.

"My first ordinance will be received with much dissent," I say. "I will have the High Elder of Awl-Feth imprisoned for treason and will not be satisfied until the Senate sees him without possibility of liberation. I will have the trade routes through Silbarran deemed safe passages for commerce again. I will have you, Centurion, paid in full for mercenary services rendered to Awl-Feth, but on a single condition."

I pause in the color-dappled light of a stained-glass triptych, warm sun against my back. Gansin is a patient man, but I sense his intrigue at the proposition.

"You'll recall that the recognition of my inheritance was not without great contest among the Senate, Centurion," I say. "But they honor your word because they respect you. I am a woman, after all. Taking up the mantle of Prince Ramus has been no easy task." My lips are pursed as I swallow my sorrow, but it sticks in my throat.

"Gods rest his soul," Gansin murmurs. He, like many L'Hestians, still believes in the old gods. The lares. Ancient disciples of Mactus would have converted all of L'Heste, had our strong armies not resisted.

I give a single, stiff nod. "Gods rest his soul." In a more peaceable time, such camaraderie would inspire me. But now it is yet another obstruction between us and the Valtan people. "I will face public opposition, even hate, if I am to do him justice. Gansin, my request to you intends to defy a longstanding tradition. I ask that you permit all able combatants, man or woman, to fight for the L'Hestian legion and win this war. For I will have you appointed Legate."

The Centurion does not immediately respond as he studies me. We have made an implicit oath, he and I, to never again speak a word of Silbarran, of the dark artifice Prince Remetus had meddled in, of the men who died on its behalf. He knows nothing of it yet and has seemed to conclude that it will remain an unanswered question.

I happen to know a little more.

Our losing war with Caenan is another question entirely, and it hangs between us.

"Forgive me, your grace," he says at last. "I do not wish to be presumptuous, but I must say that I recognized something about you upon our first meeting."

I can't help but smile. "Do not say it was the insignia of *Tharknas*."

Gansin's smile is even broader, creasing his eyes at the corners. They are wise eyes, and I am abruptly reminded of the deaths he must have seen to gain this wisdom.

"You are correct that you will face opposition," he says. "But you cannot forget that you were a soldier once. Opposition is our domain. The only life we know is one well fought for. No – I recognized something about you that I respect above all else, beyond your rank."

The voices outside the curtain are rising. They could be a battle cry as much as a reception.

"They doubt me." I frown, wishing I could recant these childish words as soon as I say them.

Gansin only walks me toward the curtain, as a father would walk a bride on her wedding day. Except my destiny is not in the shape of Ram. Now it is only a vision of myself, forging an unknown path stone by stone.

"Do you know why I did not doubt you that day?" he asks. "Because this singular quality you possess is one I have only known in the finest men. An answer to the call of duty. A potential for greatness. A fire. I see it today, in the face of a woman. And so a woman shall lead her empire."

He makes to grasp my hand in a firm pact. The certainty in his voice lifts me with its strength. I take his great hand and hold his gaze, though the shine of my eyes betrays my composure.

"I have called this bloodshed in Caenan a wasted labor under prior command," Gansin says. "But I will ready my legion. And I will be honored to end this war under your banners, my liege."

His hand releases mine, which flies to the ring against my heart. My thumb caresses its smooth facets.

"Ram had that fire," I murmur. "And more."

A divine thing, indeed, Centurion.

But just as my fingers close around the crown jewel, so my mouth closes upon further elaboration, coveting the secret I keep. A secret Ram had once whispered to me in the quietest dusk hour while I listened, smothered in the warmth of the Earthencloak and the scent of wolf. A secret only I guessed, and only the wise could suspect. And only I, a lover, could entirely understand, devoured by his touch.

And when he had explained everything he knew, a smile had stolen across his face.

Mighty men fall when they dare to rise above the heights of gods, he had said. As though I would not be the one who must catch him when he fell at last. Who must shoulder the anguish of his death. Who must assume his legacy and lead a people who will not readily follow.

But for Ram, I will readily lead. Outside, an empire lies in wait, and my fate with them.

I part the curtains. I go to meet it.

Acknowledgements

I finished writing *The Soft Fall* in a tiny café called The Muse, 2,700 miles from home. It was a surreal experience to meet such a goal and have so few to immediately share the news with. To share it with everyone is even more surreal.

My version of Diana the Huntress diverges from her more canonical roots, and though many iterations of her exist throughout history, her character is inspired by ancient Greco-Roman mythology. My regards go to many wonderful written works in the process of crafting her and her world, including Ovid's *Metamorphoses, Women Who Run with the Wolves* by Clarissa Pinkola Estés, Bulfinch's *Greek and Roman Mythology, Of Wolves and Men* by Barry Lopez, *SPQR: A History of Ancient Rome* by Mary Beard, and *The Wonderbook* by Jeff VanderMeer.

Writing is a solitary endeavor until others are willing to take the journey with you, so I must give my wholehearted appreciation to the following benevolent travelers.

Many thanks to Ellysian Press, who gave this story a home: to founder and editor Maer Wilson, for your forthright guidance, for your dedication to your authors, and for calling me a sweetie. Thank you to David Gray and S.A. Maethyn, for your valuable editorial input, smoothing out the rough edges. Thank you to Jenn Nixon for bringing your marketing skills to the team. Thank you to Joseph Murphy, artist extraordinaire – if books are to be judged by their covers, then your design makes mine a total badass.

To my dear family, who raised a wild Oregon child and avid reader with the best of care and support – as well as my family-in-law, and in memory of my grandparents – I love you with all my heart.

Infinite love and gratitude to my beta readers – Alex, Ben, Claire, Kendall, Megan, Paden, and others who gave their time and comments – without whose encouragement, I'd be lost. Thanks also to my longtime friends, Britanny, Myka, Stefani, Charneé, Neisje, and Denise, whose creativity and strength have always moved me. Special shoutouts to Mica for taking my author photos and Kim for gifting me my first fan art.

Thank you to my circle of writers, the Peeps: Donovan, Beverley, Ann Marie, Jason, Margie, Dean, Monica, and Sheila. How fortunate I am that our paths crossed. I came to you with far less life experience and a story about some rather strange and serious werewolves, and you welcomed me with warmth and mercy. Thank you for lighting my way with your insightful critiques, storytelling wisdom, and friendship.

I'm proud to call home a well-read community in the Pacific Northwest. To my fellow booksellers and to the owners of Grass Roots Books & Music, where I've been selling and shelving books for years with the dream of one day finding a place among them, and to my newfound coworkers at my local public library: Thank you for believing in me and in the power of words.

To OR-7: May your legacy echo on.

Patrick, my husband, your absolute and unshakable support for more than a decade is the compass to my path, my beginning and end. You are forever my love, who gave me my best story of all.

About the Author

Marissa Byfield was raised in the lush woodlands of the Pacific Northwest. After graduating with a Bachelor's degree in English from Oregon State University, Marissa married her high school sweetheart and finished writing her fantasy novel, *The Soft Fall*, inspired by her love of mythology and wolves.

Marissa has been a longtime bookseller and the newsletter editor at Grass Roots Books & Music, Oregon's second oldest independent bookstore. When not writing or reading, you'll find her practicing yoga, musing over tarot by full moonlight, shelving at her local library, and fighting hate with love. She lives in Oregon with her husband.

Also from Ellysian Press

Moonflowers by David A. Gray

I'm not like those other freaks. The kids who can look inside your head and bring your nightmares to life.

The weirdos who can steal your luck or make a thing true just by wishing it. The outliers born from the mess that followed Armageddon.

The ones you call Moonflowers, half mockingly and half afraid. They're the mistakes that humanity hates – and needs.

I'm not like them. I'm worse. And I'm the only thing standing between you and the legions of heaven and hell.

—Petal – The Armageddon-Lite Archives

The Clockwork Detective from R.A. McCandless

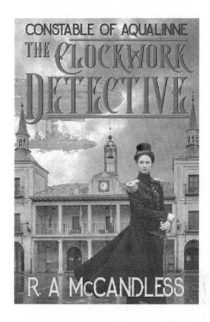

Aubrey Hartmann left the Imperial battlefields with a pocketful of medals, a fearsome reputation, and a clockwork leg.

The Imperium diverts her trip home to investigate the murder of a young *druwyd* in a strange town. She is ordered to not only find the killer but prevent a full-scale war with the dreaded Fae.

Meanwhile, the arrival of a sinister secret policeman threatens to dig up Aubrey's own secrets – ones that could ruin her career.

It soon becomes clear that Aubrey has powerful enemies with plans to stop her before she gets started. Determined to solve the mystery, Aubrey must survive centaurs, thugs and a monster of pure destruction.

"This is my kind of book: a wonderful, fully realized, utterly plausible Steampunk world with a dynamite plot, great characters, and the best dirigibles this side of anywhere. I hope there's more to come."— From James P. Blaylock, World Fantasy Award Winning Author, Co-Founder of the Modern Steampunk Genre

Exiles of Forlorn by Sean T. Poindexter

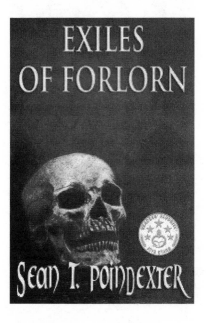

It all began when the old man died.

On a ship of exiles bound for the edge of civilization, he passes on his life's work to a band of youths. He gives each of them a piece of information that leads to a mythical treasure.

The five friends – the lord's son, the soldier, the thief, the beautiful river pirate and the wizard's apprentice – all agree to join the hunt.

They arrive on the shores of Forlorn eager to begin their journey, but find a community plagued by threats from pirates and man-eating giants. The friends must choose to either stay and help those who have taken them in or to venture into unknown lands in search of a prize that may not even exist.

Either choice promises excitement, danger — and death.

ABOUT ELLYSIAN PRESS

To find other Ellysian Press books, please visit our **website**: (http://www.ellysianpress.com/).

You can find our complete list of **novels here**. They include:

Motley Education by S.A. Larsen

Moonflowers by David A. Gray

The Clockwork Detective by R.A. McCandless

Progenie by Mack Little

Time to Live by Jordan Elizabeth

The Moonlight Herders by Stefani Chaney

Before Dawn by Elizabeth Arroyo

Redemption by Mike Schlossberg

The Elohim Legacy by Sean T. Poindexter

Kālong by Carol Holland March

Marked Beauty by S.A. Larsen

Dreamscape by Kerry Reed

The Rending by Carol Holland March

A Deal in the Darkness by Allan B. Anderson

The Will of the Darkest One by Sean T. Poindexter

The Tyro by Carol Holland March

The Shadow of Tiamat by Sean T. Poindexter

Muse Unexpected by VC Birlidis

The Devil's Triangle by Toni De Palma

Moth by Sean T. Poindexter

Premonition by Agnes Jayne

Exiles of Forlorn by Sean T. Poindexter

Relics by Maer Wilson

A Shadow of Time by Louann Carroll

Idyllic Avenue by Chad Ganske

Portals by Maer Wilson

Innocent Blood by Louann Carroll

The Boogeyman by Lillie J. Roberts

Magics by Maer Wilson

The Ellysian Press Catalog has a complete list of current and forthcoming books.

Made in the USA
Lexington, KY
30 October 2019

56329014R00255